TO LOVE AND TO CHERISH

Tempest stared at Buck. "You mean you already knew about the dance?"

"I was hoping for some hint that you'd want to go with me."

Spinning back to the sideboard, Tempest scraped another plate. "I have no intention of pandering to the town's morbid curiosity. If they want to see you so dratted bad, let them come here."

"Morbid?"

"You're supposed to be dead, remember?"

He nuzzled her neck under her ear. His beard tickled her sensitive skin, making her shiver. "Do I feel dead?" he asked huskily.

She whirled and shoved against his chest. "No. Can we get off the subject now?"

Buck didn't budge. He placed his hands on either side of her, trapping her against the sideboard. The look in his eyes set her every nerve trembling.

"*You* sure don't feel dead," he whispered, bending to kiss her cheek. "You feel warm and real and good. Kiss me, pretty lady. I haven't had nearly enough kisses in my life, and your mouth was made for the job."

He gave her no chance to object as his mouth silenced hers in the most delicious way possible . . .

Books by Charlene Raddon

TAMING JENNA

TENDER TOUCH

FOREVER MINE

TO HAVE AND TO HOLD

Published by Zebra Books

TO HAVE AND TO HOLD

Charlene Raddon

Zebra Books
Kensington Publishing Corp.

http://www.zebrabooks.com

In memory of

my mother Velda Woolsey Birt whose tales of child-hood days in dugouts on the Kansas plains inspired parts of this story.

and my sister Janyce L. Smith who has finally reached a home where flowers bloom eternally and pain is never felt.

I miss you both

ZEBRA BOOKS are published by

Kensington Publishing Corp.
850 Third Avenue
New York, NY 10022

First Printing: May, 1997
10 9 8 7 6 5 4 3 2 1

Printed in the United States of America

Chapter One

Utah—1888

Tempest Whitney stilled as the dogs barked and raced off toward the road. The diaper she'd been about to hang on taut cord strung between cottonwood trees slid from her fingers to the dirt. Someone was coming. Her heart drummed fiercely at the thought of company, in hope as well as trepidation. It was lonely at Heartsease.

Overhead, branches thrashed in a burst of wind, announcing the changing season with a shower of golden leaves and exchanging the smell of lye soap for that of sagebrush. In the house twenty-two-month-old Ethan wailed, as if he sensed his mother's unease. Angel's childish voice mingled with his cries as the four-year-old tried to soothe her brother.

Shading her eyes with her hand, Tempest peered into the distance, torn between the need to go to her children and the need to see who was coming. Shadows from the canyon walls hid the rider's features. It wasn't her father; the dogs never barked at Ronan Carmichael. Besides, now that he worked at Jonas Creedy's saloon in Harper, he rarely came home anyway, except to beg for money.

Thoughts of Jonas added to her apprehension. The man wanted her and didn't care a fig if she was willing or not. So far she'd managed to evade his grasp, but she feared her luck would run out.

Everyone in Deception Canyon had been pushing her to remarry. Hardly a month went by without some dire prediction of her fate if she stubbornly insisted on living alone. Yet no matter how lonely or how difficult it was to run her ranch on her own, she preferred independence to marriage. The men here were hard and rough, not an ounce of warmth or gentleness in them. They didn't want a wife so much as a housekeeper, field hand, cook, and human brood mare all rolled into one. At least they were willing to marry her in order to bed her. Jonas Creedy was not.

Buck Maddux halted in the middle of the road, surrounded by yapping dogs. Spook whinnied and pranced beneath him. Buck studied the huddle of buildings across the creek and soothingly patted the appaloosa's long graceful neck.

Three days of slugging whiskey in Harper hadn't fortified him enough for this. Hell, he'd rather chew off his own foot than cross that bridge and face the Widow Whitney. Her husband, now that was a different story; Buck would love to get his hands on him again. But any woman a man couldn't pay for and leave behind with a clear conscience was more trouble than she was worth.

From the looks of the place, the Whitney woman wasn't doing too well. The mere thought brought sweat to his brow. Hell, he hoped she was ugly as a mud puppy and ornery to boot. Kindness from Skeet Whitney's widow would be his undoing, considering the part he'd played in her husband's death. Besides, he was more familiar with anger and accusations.

Your life's already hit rock bottom, Buck old boy, he reminded himself. Can't go anywhere but up now. He'd repeated that maxim to himself all the way from Salt Lake City. His new life's motto.

The ranch sat on bottomland, threaded through a twisting, narrow canyon of wind-sculpted sandstone that challenged the imagination. So far, he hadn't seen a single steer, which came as no surprise; between drinks at Johansson's Saloon, Buck had learned what to expect. The widow, it seemed, raised almost everything except cattle.

He nudged his appaloosa toward the plank bridge. The road showed evidence of a recent rain. Dog tracks ringed the muddy puddles that glistened in ruts and potholes, nearly obliterating the prints of deer, raccoon, and quail. A lizard zigged onto the road and, confronted by a mongrel pup, zagged back beneath a six-foot greasewood shrub. Between steep banks, Carcass Creek flowed sluggishly, its voice as deep and lethargic as a sleepy frog's. Beyond the bridge, cottonwood trees with trunks as gray and rough as a washerwoman's knees crowded a bend where the stream widened and seemed to slumber in the September sun.

If not for the smoke spiraling up from the roof, the house would be hell to spot. It looked like a wall of rocks stacked against the slope of an old creek bed. Poles and sod formed the flat roof, the front edge rimmed with elk and deer antlers. Two mules and a donkey hung their heads over the bars of a corral attached to a lopsided barn. Between the house and barn a patch of green marked a vegetable garden. Busted wagon parts, a rusted stove with a hole in its round belly, and broken farm implements littered the yard. Buck had seen better dugouts in Kansas and had considered them poor doings.

Riding up to the house, he called out a hello. Then he dismounted amidst the barking dogs and proceeded to water his horse at a well built over a natural spring. From beneath the wide brim of his Stetson he searched for some sign of life. Finally he headed for the house, spurs jangling in his wake. His fist was raised, ready to knock, when the rough plank door swung inward and the business end of a Henry repeating rifle was thrust at his nose.

"Judas!" He jerked back and stumbled over his own big feet. A cat screeched, letting him know he had mangled its tail. The critter got even by climbing Buck's trousers. Yelping and dancing while he tried to extract the cat, Buck trampled two or three more. Easy to do; half a dozen littered the yard, along with pigs and a flutter of chickens.

"Whoa there, ma'am." He held up a hand. "Don't mean you any harm."

"What *do* you mean?" she asked.

The cat took off, its tail in the air. Buck checked for damage and decided he'd live. "That's a mite awkward to explain." He took off his hat, wiped his brow with his sleeve, and put the hat back on, buying time while he studied her.

She wasn't much to look at. The braid hanging to her waist looked as though crows had been pecking at it. Dun-colored strands fluttering about her head gave her a wild look that belied the delicacy of her face. Her large eyes were balanced by a strong chin and a mouth as stubborn as the mules over in the pole corral. A patched apron hung to her scuffed boots and hugged her legs snug enough to tell him she wasn't wearing skirts. He was wondering what might be under the apron when she spat, "Spill it, mister. I haven't got all day."

"Think you could put the gun down?" He eyed the rifle

with amusement and chagrin. "This might take a while and your arms'll get tired."

"Don't think for a second that I can't shoot this, just because I'm a woman," she drawled. "I hate it when men jump to conclusions like that. It makes me so angry I start shaking and that makes my trigger finger jittery, if you know what I mean."

Buck knew. A jittery trigger finger meant he might get shot for no reason. He eyed her speculatively. She wasn't much bigger than a colt, no problem for a man his size to handle. "I doubt you'd enjoy where they'd put you for shooting a man," he said, smiling to hide his growing irritation.

"Nobody goes to jail for defending himself, especially not a woman. You going to state your business or not?"

"Are you Tempest Whitney?"

"What's it to you?"

He sighed. "Name's Buck Maddux. I ran onto your husband two years ago. He was gut-shot and bleeding bad—"

"Maddux!" Her head snapped up, and her finger tightened on the trigger. "You yellow-bellied son of a coyote. How dare you come here? Didn't you cause enough grief robbing that stage and getting my husband killed? Get off my property before I fill you with lead the way the posse did Skeet."

He threw up his hands as she moved closer. "Easy, ma'am, I didn't come here to get you all upset."

"What did you expect?" she said. "Did you think I'd welcome you with open arms and invite you in for supper? Just because my husband let you rope him into a stupid robbery doesn't mean I have to put up with you."

That did it. Now he was angry. "Hold on a minute there." His mouth was tight, his voice hard. "I had nothing to do with that robbery, or the Army patrol who shot your husband.''

''Sure. You were just an innocent bystander who happened to be with Skeet when he was caught.''

''As a matter of fact—''

''Raspberry stickers!'' she spat. ''*You* plotted that holdup. You killed my husband as surely as if you'd pulled the trigger yourself.''

Buck's blood boiled. He told himself it was because she'd accused him of lying, not because she'd come too close to the truth, but the excuse didn't wash, adding to his fury. In one swift movement, he snatched the rifle from her, threw it to the ground and shoved her against the door jamb. He held her there with his body, her hands pinned above her head, while he stared down into amber-sparked brown eyes.

The dogs took up barking again.

''Damn, if you were a man . . .'' But she wasn't. He closed his eyes and clenched his jaw, fighting for control.

Hell. Part of him *wanted* to hurt her, wanted to make Skeet's widow pay for what trying to help her husband had cost him. He hated himself for that. Forcing his muscles to relax, he was about to release her when something latched onto his pant leg—something toothy that snarled like a wolf. Maybe a bear. He didn't dare let go of the woman long enough to look. Whatever it was, it was ragging his leg back and forth as if it was a sick rat. He kicked out and struck empty air.

''You'd what?'' the woman prompted. ''Thrash me?'' Sweet Mary, but I'm fed up with men who think violence is the only way to solve anything.''

''*You're* the one greeting folks at the door with a loaded gun,'' he said.

''What else can a woman do, with men like you around?''

Suddenly he wanted to laugh. She was better looking

than a mud puppy but every bit as ornery a mule. "Believe what you want, but I have no fondness for violence. Now, will you settle down and listen to me?" He took her silent scowl as a no. "Look"—cloth ripped somewhere below his knee, renewing his anger—"all I did was stay with your husband so he wouldn't have to die alone, and for that—"

"You said you had nothing to do with his death."

"I didn't! I found him *after* the robbery, after he'd been shot." Judas. Trying to hang onto her and shake off the wolf was more work than chopping wood with a butter knife.

"So," she said, "you simply waited until he was dead and stashed the money somewhere for yourself, is that it? You detestable, dung-eating coyote's whelp, I ought to—"

"You sure do have a thing about coyotes, ma'am."

She kicked him in the shin. Muttering a curse that lacked the color of hers, he pinned her more securely to the house, his feet spread wide so she couldn't kick him again. Checking for weapons, he slid a hand to her waist and found denim, the waistband bunched up and held on with a rope. Trousers! The woman was wearing trousers. Hell, not only did she hate being treated as a female, she hated *being* female.

"What did you do with the money?" she ranted. "It's rightfully mine now. I mortgaged my ranch to pay off what you stole, and now I'm about to lose it."

He wasn't listening. He was too caught up in the feel of her thighs squirming between his, her soft abdomen cradling his ... Christ, his blood was heating up faster than a teapot in hell, and he didn't even like the woman.

"If you're losing this"—he gave the wolf/bear/dog/whatever a vicious kick—"zoo, it's because you married a fool, not because of me. More likely it was your pestering that drove him to do something desperate like a holdup."

"Frog turds!" Abruptly she froze, awareness widening her eyes as the bulge in his trousers nudged her soft femininity. Her lips parted, and Buck feared he could see a scream working up out of her throat. It mortified him to realize how much he wanted to stop that scream with a kiss. His nostrils dilated at her feminine scent, natural and earthy like herbs and fresh-baked bread. His gaze lingered on her mouth while his body reacted to the feel and sight and smell of her.

"Let go of me," she demanded in a voice too choked to be threatening.

"Why? I kind of like things as they are." If he moved at all, it would be to add taste to the other sensations she'd already aroused in him.

In a voice sharp enough to pare flesh, she said, "Let me go or I'll tell the dog to start gnawing flesh—whatever he finds hanging between your legs."

Buck's chuckle was low and husky. "At the moment, sweetheart, *you're* what's hanging between my legs." He winked. Damned if she wasn't pretty with her eyes spitting and her mouth pouting like that. He wondered how those lips would feel beneath his. He lowered his head, but before his lips could reach hers, a small voice inside the dark house said, "Mama?"

He looked up to see a frightened little girl, a naked toddler pressed to her side.

The breath hissed out of him, along with the lust. Judas, how had the situation gotten so out of control? He'd only meant to teach the woman some manners. He surely had liked the way she felt against him, though, and the way she smelled. Most women were eager to give him anything he wanted, but those were whores. He wasn't used to dealing with decent women. Women too good for the likes of him. He stepped back, dragging the dog with him.

She rushed inside, hauled the toddler onto her hip, and

hugged her daughter to her side. The dog let go of Buck's pants and trotted after her.

For a long moment he stared at them, then stalked away. After a dozen paces, he halted, his hands on his hips as he dragged in gulps of air to cool his blood. At his feet grew a wild rosebush no higher than a handspan, its tip bowed by the weight of a large, single blossom. A touch of beauty startlingly out of place in this almost desertlike terrain. Like the woman, he thought.

Damn. He had to finish his business with her and get the hell out. Something about the Widow Whitney drove him to behave in ways he didn't like. He turned back. She hadn't moved. The toddler had his head on her shoulder and was sucking a dirty thumb. A picture of innocence and virtue that, along with the vulnerability he could see in the widow's eyes, magnified his guilt.

"Look, I apologize." He took off his hat and held it as if showing respect for her gender. "That shouldn't have happened. I only came here because I promised your husband . . ."

A new emotion flashed into her eyes. Curiosity, he thought with some relief. Maybe they could settle this reasonably after all.

"Skeet talked about me before he died?" she asked.

"You were all he talked about, actually. You, his little girl, and the baby you were expecting."

She rested her cheek on her son's head in a tender gesture that wrung Buck's heart. "What did he want you to promise?" she asked.

"To make sure you were okay. He was worried how you'd fare all alone, with no house and . . ." Buck glanced away. The idea of what she must have endured, trying to shelter her children and keep them alive in a land even Satan seemed to have forsaken, twisted his innards.

"So why did it take you so long to come?" she said.

Buck shifted on his feet, memories of the last two years hardening his gut the way sunlight hardens adobe.

"Came as soon as I could. Might not have come at all, except . . ." Again, he looked around at the ranch. "Making sure you were all right was so damned important to him he deeded me half-interest in this place to guarantee I'd keep my promise."

Her head snapped up at that, and in an instant, the vulnerability was gone. "The devil he did! You lying billy goat, your tongue's so slick a fly could use it as a slide."

Before he could object to her assessment of his character, she'd replaced the boy in her arms with a .41 rim-fire, double-barreled, Remington derringer.

"Now get off my property," she said, "and don't come back."

"Look here, ma'am—"

"I said get!"

"All right, all right, I'm going." The derringer was held so steady on his chest, he figured she couldn't miss. He mounted his horse and headed for the road, not bothering to look back.

Judas, this wasn't the way things were supposed to go. When Skeet Whitney had offered him the land, Buck hadn't been interested in owning property. He still wasn't. The last thing he wanted was responsibility. Buck Maddux and responsibility didn't go together. But fifteen years ago, he'd vowed never to break another promise, and he didn't reckon his promise to Skeet was any exception. So now he'd kept that promise. Tempest Whitney was one woman who could take care of herself. So what if she'd looked pathetic standing there all proud and stubborn and female, trying to look tough and competent. So what if she lived in nothing better than an oversized badger hole, alone except for two scared little tykes clinging to her apron. She wasn't his responsibility. And thank the Lord for that.

That's right, Buck, old boy. Life's taking you up now, remember—not down.

And Buck intended to keep it that way.

Tempest let her hand fall to her side. Now that the man was gone, the derringer she held weighed on her as heavily as her heart.

Her first assumption on seeing the stranger was that a homesteader had heard of the mule colt she needed to sell. Or had come for a cat. Horses were in short supply these days and cats downright precious, while there were enough mice to pick up the canyon and haul it to California.

But Buck Maddux was a good deal more dangerous than a farmer. His spurs and lazy, long-legged stance were typical of a cowhand, though the weapon strapped to his hip and his hard intractable face said gunman. Even in anger, however, his blue eyes weren't the cold, emotionless eyes of a killer. As he'd held her against his body, they had warmed like a hot summer afternoon when the sky presses a body down almost to the point of suffocation. Mesmerizing eyes. The sympathy and concern she'd glimpsed in them as he'd eyed her and the children had nearly unraveled her. His big body moving against hers turned her insides shivery, yet hot and butter soft.

Despite the silver streaking the ebony hair above his forehead, and the oldness in his eyes, she doubted he was over thirty-five. His body moved with a sensual, masculine grace that made her tinglingly aware of her own femininity. A mustache nearly hid the grooves time had etched around his mouth. His jaw was square and hard, the chin covered by dark, close-cropped whiskers. His face was as craggy as the sandstone walls of her beloved canyon and, in the same harsh, imposing manner, beautiful.

His effect on her senses, and the strong, inexplicable sense of safety she'd felt in his arms, frightened her. He was pure trouble.

Or an answer to a prayer?

No, he was trouble, and Tempest already had all of that she could handle.

"Mama?" Angel slipped a hand inside her mother's. "Wath he a bad man?"

"I don't think so, honey." Tempest squeezed the small trusting hand, unsure if she was trying to reassure her daughter or herself.

"Will he come back?"

"I hope not." But deep down inside, Tempest knew she was lying.

In front of Johansson's saloon Buck dismounted and looped the reins over the hitch rail. Spook stuck his long white muzzle under Buck's dusty hat, gave a wet snort in his ear, then flipped the hat into the air.

"Will you cut that out?" Buck caught the hat, slapped it back on his head, and ran a finger inside his ear to scoop out the moisture. "Day's gone bad enough without you adding your two cents."

Spook nodded, but when Buck stepped onto the walkway without saying anything more, the horse whinnied.

"I hear you," Buck muttered as he vanished inside. "Confounded beer-guzzling nag thinks he owns me instead of the other way around."

The frame building of Johansson's Emporium of Liquid Refreshment had only one floor, in spite of the false front that made it look two storied. Unlike his competitor across the street, the Swede offered only drinks and honest games—no food or females. At the moment Buck doubted the last restriction was in his favor. He could use a woman. His lack of restraint with the Widow Whitney proved that.

Three cowhands were playing poker at a corner table, the only gambling allowed. A tinware drummer waiting for the five-thirty stage was making up for the dry dusty road ahead by drowning his thirst now. Buck's stomach rumbled at the sight of a pickle crock on the bar. He was fond of dills. The drummer beat him to them, pulling out a fat pickle with a hand that hadn't seen soap in days. Buck's hunger vanished.

Johansson stood behind a bar made of two slightly warped planks set on barrels. No brass foot rail, only tarnished, well-splattered spittoons at each end. Nails held towels for wiping beer foam from patrons' mustaches. The color and smell indicated they'd seen steady use for at least six months. The saloon owner himself looked little more than average size until he emerged from the trench he'd dug behind his makeshift counter. Then he towered over everybody at the unnatural height of six-foot-six. A wall plaque proclaimed him to be Yngve Twigmuntus Johansson, a good reason for folks to simply call him Swede.

The blond giant greeted Buck in faltering English. "Hullo again, stranger. You have trouble finding Whitney place?"

"No." Buck glanced around. The smoky room reeked of tobacco juice, sweat, urine, whiskey-soaked sawdust, and vomit. "Tell me, is that woman always so sweet and compliant?"

Swede spat tobacco juice in the general direction of a spittoon, missing by four inches. "Ya, sweet as honey. A snack for eyes, as you Americans say."

Buck decided either he was crazy or the Swede was. She wasn't bad to look at, but . . . sweet? He scanned the sign tacked onto the wall: Valley Tan whiskey . . . 25 cents;

German beer . . . 15 cents; Mormon beer . . . 5 cents; Ditch water . . . free. "Give me a whiskey," he said.

The glass placed in front of Buck was dull with grime, but he needed the drink too badly to complain. He sighed contentedly as the amber liquid burned its way to his stomach. Not bad, considering it was locally made. Mormons preached against the use of spirits, but with empty stomachs and emptier pockets, they didn't hesitate to produce and sell the stuff to gentiles.

"Tell me what you know about Skeet Whitney," Buck said.

Swede shrugged. "Not be much. Harper was only stage stop when Whitney killed. I come after. He was prospector, I know." Frowning, he shook his head. "To labor so hard, look for something only few men find seems waste of time. Ya?"

"You've the right of that." Buck decided he liked the big barman. He signaled for a refill.

Swede's grin rivaled a six-year-old's for lack of teeth. "You needed that, ya? Widow gives a man crotch itch, I hear Jonas Creedy say, and he does not mean lice."

Buck sipped his whiskey, uncertain why the barman's mention of crotch itch in the same breath as the Widow Whitney tightened his innards. "Creedy's the one who owns the fancy joint across the way?"

"Ya. He tries to buy widow's land for to drive cows to pasture on top of plateau and not pay toll, but"—Swede tapped his head with a cigar-sized finger—"I think he wants widow more."

Buck peered through the grimy front window at a green and white sign across the street that read The Sagebrush Princess—Jonas Creedy, Proprietor. Fine Cigars and Liquors Our Specialty.

"Any women over there worth looking at?"

"Ya, Lacey and Big Red. You go calling maybe?"

"Maybe. Got any recommendations?"

"Depends. Me, I could marry that Lacey." Swede gave an exaggerated sigh while color mounted his long neck. "Soft and pretty as spring daisies. Makes a man feel . . . good."

Buck resisted the urge to laugh. The blond giant was obviously stuck on the girl. "What about Big Red? She doesn't come by her name because of her height, I'd bet."

A deep rumble of laughter erupted from Swede's chest. "No, not for height."

Ten minutes later, Buck left, carrying a bowl full of beer. Spook gave a soft satisfied snort, slurped up his favorite drink, then belched.

"You're the damnedest thing on four legs," Buck muttered.

Spook tried to nuzzle him with a beer-soaked nose. Shoving the horse aside, Buck crossed the street and stepped inside the Sagebrush Princess. Thirty feet of polished walnut with burl veneers, beveled edges, and brass fittings made up the bar. A painting of a nude woman draped in gauzy fabric that enhanced her attributes rather than hiding them decorated the back the bar. Leering cherubs peeked over her shoulders and tugged playfully at the cloth. A table laden with sliced ham, fresh bread, and deviled eggs tantalized Buck with its delicious aroma. A sign read Free Lunch for Patrons Only. He was hungry, all right, but right now all he wanted was another drink.

The barman had a mustache waxed into four-inch spikes sharp enough to drill holes in oranges. His crisp, clean white shirt—the sleeves held up by green garters—ankle-length apron, and string tie were downright dazzling compared to Swede's stained garb. Buck decided to test the man's skill by ordering the fanciest drink he could think of—a Sazerac, the best whiskey flavored with sugar and aromatic bitters. It would be expensive, but he felt like splurging. Lord knew he hadn't exactly been living high the last two years. He deserved a treat. While he waited he glanced around.

The place was twice as large as Swede's, three times showier, and a whole world cleaner. A nubile girl with slumberous eyes sat at a round table with a burly one-armed man with bushy gray brows and a mustache. A red plaid tam-o'-shanter covered the man's head. He tossed down a drink, refilled his glass from a bottle on the table, and tossed that one down too. Buck caught the girl's eye and flashed a grin that never failed to bring females to their knees. She smiled back. Hair like gold-streaked champagne curled about her face. If this was Lacey, judging from the smallness of her breasts, the Swede had good taste.

Ranchers, cowhands, and other businessmen lounged at the bar or at tables. Toward the back a guard with cauliflower ears and the face of a ferret sat on a high stool, wearing enough artillery to outfit everybody in town. His gaze centered mostly on the noisy faro game going on nearby, but Buck didn't figure the gunman missed much that went on in the room.

The one-armed drunk rose unsteadily and started toward a roulette table where a dealer with arms like fence posts was trying to drum up business. The girl grabbed the old timer's good arm and said something in a low, urgent voice. He shook her off and kept going. She'd started after him again when a sharp-edged voice cut across the room. "Is there a problem, Lacey?"

She whirled. "No. No, Mr. Creedy, no problem." Her fear was evident.

Creedy was descending the stairs from the upper floor. What he lacked in height and good looks he made up for in arrogance. Matchstick legs so bowed a cannonball could pass between his thighs without touching flesh supported his thick compact body. Behind him, a woman slightly older than Lacey, in a dress so daring Buck marveled at her ability to keep her ample bosom from falling out, hovered on the top step. Tension radiated from her like cheap perfume. A bruise on her cheek was beginning to purple.

Buck's chest tightened. Any man who hit a woman was the worst kind of coward there was. He had met dozens of them in the past two years. Men who liked to brag of the cruelties they inflicted on those weaker than themselves.

The fancy fabric and expensive cut of Creedy's clothes failed to disguise his mixed blood or the cold, dispassionate meanness in his narrow, raisin-dark eyes. The man was a killer. Buck had lived with too many not to recognize one on sight. He didn't know how the man had gotten his money, but he was damn sure his means hadn't been legal—or bloodless.

"If Carmichael ain't needing your company anymore, maybe you ought to find someone else to entertain, Lacey," Creedy said.

"Yes sir." Her gaze shifted to Buck. He put extra warmth in his smile to let her know she was welcome. When she reached him, he circled her shoulders with his arm and flashed Creedy a message too obvious to be misunderstood. The saloon owner glowered back.

The girl leaning into Buck's strength was warm and soft and smelled of lilacs. She was pretty, with green, slanted eyes that made a man think instantly of beds and carnal pleasures. He'd known women who effected that drowsy look purposely to lure men to their rooms, but this girl's was natural. He doubted she even knew what had likely targeted her at a very young age as a victim to men's lust.

Across the room Creedy whispered into a cauliflower ear. Buck kept the two men in sight out of the corner of his eye. Their type had been more common where he'd come from than steel bars. He had often been obliged to outwit or outfight them in order to keep breathing. His body bore the scars. When they looked his way, he stared them in the eye and stroked the handle of his .44 Army Colt. If trouble came, Buck would be ready. If not—he smiled down at the girl whose small breasts were pressed against his side—tonight might turn out as pleasurably as he'd hoped.

Tomorrow could take care of itself.

Chapter Two

Something about the sweet, rhythmic tug and pull of Ethan's mouth on her breast relaxed Tempest as nothing else could. She rested her head against the back of the rocking chair, closed her eyes, and wrinkled her nose at the odor of baby diapers waiting to be washed. Something was always needing to be done, like the cabbage and beets that had to be picked before frost got them. But she shunted such thoughts aside. These moments of nursing Ethan were the best of her day. His cuddly warmth filling her arms and his contented cooing as he suckled never failed to wash life's constant worries and fears from her mind.

In the front room Angel's shrill giggles danced in the air like dust motes in a wedge of sunlight as she played with the latest litter of kittens. How could a woman complain with the sound of her child's laughter in her ears and a bundle of love like Ethan in her arms? Not even the

scare Buck Maddux had given her yesterday could diminish
her pleasure in this moment. She wouldn't let it.

Blast the man for showing her how defenseless she was,
though. Had Skeet truly given away half her land? Half of
what she had spent the last two years slaving to make into
something nearly profitable?

The day Skeet left two years ago she had been six months
pregnant. Angel had been two and a half, and a handful.
Their cabin and almost everything they owned, except
livestock, had been destroyed by a flash flood. Their only
shelter was the old wagon with its tattered canvas top.
They had salvaged what they could: clothes, quilts, cast-
iron cookware, a backless chair, a drawer Tempest made
into a bed for Angel. The plow she had badgered Skeet
into buying was wedged in the top of a tree, too mangled
to repair. Their only material for constructing a new home
was dirt, their only tool a shovel with a broken handle.

Skeet could have sold the mare for enough to keep them
going for a few months. There were rabbits and sage hens
to eat. With the purchase of a few staples like flour and
coffee they could have gotten by until they figured out
what to do next. But Skeet insisted they keep the horse.
How would he find the Spanish gold he had come for if
he had no way to get around?

Tempest hadn't believed in his treasure. All she had
cared about was keeping her babies healthy and alive,
but Skeet wouldn't listen. He took the mare, and their
remaining cash, and rode off to buy supplies. While she
waited for him to return, Tempest began gouging a hole
out of an ancient creek bank high above the current water
level. A dugout would provide better shelter than the
wagon for the coming winter and would give them more
room. In the spring he could build a new cabin.

But she never saw her husband again.

After two weeks, Tempest began to fear that Skeet had

abandoned them. He was a good man, generous and sweet and kind for the most part, yet marriage had exposed a softness in him she knew wouldn't stand up to hard scrutiny. One day a U.S. marshal rode up with the mare in tow, Skeet's empty saddle on her back. Her husband was dead, shot trying to escape an Army detail from Fort Duchesne after robbing a stage.

Heaven only knew why he had done such an asinine thing; he hadn't enough deceit in him to pull off a robbery without getting caught. No doubt he had lost his money gambling. He was always so certain he would win. And he often did. Otherwise they might have starved before reaching Deception Canyon. Without the money, or food, he wouldn't have had the nerve to face her. Still, how could he do something as stupid as robbing a stage? Then to turn around and give away half her land to a stranger. As if getting himself killed and deserting her hadn't been enough. It made her want to shoot him herself.

If Buck Maddux was telling the truth about Skeet deeding him the land—and she had a terrible feeling he was—he would be back. This time, with the law. She didn't want to think what would happen then. She'd worked too hard to hang onto Heartsease to let some man waltz in and take it from her. No matter how handsome he might be.

The pigs were fighting over something out in the yard, squealing and snorting. An unwary rattler probably. Soon it would be time to butcher one of the pigs, smoke it, and salt it away for winter. She had hoped to get the root cellar dug first so there would be a cool place other than her bedroom to hang the hams. There never was enough time.

One day this place would be Ethan's, God willing. Horses, pigs, mules, land—Ethan's heritage, all he would ever have of the father he'd never known. Tempest would do anything to preserve his inheritance. Even kill, if necessary.

Except that she wasn't sure she could shoot Buck Maddux. For some inexplicable reason, the thought of him being killed dismayed her. She told herself it had nothing to do with his looks, or how safe she had felt in his arms. If only—

Raspberry stickers! He was a man, likely a thief, and the last thing she needed in her life. No matter how alone and lonely she might be.

Tempest had loved her husband, but that hadn't blinded her to his faults any more than it had blinded her to the faults of the other men in her life. Like Papa's drinking. Men had taught Tempest two important lessons: a man's only useful attribute was his muscles; his only reliable trait, lust. Maddux had proved no exception to the rule, and clumsy as he was, he'd probably increase a woman's workload rather than lessen it.

The sound of a horse cantering up to the house brought up her head. Had Maddux returned already? No, he couldn't have made it to Fort Duchesne, the closest point of civilization with any sort of law, and back to Deception Canyon this fast. Besides, the dogs weren't barking. Which meant the rider had to be Papa, although it was difficult to imagine his old nag moving that fast.

Tempest made herself relax, forcing away worry and dread. This was her special time with Ethan, a time to treasure while she could. In the past few weeks he had shown a marked lack of interest in milk—hers or Flopsey's. She switched him to her other breast and debated covering herself. To fetch his blanket off the bed would mean disturbing him and she was loath to do that. She decided not to worry about it. Even when he was still living here, Papa had never violated her privacy.

A few more milliseconds of peace is all I ask, Lord. And that Papa be sober.

The front door opened. No sound of voices followed.

Tempest frowned. Normally, Angel greeted her grandpa with excited chatter about kittens and squirrels and the latest's goings-on. She had known him less than a year, yet she loved him in that unconditional way of children.

"Mama?"

Tempest felt Angel's pudgy hand on her arm. Stubbornly, she kept her eyes closed, holding the outer world at bay a bit longer. "Just a minute, honey, Ethan's almost through."

"But Mama—"

"My, oh my," another voice put in, one she recognized with horror. "If that ain't the prettiest sight I've ever seen, I don't know what is."

In the curtained doorway stood Jonas Creedy, his small, buzzardlike eyes riveted to her naked breasts. Tempest yanked her shirt front together. Where was her father? The dogs would have barked if Jonas had come alone.

"Don't stop on my account, puss," he said. "I enjoyed watching."

"How dare you come into my house uninvited." Her fingers flashed as they swiftly fastened buttons. "Papa?" she called.

"Your father's watering the horses. He was kind enough to invite me out for a visit." Jonas moved closer and she shot to her feet, holding Ethan in front of her like a shield, his naked bottom nestled against her stomach. The boy had taken off his diaper again.

"Bye-bye." Ethan opened and closed his fists in a childish wave.

"No, Ethan." Angel giggled and tickled her brother's toes. "You say hello when folks come. Bye-bye is for when they go."

"That's all right, Angel, the man *is* going. Right now." Tempest's voice was razor sharp but sounded calmer than she actually felt. Why couldn't it have been Buck Maddux?

As much as she dreaded seeing him again, she would have preferred him to Jonas. *Blast! Where was Papa?*

Jonas Creedy rubbed a finger over his upper lip as he studied her. He was all cheekbones and nose, with a nub of a chin, and a thin, wide mouth. Rumor had it he was half-Apache. His small stature, barely equaling her own height, and his lack of a beard testified to the truth of the story. Tempest didn't care. Apache or white, she would still detest him.

"Problem is," he said, "you and me got business to discuss, Tempest."

"What business?"

"Why don't we sit on the bed and talk about it?"

"No." Ronan Carmichael's rotund figure suddenly filled the doorway. "Long as you're in me daughter's house, you'll treat her with respect, Mr. Creedy."

"Who's going to make me? You?" Jonas gave an ugly laugh. "You old drunk, how long do you think you'd last without my whiskey or the use of—"

"Shut yer yap, mon." Carmichael slid a mortified glance in her direction, and his bluster withered and died. "Treat her with respect is all I ask." He paused as he turned back to the front room and lifted a gentle, trembling hand to her cheek. "I'm sorry, Tara," he said, using her given name. Long before she could remember, her parents had decided that her middle name, her mother's maiden name, suited her best.

Jonas gave Tempest a smile that reminded her she needed to put more catalogue pages in the privy. With all the dignity she could muster, she started past him into the other room. His arm darted out to block the way. She stared at the expensive brown tweed of his coat sleeve, the fine percale of his shirt peeking from beneath the cuff, the dirt under his nails. And wished she had her derringer.

"Why don't you put the brat down so we can talk more private-like?" Jonas said.

"No."

"No? All right then."

Tempest gritted her teeth. Her arms tightened across the boy's plump abdomen as Jonas's hands snaked down her arms and his thumbs brushed the full sides of her breasts. Then, abruptly, his oily smile fled. "What the . . . ?"

Following his gaze Tempest saw a stream of liquid arching from Ethan's perky little penis onto the man's trousers.

"Damn that brat!" Jonas jerked back as far as he could— not much since the wall was right behind him. "Why don't you have him in a diaper?"

"I can't afford to buy enough cloth for all he needs," Tempest said. The boy gurgled happily and added insult to injury by kicking Jonas in the crotch.

The man grabbed for his privates. "Cut that out!"

"Oh, dear," Tempest murmured with exaggerated concern. "Perhaps you'd best let me past so I can get you a rag to mop yourself up with."

Grumbling, he followed her into the front room where Ronan sat before the stove, puffing furiously on his pipe. His hair was mussed, as if he had been wildly scratching his head, something he did when he was flustered. Tempest fetched a cloth, handed it to Jonas, and sat down at the table with Ethan on her lap. "Now, suppose you tell me what business you came out here to discuss," she said.

Ronan's jaw sank deeper onto his thick chest as he slanted a glance at the other man. Uneasiness crawled over Tempest. Whatever Jonas's business was, her father knew about it. And it wasn't good.

"You think I'm here to make another offer on this so-called mule ranch, don't you?" Jonas's smile was sly, almost triumphant. "Well, I don't have to now, because in five weeks it'll be mine anyway."

Tempest came to her feet in a rush. "What do you mean?"

"I mean, puss, that I'm holdin' the mortgage on this place now, a mortgage with a nice fat payment due right soon." He waved a paper in front of her. "You gonna be able to pay it?"

Tempest grabbed for the paper, but he snatched it away.

"I don't believe you. That mortgage was with the Wasatch Mountain Bank in Provo. How could you have gotten hold of it?"

Jonas's teeth showed startlingly white in his dark skin as he grinned. "It's amazing what a man can do when he's got money."

Tempest bit down on her tongue, and her rage.

"Point is," he went on, "do you have the money to pay it or not?"

She didn't have to answer. He knew as well as she did that she didn't have an extra dollar, let alone the three hundred due in five weeks. She'd been counting on getting an extension from the bank.

Ethan burped. Jonas eyed the child with contempt. His scowl, combined with his flat, twisted nose and his slitted eyes gave him a look so sinister Tempest felt sweat pearl beneath her arms. She didn't want to hear what was coming next. Her gaze flicked to the shelf above the door that held her derringer. Trying to appear calm, she set her son on the floor and pulled his dress down over his naked bottom.

"Go play with your sister, Ethan, and remember to be soft with the kittens."

The child raced off. He fell, picked himself up, giggling, and took off again. There was no such thing as walking with Ethan. Tempest paced to the open doorway, within reach of the derringer, and gazed out. "I assume that you intend to take possession when the loan comes due?"

"That depends."

She whirled to face him, hope and doubt warring within her. "What do you mean, it *depends,* Mr. Creedy?"

"You'd make me real happy if you'd use my first name, Tempest. I'm trying to fix things so we can both end up happy."

She snorted. The only way he could make her happy was to tie a rope around his neck and let his horse drag him to kingdom come. "You want my land and I refuse to give it up, so how are we both going to be happy?"

"Easy. All you gotta do is marry me."

"Marry . . . ?" She started to laugh, then caught the look of doom in her father's bloodshot eyes. The laughter died in her throat, forming a ball as solid as an anvil, past which she could barely swallow. Jonas looked smug.

"No," she said. "I'll forgo my toll for driving your herd across my land when you bring them down from the summer range. That should cover half the payment."

"That's real generous, puss, but . . ."—from his pocket he took a handful of papers—"your pa's into me for quite a bundle. Liquor, gambling, and . . . other services. They add up."

The notes said it all. Each IOU stated an amount, followed by her father's scribbled signature. Tempest made a swift calculation in her head—two hundred and seventy dollars. With the mortgage, that made almost six hundred she owed Creedy. Might as well be six thousand. And with another mortgage payment due in another six months. She wished she could throw the IOU's in Jonas's face and tell him to collect from her father. But Ronan Carmichael was a drunk who guzzled all he earned sweeping Jonas's saloon. He never had a dime. Why had she taken him in when he'd come crawling to her a year ago? She had known what she was letting herself in for. But he was her father. Now, in the unjust way of the world, his sins would be visited upon her head. She could force Jonas to take her to court, but she knew she would lose.

Fear railroaded her straight toward a precipice as the seriousness of her situation sank home. Lord, but she hated feeling helpless. She had accepted that she would always be lonely and struggling for money. But taking Jonas Creedy as her husband was more than unacceptable—it was her worst nightmare come true. Her stomach churned at the thought of his touching her. She swallowed the scream that threatened to blow her apart, like a stick of dynamite shoved in her ear, and averted her face to hide her emotions. Through a watery blur she could see outside to the scrubby land she had fought so hard to hang onto.

For Angel. For Ethan. For herself.

Definitely not for Skeet. All he had ever thought about was chasing rainbows. Claiming land under the Homestead Act had been Tempest's idea, a grasping at security in a world that seemed entirely too uncertain. A thousand times since Skeet's death, she had thanked a God she wasn't sure she believed in anymore, for helping her to provide her children a permanent home, such as it was. Even Skeet had admitted that without the land they'd likely have starved that first year. While he hiked the canyons and plateaus hunting lost treasures that didn't exist, she had hunted roots and herbs, rabbits and sage hens. Skills she'd perfected since then, with the help of an old Ute Indian woman.

"Well, Tempest?"

Jonas Creedy's voice jerked her back to the present. The man was waiting for an answer, his thin lips forming a smug, arrogant smile. Tempest shut her eyes and chewed her inner lip.

All the work, the fear, the never-ending loneliness, the pain and hunger would be for nothing if she lost Heartsease. But to marry Jonas? Could she do it? Could she let him put those sweaty brown hands on her? She would rather die first, although she was more inclined to kill him. Joint by joint her fingers curled inward until her fingernails sliced into her palms. Her jaw clenched as she summoned all her sorely tried courage and strength. She raised her chin, her lips parted.

Jonas put up a hand. "In case you're thinking 'bout refusing my proposal, best ask yourself how you're gonna feed them stinking brats once you leave here. You'll be forfeiting all your livestock to me, you know. Your house, this trash you call furniture"—he kicked a mended stool across the room—"the very clothes on your back—mine."

His smile was triumphant. Evil. "Course, I'll help you all I can. There's an extra room upstairs at the Princess. Bit of guidance from Lacey and Red—and a lotta time on your back—you might be able to pay me off in, oh, five years or so."

Bile geysered into Tempest's throat. She considered snatching down the derringer and emptying it into Jonas Creedy's vile body—and hated herself because she knew she couldn't. She couldn't shoot any man. Her resulting rage was aimed almost as much at herself as it was at Jonas. "You no good, slimy—"

"Uh-uh. Careful, little puss. Don't want to make me withdraw my proposal now, do you?"

But she did. Desperately. And why not? She didn't need him. She had managed all by herself after Skeet vanished. Built the dugout with her own hands, for the most part. Given birth to Ethan, with only Angel to help. And she had survived. Two long, lonely years, during any moment of which she would have sold her soul for a good, strong man to love her, ease her fears, banish vermin like Jonas Creedy, build her a real house with real windows and a real floor. But there were no men that good or that strong.

Tempest had learned to endure without one, and saw no need to knuckle under now.

Angel wrapped her arms around her mother's leg and looked up at her with saucer-sized brown eyes. "Mama? I'm hungry. Are we gonna eat thoon?"

Tempest looked down at her small daughter, and crumpled inside. They'd had nothing to eat in those first days after Skeet left, except roots, an occasional sage hen or rabbit, and lizards. She couldn't put Angel through that again. And there was Ethan now. She had to think of them. Above and before anything else, she had to think of her children. "You'll tear up my father's IOU's and keep him on at the Princess?" she asked, her voice low and strained.

"Agreed."

"What about any future debts he might run up?"

"Anything he wants at the Princess is on the house the moment you say 'I do.'"

Ronan's gaze lay heavily on her shoulders. She wished she could tell her father to go to hell. Or, at least, to one of her brothers. But Rule had vanished during the war, and the reason her father had searched her out in the first place was because Dirk had gotten tired of supporting the old man and had run off to Lord knew where. She had no kin, no friend to help her. Without the land, where would they go? She didn't even have money for a stage ticket. How would she feed her babies?

The image of a tall man with summer blue eyes and silver-streaked jet hair swept gallantly into her mind. Half a ranch would be better than none at all. Maybe Maddux could pay off her debts. No! Jerking her chin a notch higher, she shoved the thought away. Tempest Whitney did not take charity. Besides, Buck Maddux was gone now. She didn't know how to find him. And even if she did, she would never allow herself to sink low enough to seek the man out.

Only one choice lay open to her. But the words that would seal her to Jonas for eternity would not come. Her tongue refused to form them. She made do with a curt nod, and turned away.

Grinning, he rubbed his hands together in triumph. "I'll ride to Price in the morning to fetch the preacher. We'll have the wedding at my house Thursday afternoon at four."

Tempest swung toward him, panic churning inside her. She needed more time. "No! In five weeks, Jonas, the day my note comes due . . . that's when I'll marry you, not one day sooner. And I want a priest. I am Catholic, you know. I want my marriage recognized by the church."

His thin lips twisted. He stalked her across the room until his bent nose was only a foul breath away. "In *three days*, bitch. And no priest. Or you'll lose this land, and instead of taking you as my wife, I'll just make you my whore."

Chapter Three

For the third morning in a row, Buck Maddux awoke in an upstairs room of the Sagebrush Princess Saloon and told himself it was time to move on. He never stayed in one place for long. He'd work roundup at one ranch or another, in Texas or Colorado or Montana. Then he'd winter in a town, tending bar at a saloon or riding shotgun on a stage. In the spring he would travel on, a job here, a job there, restless, eager to see what lay beyond the next hill. Usually when he got there he found it wasn't much different than the last hill, and he'd feel a little disappointed. But the restlessness would begin again, and off he'd go.

He had vowed, in the dark days of prison, while the blazing Utah sun baked his brains to a useless mush and the winters threatened to turn him into a black and white-striped glacier, that the first thing he'd do upon being released would be to visit the wonders of southeastern Utah, then Arizona and California.

As a child, fascinated by the power and wildness of the sea after a visit to Pensacola, he'd yearned to become a sailor. As a young man, he wanted only to see the ocean again. Once he had come close. The pain of that time still had the power to bring Buck to his knees. To avoid the memories, he had put aside his dreams of the sea. But prison had reawakened them. Nowhere else would he find enough water to wash away the filth of his incarceration, enough fresh air to banish the stench of jail from his nostrils. He'd made up his mind never to allow anything to interfere with that goal again.

Yet each morning found him still in Harper, reluctant to leave, and without the slightest idea why. His thoughts drifted to the defiant thrust of a delicate chin, a tangled braid, and brown eyes that spat amber sparks.

"Judas," he muttered, shoving himself up in bed. Beside him, Lacey moaned and opened her eyes.

"Sorry," he said. "Didn't mean to wake you. Go back to sleep." He tucked the blanket around her bare shoulders, then swung his long legs out of bed.

Lacey scooted into a sitting position. She watched him go to one of the windows he insisted on leaving open at night. Leaning on the sill, he dragged in deep drafts of air as if he were suffocating. There was something different about him this morning, a restless energy that sank her heart to her toes. "Buck, honey, you hungry?" Yawning, she stretched, allowing the covers to drop and expose her small upturned breasts. "I can get us something from the kitchen."

"No, thanks." Ignoring her display, Buck walked over to the commode and splashed water on his face.

"We could eat right here." She patted the rumpled bed.

Buck blinked water from his eyes and glanced at her in the mirror. She looked like a sleepy child. In truth, she was nearly young enough to be his daughter. Nearly the same age, in fact, as ... He didn't let himself finish the thought. Instead, he kicked himself for the hope in her eyes that hadn't been there three days ago. Lacey had the body of a woman, and knew how to use it to fulfill men's fantasies. But she was still enough of a child to entertain fantasies of her own. He had known from the beginning that she harbored an affection for him beyond what was usual for one in her business. The older he grew, the more difficult it became not to grab on when some bit of affection came his way. It had been so long. But staying with Lacey and allowing her to hope had been cruelly selfish. Feeling twice his thirty-five years, he said, "Look, Lacey ..."

Her smile fled. "No, Buck, don't say it, don't say you're leaving. I was hoping—"

"It's way past time." The money he'd earned riding shotgun for a freighter in Provo before heading to Harper was vanishing at a rapid pace. Smelling of sex, cheap whiskey, and long-lost innocence, she came and pressed her body against his naked backside, entwining her arms around him like a vine.

"Please, Buck, not yet." Her hands tangled in the hair around his navel, then trailed downward. Buck groaned silently while he watched her fondle him in the mirror. He hated hurting women. Dammit, when would he ever learn?

Moaning at his lack of response, Lacey moved in front of him and went down on her knees to try something more arousing. Buck drew her to her feet. "Don't, Lacey. Don't demean yourself that way."

"Why not?" She flounced away from him. "I'm a whore. How can I get any more 'demeaned' than that?"

Hearing her bitterness and feeling lower than a lizard's belly for having used her to scratch an itch she hadn't created, he said, "I can't lay around forever. I'll be broke soon if I don't find work, and there isn't any around here."

She looked at him pleadingly. "You could—"

Buck shook his head. "I'm a drifter, Lacey. I never stay in one place long enough to wash my socks, let alone keep a woman happy. Ah hell, honey, I'm no good for you. I'm no good for any woman."

Thrusting out her lower lip, Lacey sashayed across the room. It was the practiced walk of a whore, but on her it reminded him of a child playing dress-up. She hadn't developed the usual hard crust, but her smile was the same strained smile he'd seen on countless other whores. "Don't you worry about me, sugar," she purred. "Just remember to drop by if you ever come back this way. Lacey's door is always open."

Buck heard the quaver in her voice. He cursed. "Look, you're a sweet, beautiful girl who deserves better than a drifter like me. Why don't you get out of here, Lacey? Go to Provo or Salt Lake City where you'd have a chance to find decent work."

Her laugh was brittle. "Sure. I bet those goody-goody Mormons up there are lined up all along Main Street just waiting for the chance to hire an out-of-work trollop."

"They won't know how you earned your living before you came there. You could start over, maybe even get married." He hated himself for the lie, but he couldn't bring himself to walk away and leave her so dejected.

"How, Buck?" She crossed her arms beneath her bosom and glowered at him. "You tell me how, dammit. I've worked for Jonas five months and I don't have enough money to buy breakfast, let alone a ticket on the stage. By the time he deducts what he calls 'living expenses' there's nothing left. Anything we buy goes on his account, and we have to pay it back at ten percent interest."

"Judas. The man ought to be strung up."

"Let me know what time to be at the hanging," she said, flopping onto the bed.

Buck took his trousers from the chair where he'd thrown them the night before and fished out a quarter-eagle gold piece worth two-fifty, nearly twice what it cost to spend the night with her. "Here, stash this away somewhere. Every tip you get from now on, add it to this and give the rest to Jonas. When you have enough for that stage ticket, just go. To hell with Jonas and his accounts. You wait till the last minute, walk out, get on the stage, and go."

Tears glistened in her eyes as she took the money. "Thank you, Buck. I-I'll never forget you."

"I won't forget you either, Lacey," he lied.

A few minutes later Buck descended the stairs to the saloon, his head full of ideas about where to go from there. Farther south were sandstone formations he'd heard were more fantastic than those in Deception Canyon—miles of sheer, ragged walls sculpted by wind and rain into spires, fins, pillars, and mazes. Slickrock canyons, natural stone bridges, ancient Indian dwellings built on the ledges of perpendicular cliffs, and still farther south, a canyon so deep a man could stand on the edge and barely see the silver thread of the Colorado River flowing through the bottom. But what came most to mind was San Francisco. And the Pacific Ocean.

"You leaving us?" Stud stood behind the bar, his mustache so stiff he could have used it to pick his teeth. In spite of a face smallpox had left looking like the result of a buffalo stampede, the man insisted he'd gotten his nickname by being run out of Texas by a posse of jealous husbands. Buck didn't doubt it; there was something about Stud that drew people to him.

"Yep. You keep that mustache of yours sharp, Stud. Never know when you might need it."

"That I will, friend, that I will."

Halfway to the door, Buck stopped. The one-armed Scotsman he had learned was Tempest's father was passed out at one of the tables. The sight bothered him. Being crippled was no excuse for not taking better care of his daughter. Buck considered talking to the old man, then reminded himself it was none of his business. Nor would Miss Stubborn and Proud thank him for his efforts.

The door opened and Jonas Creedy entered, accompanied by a dark-frocked man with the stern face and the white-rimmed eyes of a religious fanatic. Jonas looked particularly pleased with himself.

"You ain't staying for the celebration, Maddux?" Creedy asked, eyeing the saddlebags slung over Buck's broad shoulder.

"What celebration?"

"Why, my wedding, of course."

A frisson of unease skinned down Buck's back. "You're getting married?"

"Ain't the girls told you?"

Buck had noted the man's absence the past day or so, but had spared it little thought. The less he saw of Jonas Creedy the better he liked it. "Not a word. Who's the lucky bride?"

"The Widow Whitney." Creedy smacked his lips and rubbed a hand over his crotch. "My wedding night is hours away and I'm already hard as a railroad spike. I been waiting a long time to get my cock in her—and tonight's the night."

Buck's eyes narrowed. The man's filthy mouth sickened him.

"Yessir," Creedy continued, "wedding's at four this

afternoon. Too bad you won't be there. Festivities won't soon be forgot 'round these parts."

Creedy had the personality of a wolverine and the habits of a turkey vulture. Biting back his disgust, Buck headed for the door.

"Lacey's gonna miss you," Creedy called after him. "Them whores is both gonna be lonesome after today."

Judas Priest, but Buck detested the man. How could Tempest Whitney even consider marrying a maggot like that? The idea turned Buck's stomach. Abruptly, he pivoted and went back inside. Creedy had vanished, gone upstairs to bid his favorite whore farewell, probably. Buck marched over to Tempest's father and gave the man a shove. "Wake up, Carmichael."

Ronan Carmichael groaned. Buck shook him again.

"Leave off, mon." The Scotsman tried to push him away.

"Don't you go closing your eyes again, you miserable excuse for a father. Are you aware that your daughter is about to marry the sleaziest snake on two legs?"

"Eh?" Carmichael blinked bloodshot eyes. Liquor slurred his words. "Ye mean Jonas? Ain't naught to be done about it. Lemme be."

"What do you mean, there's nothing to be done about it? You could stop it, for hell's sake."

"Nay, too many debts. Me only daughter, and I failed her, same way I did her sweet mother." Grabbing onto Buck's coat, he said, "You be a good lad, or ye wouldn't be frettin' o'er me girl. Save 'er. You've the strength and courage for it, I see it in yer eyes. Go, save the lass. You can do it . . . but not me. Not me."

The drunken Scotsman sank back down onto the table, his open mouth emitting noxious fumes that made Buck want to retch. Over in the corner, the piano player struck up a tune about a man going to war in a cloud of glory. The faro dealer called out, inviting customers to come challenge the "tiger." Cursing, Buck took up his saddle-bags and headed once more for the door.

The old man was crazy, expecting him to play hero. It wasn't in him. Besides, Tempest Whitney's choice of husband was none of his business. At least she'd be housed, dressed, and fed better than she was now. Buck had kept his promise to Skeet. Now he was free to pursue his own interests, and regardless of the fantasies that had haunted his recent nights, Creedy's bride-to-be definitely had no place in Buck's plans.

Tempest arrived at her wedding atop the old black mule Othello, Ethan before her and Angel clinging to her waist from behind. No one would ever know how desperately she wanted to run away instead. To a place she wouldn't have to deal with Jonas Creedy or any other man, only Angel and Ethan and herself.

Several yards away, cowhands tended a side of beef spitted above a fire. The smell of burning sagebrush and sizzling fat blended with the tangy aroma of the sauce brushed onto the meat. Sheets covered several tables, the corners flapping in the breeze like cheerful banners. Tempest took in the elaborate preparations and felt her heart crumble.

All night she'd lain awake searching for a way to avoid marrying Jonas. Her father had no money. No one else in the canyon did either. They might dress better and eat better, but they had nothing left over to share. Not even her dear friend Viola. Tempest's grandparents were in Scotland, and Skeet's parents had despised her on sight. No one knew where her brother Dirk was. There was no one else for her to turn to.

There had never been a man in her life she could count on. At seventeen she had run away rather than watch the boy she loved—who had vowed she would be the only woman in his life—marry someone else. Then charming, gentle Skeet had walked into the restaurant where she'd worked, and promised her the moon. What she'd got was disappointment. Skeet had tried, but all he knew how to do well was play. No sooner had he vanished from her life than her father had stumbled in—drunk, broke, and hungry.

No, she had no choice but to take her chances with Jonas and pray he had more kindness in him than she suspected. No sooner had that thought left her mind than Jonas emerged from the big log house and hurried toward her, scowling at the sight of her black-stockinged legs dangling below her shoved-up skirts.

"Gawddammit, woman, you trying to shame me, riding astride like that? Where's your dogcart?"

"I left it for Papa since I won't need it after today."

He snatched Ethan out of her arms. Before she could dismount, he noticed the dull black fabric of her gown, the crepe, the lack of adornments, all indicative of mourning.

"You bitch," he snarled. He plunked Ethan on the ground so roughly the toddler toppled into the dust. "You wore that witch's rag on purpose."

Tempest's mouth tightened. When he reached for her, she evaded his hands and slid to the ground. "This is the only dress I own, Jonas. If you find me too much of an embarrassment, I'll be glad to find another way to pay off my mortgage. Maybe you could give Papa a job—here on your ranch—that pays more than room and board."

"I ain't having that worthless father of yours on my ranch. And I ain't calling off our wedding either." He jerked her close, whispering in her ear as he squeezed her breast. "I been looking forward to tonight far too long. Your defiance will cost you, though, see if it don't. I'll ride you so hard tonight you'll forget you ever had a life without me in it—without *me* inside *you*."

Bitter acid flushed into her throat as guests stepped out onto the porch and watched him maul her like a common whore. Her own neighbors and friends. The ones she hadn't been able to face since agreeing to marry him. Everyone except her father, who hadn't bothered to come. She'd thought she couldn't hurt any worse. Now she knew better. Drawing her pride around her, she thrust her chin high. "Odd, I don't recall anything in our agreement about sleeping together."

In his shock, his hold slackened, and she shoved him away. He muttered a foul curse as she lifted Angel from Othello's rump. She half expected him to strike her. When he didn't, she released her breath, took her children by the hand, and headed for the house that would be her prison for the rest of her life.

"Wait just a gawddamn minute." Jonas blocked her way. "If you think I'm gonna let you get away with that, you're crazy. A man don't have to map out sleeping arrangements when he asks a woman to marry him."

"You didn't ask me to marry you, Jonas. You blackmailed me into it, and that allows for a whole new set of rules."

"We'll see about that. A man don't have to ask his wife permission to diddle her. You hear me?" His voice rose as she stepped around him and walked toward the house. "By gawd," he bawled at her back, heedless of the people on the porch, "I'll bed you tonight if I have to hog-tie you to do it. You belong to me now, and I'll damn well take what I want from you, any way I have to."

At Tempest's side, Angel looked up with big soulful eyes full of questions her mother couldn't answer. Ethan whimpered and tugged on his mother's hand. "Baba, 'orsy. Bye-bye." She smiled sadly at her son who couldn't tell the difference yet between a horse and a mule, and had always been sensitive to stress. "Later, sweetheart. Right now we have to go inside."

The house was huge with a wrap-around porch and leaded-glass windows, the kind of house Skeet had promised her. At least she wouldn't have to worry here about the children being bitten by rats while they slept. That might, just *might,* justify saddling them with a stepfather who hated them. Closing her eyes, she sent silent thanks to her friend White Cloud Woman for telling her the Ute secret for preventing conception. No children would be born of this union. Tempest would see to it. She knelt and retied Angel's drooping bow, then straightened the collar on Ethan's dress. "See what a pretty house this is? We're going to live here from now on. Won't that be nice?"

"No. Eef'n bye-bye, 'orsy." He imitated a whinny, then began to cry.

"Christ! Shut him up," Jonas ordered. "We have guests inside."

"*You* have guests," she said, glaring at him. "Most of whom are outside, rather than in. I'm here against my will. I have no intention of letting you forget that."

With a curse, he stalked into the house. Left behind, Tempest met the curious gaze of each guest with uncompromising directness until the starers colored and slunk back inside. Then she hugged her small son tightly and buried her face in his warm neck, seeking reassurance in the familiar, powdery-clean smell of him. A small hand slid inside hers and she looked down.

"It'll be all right, Mama," Angel assured her in an entirely too-adult voice.

"Of course it will, honey." Lifting her chin, Tempest led her small family into the shadowed foyer of their new home.

Almost two dozen residents of Deception Canyon and its vicinity waited in the parlor to witness the joining of a prosperous but ill-liked half-breed and a woman everyone respected and admired. Tempest nodded at Hildreth and

Archibald Eisenbein who sold her herbs and vegetables in their general store, and at John Bennet who handled the sale of her mules at his livery. Then Viola Sims, who ran the Boston Eatery, rushed toward her, a gun belt strapped as always around her ample waist.

"Oh, Tempest, dear. The moment I heard, I wanted to come, but I didn't dare leave the restaurant. I cannot believe you truly intend to marry that man," Viola trilled in her soft Boston accent. Her bad eye twitched, exposing her distress. "Are you sure this is what you want? He's so, well, so . . ."

"Charming and kind?" Tempest offered sardonically.

Viola was several years older, and Tempest's only friend now that White Cloud Woman was gone. "Oh, dear," she said, "you dislike Mr. Creedy, I see it in your eyes. Well, of course you dislike the man, how could anybody not dislike him? I told that nice Mr. Maddux this morning, this had to be some sort of mistake."

Tempest stiffened at the mention of Buck Maddux, but Viola didn't notice. Was he still in town? Would he help her if he knew? No, of course he wouldn't, except perhaps to protect his interest in her land.

"What are you going to do?" Viola asked. "I'm afraid Mr. Creedy truly expects you to marry him." Speaking to the empty space beside her, she said, "I know you assured me everything would turn out all right, Mr. Sims, but at this point, I truly don't see how."

Tempest didn't bat an eye as her friend argued with her dead husband; it had been like this ever since Mr. Sims was killed by robbers a year ago, the same time Viola's left eye was permanently damaged. Since then she had taken to wearing an old training pistol—at Mr. Sims's suggestion, she claimed. Viola had never used his Christian name, always addressing him as Mr. Sims—out of respect, she explained. Even in death she had been unable to let go of him.

"Mr. Sims says for you not to worry, dear. He insists all will go well." Viola heaved a sigh which lifted her considerable bosom nearly to her chin. "I certainly hope he's right."

Over the plump woman's shoulder, Tempest saw Jonas start toward her with a somber man she guessed to be the preacher. "Don't worry about me, Viola. I'm sure Mr. Sims is right. Would you keep an eye on the children for me? I think they're ready to start the ceremony."

"Certainly, but . . ."

Tempest acknowledged the preacher with a nod as Jonas led her to the front of the outlandishly opulent room. The multitude of flickering candles and lamps placed about to dispel the shadows of the towering canyon walls failed to lift her gloom. Her mind spun as the preacher began the service, the words booming out of his thick chest. His stony gaze speared Tempest as if he knew she had no intention of keeping any pledges made to the man at her side.

A part of her was silently screaming No! Sweet Mary, Mother of God, don't let this happen. In spite of her brave words earlier, she knew there was no way to prevent Jonas from consummating the marriage. She shuddered in revulsion, wishing she'd never been born.

At the back of the room a child began to cry. The sound pierced Tempest's agony. Whirling, she pushed through the crowd. Behind her, Jonas called out, demanding she return to her place beside him. All around, voices buzzed with excitement and anticipation. Finally she found Viola, Ethan struggling in her arms and wailing for his mother. Moisture pricked the backs of Tempest's eyes. She clutched her son fiercely, willing the tears away. Emotional rain, her mother had called tears—an unaccountably poetic term for a woman so critical she never offered her daughter a single word of praise. Ethan calmed, nestled his head in the crook of her neck and slid a thumb into his mouth.

"Mama," Angel said, "can we go home now?"

Jonas forestalled her reply. "What's the meaning of this, Tempest? You're creating a scene. Get back over there and let Pastor Kane finish the ceremony."

Silently, she started back to the waiting preacher. When Jonas attempted to take Ethan from her, she sent him a murderous look she knew she would pay for later. Head high, she resumed the bride's place, her son riding her hip and sucking a thumb. Jonas's voice vibrated through the room, rich with satisfaction and pride as he said his vows. Then it was her turn.

"I, Tara Tempest Whitney, do take Jonas Creedy as my husband, to have and to hold . . ." The words stuck in her throat. She could feel everyone staring at her, expectation thick as summer mosquitoes in the air. Her gaze fell from the preacher's glowering face to the holy book he held in stout hands better suited for hauling manure. Jonas shook her arm, his fingers digging cruelly into her flesh.

"Finish it, Tempest. Finish it, or . . ."

The front door swung open with such force it struck the wall at the back of the room.

A ripple of gasps punctuated the silence.

Beside Tempest, Jonas stiffened.

"Let go of her, Creedy," said a voice as hard and lethal as a rattler's venom.

Jonas muttered an ugly oath. At first, Tempest saw only the backs of the guests facing the open door. Then they parted and Buck Maddux strolled into view, his icy blue eyes glinting like sunlight on steel.

"I said, let go of her," he repeated.

A shiver, half-fear, half-elation, etched Tempest's spine. She tamped down the urge to run to him. To seek the safety of his strong arms.

"Whaddya mean by this, Maddux?" Jonas demanded. "You're interfering in something that don't concern you."

Buck looked at him, his hands on his slim hips, his feet spread, head slightly cocked. As casual as a cornered cougar. "This wedding very much concerns me. You see, Tempest is my responsibility."

"What in hell you talking about? How could she be?"

Buck's gaze met Tempest's. She tried to read the message reflected in the blue depths, and failed.

"Simple," he said, flashing a satanic smile. "She's my wife. Two years ago I was known as Skeet Whitney."

Chapter Four

Judas Priest but he was a stupid son of a bitch. Idiot. Imbecile. Jackass. Buck couldn't come up with enough foul names to call himself, though he said none of them aloud, what with Angel riding in his lap and Tempest alongside on her old soot-colored mule, holding Ethan.

Why had he done such a fool thing? He was the last man on earth to be playing white knight to a woman who didn't even look grateful. Not that he'd done it for gratitude. He'd done it to salve his own conscience. Buck couldn't abide seeing a woman abused, and Jonas Creedy didn't know any other way to treat one. Buck didn't like thinking what having Creedy as a father might do to the widow's kids either.

The child seated in front of him squirmed. In his anger and frustration he had tightened his grip on her. He forced himself to loosen his hold and eased his temper with a few deep breaths. She was a cute little thing, like his sisters, Lize and Larken, had been when he'd last seen them fifteen years ago. It amazed him to realize how much he still missed them. Usually he kept the pain and loneliness of having been cast from his family sunk so deep in his soul he rarely thought of them. Now, feeling the warm, wriggly little girl in his arms, the memories gushed back with alarming force and clarity. He swallowed the sudden itch in his throat and glanced to see if Tempest noticed his momentary weakness. Her gaze seemed fixed somewhere between the long ears of the mule she rode, and she looked as though she'd been chewing nails and was about to spit them out, sharp end first—right at Buck's heart.

While Mrs. Sims shooed away curious wedding guests, Jonas had demanded to know why—if Buck truly was Skeet Whitney—he hadn't come forward sooner. Why had he lied about who he was? Buck said the only thing he could think of, that before disclosing his presence, he'd wanted to make sure she hadn't remarried and might welcome him back.

"Well, she's promised to be *my* wife now," Jonas had retorted with a sneer. "So you can go back to playing dead."

Buck's smile could have frozen hell. "I don't think so, Creedy. See, I don't like you. I don't like the way you treat your women, and I sure as thunder don't want scum like you raising my children."

Jonas's hand shot to his waist, but he'd left his gun belt off for the wedding. The veins in his temples bulged with fury. "You white-assed sonuvabitch. She might be a little less glad to welcome you back in her bed if she knew where you been sleeping the last three days. Tell me, does she squeal and pant and beg for more the way Lacey's done every night since you come to town?"

That was when Buck knocked the ugly bastard on his ear, but he wished he'd done it a few seconds sooner— before Tempest was humiliated in front of her friends.

He glanced at her again. With her amber-flecked eyes flashing and her cheeks flushed with anger, she was actually kind of pretty. He hadn't recognized her at first in her black dress and bonnet and prim gloves. Then it had taken all his self-control not to laugh in Jonas's face, making a bad situation worse. What other woman would wear widow's weeds to her own wedding? That she could look so feminine all dressed up proper surprised him. The bodice molded to her curves, revealing what her baggy shirt and apron had hidden before. The skirt, hiked up to ride astride, showed gently rounded calves and slim ankles sheathed in black wool stockings. Of course, the scuffed-up boy's work boots sort of ruined the image, but he found them comforting; they assured him this truly was the Tempest Whitney he knew and disliked.

"Go on," he said, encouraging her to nourish his antipathy. "Nail me to the cross. Been done before."

Tempest glared. She knew she should be grateful to him, but having to feel beholden to any man rankled her. And, ridiculous as it might be, she was mortified that everybody knew he'd been sleeping with Jonas's fallen doves. "Don't tempt me, you snake-eyed sneak-in-the-night. What in purple petunias did you think you were doing back there? You have any idea the mess you've made?"

Buck grinned. He had never met anybody better at name-calling than Tempest Whitney. The urge to provoke her a little more was irresistible. "Only petunias I ever saw were pink, but they don't grow in this desert. Sure you don't mean prairie flax?"

Tempest snorted. "What would a two-legged, offal-eating skunk like you know about flowers?"

He leaned closer, giving her the smile prison guards called his devil's grin. "You'd be surprised what I know. Care to find out?"

"No, and don't try to sidetrack me, Mr. Maddux. The

subject was your breaking in on my wedding and announcing to the world that you were my husband. If you think
this is going to get you the rest of Heartsease you failed
to bamboozle my husband out of, you'd best think again.''

Her accusation jabbed his innards like a ten-inch prickly
pear spine. Maybe he was a no-account; he'd made plenty
of mistakes in his time, he'd grant that. Mistakes that still
gave him nightmares. But he'd never knowingly cheated
a soul and had no intention of starting now. Something
he would make very clear to Tempest Whitney. In one easy
motion, he bent from his saddle, grabbed her reins and
brought their animals to a halt. Spook tossed his head and
whinnied in protest at being crowded so close to the mule,
but Buck ignored him.

"Dammit, woman, I didn't bamboozle anything out of
that fool you married and there's nothing I want from you
either. You got that?''

Pinned by his burning gaze, Tempest could only stare
back at him. He had gone from a devil-may-care womanizer
to a hard-eyed demon even a Ute warrior would hesitate
to tangle with, all in an instant's time, and without warning.
It was plain as summer lightning there was more to Buck
Maddux than met the eye, more than he wanted her to
see.

In her lap Ethan squirmed and whimpered. She patted
his leg with her free hand, her gaze falling away from
Buck's. Her fury waned. Truth to tell, she wasn't sure why
she'd felt so angry. Except that she was scared, and whenever she got scared, she got angry. If the Lord had set out
to teach her exactly how helpless she was without a man,
He had gone about it right, but she sure didn't like it.
Viola Sims was on her own and nobody bothered her. Why
did Tempest need a husband, if Viola didn't?

*Viola is fifteen years older, has a bad eye, wears a pistol, and
talks to her dead husband as if he were still alive.* Well, so what?

Tempest was no prize herself. And she had a derringer; all she had to do was carry it.

That wouldn't have kept Jonas from using your mortgage to force you into marriage. Tempest couldn't argue that. Neither did it explain Buck Maddux's heroics. "If you don't want anything from me, why did you interfere?"

"Damned if I know. Call it insanity." Releasing her, he spurred Spook away from the mule and they began moving again. "I promised your husband I'd make sure you were all right, and being married to Jonas Creedy wasn't my idea of all right."

His voice was still hard edged as a razor, though he looked more frustrated now than angry. For the first time since he'd burst into Jonas's house, Tempest thought of what it had cost him to help her. He'd given away every cent he had and had put himself in an awkward situation, since he was now forced to pretend to be her husband. Why had he done it? Because of a promise? It was safer to assume he was greedy for her land ... or feeling guilty over the stolen money—if the man *had* a conscience.

"No one in town could tell me anything about Skeet," he said after a moment. "Said they'd never even seen the man. Reckon that's what put the idea in my head." He took off his hat and rubbed his neck. "Must be someone here who knew him, though, and can put the lie to my claim. So you're right, it was a damn foolish thing to do."

"I'm surprised you didn't tell Jonas that marrying me would only get him *half* my ranch," she muttered, "since you claim to own the other half. It would've been easier, and we wouldn't have to pretend to be married."

"Might have ... if I could have proved it."

"You mean Skeet didn't sign anything giving you half the land?"

Cramming the hat back on his head, he growled, "No, I mean I tore the blasted paper up after he died. Anyway, it was my understanding that Jonas wanted more out of this deal than your land. I couldn't risk having him settle for half the land . . . and you. Reckoned it was safer to say I was your husband."

Tempest had no doubt Jonas would have done exactly what Buck had anticipated—take half the land and her, then figure out how to get the other half from Buck. Jonas's words came back to her, reminding her of what Buck had saved her from. *I'll ride you so hard tonight you'll forget you ever had a life without me in it— without me inside you.* She shuddered.

"Is the idea of pretending to be my wife that repulsive?" Buck asked.

His sensitivity surprised her. So did the flash of pain in his eyes. She started to tell him it was thinking of Jonas that made her shudder, not him, then snapped her mouth shut. Let the arrogant rogue think what he wanted; it might keep him away from her. For all she knew he might have a real wife somewhere.

"First building in Harper didn't go up until last year, after Skeet died," she said, switching the conversation to a more comfortable track. So what if he was married? All Tempest wanted was his protection for a few weeks until she could pay off the loan. "There is Melba Washburn, she'd know him. Only she lives too far away to be any real threat." Under her breath she added, "Or help, depending on how you look at it."

"How do *you* look at it, Tempest?" he asked. "You want me to ride on? You could tell folks you kicked me out. They'd understand, under the circumstances."

Silently, she cursed his good ears. "An absentee husband wouldn't keep a hungry buzzard like Jonas at bay for long." Quickly, she added, "That's the only reason I'm not sending you packing, though. Don't get any ideas about how things will be between us. This is a pretend marriage, nothing more."

His eyes were like frozen bits of sky. "I told you, woman, I don't want your land . . . or you."

She didn't believe him. All her life men had wanted something from her. With her father and brothers it had been cooking, washing, and mending clothes. Skeet had needed a mama. He'd tapped into her strength, the way Indian paintbrush taps into the roots of other plants to steal their food, and he'd nearly drained her dry. Buck Maddux wasn't weak like Skeet. He was too hard, too self-reliant to lean on a woman. He was also too much of a devil to trust. She had seen the desire in his eyes the day he'd come to the dugout and pinned her against the wall with his body. He may not want her land, but he did want her.

And you want him.

No! I want a man who will love me for what I am, instead of sucking the strength from me. Using me.

Then why does thinking about him heat up your body like a spring fever?

"What about your father?" Buck said, ending her inner argument. "Will he go along with this ridiculous charade?"

"I was living a hundred miles from home when I married Skeet. My family never met him. Papa may have questions like everyone else about why you came here claiming to be someone else at first, but he can't prove you aren't Skeet."

"Might work then." Again he pinned her with those keen, blue, blue eyes. "If you want it to."

Tempest averted her gaze to the sculpted canyon walls she loved. "I don't want to marry Jonas," she said softly.

"I'll take that as a yes." The satisfaction that filled him also frightened him. "What about the money? Any idea how we can come up with it?"

Her chin dipped; then she forced it back up. "I could go to Provo and try for another loan."

He didn't bother to point out how unlikely she was to get one. "No family to borrow it from?"

"No. All I've got is Papa . . . and the debts he runs up for me."

"I'll see to it he stays out of the saloons. How do you buy supplies?"

"I keep the Eisenbeins and Viola Sims supplied with produce from my garden, and I sell jams and jellies and herbs. The mule colts I've raised paid the loan payments until now, but Papa found what I'd hoarded up over the summer and spent it on liquor and gambling." Ethan squirmed in her lap, trying to reach a butterfly. "Sit still, Ethan, you'll fall off." The hopelessness of the situation made her want to cry. Or scream. She shoved away both impulses.

Buck muttered something vile about her father and rubbed his neck. "We'll find a way out of this somehow. We have to."

They lapsed into silence. Out of the corner of her eye, she studied him, pondering how far he might try to carry their "charade." His use of "we" troubled her, not only because it made her question again what he expected from her, but also because the sound of it pleased her. The man was good-looking; she had to admit that. His forearms, exposed by the rolled-up sleeves of his chambray shirt, were tan and rough with dark hair. The veins in his large, strong hands were thick and blue with the blood that pulsed through them in a throbbing echo of her own heartbeat. How many women had felt the touch of those hands—besides Lacey? Were they gentle and tender, or grasping and selfish as Skeet's had often been? Certainly they wouldn't be cruel like Jonas's. The thought of Buck's hands caressing her caused a tingling low in her body. She tried to look away, to put the inappropriate thoughts from her mind, but she couldn't help watching him, and wondering.

Angel leaned over in his lap to hug the dappled horse they rode. Muscles rolled across his shoulders under his shirt and leather vest as he reached to keep the girl from falling. The action showed Tempest exactly how gentle his hands could be. It stood to reason that a gentle man would also be a giving man. Something she'd yearned for, though she hadn't dared to hope to really find it. But Buck Maddux was a drifter, an arrogant devil of a rogue. She couldn't allow herself to think of him as anything other than a temporary means to an end. Living in the same house with him long enough to solve their dilemma was more than unthinkable. It was insane.

So why do I feel this secret thrill inside?

Buck guided Spook down the sloping bank of a dry gully carved by the rushing water of a flash flood. The big appaloosa climbed easily onto the road again and Buck turned to make sure the mule maneuvered the crumbling bank without difficulty. Tempest had fallen behind. She was nursing her son, shielded by the crocheted wool of her shawl. The naked bliss in her smile as her son suckled her breast, cooing his contentment, lit a spark that seared Buck's innards. It also left him feeling set apart, empty and bereft. He told himself it was the same old loneliness he'd lived with half his life. The same hunger for a home, hearth, and family that could never be his. Whipping around in his seat he stared morosely forward, wondering how long it would take to shake loose of Tempest Whitney and her mewling brats.

"Mithter Buck?"

He squirmed as he looked down at the tiny child in his

lap, a riot of pale curls swirling about her sweet face like a wind-tossed halo. Judas, he didn't want to have to talk with her. What did a man say to a four-year-old? "Yeah, Angel?"

"Are you really my daddy?"

Buck cursed silently. He hadn't been around children in years and had given no thought to how this ruse would affect Tempest's. Now new guilt and doubts riddled him. He surprised himself by thumbing a chocolate smudge off her button mouth. The girl hadn't hesitated to make free with the wedding cake while the adults argued after Buck had disrupted the ceremony. "No, honey. I'm only going to be a pretend daddy for a while, till your mama can handle things on her own again. It'll be like a game, a secret game no one will know about except you and me and Ethan and Mama, all right?"

For thirty seconds Angel chewed on that. Then she looked up again. "Ethan and me ain't got no real daddy."

"I know." A shocking, bittersweet mixture of pleasure and pain skewered his heart. Pleasure that she might want him, pain because he would never have little ones of his own. "Doesn't mean we can't be friends, though. Okay?"

"Okay." The soft wistfulness in her voice found a corresponding note inside his soul. Swiftly he stamped it out. There was no room in a drifter's life for angels. Or for widows either, no matter how fetching he might find them.

When they reached Heartsease, Tempest took the children into the dugout and started supper. Buck lingered in the barn, tending to Spook and the mule. There were matters to be settled yet between him and the window. Like how they would come up with the cash to pay off Creedy and regain their freedom. Matters he didn't relish facing because he knew, with a woman like her, it would mean arguing. Tempest Whitney wasn't the type to make things easy for a man.

The only thing Buck hated more than arguing with a woman was hearing one cry. There was a wealth of female sobbing already locked in his memory he'd never be able to shed. Wails of terror and grief that haunted his nights. Buck prayed Tempest Whitney wouldn't add to those nightmares, that he wouldn't regret having saved her from Jonas more than he already did. He told himself he could climb back on Spook and simply ride off. Trouble was, his conscience wouldn't let him. Besides, he didn't have a dime. Tempest's thwarted bridegroom had screeched at the top of his lungs that "that bitch" wasn't going anywhere until she repaid him some of what she owed him. Like an idiot Buck had emptied his pockets onto the table.

"That's all there is, Creedy," he'd said. "Twenty-four dollars and six cents. You might be able to get a judge to award you some of Tempest's land for the rest of it. 'Course that would take time, and you'll be getting the whole ranch anyway when we fail to make the payment, won't you? All you need is patience."

Creedy had pocketed the money and ordered them off his land.

Twenty-four dollars and six cents. No fortune, but enough to get Buck the blazes away from Harper, Utah, and the Widow Whitney. What would happen now? Would Tempest expect him to stay here, with her? He didn't have a dollar for a room at the Harper Hotel. Or the dollar-fifty he'd need to spend the night with Lacey, which, of course, was out of the question now.

He had just become a married man.

Panic accompanied the thought, along with a frisson of longing. Buck shrugged them both away. Marriage, love, children—those were only dreams. Dreams that would never come true for him. He'd had his chance—and bungled it.

Finding work in Deception Canyon was about as likely as being named a prophet in the Mormon church. The thriving metropolis of Harper consisted of two saloons, Eisenbein's store, Bennet's livery, the hotel and the Boston Eatery. The one ranch other than Heartsease that was owned by a gentile—what Mormons called non-Mormons—and was large enough to employ more than a hand or two, was Creedy's. Mormons needed the money gentiles brought into their precious Zion, but they stringently avoided giving their business, their jobs, or their women to nonbelievers.

Buck was straight-out broke, and had just taken on the responsibility of a woman and two small children. Buck Maddux, who'd spent his life, since the age of twenty, making sure he wasn't accountable to anybody. Hell of a fix. One he had to get out of, before it became worse. He grabbed up his saddle and was about to plunk it onto Spook's back when a high, lisping voice halted him.

"Mithter Buck? You aren't going nowhere, are you?"

Guilt shafted through him at the sight of Angel's moonbeam curls and worried little-girl frown. He put the saddle down. "No, Angel. I'm not going anywhere."

"I'm glad." Her face blossomed with a smile sweeter than peppermint sticks. "I came to tell you thupper's ready. Mama made fried taters and onions."

"Sounds great." Feeling inexplicably cheerful all of a sudden, he lifted her high in the air until she squealed, then lowered her to his shoulders. Her hands knotted in his black, silver-streaked hair as she straddled his neck. "Reckon we oughta wash up?" he said in mock seriousness as he headed for the house. "Little mud and horse droppings won't hurt nothing, will it?"

Angel giggled. "Mama makes uth wath all the time."

He chuckled at the disgust in her lisping voice. "Little girls are supposed to like being clean. You are a little girl, aren't you?"

"Yeth, but being clean *all* the time ith thilly."

"Tell you what," he said as he lifted her down and held her in front of him. "We'll just wash off the top layer and not tell a soul. How's that sound?"

To his surprise, the girl framed his face in her two small hands, then kissed him full on the mouth. "I like you, Mithter Buck. I hope you can be my daddy forever."

A tiny door inside him unlatched. He set her down next to the bench which held a wash basin and a bar of homemade lye soap. "Being friends is better."

Angel took up a pitcher of water he would have thought too heavy for her, and filled the basin without spilling a drop. Handing him the soap, she gave him a quizzical look. "How?"

Bending from the waist, he put his nose close to hers. "Because if I were your daddy, I'd have to make you scrub off all the dirt instead of only the top layer. That's what daddies do."

"Oh."

While she contemplated that, Buck stripped off his shirt and set it aside. He splashed water on his face, soaped up his hands, and scrubbed hard. After rinsing off, he opened his eyes to see Angel gaping at him in disgust.

"You tell whopperth, Mithter Buck."

"What, me?" he uttered in shocked amazement. "How can you say such a thing?"

"I can thay it cauthe I theen you rub off *all* the layers, even behind your ears and the back of your neck."

Buck felt his ears and neck with his hands as though terrified he might find them missing. "What do you know, I believe you're right. Think I ought to sprinkle a little dirt on 'em?"

"That won't be necessary," said another voice.

Tempest stood in the doorway. Her braid was still coiled neatly at her nape, but the black gown had been replaced by the loose denims, sacklike shirt, and long apron she'd worn the day he met her. She was smiling, and he realized it was the first time he had seen the sight. Damn if it didn't make her look fetching. Then her gaze lowered to his bare chest and the smile fled. Her throat convulsed as her eyes followed a bead of water from his neck onto the rugged plain of his chest where it caught in a brake of black hair. The pulse visible in the hollow of her throat kicked into a lope as she watched the droplet slide free and venture lower, over his rib cage onto his belly. When it vanished inside his navel, she licked her lips, and Buck's veins turned to liquid fire.

She jerked her gaze away and met his. To keep from reaching for her, he retreated behind the mask he used to hide his pain and loneliness. He flashed her a devilish, knowing grin and winked. Her unfashionably tanned face took on a rosy hue that delighted him. He expected her to whirl and storm back into the house. Or call him some new, inventive name. Instead, she held firm, refusing to look away first.

"We have serious matters to discuss, Mr. Maddux . . . if you're through teaching my daughter your bad habits."

Buck expanded his grin, this time in genuine enjoyment. He sketched her a low bow. "At your service, ma'am."

Her snort was as delicate as he'd ever heard. "Angel, when you come inside I expect to see *every* layer of dirt gone. You hear?"

"Yeth, Mama."

"And don't forget to get Ethan washed up."

With that Tempest disappeared into the house. Buck toweled off and took up his shirt. He winked at Angel as he slipped his arms into the sleeves. The girl grinned back as if they shared a secret, then went to fetch her brother. As Buck approached the doorway, a dog the same faded yellow ocher as the dirt lifted itself from the ground as Buck approached the doorway and bared its fangs in a snarl.

"Hello, fella," Buck crooned. "You the one tried to rip the britches off me the other day?"

The dog barked and made a mock lunge at him. From inside the dugout Tempest yelled, "Down, Rooster."

The dog backed off reluctantly and flopped against the wall again.

"Rooster?" Buck removed his hat, ducked beneath the low doorway and entered the house, the clanking of his spurs seeming unnaturally loud within the thick walls. "What kind of name is that for a self-respecting hound?"

"He howls every morning when the sun comes up. Angel named him," she added as if that explained everything. Which it did.

"Doesn't much care for daylight, huh? My kind of dog. Too bad he doesn't like me."

Tempest felt the man's presence with every nerve in her body. He filled the room, like the musty air surrounding her. Touching her, embracing her. Her pulse sped up. She glanced over her shoulder, certain he was hovering behind her. Instead he stood in the center of the room, several feet away, his head bowed to avoid brushing the ceiling.

Buck felt the walls of the small room close in on him as he studied her pathetic, patched-up furniture. A battered sideboard with a broken mirror shared one end of the room with the cookstove which had been placed as close to the bedroom doorway as possible for heat distribution. A table took up the center of the room, while the far end was occupied by a narrow bed. Dried herbs hung from the ceiling, along with strings of onions. There was no sofa or divan. No comfortable chair. The rock wall between the two rooms had been roughly plastered with clay and decorated with pictures of flowers cut from magazines. The only flowers on the place, he noted; all else was brutally plain and practical. It hurt him to imagine the harshness of a life whose one concession to the typical, feminine need for beauty had come so cheaply, and secondhand to boot.

Tempest's face flushed as his glance shifted to her. For the first time she was glad of the dimness of the light filtering through the velum that acted as window panes. In bright light her home and possessions would appear even meaner. The open door did little to alleviate the darkness. Tempest loved Heartsease. But she hated the dank, fusty dugout. Heaven, she was certain, had smooth, wooden floors, real glass windows, and walls that kept out snakes and insects.

Taking a deep breath she tried to relax. Her nostrils filled with the aroma of wood smoke, onions, and coal oil. Familiar smells. Comforting smells. But now there was a new scent—the potent, masculine scent of Buck Maddux.

He stepped into the back room and peered into shadowed corners. A single bed crowded the far corner, a small table beside it. The only other contents were a dresser, a trunk, a rocking chair, and a wash tub. The house was as dank and depressing as a cave, the furnishings as sparse as they came. Yet it was the scarcity of feminine trappings that tore at him most. He felt a strange and mortifying urge to haul her and her children out of there and see them settled somewhere decent. Finally he turned and met her gaze.

Tempest was aware on some level of consciousness of the potatoes sizzling in the fry pan, the wood popping on the fire, the faint trill of children's laughter outside. Yet the silence had never seemed so deep. It thickened until she could barely breathe. She tried not to imagine him in that bed, her bed, and heat rushed to her face as well as other places that had never felt so fevered before. Still, she couldn't look away. Her knees puddled beneath her apron, threatening to dump her on the floor. No other man had done that to her.

"Who are you?" she whispered. "Where did you come from?" *Do you already belong to some other woman?*

His eyes flicked back to the big bed; then he walked toward her. The room shrank. The world shrank. To only the two of them, staring at each other, trying to divine the other's thoughts.

"Nobody," he said, his voice deep and husky. "A drifter who's been most everywhere, done most everything"—he halted an arm's length away and Tempest stopped breathing—"and accomplished nothing."

His hand lifted and his fingertips lightly grazed her cheek. A dragonfly's touch. His gaze on her mouth was like a moist, heated caress. Hungry, somber eyes lingered. Eyes full of darkness. Then his hand fell away. "Whatever happens now, pretty lady, is entirely up to you," he said gently. "I don't force myself on women."

Then he spoiled it with a licentious grin. "I only seduce them," he whispered.

The change was so sudden it took her a moment to take it in. The gentle, sensitive man was gone and the charming devil was back. She tried to smile to show she wasn't afraid of him, and failed. There were other questions she needed to ask, but she couldn't think of them. Not while he stood so close, overwhelming her with his size, his scent, his dark sensuality. "Supper's nearly ready. Sit down," she said, pleased she'd managed not to stammer.

An assortment of crudely fashioned stools flanked the table. Buck chose the strongest. Wishing she had meat to serve instead of only potatoes and onions and turnip greens, she busied herself setting buttermilk, hot golden-browned biscuits, a jar of sorghum, and last year's elderberry jam on the table. Not a dish, cup, or glass matched. Neither did the flatware. She had never cared before, and cursed herself for letting it matter now.

Marmalade came and sat at Buck's feet, staring intently up at him. Tempest hid a smile to see the man squirm beneath the cat's green-eyed scrutiny. Then Marmalade leaped onto his thighs.

"Whoa! Wrong lap." He shoved the cat away with a look of abhorrence.

"Don't you like cats?" Tempest asked.

"Can't abide the sneaky little fleabags."

"You're in trouble then. Marmalade loves a challenge and never accepts no for an answer."

"Takes after you, huh?"

Tempest smiled in genuine enjoyment. "Not at all. Not only do I accept no for an answer, I make frequent use of the word myself."

"That's what I figured," he muttered.

The children came in and they sat down. Buck was hungry enough to eat one of the mules out in the corral and maybe a dog or two along with it. An ornery yellow dog. He reached for the potatoes, only to pull back empty-handed as Tempest, Angel, and even Ethan, folded their hands and bowed their heads. In her sweet, lisping voice, Angel asked a blessing on the food. "And pleathe make Mithter Buck thtay here with uth, Lord, cauthe me and Ethan need a daddy real bad."

Tempest's head snapped up and she dropped her hands to her lap. "That's enough, Angel. Say amen now, and put your napkin in your lap where it belongs."

Throughout the rest of the meal Tempest avoided Buck's gaze. When they finished eating, she changed Ethan's diaper and the children went outside to play. Tempest scraped the plates and carried the scraps out to the small herd of pigs, dogs, and cats. She came back in to find Buck filling the wash basin with hot water from the reservoir in the cookstove.

"What are you doing?"

"What does it look like I'm doing?"

"You don't have to do that."

"I know. Want to wash or dry?" He grinned, pleased that he had taken her by surprise. It wasn't good to let a woman get to know a man too thoroughly. Keep them off balance was Buck's theory on the best way to control females. They never knew quite what to expect that way, which made them less likely to make demands a man wasn't prepared to meet.

"I'd better wash," she said. "You'd probably only scrub off the top layer."

Buck gave her his devil's grin. Sidling up close, he murmured in a husky drawl, "If a woman were to give me a good reason, I'd go down to the creek and scrub my whole body till it shone brighter than the moon."

"Don't bother. You'd simply get it dirty again sleeping in the barn with the pigs."

"Damn!" His warm breath caressed her cheek. "You wouldn't really do that to me, would you? I'm your husband, remember? Cost me twenty-five dollars in cold cash to prove it today. And I've been gone two long, lonely years."

"Twenty-four dollars and six cents," she corrected. Enjoying the game, she gazed at the newspaper-lined ceiling, a slender finger tapping her lower lip as she pretended to reconsider his request. "You're right," she said finally with a coy smile, "making you sleep with pigs would be unseemly."

"Not to mention ungrateful," he provided.

"The wind has whipped up rather fierce out there, and the barn's terribly drafty."

Buck's grin returned. But it was short-lived.

"You can use Angel's bed instead," she concluded, gesturing to the cot in the corner. "She can sleep in the back room with Ethan and me while you're here."

Watching her sashay across the room, her hips swaying seductively, he cursed.

Chapter Five

Lacey hummed softly as she stemmed dark blue elder-berries for a pie. The fragrance of the tart juice permeated the air, adding to the delicious aroma of pie crust baking in the big oven. A small, dreamy smile curved her mouth. Inside her head, she wasn't in the kitchen of the Sagebrush Princess. She was in a snug home of her own, with a husband who resembled Buck Maddux seated across from her, telling her how much he loved her.

"Ya about done, honey?" Big Red's soft Southern voice burst the bubble of Lacey's vision, yanking her back to reality.

Glancing up, Lacey watched Red plunge a blunt needle threaded with jade green yarn into the fine-meshed needle-point canvas on her lap. "Oh, Red, that pillow's going to be beautiful. I can't believe what you can do with a few bits of yarn. Wish I had some sort of talent."

"Don't ya be putting yourself down, Lacey. Ya can cook,

and cooking's everythin' to a man, ya know. Ah cain't even boil water.''

"Well, cooking's not enough to get me out of this hell-hole.'' Lacey sighed. "I wish these berries weren't so dang small, but I'm about done. Finally.''

"Good.'' Red turned her needlework over and secured the tail of her yarn beneath the backs of the finished stitches. "That smell's making me hungrier than a pregnant possum in a pear tree.''

Lacey giggled. "There aren't any possums in Utah, Red.''

"Don't ah know it. Just thinking 'bout 'em makes me feel closer to Georgia, though.''

"You miss home that much?''

"Not home,'' Red said with a snort. "Just Georgia. Ah surely don't miss that hovel ah came from. Or my pa and his razor strap.''

Bitterness salted the slightly older girl's voice. Lacey's eyes widened. "He beat you?''

"With a vengeance.''

"Was that . . . all he did?''

Red looked up. "Why, Lacey, ya got fear in your eyes. Your pa beat you, too, didn't he?''

Lacey turned away, shame heating up her cheeks. "No. Not . . . not unless he had to.''

"What do you mean, less'n he had to?''

The girl didn't answer. The words were too ugly to speak aloud. She covered her face with juice-stained hands and tried to blink away the tears. Wood scraped against wood as Red left her chair and moved to stand beside Lacey.

"Ya mean, less'n ya refused to give him what he wanted? Aw, Lacey honey. What'd that awful old man do to ya?''

The sincerity of Red's empathy and the gentleness of her hand lightly squeezing Lacey's shoulder was the girl's undoing. Lacey sobbed as she hadn't since that first terrible visit her pa paid her in the middle of the night when she was five. When Lacey finally quit crying, Red gave her one last squeeze, then went to the stove and poured coffee for them. Lacey dabbed her eyes with the hem of her apron and began stemming berries again. To her relief, nothing more was said about her pa.

Whoops of laughter from the saloon penetrated the walls, demolishing the women's peace. Someone belched loudly and fists banged on the bar. Until that moment the kitchen had been an island of calm in the sea of revelry going on in the saloon. Now not even the thick oak of the door kept out the noise.

"Gawd," Big Red muttered, "listen to 'em out there, like a swarm of flies on a fresh carcass."

"Can't blame them," said Lacey. "Jonas getting left at the altar is even funnier than the night Doc got caught with you and told his wife it was his job to make sure he'd healed up that Cupid's itch you got off a sheepherder."

"Ah fail to see how you could call that funny. She shot the poor old swillpot right there in my bed."

"I know. Lucky his ass was so well padded or that bullet might have gone clean through and nailed you too."

Red stood abruptly, went to the sink and tossed out her coffee with such a vengeance the cup flew from her hand and shattered. "How am ah gonna stand it, Lacey? Ah thought ah was free of Jonas, thanks to that little widow. But now . . ."

The door swung open and Stud Wiley stuck his head around the corner. "Lacey, you're wanted out here."

"Who?" she asked.

"Hitch."

Lacey squeezed her eyes shut and groaned. Of all the men who came to her, Hitch Conners was the most difficult to bear. "Be there in a minute."

At the sink Lacey cleared out the broken crockery and

scrubbed berry juice from her hands with a bar of lye soap. She dried off on a piece of toweling, then turned to Red. Without a word, they hugged.

Lacey had barely entered the bar when the front door opened. The wind wrenched it out of Jonas Creedy's hand and slammed it against the wall, letting in a cloud of dust. Every head at the bar swiveled to see who had come in, and a silence more profound than a minister's pause descended on the saloon. Jonas slapped his hat against his leg to knock off the dirt and glowered at the solemn crowd. "What're you staring at, you whiskey-soaked jackasses?"

At once the men pivoted back to the bar and picked up their glasses. They coughed into their hands, cleared their throats, and gulped their drinks. Stud Wiley polished glasses. "Well, gentlemen, who can tell us the latest on the boxing circuit?"

"Saw a good match in Salt Lake City last week," said John Bennet, "between a big black soldier from Fort Union and a runt no taller than Swede's kneecaps. That little no-account proved more slippery than a greased eel. Before the black landed a single punch, the runt had him out cold. Never saw the like of it anywhere."

Jonas stalked over to Lacey. "Red got a customer upstairs?"

The girl studied her small hands. "No, she's in the kitchen."

"Dammit, is she sewing again?"

"It-it's called needlepoint, Jonas."

"I don't give a pig's pink ass what it's called," Jonas muttered as he headed for the kitchen door. "She's supposed to be upstairs taking care of customers, not sitting on her rear in the kitchen. 'Bout time she learned her place once and for all."

He closed the kitchen door behind him, but everyone at the bar heard him yelling. He came back out, dragging

Red by the arm. For a few minutes after the door to Big Red's room banged shut upstairs the only sounds were the slurps of men guzzling liquor, and awkward cough, shoe leather scuffing the brass rail, and the metallic splatter of tobacco juice in spittoons.

"Hot today for September," Stud said after a while.

Moose Hoffstetter nodded. "Too hot."

"Wind'll cool it off." John Bennet set his empty beer glass down with a clunk. "Got critters to feed."

"Yeah, I got work to do too."

Together, Bennet and Hoffstetter headed for the door. It was like opening the floodgate on an irrigation ditch. Within five minutes the saloon was empty except for Stud, Lacey, and a few no-goods who were reluctant to miss the very show the others wanted to avoid. Everyone knew what was happening upstairs and how it would end—the same way it always ended when Jonas went to Red's room full of anger. Red would be wearing bruises when she came back down. The tension was thick as axle grease, the silence ominous. Lacey wished with all her heart she could escape like Bennet and Moose and the others.

Hitch left his place at the bar and sidled up to her. He ran a dirty finger up her bare arm to the cap sleeve of her dress, then underneath the fabric and down toward her breast. "Why'n't we go up to your room fer a spell, Lacey, see what comes up, eh?" He laughed at his joke, expecting the others to join in.

Lacey averted her gaze from the puckered scar that pulled his mouth down on one side, deforming his smile. She had given up hope that she would stop feeling repulsed every time a man asked her to lift her skirts for him. With Hitch, it wasn't the scar that repelled her; it was his smell, his crudeness, and the fact that his lank, greasy hair housed more lice than a hound's belly.

"Sorry, Hitch," she said. "Scotty Carmichael fell asleep up there and hasn't come down yet."

"Well, hell, you jest prance up there and wake him up, girlie. He got what he paid for. Now it's my turn."

"He isn't feeling well. He's old, you know, and he was really upset about his daughter . . ." Her words faded.

Pain lanced Lacey. Buck hadn't been honest with her. Maddux wasn't even his name. It was Skeet Whitney, and he was married to Scotty's daughter. He was the finest man who'd ever come into her life, and he had lied to her. Or had he? He hadn't acted like a man who had a wife nearby. He hadn't acted like a married man at all. But if he wasn't Skeet Whitney, why had he said he was? The whole affair confused Lacey. Whether he was married or not, she was a fool to have hoped he would take her away with him. But then, the world was full of fools.

Hitch opened his twisted mouth to argue with her, but at that instant a scream ripped through the building.

Big Red's panicked voice came down to the men and the young whore listening below. "No, Jonas. Please . . . Oh God, oh God. *No!*"

Lacey clapped her hands over her ears as that last frantic, pain-filled cry died away.

Hitch giggled and elbowed his friend in the ribs. "That ol' boy's getting him some good stuff, jest like I tole you he would. Shit, but I'd love to be a fly on the wall up there. That'd be some gawddamned sight to see, wouldn't it?"

Stud whirled toward the two cowhands, his mouth carved in a snarl. "You got more filth in your brain than on your boots, you know that, Hitch? I think you've drunk your fill here. You want anything else, go across the street to the Swede's place, it's more your style anyway."

The cowhand had no chance to reply. This time the interruption came from a gunshot, exploding overhead.

* * *

"Your bath's waiting, Angel." Tempest scooped up Ethan and herded her small daughter toward the bedroom. "You can play with Buck tomorrow."

"Need any help?" Buck asked.

"No thanks."

Tempest sat down in the rocker and began to undress her son, ignoring Buck when he came and leaned against the wall, his gaze sweeping the crowded room. The kerosene lamp exposed inadequacies he might have missed in his first viewing. The wooden wash tub stood on a scraped hide just inside the curtained doorway where the heat could reach it from the cookstove. A stool held flour-sack towels and a bar of lye soap on a cracked saucer. Tempest knew it wouldn't look like much to a man who had "been most everywhere" and "done most everything." It wasn't the nicest place she'd ever lived in either. But it was hers, and she intended to keep it that way.

Angel was struggling to pull off her dress. The skirt was over her head, and her arms were tangled in the sleeves. Before Tempest could finish with Ethan and help her, Buck walked over and freed the girl. Underneath, Angel wore a pair of flour-sack drawers. Buck hesitated, as though reluctant to touch such personal garments, even on a child. Unaware and totally uninhibited, the four-year-old stripped herself naked. The tender amusement in Buck's smile as he watched Angel skip over to the tub and climb inside brought a lump to Tempest's throat. A natural, everyday family scene. Yet nothing could have been further from the truth.

She dropped Ethan's diaper to the floor and set him in the tub beside his sister. The boy laughed up at his mother as she scrubbed him down. Then she hauled him out and handed him to Buck. "Here, dry him off."

"Me?"

His horror answered a question she'd been afraid to voice; he had no children of his own. "It won't hurt you to make yourself useful."

Awkward as a pig in satin slippers, Buck took the dripping boy and wrapped him in a towel.

"I want Mithter Buck to wath me, Mama," Angel said.

"Forget it. You're not climbing in my bed until every layer of dirt is gone."

"She could sleep out front," Buck suggested with a leer. "That way there'd be room in here for me."

Tempest almost smiled. He didn't act like a man who had a wife either. At least his libidinous suggestions were easier to deal with than his sporadic moments of gentleness that nudged at her heart. She shafted him a look that would have scalded the hide off a buffalo at twenty paces. "Do you know how to put a diaper on?" she asked. Buck cast the boy a nervous glance as though wondering when Ethan had last wet. "Never mind," she told him. "I'll diaper him while you dry Angel."

Angel's drying session turned into a tickling session. The devil had her laughing so hard she got hiccups. Melancholy tinged Tempest's smile. Skeet had always been too busy to play with his daughter. It hurt to know the man responsible for the new joy in Angel's eyes would soon be gone, leaving Tempest to deal with her daughter's sorrow and confusion. Suddenly irritated, she said, "That's enough. You'll have her sick, or so wound up she'll never go to sleep."

Ethan, on the other hand, was already asleep in the big bed. Tempest helped Angel into her gown, then tucked her under the covers. Ethan was making soft noises midway between a hum and a coo. Buck walked over and looked down at the boy in the dim light, a frown marring his brow.

"He always sounds like that when he sleeps." Tempest hung up Angel's dress and took down her own nightgown.

Buck turned from the bed. "Want me to empty the tub?"

"No, I'll add some hot water and use it myself first."

He glanced again at the children sleeping in the bed and Tempest thought she saw a deep yearning in his eyes. One that had nothing to do with her or sex. A haunted sort of yearning that spoke of pain and loneliness and loss. Then he blinked and it was gone. His gaze circled back to her, his devil's smile firmly in place again. "Don't suppose you want any help," he offered wolfishly. "I'm mighty good at scrubbing backs."

The tiny smile that curved her mouth came unbidden. He was such an enigma. Dark and haunted one moment, light and flippant the next. Every time she thought she had him figured out, he switched horses on her, until she didn't know what to expect. She suspected that he used deviltry to conceal the goodness in him, as though he had some perverse need to be seen as nothing more than an aimless, womanizing drifter.

He was taller than Skeet, more muscular but no better looking. Skeet had been beautiful, with a classical face and golden blond hair that curled when it got damp and fell into his eyes. He had been sunshine and summer grass. Buck Maddux was a moonless midnight with dark promises hidden in sultry shadows. Compared to Buck, Skeet had been a guileless boy, an innocent. Tempest thought of all she had suffered because of that artless boy and shuddered to think what a man like Buck could do to her. Her smile died. "I'll scrub my own back, thank you."

She shoved him through the doorway, devil's smile and all, then yanked the curtain shut.

"I'll bed down outside," he said through the thin fabric.

"I'm used to it, and you'll be more comfortable with me out of the house."

There he went again, changing horses, from licentious rogue to solicitous guest. Still, she was relieved. "Thank you, Mr. Maddux."

"Call me Buck." He paused. "Don't reckon my 'wife' would consider giving her husband a good-night kiss."

She couldn't help laughing. Whatever else Buck Maddux might be, he was entertaining. "No. Do you need any blankets?"

"No, my bedroll's in the barn, but thanks for asking." She heard him walk across the room.

"Wait, Mr. Maddux." She peeked out. His hand was on the latch.

"Buck."

"Buck." She hesitated. "Did Skeet tell you anything about where he hid the stolen payroll?" It wasn't what she'd meant to ask, but she did want to know. Just when she had decided he was innocent of the robbery, she couldn't say.

"A few words that made no sense," he said. "The Army made a thorough search and couldn't even find the place, let alone the money. If they couldn't find it, don't reckon we could."

"I suppose not. Well, good night."

"Good night." He started to close the door, then stopped. "I have a question for you. Why *Heartsease*?"

Surprised, she explained, "It's a flower, a viola. Some people call it Johnny-jump-up. It's made into a syrup for curing pleurisy, falling sickness, inflammation of the lungs and"—she blushed—"certain male afflictions."

He grinned. One brow rose in challenge. "Such as?" When she looked away and refused to answer, he said, "Cupid's itch? French gout? Ladies fever? Or—not quite so fancy—plain old pox?"

Scowling, she said, "There's no need to be crude, Mr. Maddux."

"Buck." His smile faded and he looked chagrined. "Look, you're right. Afraid I'm not used to company as . . . genteel as yours. I apologize."

Mollified by the genuineness of his apology and the sudden loneliness in his eyes, she regretted her grumpiness. "Buck?"

Turning, he waited.

"After years of being dragged from town to town while Skeet gambled, I was sorely in need of something . . . secure," she said diffidently. "This land isn't much, but it has eased my heart."

He nodded and empathy softened his expression. Taking courage, she said, "I hope staying here won't cause you any problems. I mean, if there's someone waiting for you . . ."

"Like a wife?" he asked, his eyes darkening.

Tempest nodded, alarmed by his pain and anger.

"No," he said curtly. "My wife's dead." He shut the door and was gone.

For a long time Tempest stared at the door. Such a complex man. She doubted she would ever understand him, even if he stayed long enough to get to know. He had asked her for a kiss. It had been so long since anyone had kissed her, except for the children. She brushed her fingers over her lips, wondering what it would be like. Heat swirled inside her body. Shaking away the forbidden image, she began to undress.

Midnight found Buck tossing and turning on the bed he'd laid out under a cottonwood tree near the creek. He could hear the sluggish gurgle of the water and see the stars that dotted the sky like scattered grains of gleaming white sand. Sights and sounds he'd learned to treasure during the hell of the last two years. But tonight they did little to ease the restlessness in his soul.

It was just as well she hadn't invited him into her bed. Not only because he didn't dare become involved with a woman like her, but because he was afraid he would have made a fool of himself. For two years he'd slept in a windowless cubicle barely big enough to house the two bunks that hung on its wall. The stench of the open buckets that served as chamber pots and the soft night noises of scavenging rats defied a man's efforts to sleep. At Lacey's he'd been able to leave the two big windows open so he could feel the breeze on his face and see the stars. But there were no windows in Tempest's bedroom. Hell, what hope did he have for a normal life when he couldn't even accustom himself to sleeping indoors?

Coyotes announced a kill up one of the draws, filling the night with eerie yips and howls. Closer by, an owl hooted. Buck sighed. The air was brisk, clean. No prison stink. High above, the dark silhouette of the canyon wall was like a jagged rip in the deep indigo sky.

The clopping of iron-shod hooves on the wooden bridge ended Buck's musings. Tossing his blanket aside, he snatched up his six-shooter. He didn't bother with his boots. Keeping to the shadows of willows and greasewood, and hoping he wouldn't stumble into any prickly pear cactus, he crept closer.

Ronan Carmichael rode a mule more grizzled than himself. A swaybacked nag so ugly Buck thought it might be a kindness to put a bullet in its head. A snail moved faster. Probably took the man two hours to travel the four miles from Harper.

The Scotsman halted in front of the dugout. Clumsily he dragged his leg over the mule's back and slid unsteadily to the ground. At least one foot was on the ground—his left foot was hung up in the stirrup. Tempest's father was still trying to get his foot free when Buck walked up on the far side of the mule and rested his forearms on the animal's swayed back. The old Scotsman danced about, awkwardly trying to liberate himself and muttering what Buck supposed were Gaelic curses. When the foot finally came free, Carmichael lost his balance and would have fallen if he hadn't been hanging onto the saddle. He spotted Buck on the other side of the scrawny mule and peered blearily at him through bloodshot eyes.

"Who're you?" he slurred.

Remembering his new role, Buck replied, "Your son-in-law, Skeet Whitney."

"Ach." Carmichael waved a hand at him. "Mon's dead, lemme alone." He swung about, wove dizzily, and fell. On hands and knees, he vomited into the weeds.

Buck cast heaven a disparaging glance.

When Carmichael quit retching, Buck helped him up and aimed him toward the house, following in case he fell again. It was a long journey. He had to help his "father-in-law" up twice more before they reached the front room, where Carmichael curled up fully dressed on the floor near the stove and began to snore like a three-hundred-pound hog rooting in slops.

Buck stared at the pathetic drunkard and wondered for the thousandth time what he had gotten himself into. A smart man would pack up and get the hell out. Christ only knew what sort of retaliation Jonas Creedy might attempt. Buck could find himself fighting for his life, as well as those of the woman and her kids. Hadn't he sacrificed enough for Skeet Whitney? Dammit, he had his own life to live, and he sure as Hades didn't intend to spend it here.

What would happen to Tempest if he left?

Quietly, he slipped into the back room. Her pale face

barely showed in the flickering light of the candle he'd
lit, her unbound hair a dark shadow on the pristine pillow
slip. She looked younger, the strain of providing for her
family in this rough land gone, leaving only beauty and
vulnerability behind.

Buck resisted the urge to stroke her satiny cheek and
forced himself from the room. He would stay a while
longer. Only, he told himself, because he had promised
Skeet.

Chapter Six

The sky was a rich deep sapphire when Buck awoke the next morning to the baying of a hound. Tempest's yellow dog, Rooster, was announcing the dawn. Buck got up and watered a greasewood shrub. He disliked privies. Too closed in.

The morning was still, crisp, heavy with the scent of rabbit brush and the junipers that locals called cedars. The colorless sky over the eastern cliffs gained intensity as it traveled westward to become a washed-out indigo. In the inky shadows of the deep canyon a man could barely see where he was walking. The crickets were silent, the breeze had yet to stir the leaves. There was something almost mystical about such a morning, Buck thought. If he closed his eyes and gave his senses free rein, he suspected he would hear the morning songs of a people long since dead. The ones who had left their marks on the canyon walls. A strange, deep peace invaded him. A sense of belonging, of coming home. But Buck Maddux had no home.

Rooster trotted over. Buck tensed, waiting for the mutt to try to breakfast on one of his calves. Instead, the dog sniffed the bush Buck had wet down, lifted a leg and covered Buck's scent with his own, reclaiming his territory. Spook nickered a greeting from the corral. Buck walked over and rubbed the appaloosa's neck. "Mornin', old boy. You eager to get out of there?"

The horse whinnied. Othello tried to nudge him aside. Spook nudged back. Buck had a hunch it wasn't their first dispute. Giving up on ousting his rival, the mule hung his long-eared charcoal-black head over the fence and begged to be petted. Buck rubbed Othello's nose and the mule closed his eyes in ecstasy.

With a snort of disgust, Spook pranced off.

About that time, Ronan Carmichael shuffled up, looking peaked yet more fit than Buck had expected. The Scotsman rubbed the stump of his missing arm as though it pained him. He wore the same stained undershirt and trousers he'd passed out in. The woolen undershirt had grayed to a sick shade of dun, and smelled of whiskey, pipe smoke and, vomit.

"Who might you be, lad?" the man asked.

"Introduced myself to you last night," Buck answered curtly. "Although I'm not surprised you don't remember, booze-blind as you were at the time."

Tempest's father frowned. "Ye spent the night here? With me daughter?"

"That's right." It suited Buck to let Ronan stew. The man's drunkenness had doubled Tempest's burden and nearly landed her in Jonas Creedy's bed, enough in Buck's book to condemn the man.

" 'Tain't like Tempest to have male guests."

Buck smiled. "I certainly hope not."

Ronan's frown deepened. "Well, mon, are ye goin' to

explain yerself and tell me who ye are, or must I ask me daughter?''

"Suit yourself, she'll just tell you she's been married to me for over five years. I'm your son-in-law.''

"Son-in-law? 'Tain't possible. Skeet Whitney's dead.''

Buck's smile wore the devil's brand. "You mean folks *thought* I was dead.''

Ronan's face flushed with anger. "If ye truly be Skeet, then I have to tell ye I've no respect for a man who abandons his wife and bairns the way ye done. I've no say 'bout ye staying here, but ye'd best know I won't let ye take further advantage o' me girl.''

Buck calmly took out cigarette makings and tapped shredded tobacco onto thin white paper. "Me, now . . . I find it difficult to admire a man who lives off a woman, drinking up her hard-earned money and not lifting a hand to help her.''

Ronan's ruddy face was vermillion now, his eyes glowering. "And where were you the past two years when she needed ye?''

"That's between me and my wife.'' Buck fished a match out of his vest pocket, struck it on the edge of his spur, and lit his cigarette.

Ronan raked a hand through his grizzled hair until it resembled a wind-whipped wheat field. Buck could see where Tempest had gotten her stubborn mouth. She'd also inherited her father's brown eyes, though hers were more amber-flecked and thickly lashed. Hers weren't faded, puffy, or bloodshot either. Buck imagined Ronan Carmichael had been a good-looking man in his day. Might still be, if he sobered up and let good health erase the effects of a dissolute life. The two men stared at each other until the aging Scotsman gave a nod and, with slumped shoulders, headed for the privy, rubbing again at the stump that was all he had for a right arm.

Buck leaned against the pasture fence and watched him go, recalling horror stories he'd heard of the War Between the States. Folks said the severed limbs were piled high as haystacks, and the men who lost them suffered the pain of it to their dying day. Buck drew deeply on his cigarette and told himself he had no right to reproach anybody. At least Ronan Carmichael hadn't killed his own wife and baby.

The cigarette suddenly tasted like gall. He tossed it down and ground it into the dirt with his heel, wishing he could do the same to himself. Othello nudged Buck's arm off the corral rail, giving him a sorrowful look from deep brown eyes.

"Yeah, I know," Buck told the mule. "Brooding over the past doesn't do any good." He crooked his arm on the rail again. Othello knocked it off. Buck chuckled and scratched behind the mule's long ears. "Bet I could teach you a few tricks, eh, boy?"

A white cow-hocked mare ambled over, her hind legs nearly touching at the hocks, then spreading at the pastern joints the way a cow's would. She greeted the big mule with an affectionate nose rub. A smaller pasture east of the barn housed a burro, a billy goat, and Flopsey the milch cow. Buck shook his head and grinned. Tempest had enough variety to start a zoo. Heading for the house, he found Angel feeding chickens.

"Morning, Mithter Buck. Wanna help gather eggth?"

It was the last thing he wanted to do, but her smile was so sunny he couldn't say no. Angel knew where each nest was hidden—in straw inside the barn, under bushes, in the weeds at the foot of a corral post, among piles of worn-out tack, even under the bench where Tempest kept the pan for washing up.

"It's a wonder the pigs don't eat these," Buck said, placing an egg in the girl's basket.

Angel looked up with big eyes far too wise for a child's. "They don't like eggth much, Mithter Buck."

He squatted in front of her and tapped her nose with his finger, surprised to realize he was enjoying himself. "How come? Most pigs love eggs."

She grinned and batted the finger away. "When they were little, Mama had me clobber 'em on the thnout every time they went near any eggth. They get thome, but not very many. Mama thays I'm the best thnout thmacker in the county."

"I just bet you are." She was also the most adorable creature he'd met in a long time. As adorable as the child he'd once dreamed of having. *Watch it, Buck, old boy. She'll steal your heart.* He suspected it might be too late.

Tempest stepped from the dugout, Ethan riding her hip. As if her entire being were tuned to his presence, her gaze went unerringly to the big man hunkered in front of her little girl, both of them wearing impish grins. As she watched his shirt stretch taut across his broad, muscular back, she wondered how his wife had died . . . and if that caused the haunted look in his eyes. Morning sun glinted off his thick jet hair. Her pulse couldn't help but accelerate at the sight of him. But the warmth invading her body came from more than sensual awareness of a man. Life in the canyon was hard, forcing her little girl to grow up much too fast, feeding chickens, collecting eggs, watching over her brother, making beds . . . But, under the spell of Buck Maddux's grin, Angel was a child again. Tempest could love him for that alone.

Jonas had gone to a great deal of trouble to track down and buy her mortgage, as well as to get her father in debt to him. How far would he go to get his way? Tempest had to find a solution before matters worsened and someone got hurt. Buck Maddux was as maddening and arrogant as he was handsome, but he didn't deserve to be shot for protecting her.

Watching him laugh with her daughter, Tempest almost wished he could stay with them forever. She banished the thought immediately. Gratitude was all she felt for the man. He had bailed her out of a horrible mess with Jonas, he made her daughter laugh and . . . Tempest shut off her thoughts before she could dwell on the lonely place in her heart which felt lighter since Buck Maddux had entered her life. He looked up then, his mouth wide with the grin he was sharing with Angel. His laughing blue eyes met Tempest's, then went to Ethan on her hip. Sudden heat burned in his gaze, and his smile ebbed. Tempest glanced down to see her shirt gaping open, her son's small hand inside on her naked breast.

How could she not have known what Ethan was doing? Was she so accustomed to having her son's hands on her that she didn't even notice? Blood rushed to her face as she snatched the boy's hand away, set him down, and attempted to button her shirt. She sensed more than saw Buck rise to his feet and amble toward her. Desperation made her fingers awkward. The harder she tried, the more the buttons refused to cooperate. His torrid gaze captured hers, and she felt as if his big, callused hands were already caressing the rounded flesh she was trying to conceal. A tingling sensation uncoiled in her feminine regions, and her heart pounded. As her nipples tautened, milk dampened the worn cotton of her shirt. The wet fabric stuck to her skin, exposing the hard nub of flesh underneath.

Tempest wanted to run, but her feet had taken root in the dry dusty soil. Her pulse drummed louder with each step that brought him nearer.

Barely a foot separated them when he finally came to a halt and she saw an odd look of reverence in his eyes. Her heart stopped. A curious sense of unreality gripped her as he nudged her hands away, then slowly fastened each button until she was covered to her chin. The hunger never left his eyes, but dark shadows clouded the compelling blue of their irises. In their depths she saw such black torment that she wanted to reach out and touch him, soothe him, love him—anything to banish that awful sadness. But her hands remained at her sides, frozen.

Gradually, she became aware of Ethan tugging on her pantleg and making ''Bock, bock'' sounds for chicken, reminding her of her reason for coming outside. Tearing her gaze from Buck, she picked up her son and croaked, ''Breakfast is ready.''

As she vanished into the dim interior of the dugout, Buck closed his eyes. His body sagged. The sight of Ethan's hand on his mother's breast, the milk that had dampened her shirt, had reopened a wound that had festered inside him for fifteen years. Needs and desires normally held tightly in check avalanched over him, bringing with them a return of the melancholy he had nearly succumbed to so long ago, in the black days following Ellen's death.

Forget it, he commanded himself. He didn't deserve what Tempest Whitney and her children made him want. He'd had his chance. Never again would he let another woman down as he had Ellen—nor would he risk a child's life with his selfishness.

''Mithter Buck. Come on, Mithter Buck.''

Angel's sweet lisping voice pierced the black vortex of his mind. Her tiny hand slipped into his. He swallowed the knot in his throat and masked his emotions with his usual grin as he let her lead him to the house.

When they entered, Tempest was trying to spoon scrambled eggs onto plates and shoo flies at the same time, reminding Buck of his mother who had abhorred flies. The sudden memory of her naming him Official Fly Swatter swooped into his head before he could ward it off as he did most remembrances of home and childhood. He still recalled how proud he had been to receive her praise for a task well done. But a man couldn't allow himself to dwell in the past. Especially when that past was so filled with pain it robbed him of the will to live. Ruffling Angel's bright hair with his hand, Buck took his seat, carefully keeping his eyes off Tempest. His control was too uncertain at the moment to chance looking at her.

At his feet the mother cat eyed him with calculated determination in her slanted green orbs. Buck glowered at her.

"Gampa!" Angel flung herself at the dour old man who came through the door. "Gueth what, Gampa? We got married yeth-terday, and me and Ethan got a new daddy, 'thepting he'd rather be a friend tho we won't have to wash tho much."

Buck tensed. The spoonful of eggs Tempest was transferring to his plate quivered, then plopped onto the plate. Seizing the moment, Marmalade leaped onto his lap. "Off, fleabag," he growled, jumping to his feet.

"Get down, Marmalade," Tempest said at the same time, more worried about the cat than the man.

The cat clung to his Levis, green eyes narrowed in warning as he and Tempest worked to free it. Her hand brushed his inner thigh near his crotch, and he stiffened. Their eyes met. Lightning crackled. Flushing, Tempest jerked her gaze back to the job at hand, only to find herself staring at the tighter fit of his trousers. Spinning away, she tried to hide her mortification. *Please, Holy Mother, don't let Papa have seen.* She forgot that, to Ronan, Buck was her long-lost husband who had been away for two years.

Having lost their attention, Marmalade gave up and let go. With her tail high in the air, she stalked back to her kittens in the corner. Buck sat down to hide his arousal.

He grabbed his coffee and took a swig. Six-shooter coffee, strong enough to float a revolver, the way he liked it. Unfortunately, it was scalding hot. He cursed as he slammed the cup down on the table. Ronan gave him a small, inquisitive glance Buck chose to ignore. Finally peace reigned once more in the room. Ronan seemed to have forgotten Angel's odd announcement, and all went well until Angel opened her sweet button mouth and stirred the hornet's nest again.

"Gampa, where do daddies thleep?"

Ronan licked a drop of well-sugared coffee from his mustache. "With their wives, wee lassie. Where else would ye be havin' 'em sleep?"

Angel frowned. "Mama thays they thleep out front, but I want Mithter Buck to thleep in back with uth."

"*Buck,* is it?" Ronan glanced from his daughter to Buck, his expression unreadable.

"That's the name I've used the past two years . . . Buck Maddux. It's what I'm used to."

"Still, 'tis an odd way for a lass to address her papa."

Tempest blushed an appealing pink at the look her father sent her, which questioned more than the name Angel used for her "father."

"Skeet's been gone a long time, Papa. The children and I need time to get used to having him back."

Plastering a grin on his face, Buck pulled Tempest onto his lap and gave her a quick kiss on the mouth. He was playing with fire, but it was hard to think straight with his body aching for more than a kiss. "Told you I would've been back sooner, sweetheart, if I'd known I wasn't wanted by the law anymore. It wasn't until I came back that I learned you'd mortgaged the place and paid off what I stole. You forgive me, don't you?"

"What difference does it make?" she growled sweetly,

struggling to get up. "You're my husband. We simply have to work it out."

He recognized her fury, but refused to let her go. She felt too good, her soft bottom squirming against him and sending the blood pulsing to his groin. "Knew you'd see it my way." He couldn't help it. He kissed her again.

Tempest didn't dare resist; her father wouldn't understand a woman slapping her husband for kissing her. But she knew she was only using his presence as an excuse to find out what kissing Buck was like. Heaven. His mouth was firm, yet soft. Gentle. He tasted of coffee and honeyheated passion. Her every nerve ending leaped to life, and she was tingling in places she'd forgotten she even owned.

Buck probed her lips gently with his tongue, and she opened to him. He imagined her thighs parting just as sweetly, experienced a fierce thrust of desire. He plunged his tongue inside her mouth—the way he wanted to plunge into her body—and explored every surface, savoring the tastes and textures secreted there. It lasted only a few heartbeats, but in that tiny space of time, Ronan Carmichael ceased to exist. The children ceased to exist. The world pivoted on their two joined mouths and the fevered places where their bodies touched.

Tempest felt as if she were being consumed, and she reveled in it. She wanted to lose herself in this man, to climb inside his warmth, wallow in the comforting safety of his arms, the bliss hinted at in his kiss. It had been so long since a man had kissed her, and even then, it hadn't been like this. The heat and intensity of the passion erupting between them thrilled and frightened her.

Buck was no less shaken than she. As lonely as his life had been, wandering from ranch to ranch from Texas to Montana, herding cows, bartending, riding shotgun, or driving freight wagons, there had been plenty of women. Whores mostly, a widow or two, women whose names he forgot five minutes after leaving their beds. None had tasted like Tempest Whitney. None had aroused him so fully, or left him with such a gut-wrenching need for more. He watched her fluttering breasts lift the fabric of her shirt with each heartbeat and yearned to caress them. As though she'd read this thought, she leaped to her feet and began clanging pots at the sideboard.

"There now, lass," the old man told his granddaughter, "all's well with yer mama and yer Papa Buck. Doubtless ye'll all be sleeping in back together tonight as ye wanted."

Buck closed his eyes and squirmed in his chair as his body reacted to the image painted in his mind by Ronan's heavenly prediction.

The fried eggs, flapjacks, and mush were nearly gone, and Buck was thinking he'd never eaten a finer breakfast, when Tempest announced she would be going into town after her morning chores. The elderberries were ripe, and she needed paraffin for bottling the jam she intended to make. Ronan looked up from his nearly untouched plate. "There's something happened in town last night ye'd best be knowing about first, lass."

The ominous tone of the man's softly burred voice sent a tremor of unease down Buck's spine.

"Jonas fired you, didn't he?" Tempest heaved a martyred sigh as she gathered up the dirty plates. "All right, Papa, you can stay here, I don't have the money for you to stay in town."

His ruddy face blushed crimson. "I still have me job. I didna' come to beg money. But Jonas was shot last night, and it'd be best if ye stayed clear of 'im."

Carefully, she set down the dishes. Her expression was guarded, but her heart thudded like stampeding cattle. "Is he dead?"

"Nay, lass. The bullet grazed his side is all. Likely he's up and about t'day, but 'tis a nasty temper he'll have."

Turning to the sideboard, she crossed herself and asked forgiveness for having wished for another soul's death. To be rid of Jonas would solve all her problems, but she should have known it wouldn't be that easy. "What happened, Papa?"

"He had a . . . disagreement with one of the lasses who work for him. She got hold of his firearm somehow. I doubt 'twould be wise for ye to go into town for a wee bit."

"Nonsense." She began clearing the table again. "What does it have to do with me? The woman probably had good reason for what she did. Working for a man as vile as Jonas can't be . . ." She stopped and stared at her father. "You believe it does have something to do with me, don't you?"

Ronan glanced down at his lap, looking uncomfortable.

"What could it possibly . . . ?" Her eyes widened and she spun away. "Never mind." Heat flushed her face as she realized what her father hadn't said. Jonas had expected to bed *her* last night. He'd gone to one of his whores to get what he'd been cheated out of and was shot instead. Holy Mary, what had he been doing to the girl that she would do such a thing? And it was her fault. Her knuckles whitened as she gripped the edge of the sideboard and closed her eyes against the guilt.

"It's not your fault, sweetheart." Understanding softened Buck's voice. For him to so easily discern her emotions left her feeling exposed, vulnerable.

"Of course it isn't," she snapped, all business again as she scraped dishes with a vengeance. "I'm not to blame for what happens between Jonas and his . . . women. As for staying out of town, I've no intention of hiding out as if I'd done something wrong."

Buck smiled inwardly as her chin came up and her

mouth tightened with predictable tenacity. No good would come from arguing with her. Ronan's worried gaze met his. Buck signaled for him to take the children outside. Shrugging his rounded shoulders, Ronan rose and lumbered out the door.

Outside, the children shouted in high, excited voices for their grandfather to come see the bug they'd found. Ronan's footsteps faded. Buck sipped his coffee while he debated how to deal with Tempest. In the corner, a kitten mewed a protest as its mother laved it with her rasplike tongue, interrupting her offspring's play. A fly buzzed the slop bucket. Tempest muttered an epithet and viciously swatted the insect.

"Reckon I'd best get going if I'm to find work today." Buck's spurs jangled as he got to his feet. He took his hat from the wall peg and began to reshape the brim. "Unless you've thought of another way to get the money we need."

"No." Without looking up from her chore, she added, "I was hoping you might fix that broken latch on the privy door for me, though."

"All right." It felt good being asked to do things, as if he truly was the man of the house. Reminding himself that that kind of thinking would only make matters worse, he said, "I'll do that first, then ride into town. Make up a shopping list and—"

"No!" Tempest straightened, spearing him with a fierce glare. "I'll get my own supplies, thank you very much. I can take care of myself." Besides resenting being bossed by him, she wasn't about to let him go into town without her. She squashed the inner voice that accused her of worrying only that he might visit his soiled dove at the Sagebrush Princess.

Buck's brow rose and his mouth tightened. "Don't need me hanging around here then. I'll fetch my plunder and head for California."

He'd made it halfway to the corner where his saddlebags and personal possessions were stored before her bitter, saw-edged voice brought him to a halt. "Blast you, Buck Maddux. You know Jonas will be here three seconds after you leave. Only there won't be any offer of marriage this time. He'll simply make me his whore instead."

Buck swallowed the curses singeing the tongue he'd already burned on coffee. He counted to ten, then turned to face her, hoping he seemed more calm than he felt. The thought of Jonas Creedy putting his hands on her bunched Buck's muscles into tight knots. The veins in his temples pulsed. "You saying you want me to stay?"

Tempest tossed her head like a high-strung filly, looking everywhere but at him. "Yes, dammit."

He started toward her, determined to make it clear that he, and he alone, would call the shots in this partnership. He couldn't risk letting her endanger herself. "Say it."

She glared at him. "Say what?"

"That you want me to stay."

Hands clenched at her sides, she held her ground as he came to a halt in front of her. "I see no need—"

"Say it," he ground out. He stood close enough to smell her sweet breath and count the amber flecks in her angry brown eyes. As she faced him, nose to nose, unwilling to give in, he stifled an urge to throttle her. Damn her stubborn pride. Never had he known a woman more mule-headed. Or more tempting. His gaze went to her lips, which were clamped tighter than a spinster's knees. He thought of easing them open, slipping his tongue inside. Imagined what it would be like to join their bodies in a more intimate manner. He wanted to taste her passion, feel her tighten around him, hot and wet and hungry. Her lips parted on a soft gasp, telling him she'd read his desire. She shoved a restraining hand against his chest and started to back away. "All right, all right, I'll say it. I want you—"

"*That's* what I wanted to hear," he said. Dragging her close, he brought his mouth down on hers. The kiss was hard, quick and bruisingly commanding. Then he put her from him before he lost total control and took her there on the floor.

"You *will* stay out of town, Tempest, until I decide it's safe. Meanwhile, if you so much as look like you're considering defying my orders, I'll strip those trousers off your pretty little bottom and paddle it black and blue." *Among other things.* "Understand?"

Glowering, she snarled, "Yes, I understand . . . *master*. Will that be all, *master*?"

Buck grinned like the devil he liked to pretend he was. The idea of her submitting to his every whim racked his body with white hot desire and made his voice low and husky. "Until tonight, anyway." He winked.

Seeing her eyes darken with purpose, he ducked swiftly through the doorway, sidestepping the fry pan that followed him out. The cast-iron missile landed in the dirt, skidded a few feet, and nearly plowed into Rooster who had sought warmth in a weak patch of sunlight. The dog yelped and took off as though a blazing rocket had been tied to his tail.

Laughing, Buck kept walking.

Sunlight glinted off steel high up the steep juniper slope above the Whitney ranch, but the man crossing the ranch yard never noticed. Jonas Creedy took his eye from the rifle sight and eased his finger off the trigger. The three gunmen crouched next to him did the same.

"Why didn't you do it, boss?" asked a bespectacled man in a suit that was unbelievably tidy and clean for someone in his line of work. "One shot and you could have gotten rid of this Whitney guy for good."

Jonas walked to his horse and shoved the rifle in its scabbard, wincing as pain speared the bullet wound in his side. "Because, Howard, everyone would blame me. You may look like a city lawyer, but you ain't got the smarts of one."

A tall man, more arms and legs than anything else, rose to his feet. "You leaving, Creedy?"

Jonas pinned the gangly man with a glare that could have gutted a fish. "It's *Mister* Creedy to you, Spider."

Spider held up sticklike arms. "Sorry . . . Mr. Creedy."

"I want you three to plant your asses here and keep an eye on Whitney." If the man down below *was* Skeet Whitney, Jonas wasn't so sure. "If he as much as leaves the ranch yard, follow him. If he starts doing any digging, one of you come get me pronto. Got that?"

"When are we supposed to sleep, Mr. Creedy?"

"Figure it out for yourselves." Jonas tightened the cinch on his horse. The bay gelding didn't have a name. He saw no reason to name animals as if they were children. "Morg, you're in charge. I'll expect a full report every morning. If Whitney so much as shits, I want to know about it."

"Sure thing, Mr. Creedy." Morgan Paine, still squatting on the ground watching the ranch, pulled a twist of chewing tobacco from his pocket and gnawed off a hunk. "What about the woman?" he mumbled around the chaw in his mouth. "Want us to dog her too?"

Spider guffawed. "I'd like to 'dog' her." He bent and pumped his hips in a vulgar demonstration of a dog on a bitch.

Before the man could straighten up, Jonas had him by the throat. "The woman is mine," he ground out between clenched teeth. "You got that?"

In spite of the variance in their heights, the two men

were a matched set; both ruthless, deadly, without a shred of conscience. "Yeah, I got it. And you're gonna get it, too," Spider snarled, reaching for his six-shooter. Before his revolver cleared leather a sharp pain in the groin stole the breath from his lungs. He screeched and clutched at his groin. "He cut me, he cut me. Make him let go, Morg. Make him let go."

Morgan Paine never moved. Jonas let go of Spider's skinny neck, cleaned his bloody knife on some weeds and returned it to its sheath.

Spider crumpled to the ground. Blood spread quickly from his crotch down his thin leg. Whimpering, he unbuckled his gun belt, shoved trousers and underwear to his knees and tried to examine the profusely bleeding wound. An inch to the left and he would have needed a new way to piss. "Oh, Jesus. Oh, Jesus." Pulling a kerchief from around his neck he wadded it against the cut to stem the bleeding. "Look, Howard. He nearly cut off my cock. It's bleeding bad. Think I'll still be able to bugger whores?"

"Look at it yourself," Howard muttered. "You're lucky he missed that pea brain you got down there."

"Doesn't matter anyhow," Morg put in, watching the gush of blood from Spider's groin. Creedy had obviously cut a major vein. "You're a dead man, Spider. You ain't never gonna bugger anyone again."

Without giving the injured man a second glance, Jonas eased into his saddle. "Reckon I got my point across. I don't care what you do to the old man or the brats, but *no one* touches the woman."

Howard hunkered down and took the binoculars from Morg. Seeing how intently he was staring at the ranch, Jonas said, "What are you looking at?"

"Prettiest little girl you ever saw," the tidy little gunman said with soft reverence. "Hair like champagne, and a rosebud mouth."

Jonas snorted in disgust. "Heard 'bout your liking for little girls. Just don't go screwing up my plans, Howard. I don't care what you do with the brat, long as I get what I want first."

"I've never failed an employer yet. I won't fail you."

"See that you don't." Glancing at the man lying on the ground, Jonas said, "Dump him somewhere a long way from here. And get a man to replace Spider.

"You want us to bury him, Mr. Creedy?"

Jonas shrugged. Taking a man's life was no longer the thrill it used to be. "Suit yourselves." With a flick of the reins, he guided the bay gelding down a ragged coulee to the road, keeping out of sight of the Whitney place. His injured side throbbed with pain. When he was far enough away to ensure that his dust wouldn't be noticed, he kicked the bay into a lope. At Gates Canyon he turned north, heading for Fort Duchesne. Flipping open his watch he smiled. Good, he should be at the fort before dusk. With luck, he would have a nice surprise tomorrow night for the man calling himself Skeet Whitney.

Inside the dainty locket he used as a watch fob was a likeness of a white woman in a fancy bonnet. Jonas's mother. Her yellow hair and the way she'd cried herself to sleep every night was all he remembered of her. When the soldiers came she denied having given birth to a "filthy, murdering savage." Jonas was left behind. No one knew his father's identity. The entire raiding party had taken turns between her legs. The old woman who took him in after his mother left was the only person he ever loved. As she lay dying, in Jonas's tenth summer, she told him to find his mother, saying he would be better off with the whites. Jonas swore if he found his mother, he would show her how little she meant to him.

The whites—except the missionary who had housed him and taught him to read—hated him. In return, his enmity for them grew like a festering sore. Still, he determined to be like them, to own the fine things they had and become a big man among them, one they would respect.

Snapping the locket shut, Jonas returned the watch to its pocket. Having Tempest Whitney as his wife would go a long way toward helping him attain his goal. And he would have her. His sons would grow in her fine white woman's body. They would nurse at her milk white breasts. And she would never abandon them. Jonas would kill her first.

The same way he would kill any man standing in his way—starting with the one posing as her husband.

Chapter Seven

Twenty minutes after Buck left for town, Tempest hung the last of Ethan's freshly laundered diapers on the line and removed her apron. Angel was rolling a ball for her brother to catch. Tempest paused to watch Ethan grab for it. He fell, picked himself up, and ran after it.

"Ba!" he squealed in delight, holding up the toy for his mother to see. "Ba."

"Yes, Ethan, you caught it. Good boy. Throw it back to Angel now."

He raised it above his head, but let go too soon. The ball fell behind him with a dull thunk and rolled away. Tempest couldn't help but laugh at the surprised look on his little face.

"No, thilly," Angel called to him. "You're thupposed to throw it, not drop it."

Hiding her smile, Tempest chided the girl. "Don't call your brother silly, Angel. Now, make sure he has a diaper on and wash his face. Then get your coats on. We're going for a ride in the dogcart."

Angel hurried after her mother. "Are you going to pull it, Mama?"

"Pull what?"

"The cart."

"Of course not. Othello will pull it."

"No, he won't."

Tempest halted. "What do you mean? Why won't Othello pull it?"

"Cauth he'th not here, Mama."

Tempest pivoted toward the pasture. Sure enough, it was empty. There was no sign of Othello anywhere. Or the mares, or the donkey. Buck had even taken Grunt and Flopsey. If he hadn't been so angry, she might have laughed at that last bit of insanity. Instead, she clenched her fists and headed for the barn.

"Then I'll pull it myself," she mumbled. She'd show him, the sneaky, split-tongued devil. She wouldn't allow him to rule her as if she were a child.

The dogcart was exactly where it should be, except that it had no wheels. Tempest cursed and kicked at the loose straw on the floor. Her shoe slid on a bit of chicken manure, her feet went out from under her and she found herself on her bottom. The big floppy boy's hat—she considered it more practical than the more feminine bonnets other women wore—fell off. She snatched it up and jammed it back down on her head. Angel and Ethan were waiting for her when she stormed out of the barn.

"Papa Buck thaid he knew better than to truth you. What did he mean, Mama?"

"Never mind what he meant." Tempest ground her teeth in an attempt to spare her children the brunt of her growing temper. She wasn't sure when, if ever, she'd been more angry. When that two-legged road apple came home, she'd have a few things to say to him. None of which he'd like.

But Buck didn't come back.

The sun set, leaving behind a copper sky and a hint of frost in the air, and still there was no sign of him. Tempest wondered if he had gone for good. The man was a drifter, after all. Lord only knew where he'd been or what he'd done before showing up in Deception Canyon. There certainly was some mystery as to why it took him so long to check on her, as he'd promised Skeet he would do. She had no doubt he was capable of stealing her animals and leaving her with nothing—damn him and his Satan's smile.

He could be at the Swede's place, drunk as a Ute squaw with her first taste of whiskey. Or he might be—Sweet Mary, why should it hurt so much?—he might be with that girl at the Princess. Tempest wondered if it was the busty one or the one who looked barely past puberty. No doubt either would welcome him. What woman wouldn't? He probably had a woman in every town he wandered through. It meant nothing to her. Still, the thought that at that very moment he might be doing to one of Jonas's girls all the audacious things his eyes so often promised to do to her infuriated Tempest.

By the time the dogs set up a ruckus, letting her know someone or something was outside, she had worked herself into a high choler. Armed with the Henry repeater, she stormed out into the night, determined to force him to return her stock and get out of her life. If Jonas came anywhere near her after that, she'd simply shoot first and ask questions later. A fine notion, as long as she didn't examine it too closely.

A horse stood in the darkness of the yard, its speckled white rump luminous in the light of a full moon. Spook nickered as she approached, the rifle held to her shoulder.

"Is that you, Buck Maddux?"

"Yeah, sweetheart, it's me. You gonna shoot me or just threaten me some more?"

"I don't know. Where have you been?"

Leather creaked as he eased himself from the saddle. Spurs jangled as his boots touched ground. Spook snuffled softly, and danced to the side. Buck soothed him with a few quiet words.

"Buck?"

"Haven't gone anywhere."

"I can see that," she said with a snort. "What I want to know is where have you been?"

"Oh, been having me a grand old time." Irony laced his deep, craggy voice. He sounded tired, his words slurred as if he'd been drinking. Fresh anger surged through her. While she was worrying whether he was even coming back, he was out drinking . . . and Lord only knew what else. Then he turned and a shaft of moonlight illuminated his face. Tempest gasped. His lower lip was swollen and a dark smear high on his cheek looked suspiciously like blood. His clothes were filthy and torn. She dropped the rifle and hurried over to him.

"What happened?" She was too upset to hide her concern.

"Some of Jonas's boys invited me to a party I couldn't refuse."

"You mean . . . they waylaid you?"

He nodded. "Between his place and here. Think we could talk about it inside? I'm a bit shaky and I sure could use a drink."

Bracing him with an arm about his waist, his arm around her shoulders, she helped him into the house. There was no scent of whiskey on him, only the smells of dirt and horse and blood, filling her with guilt for having doubted him.

Buck drew her tightly against him, more than willing to

accept whatever sympathy he could get. Her firm breast brushed his side. He breathed in her sweet, feminine scent and decided that getting the stuffing knocked out of him wasn't so bad after all.

Ronan was sitting on the cot when they entered. His face shone with sweat, despite the coolness of the house, and his entire body was trembling. One look told Buck that Ronan had found no way to appease his thirst that day. Tempest lowered Buck to a stool. He slumped back gratefully, stifling a groan, and nearly fell off. Judas! Tomorrow he would make them a chair with a back. Tempest filled a basin with hot water, then washed the blood from his face.

"At least you won't need any stitches." Her tone made it clear she didn't consider that much of an accomplishment. Buck might have chuckled if it wouldn't have hurt too much.

"I hope you managed to get in a few punches," she said sardonically as she rinsed the bloodied cloth in the basin.

"Did my best."

"How many were there?"

"Three."

"About what I'd expect of Jonas . . . three against one. Was he one of them?"

"No, but he sent a real friendly message—get out of Deception Canyon or wind up as dead as I'm supposed to be."

"The maggot-eating vulture." Tempest set the basin down so hard, the water sloshed over the side onto the counter top.

In spite of the pain it caused him, Buck couldn't keep from smiling. She went into the bedroom and came back with a clean flour sack which she quickly tore into strips. He wanted a cigarette, but wasn't sure how she would react to his smoking in her house. Of course, he was never sure how Tempest Whitney would react to anything.

Tonight's attack had not been unexpected. As Tempest said, it was exactly what a bastard like Jonas would do. Nor had Buck been surprised to see a rifle-toting Tempest fly out of the house like the cork from a popgun when he'd arrived home. She'd probably called him every foul name she could think of when she'd found her livestock missing. But tonight, when she had seen his condition, the anger had drained from her face, along with her color, and her eyes had filled with concern. The sight had done strange, giddy things to his heart.

"Stand up," she said. Obeying, Buck pushed to his feet. Halfway up he clutched his ribs and groaned.

Clucking her tongue at his grimace of pain, Tempest unbuttoned his shirt. He glanced at her father, sitting on the bed and looking calm as a trout in hot butter. "Think you're up to unsaddling my horse, Ronan? Might be something in the saddlebags that'll ease your shakes a bit." Buck wanted Tempest to himself—no audience.

The older man fumbled to his feet and shuffled out. Tempest stared at Buck. "Sweet Mary! Surely you didn't bring him back a bottle." She knew he had been trying to help her father give up the whiskey, but this seemed a strange way to do it.

"Don't worry," he said, "it's half water and mostly empty, barely enough to keep him from climbing the walls. I'm bringing him down off it slowly."

"I hope it works." She tried to pull his shirt out of his pants so she could finish the unbuttoning, but they were too snug. He waited for her to realize why. When she did, her face flooded with color. Her gaze leaped to meet his, only a few inches away.

"Been a while since a woman's undressed me," he said hoarsely. "I'm enjoying the hell out of it."

Tempest spun away. "Do it yourself, you dung-eating—"

"Coyote?" he supplied, grinning. He undid the top two buttons on his pants and drew out his shirttail. Then he shrugged out of the garment and let it fall to the floor. Purposely leaving the trouser buttons undone, he announced, "I'm ready."

Tempest told herself she could do this. She could ignore the sweet, tingling ache in her most feminine regions, could resist the temptation to look her fill of him, to sate the itch of her hands to explore his body. She could pretend disinterest. But when she turned and saw the magnificence of his naked chest and the inviting vee of his half-opened pants, she knew she'd been wrong. Pride forced her to pick up the bandage and wrap it around his midriff. The task was accomplished with more speed than efficiency, but she didn't care. The sight of dark curly hair frothing about tiny masculine nipples had her hands and knees shaking so badly she wasn't sure how much longer she could remain on her feet. It infuriated her that he could effect her this way. No matter how deeply she scoured her memory, she unearthed no recollection of wanting to touch Skeet the way she did Buck Maddux. Self-defense alone caused her to twine the cloth strips higher and higher to shield his chest from her view.

"Aren't you going to check my ribs to see if I even need binding, before you make a mummy out of me?" he said.

Tempest hated the wry amusement in his voice. Blast him, he was determined to humiliate her. His chest rose and fell in rhythm with the slightly ragged sound of his breathing. She felt his gaze on her, hot and intense. Waiting.

Savagely she ripped the cloth binding off him, enjoying the pain it caused. She made no attempt to be gentle as she examined him, only to be swift and impassive. Foolish woman. His skin was warm and soft. She hadn't expected the softness. Even the hard muscles underneath were malleable. She wanted to linger, stroke, massage. Holy Mary, she wanted to taste him.

Tempest closed her eyes, fighting back a sudden wrenching need to be wrapped in those arms, to be kissed, to feel like a woman again.

Snatching her hands away, she said, "You're fine, nothing broken."

When she would have stepped away, he grabbed her wrists and imprisoned her open palms against his chest. His voice flowed over her like warm honey. "Are you sure? That was awfully quick. Maybe you should check again."

Her traitorous fingers tunneled into his hair. He moved her hands over him in slow erotic circles until she gave up all pretense at disinterest and succumbed to the glory of his smooth, resilient flesh, the tiny nubs of his nipples, the firmness of well-toned muscle. He slid her hands lower. Her fingers dipped beneath the gaping waistband and she gasped at the white-hot fire that exploded inside her. His hands glided up her forearms to her shoulders, then down her back to her hips. She didn't resist as he drew her against him, so close she couldn't mistake the extent of his desire for her. Her own body reacted in ways foreign to her. It came alive and clamored for more—of him, of whatever he would give her, of whatever would ease the growing ache inside her.

"Tempest." His voice was rough with passion, demanding in a soft sensual manner she could not refuse. She looked up and his mouth claimed hers.

Tempest thought surely they would be incinerated by the heat of that kiss. Her insides melted. Her entire body became a river of fire, eager to converge with his in the most primal way. It was crazy, insane. Yet she could not pull away. Their tongues mated and she tasted that distinctive flavor she would never forget. Like his scent. Clean, pure, masculine.

The door opened and they sprang apart.

As Ronan Carmichael lumbered inside Tempest busied herself with the bandages, too embarrassed to meet her father's gaze. He cleared his throat and went to sit on the cot. Out the corner of her eye, she saw that his entire body was trembling. Due to the cold outside or the absence of alcohol in his system, she wasn't sure.

"Probably don't need this," she told Buck, her voice strained as she tied off the binding, "but it might ease the discomfort."

"Thanks." He reached for his shirt.

Ignoring the pain it caused him to don his shirt without help, she picked up the remaining bandages and fled to her bedroom. "Good night, Papa."

Buck buttoned his shirt and walked to the door. He was putting on his hat when Ronan's voice stopped him.

"Go to yer bed, lad, yer horse is fine. I hung up yer tack and fed him. Ye've no need to check on him." He made no mention of the watered-down whiskey his "son-in-law" had brought him.

Buck nodded. He understood the pride that prevented the older man from verbally expressing his gratitude. As he closed the door behind him, he saw Ronan's brow beetle in confusion and disapproval. Buck wasn't about to explain why he was sleeping outside. Let the man's daughter do it.

In the middle of the night Ronan awoke, screaming of centipedes. His howls of terror reached Buck in his bed under the trees. Buck cursed, threw back his blanket and grabbed for his pants. He didn't bother with his boots. Obviously the liquor he'd given the man hadn't been enough to prevent the hallucinations of alcohol withdrawal.

Ronan was huddled in the corner on top of his bed, swiping desperately at his face, his head, his shoulders. "All over me. Buried alive in 'em. Get 'em off me. Get 'em off me."

Tempest stood in the doorway to her bedroom, one hand over her mouth, her eyes wide with horror. In her other hand she held a candle, the flame flickering wildly. Buck wanted to go to her, to comfort her, but first there was Ronan to tend to. "It's all right, Ronan, I'll get them off. Easy, now."

Buck got him back in bed. The man was shaking violently, his hand clawing the bedclothes fitfully. Sweat dotted his pale face. Buck told Tempest to fetch the laudanum. He held Ronan's head up while she helped her father drink the medicine. After a few moments Ronan's eyes closed. The trembling eased, and he drifted off to sleep.

"He'll be all right now." Buck rose wearily to his feet and looked at Tempest. For the first time he noticed her disheveled hair and the rumpled cotton nightgown that failed to conceal her curves. She looked young, seductive, and scared. Her vulnerability reached out to him, twining invisible threads about his heart in a way that her sensuality never could.

"Why are you doing this for us?" she asked, meeting his gaze.

Buck shrugged. "Needs doing, doesn't it?"

She paused, seeming to choose her words carefully. "We're nothing to you, not kin, not even friends. Yet you've patched and repaired and mended. You gave up your freedom and every cent you had, knowing you wouldn't be paid for your trouble. So tell me, what do you get out of all this?"

Shifting on his feet, he looked everywhere but at her.

"You're going to catch cold dressed like that. Get back to bed. I'll see you in the morning."

He headed for the door. The speed with which she beat him to it astounded him. Leaning against the wooden panel she repeated, "Why?"

Rubbing a hand over the back of his neck, he growled, "Dammit, woman, what do you want from me? I told your husband I'd look out for you, that's all there is to it. What more can I say?"

"I'm not sure. Who are you, Buck? Where did you come from? And why are you still here? How much of the pain and anger I see in your eyes when your guard's down have to do with Skeet? And what exactly is it you want from me in return for your help?"

His mouth was a grim slash in his bearded face as he glared at her. Slamming a hand against the door on either side of her head, he thrust his face into hers. "An ex-convict," he ground out. "That's who I am. Happy now? I spent the last two years in prison, thanks to *your* husband. Still want me to stay on here, contaminating your kids and threatening your pristine virtue?"

She stared at him, aghast. Before she could pull herself together enough to speak, he continued: "Do you know what prison is like, Tempest? It's slimy, dank walls without windows. Darkness blacker than death itself. The stench of vomit and urine and feces every hour of the day. It's lice and rats . . . the two-legged as well as the four-legged kind. It's brutality more ugly and savage than anything you could imagine. And there wasn't a day of it that I didn't yearn to get my hands on Skeet Whitney so I could see him dead again. Finding out what you've been through because of him hasn't made me any fonder of the man. If he walked through the door right now I'd happily throttle the life out of him."

Her stomach jerked spasmodically as his heated gaze

went to her mouth and lingered there. "He didn't deserve you," he muttered as his mouth came down on hers.

The kiss was fierce and desperate, demanding more than Tempest knew how to give, but she met it with equal fervor. Or would have, if he hadn't ended it as abruptly as it began.

"Unfortunately," he whispered huskily as he drew away, "neither do I. But I'm a lot more hungry than before I went to prison—and more uncivilized. So get out of my way, lady, or I'm going to haul you out to that bed under the trees and *show* you what I want from you."

Roughly he grabbed her by the arms and shoved her aside. A rush of cold night air chilled her flushed skin through her thin nightdress as the door banged shut behind him, leaving Tempest alone to ponder his words. He'd left her with more questions than she'd started with, an aching need she didn't know how to sate, and a ruthless desire to know every facet of this enigmatic man so she could banish the shadows from his eyes and fill the cold, cold void she had glimpsed deep in his soul. A void she very much feared she had fallen into, head over heels, and would never get out of again.

Chapter Eight

The next day began with another argument. Tempest demanded Buck put the dogcart back together and return her livestock. He refused. Frustrated and disgusted, she snatched up his unfinished breakfast and tossed it into the slop bucket. Buck was too relieved, in light of last night's confession about prison, at the lack of revulsion in her eyes when she looked at him to get very upset over a bit of food, even if it was a hundred times better than prison fare. "Good idea, sweetheart," he said, patting his flat stomach. "Spook's been complaining about the weight I've put on, eating so well here."

"Fine! You can fix your own meals from now on. And provide the means."

Grinning, he dragged her onto his lap, ignoring the pain it caused his battered ribs. "Now, sweetheart," he crooned as he held her against him, her arms imprisoned at her sides, "you know you don't mean that. I've been trying to find a job, and I have managed to bring home some game. If you aren't careful, I may get the notion you aren't glad to have me back. You don't want me riding off again and leaving you to the mercy of Jonas Creedy, do you?"

"Mama," Angel cried from her place at the table, "please don't let Papa Buck go away again. We need him."

Reacting to the tension in the room, Ethan banged his spoon, splattering mush. "Nee-im, nee-im," he mimicked.

Buck's heart lifted. Fifteen years had passed since anyone had really needed him, and it felt good. "See, sweetheart? You've got the kids upset. You know how sensitive Ethan is to friction. Tell them you didn't mean it."

"I meant every word and you know it," she ground out between clamped teeth. "Now let go of me." Lifting her leg, she brought her heel down hard on the toe of his boot.

Buck bellowed like a cow in labor. He shoved her from his lap, so hard she nearly ended up on the floor. Then he pulled his foot onto his knee and cradled it in his hands, gently applying pressure to the injured toes to ease the pain.

"Oh, dear," Tempest crooned with a false smile. "Did you hurt yourself?"

His eyes promised retribution. "You win this round, woman, but you're still not going to town before I say so. Got that?"

Smiling demurely, she said, "Yes, master."

With another groan he hobbled out the door. The children fell in behind him as he headed for the barn. They had taken to following Buck like puppies. Spook and Othello were almost as bad. Tempest smiled at the picture they made: the tall man trailed by a skipping four-year-old and a bare-bottomed toddler, running, always running; then Rooster who never let the children out of sight, and the appaloosa and the mule, fighting for position. Marmalade or one of the pigs usually brought up the rear.

Tempest's amusement faded. Her children had become terribly fond of Buck, especially Angel, and it frightened her to know he would leave them someday and break her babies' hearts. *And maybe my heart, too.* All the more reason to hang onto her independence, she told herself.

While she baked bread and set pinto beans to soaking for supper, she thought about how awful it must have been for him to be locked away in a prison. The image of him in a tiny, filthy cell, peering out through iron bars, tore at her heart. So many things were clearer now. The stiff pride and fragile arrogance, the mask he hid behind, safeguarding his emotions by pretending to be a carefree rogue. The sense of danger, the hint of ruthlessness and barely sheathed violence. The rare glimpse of vulnerability. His aversion to small spaces—like privies.

But why, if he'd had nothing to do with the robbery— as he insisted—had they put him in prison? She wanted to believe him. After all, she was a mother, she couldn't very well expose her sweet babies to the ill manners of a thief, could she?

Frog turds! She wanted to believe in him because she cared, blast him. To think of him suffering something so terrible made her heartsick. He was a drifter, a cowhand, and Lord only knew what else. A lascivious scoundrel, that was certain. Yet she had seen more in Buck Maddux. Warmth, kindness, sensitivity. A lost little boy desperately in need of love. Tempest shoved the thought aside. She couldn't afford to even think of loving Buck Maddux. He would never stay in Deception Canyon, never settle down. *But he had settled down once. He'd been married. What had happened? How had his wife died?*

It didn't matter. She didn't want him to stay. She liked her independence, liked knowing that all they had, poor as it might be, came from the labor of her own hands. It was an accomplishment in which any woman could take pride. No, Tempest Whitney had no need of another man in her life.

Buck Maddux had gotten the best of her. He'd proven he could bend her to his will. But this was a new day, and he was about to find out she had a few tricks of her own. Grabbing the rifle down from its perch, she stalked out the door.

Buck was striding toward the barn, ax in hand, when Tempest found him. He'd shed his shirt and hat. At first, all she could do was admire his muscular body, bandaged ribs and all. Then she forced her mind back on her task. The children were haphazardly stacking the wood he had chopped. When he was safely away from them, she put the rifle to her shoulder and called for him to halt.

"What do you think you're doing?" he said, maddeningly calm as he stared at her down the length of the rifle barrel.

With her eye to the sight, she smiled. It felt good to be in control. "I'll put it down . . . the minute that cart's in one piece and drivable again. Now get busy."

It bothered her that he didn't appear frightened. With a hand propped on his hip, one long leg cocked, and sweat glistening on his naked chest, he was devastatingly handsome. And all male. But those big, calloused hands were entirely too close to his Colt to suit her.

"Take the six-shooter out of your holster and drop it, Buck."

One corner of his mouth crescented in a smile. "I don't think so, sweetheart."

"Don't push me, Buck. I'm serious. Now drop it."

He dipped his head, hiding his face. "The rifle isn't loaded, Tempest."

Her head straightened and she glared at him. She had the terrible feeling he was laughing at her. "What do you mean, it isn't loaded? It's always loaded."

His hand moved to the back of his head and he rubbed his neck. "You think I'm fool enough to leave a loaded weapon within reach of a termagant like you who's just itching to get the best of me?"

Damn him. Damn him! Tempest jerked the rifle from her shoulder and eased the lever back enough to see into the chamber. Empty. This time she cursed out loud. Spurs jangled as he walked toward her. The gravelly dirt crunched beneath his boots. Desperate now, she tried to lever a cartridge into the chamber. Nothing. Buck reached her and gently took the gun from her hands.

Tears stung the backs of her eyes, fanning her anger. Refusing to let him see her defeated, she lifted her chin and stared him in the eye. "You have no right, Buck. That dogcart doesn't belong to you. *I* don't belong to you."

A corded arm snaked out and coiled about her waist, pulling her flush against his hard body. "No, but we could change that."

He lowered his mouth to hers. In spite of his split lip, he kissed her until she trembled and melted in his arms. Her mouth opened. He ravaged it with his tongue, let her ravage his. Neither had a thought for the children nearby who were making a game out of stacking logs. The entire world had narrowed to these lips, these tongues, these arms binding each other close.

Tempest matched him thrust for thrust, tasting tobacco and coffee and the unique flavor that was undeniably his. Inside her head she cursed him over and over. Then cursed herself for enjoying his kiss, and desperately wanting more. But she refused to sacrifice her pride to get it. She dragged her mouth from his. They stared at each other, panting for air, trembling with need. Blood oozed from his lip, but she ignored the instinctive urge to nurse his wounds. "You won't always have the upper hand, Buck Maddux," she whispered brokenly.

"No. One of these days I'll be gone."

Shoving her from him, he threw the rifle to the ground and stalked to the barn. Still fighting for breath, she watched him disappear into the dim interior, wondering why those words left her feeling so empty and scared.

When Buck rode off later to milk Flopsey at the cow's temporary hideout, Tempest quickly considered and then abandoned the idea of following him. She'd have to take the children, and they would be bound to give her away. She made another effort to locate the missing wheels off the dogcart instead. To entertain the children and gain their help, she turned the search into a new game. But no one got the prize; the wheels remained hidden.

At supper that night, Buck announced he would take Tempest into town in the morning. The situation was getting worse day by day. He'd done a lot of thinking during that afternoon and was no longer sure that taking her body would be enough to ease the ache inside him. The children, the rugged, fantastical canyon—dammit, even that yellow dog and the long-eared mule that had become his shadows—were beginning to mean too much to him. He was enjoying playing husband, father, homesteader. It was everything his heart had longed for. His craving to see the ocean was nothing to his yen for a family. This family. Fifteen years he'd managed to keep the yearning buried. Until Tempest. If he didn't find a way to end this farce soon he was going to wind up facedown in a bigger barrel of trouble than he could swim his way out of. He'd tried his darnedest to convince himself to get on his horse right then and ride as far and as fast as he could—before he ruined any more lives. His conscience wouldn't let him.

But, dammit, he'd decided, this had to end. If that mule-headed female wanted to go into Harper so goshdanged bad and thumb her nose in Creedy's ugly face, then fine— let her wreak as much havoc as suited her. She'd certainly wreaked enough with his peace of mind. As usual, though, she reacted in exactly the opposite way to what he'd expected.

"I don't need you 'taking' me into town," she spat out.

Unperturbed, he slathered fresh butter on a steaming biscuit. "Fine with me. Won't have to bother putting the cart together then."

Only the sound of his knife and fork clinking as he cut off a hunk of roasted rabbit kept the silence from deafening them all. Before he could get the meat in his mouth, Tempest jabbed it with her fork.

"You *will* put it back together," she said, each word low and distinct.

Buck met her challenge with a look that could freeze the sun. "And I *will* take you into town."

Clamping his hand over hers, he guided her fork to his mouth. He slid the morsel off the prongs with his teeth, turned her hand over, and kissed the sensitive inner side of her wrist.

Tempest yearned to ram her fork into his hand, but she was shaking too badly. Her entire body tingled with pleasure at the feel of his lips on her skin, the scab on his lip adding to the sensation. She hated him. She hated his handsome face, his hard-muscled body, his cocky arrogance, the way he mocked her at every opportunity. Most of all, she hated the way her stomach flip-flopped and her nerves sizzled when he looked at her with those hungry blue eyes that seemed entirely too aware of all she was thinking, all she was wanting.

Buck was smoothing wrinkles from a saddle blanket on Spook's back when Tempest arrived at the barn the next morning. His saddle waited nearby, slung over the top rail of the corral. It hadn't taken Tempest as long to get ready as he'd expected. He had barely finished putting the wheels back on the cart—not an easy chore with bruised ribs—and it still had to be hitched up.

Othello hung his head over the corral rail and greeted her with his hiccuping bray. Spook tossed his head and whinnied, making Buck smile. The two animals were always trying to outdo each other. Like a couple of people he could name.

She wore her usual pants and oversized shirt, the tails left hanging to her knees. Wisps of hair flew about her face, despite the floppy, wide-brimmed hat crammed on her head. Damn, it was as though she purposely made herself as unattractive as possible. Not a bad idea when she was going into town, but—Judas—he sure would like to see her in a dress again. Only not that black rag she'd worn for her wedding. Amber, he thought, to match the flecks in her eyes.

On one arm she carried a basket of vegetables from her garden. Mewling sounds came from a second basket.

"What are you going to do with the kittens?" he called as she vanished inside the barn.

Her voice drifted out with the jingle of harness gear and the creaking of wheels. "Sell them to stage passengers as mousers so I can pay something on my bill at the store."

He frowned. "I thought you traded vegetables for what you needed from the store."

Tempest emerged, dragging the dilapidated, two-wheeled cart by its shafts. The body was little more than a black wooden box, four feet by four feet, with an upper body of tattered, yellow wickerwork and bench-type seats along the sides. Two of the spokes in the wheels had been repaired with splints.

"I do trade goods." She let the heavy tack draped over her shoulder fall to the ground. "I also sometimes trade one animal for another. By the time the Eisenbeins came here and opened their store I needed so many things. The flash flood that destroyed our house destroyed everything else too, or washed it away. The children and I were practically naked. I found a pair of Skeet's pants and a shirt, so I used my dresses to make clothes for Angel and Ethan. And diapers, though they weren't very effective." She gave a dry, humorless chuckle. "One layer of wool doesn't absorb very much."

Buck had been caught out in enough rainstorms without a slicker to know the truth of that. He clenched his jaw tight, thinking of all she had suffered. The knuckles of his balled hands whitened. How he wished he could wrap them around Skeet Whitney's throat and just squeeze, squeeze, squeeze.

"An old trapper who comes through here now and then made us coats and moccasins from deer hides," she said. "He helped me finish digging out the house and lay the rock walls. We wouldn't have survived that first winter without him."

The knowledge that she'd had some help made Buck feel better about all those months she'd been alone here, though he wished it had been him. She headed back into the barn for the rest of the harness, and he followed, taking the heavy gear out of her hands.

"You want me to corral Rooster for you?" he teased.

"Don't be ridiculous, I'll use Othello, like I always do. I would appreciate it if you'd do the harnessing, though."

Grinning, he asked, "Would it earn me a kiss?"

"Why don't you get busy and find out?" Her voice was sweet as flapjack syrup. Judas. The woman was flirting with him. It set his blood to humming.

Employing his devil's grin, he winked. "Reckon I will. Round up the kids. I'll be ready to ride quicker than a frog can tongue flies."

Still smiling, she walked away. Something about her sudden affability bothered him, but he elbowed it aside and, whistling, set to work. While he was in town he would inquire about wild horses. If there were any herds in the area and he could catch a few, their sale to local ranchers could net him enough to make a fair dent in Tempest's debt to Jonas. During the night he had spent some wakeful hours seeking answers to his problems, which at the moment all centered around their need for cash. The missing money stolen by Skeet two years ago seemed a perfect answer, but where was it?

Since the soldiers' payroll made up most of the stolen money, they had left no stone unturned in their search for it, but without success. Buck had scoured his memory repeatedly for anything Skeet might have said or done that would give him a clue, other than the worthless message he had given Buck for Tempest. He came up with nothing.

There was no sign of the children when Tempest came back a few minutes later. The shawl wrapped around her shoulders looked so inappropriate with her baggy shirt hanging to her knees beneath it that he almost laughed. "Where are the kids?"

Tempest opened the rear door of the cart, climbed inside and placed the basket of vegetables on the floor at the front. "Hand me the kittens, will you, Buck?"

Irritated at being ignored, he snatched the basket off

the ground, inciting a round of anxious mews from inside, and set it next to the first one. "Now get the kids like I asked. And make sure Angel visits the outhouse first. I don't want to have to make any stops on the way into town."

Instead of doing as he'd asked, she seated herself and took up the reins. "I thought I'd leave them with you so I could get done faster."

"What?"

"Bye." She flicked the reins and Othello started toward the bridge.

"Tempest?" he shouted, "stop that thing right now and get back here."

She lifted a gloved hand in a wave. "Do try to keep a diaper on Ethan, won't you?" she said, her tone still syrupy sweet.

"Dammit, woman, I said get back here. Your father isn't here and I have no intention of . . . Hey!"

Furious, he ran after her. The cunning little vixen had conned him into doing the harnessing so he couldn't finish saddling Spook. She'd tricked him, and he'd fallen for it, the same way he'd fallen once before for the games of a slick shyster. Now another woman was in danger. It proved what he'd known for fifteen years—he was completely worthless at protecting women and children.

Children. He came to a halt.

"Hey!" he yelled again. "What about the kids? I don't know anything about taking care of them. How do you know I won't roast them in the oven while you're gone?"

"I've seen the way you look at them," she shouted back. "You won't let them get hurt."

Buck raced back to the barn and was getting ready to leap onto Spook's bare back to go after her when a terrified wail came from the house. With one foot in the stirrup,

he looked from the cloud of dust swallowing Tempest and
the dogcart, to the house and then back to the road.

"Papa Buck," Angel shouted. "Papa Buck, come quick."

Judas Priest. Tempest wasn't even out of sight yet, and
one of the kids was in trouble. Freeing his foot, he sprinted
toward the house.

Chapter Nine

Tempest parked the dogcart between the mercantile and the hotel, intending to avoid the Sagebrush Princess on the far side of the hotel.

The thought of how furious Buck must be with her right now brought a smile to her lips. She envisioned the sparks dancing in his blue eyes, like sunlight striking water, and the loose-hipped way he probably stalked off, muttering to himself. There would be hell to pay when she returned home. She wondered if he would try to paddle her.

He was right, of course, about the danger of coming to town alone. She had heard rumors of Jonas's brutality with women. Once, when a part-Mexican, part-Ute woman who worked as his ranch cook and housekeeper tried to leave, Jonas used his fists to convince her to stay. His cruelty was visible in his eyes. Exactly *how* cruel he could be was Tempest's concern. For him to beat her, even attempt to rape her, would come as no surprise. Was he also capable of killing her?

But she couldn't stay home cowering behind a man who would not always be there to protect her. She had to learn to fend for herself. Pretending to have a live husband to evade marriage to Jonas was one thing. Letting that half-breed think her afraid of him was another. That would grant him more power over her than she could afford to allow. Still, she was not foolish enough to invite trouble by flaunting her presence in front of Jonas. Losing one woman he had hoped to marry, then getting shot for trying to bed another, was undoubtedly more than his pride could suffer for one week. So, before leaving the house, she pocketed the .41 Remington derringer Skeet had carried whenever he went gambling. It's weight against her hip gave her a measure of security that helped bolster her courage.

In the seclusion of the alleyway between the store and the hotel, she waited for the morning stage to arrive out front. While the horses were being changed at the livery across the street, she approached the passengers with her basket of kittens. None of the men was interested in a good mouser, but she managed to sell one to a Mormon family planning to homestead near Price.

Next, she found Beaner Bennet mucking out his father's livery and turned the remaining kittens over to him. After the lanky twelve-year-old took his cut, she would earn only six cents per cat, but that was better than nothing. And better than coming to town herself each time a stage was due.

"I wonder if you'd mind doing me one other favor," she asked the boy.

"Sure, Miz Whitney." He grinned at her, his calf eyes drinking her in as they always did. He'd had a crush on her ever since Christmas when she'd caught him under the mistletoe at the store and given him a kiss on the cheek.

Smiling, she handed him the other basket. "Take these vegetables to the store for me. Tell Mr. Eisenbein the packets of dye are for Mrs. Weeks at the Double Bar D. There are some herbs here too: beebalm, ground yarrow, and red elderberry bark. Ask him to please fill the order on this list and load it into my cart. I left it in the alley by the back entrance. And pick out a penny's worth of candy for yourself for your trouble."

"You bet, Miz Whitney. Thanks."

"No," she corrected with a smile. "Thank *you.*"

As Tempest left the livery, Viola Sims emerged from the eatery across the street, broom in hand, and began sweeping the porch. Beneath her gun belt Viola wore a dress the same blue as the wild larkspur that bloomed each summer near the dugout. Smoke from her pipe wreathed her head as she swept away the dirt yesterday's wind had left behind. The sight of her friend filled Tempest with peaceful joy. Her mother had never been much on affection. In truth, Adelle Carmichael had been a hardworking but severely critical woman, cold and without mirth, who'd seen no need to praise a lonely, love-starved daughter. Whatever the cause of her mother's indifference, it created in Tempest an insatiable hunger for affection that only Viola Sims had appeased.

For a few moments she allowed herself to pretend everything was normal. She wasn't on the verge of losing her ranch. Her home hadn't been invaded by an arrogant, irksome devil whose motives eluded her grasp and who made her body hum with a yearning she'd never known, a man whose presence threatened her peace of mind as nothing else could.

But pretending wasn't enough. Desperate for Viola's soothing homespun brand of nurturing, Tempest hurried across the street, calling her friend's name. That she was passing in front of the Sagebrush Princess never crossed her mind. All she thought of was being with Viola. Seeing her, Viola snatched the pipe from her mouth and set her broom aside.

"Tempest, you're a breath of spring air." Viola clasped the younger woman's hands in hers. "And mighty welcome too. It's a wonder I'm not bald, the way I been tearing at my hair, worrying about you. If I had anyone to help me run this place, I would have driven out to see you." Turning as if looking at someone next to her, she said, "What? Oh, I will, I will." She turned back to Tempest. "Mr. Sims is a little confused, dear. He says Skeet Whitney isn't alive at all, that he's there with him."

The smile froze on Tempest's face. This wasn't the first time Viola had known something impossible to know and had attributed it to her dead husband. Tempest had always found plausible explanations: Stage wrecks weren't uncommon, after all, and any prediction of an unborn baby's sex had a fifty-fifty chance of being correct. Viola had predicted the surrender of Geronimo six months before it occurred in 1886, but everyone had known his capture was inevitable. That Viola knew the exact date had been a lucky guess. But why would she want to claim Skeet was dead?

"That's ridiculous, Viola." Taking the older woman's arm, Tempest guided her toward the restaurant door, a strained smile on her face. "You met Skeet at Jonas's after he stopped the wedding. You spoke to him yourself."

A tender and knowing smile curved Viola's crinkled mouth. "If you say so, dear. I only hope you know you can confide in me. I'm not so addlepated yet that I can't see the necessity for keeping your little secret."

The hurt look on her friend's face nearly broke Tempest's heart. Lying to Viola was worse than lying to the other townspeople. Tempest wanted—needed—to tell her the truth, to throw herself into Viola's comforting arms and let the older widow tell her what to do. Suddenly she was so tired of it all: the lies, the worry, the fear. Tired of fighting off Buck's constant attempts to seduce her, when what she truly wanted was to bind him to her forever.

Holy Mary! Had she actually allowed that thought into her head? Had she come to care that deeply for Buck? No, it was only fear and exhaustion making her think such nonsense. Not having to be so strong all the time, letting someone else assume her burdens and take care of her for a change, was an enormous relief. That was all there was to her attraction to the man.

"Oh, dear, I'm so sorry." Viola came to a stop and looked at her with distress and sympathy. "I didn't mean to make you cry."

Tempest stiffened and lifted her chin. "Don't be ridiculous, I never cry. Tears are nothing but emotional rain— and a waste of time."

"Of course, dear. The only two raindrops to fall this month merely happened to land on your cheeks."

Tempest laughed, but inside she felt ready to explode from the pent-up emotions roiling inside her. "Oh, Viola . . ."

A noisy farm wagon lumbering up the street drowned out her words. "Come inside where it's quiet, dear," Viola shouted. "You can tell me all about it over coffee and cinnamon rolls."

Fortunately, it was too late for the breakfast crowd and too early for lunch, so the only customers were a couple of cowhands from the Red Butte spread, guzzling coffee and arguing about the best way to rid cows of burdock stickers. Viola poured two cups of coffee, dished up sweet rolls and set them on the table closest to the kitchen. "Now, tell me everything."

Tempest did. She couldn't help herself.

Viola's hand moved to the butt of her pistol as she heard how Jonas had gotten hold of Tempest's mortgage and threatened to evict her unless she married him. "Why, I never heard of such villainy." In an aside she said, "Do calm down, Mr. Sims, or you'll likely have a seizure of some sort. Oh, yes, I forgot you're no longer susceptible to seizures. Well, never mind. Go on, Tempest, tell us how this Mr. Maddux became involved."

When Tempest finished her tale, Viola peered at her speculatively out of her one good eye. "I do hope you're expending every effort to make him happy, dear. Mr. Sims agrees it would be a dreadful mistake to let such a good man get away from you."

"Huh!" Tempest retorted. "He's a devil is what he is. Always scheming to get into my bed. All I want is to get this mess cleared up so I can have my privacy back. You know I don't intend to marry again, Viola. Buck Maddux hasn't changed my feelings about that."

"Are you quite sure, dear?"

"What do you mean?"

Viola smiled. "Only that I can't recall seeing you quite this dead set against marriage before. You were mostly indifferent to the subject. Now you're carrying on like a balky steer in a loading chute. Could it be that this Buck has you running scared?"

"Of course not. Don't be buffalo-brained."

"I see nothing stupid about it. He's a handsome man. One you certainly would not be able to wrap around your little finger, which is exactly what you need." Glancing about secretively, Viola leaned across the table. "I wouldn't want Mr. Sims to hear this, but I would happily let Mr. Maddux change *my* mind about marrying again . . . if only my bosom hadn't sunk to my waist and my derrière to my knees. Are you positive you aren't attracted to him?"

Tempest's laugh was hollow. To say she was not attracted to Buck would be a lie. To say she was would leave her entirely too exposed.

Viola leaned back with a sigh. "At any rate, it's a lucky thing this Buck Maddux came along. You can't count on that father of yours to protect you, that's certain. I saw him not more than fifteen minutes ago, going into the Princess. You'd think, after the problems he's caused you, he'd make sure he didn't bring any more ills down on your pretty head."

"You know Papa works and rooms there."

"Still? Mr. Creedy must be growing soft if he hasn't fired him yet. It isn't like him."

Watching her friend delicately uncoil her iced pastry and eat it inch by inch, Tempest moaned inwardly. Viola was right, it wasn't like Jonas to let her father stay on after what happened. "Papa told me this morning about Jonas being shot."

"I wondered if you knew. It was the older one who did it, you know. The one they call Big Red who looks as though she ought to have been a milch cow instead of a female."

"A cow *is* a female, Viola."

"Oh, you know what I mean." Viola flapped a hand, flicking bits of icing off her fingers onto the table. "That scoundrel was doing something awful to the poor girl, you may be sure of that," Viola said. "Mr. Wiley told me they heard her screaming clear down at the bar. Somehow she got Mr. Creedy's gun and shot him. The bullet only grazed his side, here, above his waist, so it wasn't a bad wound." Viola helped herself to one of Tempest's untouched rolls. "Not bad enough to prevent him from beating that woman half to death anyway. Mr. Wiley and the younger girl sat with her all night, afraid she wouldn't make it till morning."

Tempest had seen Jonas's soiled doves around town, but had never spoken to them. Both girls were young and pretty, Red being the oldest at nineteen. In spite of how they earned their living, Tempest felt bad to hear of one of them being beaten. "Is she going to be all right?"

"Mr. Wiley said this morning that she'll be fine eventually, if they can keep Mr. Creedy away from her long enough for her to heal up."

Somehow that didn't help Tempest feel better. She looked at the gooey white frosting on the bit of roll left on her plate, her stomach felt a bit queasy.

"Oh, dear, this has upset you, hasn't it?" Viola stuffed the last of her roll into her mouth.

"What happened to that girl is my fault," Tempest said. "If I'd married Jonas that night, he wouldn't have had to take his lust to Red and she wouldn't have been hurt."

"Nonsense, dear. You put that sort of thinking right out of your head. From what I hear, this isn't the first time the brute has beaten that woman. And it's not likely to be the last. He has a cruel streak in him. If he were a wolf or a bear, someone would have killed him by now to protect folks. Because he's a man, no one does anything."

Viola refilled Tempest's cup. "Come now, let's talk about something else. There's going to be a dance Saturday night in Samuel Stefan's barn to announce the engagement of their oldest girl to Ivan Volynskji. You'll come, won't you? You and your handsome Mr. Maddux?"

"Klara's going to marry Ivan? But he's Russian, isn't he? A Swedish girl marrying a Russian?"

"Ukrainian, to be exact," Viola corrected. "And as Mr. Sims says, we're all Americans now. Besides, Russian, Polish . . . it doesn't matter once the lights are out, now does it?"

Tempest couldn't help laughing. "Viola, you say the most outrageous things. That's one of the reasons I love you so, you always keep me laughing." She picked up her driving gloves and scooted back her chair. "Thanks for the coffee and rolls. I've got to be going."

Viola grunted. "No need to thank a body for something

you didn't even touch. Here, I'll wrap some up for you to take home. I'm sure Mr. Maddux would enjoy them, and the children too, of course."

"Thank you. I guess I've got too much on my mind to eat."

"Now you mind what I said, and be nice to Mr. Maddux, dear. He may be your only hope, you know. And take advantage of the fact that you're living with him, show him what a good wife you'd make. Perhaps he'll decide to stay."

The thought of living with Buck Maddux for five whole weeks until her note came due—maybe longer—set Tempest's pulse racing. At the same time, nausea rose in her. She felt as though she were teetering on the edge of a precipice. On one side was heaven, on the other side hell, and they both wore the face of Buck Maddux.

The Boston Eatery, which had originally been a boot shop, had been built smack up against the side of the Sagebrush Princess. Beyond the saloon was the hotel and then the narrow alley where she'd left Othello and the dogcart. Skirting a mountain of liquor bottles and trash tossed out the door by the barmen, Tempest walked past the saloon's rear entrance, thankful that, according to Viola, Jonas Creedy was not in town.

The ground had been packed hard and cleared of weeds by the constant tramping of feet to storage sheds and privies, and by horses' hooves and wagon wheels. Beyond the alley, paths crisscrossed through the greasewood to vanish on the rising hillside. The delicious aromas of Viola's kitchen were banished by the stench of rotting food not yet scavenged by dogs or pigs, by the stink of human waste and vomit.

She reached the thin gap that separated the saloon from the hotel, her mind pondering the strangeness of knowing that someone other than her children waited for her at home. A thrill skated down her spine. Her steps quickened with a sudden urge to get back as quickly as possible. Only, she told herself, to see her babies.

In five weeks, or sooner if she could get the money to pay Jonas, Buck would be riding out of her life. Which was exactly what she wanted. She had tried marriage and it had fallen far short of her foolish, youthful dreams. Men were a trial women endured merely to get the babies they craved. There certainly wasn't much else Tempest could see that hooking up with a man offered.

Behind her a stone skittered into the wall. At the same moment the hair at the back of her neck lifted. As Tempest whirled to see what was there, she assured herself it would be nothing more than a cat or a dog scrounging for food. It couldn't be Jonas. He wasn't even in town.

But she was wrong.

Jonas's thin lips stretched into a smile. Not a teasing, tantalizing grin like Buck Maddux's, but an evil, diabolic leer.

"Looking for me, puss?" The nostrils of his flat, bent nose flared like that of a dog sniffing out a bitch in heat.

She tried to hide her fear. "I don't have time to talk, Jonas. Skeet's waiting for me."

"A few minutes won't make much difference. Must be some reason you're skulking out here behind my saloon. Maybe you wanted to discuss how you could pay back the money you owe me. I've got some damn good suggestions," he said as he moved closer.

"Sorry, it'll have to be some other time. Come out to the house. We'll talk there." Every instinct told her to run, but running only incited predators. Trying to remain calm, she turned her back on him and walked away. She could dart into the rear entrance of the hotel, maybe find Catherine cleaning rooms or Todd fixing a broken doorknob.

"Where you going in such a hurry? Don't you wanna know where I been?"

"Why should I care where you go?" He was keeping pace with her. She could almost feel him breathing down her neck.

"Rode over to Fort Duchesne," he said.

Tempest stumbled and caught herself. Would the Army have records there of Buck's arrest? Something that would prove Buck wasn't Skeet? Against her will, Tempest slowed. Her stomach squiggled with worms of dread.

"Talked with the major in charge up there," Jonas continued.

"Why should I be interested in that?"

If evil had a sound, it was Jonas's laugh. "Because I went there to check into your husband's death. Wanna know what I found out?"

Tempest shrugged, hoping to look unconcerned. "What's to know? When the posse caught up to him, he was burying a man named Buck Maddux who had tried to take the money from him. Skeet took the man's identity, lit out for Colorado, and lived on the stolen Army payroll until he learned he wasn't wanted anymore. You're wasting my time, Jonas. I have to go." Again she headed for the dogcart, her heart thudding in her chest.

"I figured they might like to know they buried the wrong man, and that the real thief was back." Jonas was right behind her. Tempest hurried faster.

"Damn thing is, the case was closed when you paid back the money from the missing payroll. The major did tell me a real interesting story, though, 'bout that Maddux fella. Seems he was arrested as an accomplice in the robbery and sent to Provo. The major thinks he ended up in prison."

Tempest's heart tumbled. How much had Jonas learned? He obviously thought he knew something incriminating or he wouldn't be taking such pleasure in baiting her. Panic vibrated through her. Buck and Skeet looked nothing alike. Could Jonas have gotten hold of descriptions that proved who was who? If so, nothing would save her from Jonas. Beneath her shirttail, her hand went to the slight bulge of the derringer in her pocket.

"Is that where your husband's been the last two years, puss? Prison?" Jonas edged closer. "Did he come back for you . . . or for the money he musta stashed after the robbery?"

Tempest expelled the breath she had been holding. He didn't know Buck wasn't Skeet. She was safe. Or would be if she got out of this alley in one piece. She eyed the hotel entrance a dozen steps away. Maybe she could distract him long enough to make it inside. "All right, Jonas. It's true, Skeet was in the State Penitentiary," she said, walking again. "But when he went to get the money, it was gone. He thinks one of the soldiers found it and didn't report it."

"And you believe that?"

The hotel entrance was close, so close. Eight feet. Six. Three.

Two feet from the door his hand clamped on her arm, spinning her about. "Hold on, you little bitch, I'm not done with you yet."

Off balance, she fell against him, losing her hat. Chuckling, he clutched her tightly to his stocky body. The fear she'd felt before was nothing to what coursed through her now.

"That old sot of a father of yours told me you wasn't letting Skeet in your bed. What's the matter, can't he satisfy you no more?" Slobbering lips left a trail up her neck, along her jaw toward her mouth. Tempest shuddered. The distinctive smell of his saliva reminded her of stagnant pond scum. Her arms were pinned between them, her hands on his chest. She would never be able to get to her derringer. She had to loosen his grip on her. "Wait, Jonas."

"What for?" One hand cradled her bottom while he rubbed his erection into her pelvis. "Seems to me I waited too damn long as it is."

"Maybe we could make a deal."

Grinning, he drew back slightly, but not enough. "Maybe we could at that. This ain't the best place for what I aim to do to you. With your man sleeping outside, oughta be no problem for you to get out, though. You can come to the ranch house."

"My children . . . I can't—"

"I don't give a damn about them brats! Forget about 'em." Jonas bit hard on her earlobe. "Once you get a *real* man 'tween your legs, you won't care 'bout nothing 'cept keeping me there. And I'm the one belongs there, too. You know that now, don't you?" His voice hardened. "You ain't gonna be asking *me* to sleep outdoors, you'll be too busy begging me for more."

Her ear hurt and she was aware of blood dripping down her neck. Fighting him would only arouse him more. Forcing her mouth to curve upward, she rubbed her hands over his chest, easing them down toward her derringer. "What did you do, bribe Papa with whiskey to tell you what was going on in my house?"

"Clever, ain't I? Um, I like that. Keep going." His hold loosened as he gave her room to stroke his chest and stomach. One hand still cupped her bottom while he squeezed her breast with the other. Tempest's breath snagged in her chest as she slid a hand down his hip and felt the hardness of the derringer in her pocket. She edged her fingers beneath the hem of her shirt, praying he wouldn't notice.

Jonas's mouth left a sticky trail down her neck. His hand moved from her breast to the buttons of her shirt. The derringer's walnut stock felt cool to her hand. Carefully, she drew it upward.

Suddenly, Jonas grabbed her hand, twisting it painfully as he wrenched the weapon from her.

"You little bitch," he snarled. "Shoulda knowed I couldn't trust you."

Death peered at her through the stygian orbs of his eyes. She clawed his face, panic scouring her insides. Jonas cursed and jerked backward. The derringer kerthunked as it hit the ground, too far away for her to reach it. She pulled free, but before she could dash into the hotel, he seized her again and spun her about. She tried to duck the fist she saw coming. Suddenly the world exploded and went dim.

Through the pain-filled haze that followed, Tempest was barely aware of Jonas's ragged breathing in her ear. The click of a door opening. Her heels dragging across the bare wood floors of the hotel's rear hall. The squeak of a mattress that gave beneath her body as she was tossed down.

Slowly Tempest's head cleared. Coolness blew across naked skin. A deep voice grunted and groaned. She lay on a bed in a back room of the hotel, Jonas atop her. Her shirt and chemise had been torn open, and he was suckling her breast. A hand probed painfully between her legs, through her denims. Bitter acid surged into her throat. Panicked, she fought.

"Be still, you blasted wildcat," Jonas growled. "I'm only taking what's rightfully mine. Relax and enjoy it."

"He'll kill you," she gasped, wishing Buck would appear as suddenly and conveniently as he had at the wedding. But she couldn't count on him to rescue her this time, she had only herself. And she was terrified.

He laughed cruelly. "He can try. If you're smart, though,

you'll keep your mouth shut. Otherwise, you might find yourself missing a brat. I've got a new man who has a real fondness for little girls like yours. Know what he does with 'em? He strips 'em naked and then he—"

Tempest's panic soared. She dug her fingernails into his face. "You touch my children and *I'll* kill you," she panted.

"Dammit, that hurts!" His fist connected with her jaw. Pain cleaved her head in two. The world spun, deadly dark except for the bright colors that slashed at her eyes. He was tearing at her pants. She had to get free. Stretching her arms out to the sides, she felt for something, anything, to use as a weapon.

"Shit. Why in hell can't you wear skirts like any other woman?" he muttered as he jerked on her waistband. Fabric tore. With a satisfied grunt, he rammed his hand beneath the denim and palmed her feminine mound, moaning rapturously. Fingers dug at the muslin that barred him from the reality of her soft flesh. Then he cursed. "What the gawddamned hell you got on under your pants?"

A memory of Buck fingering the legs of her combination chemise and drawers as they hung on the clothesline came to her. She heard Buck's low, gruff voice pondering who it was that thought up such things as back flaps for keeping men from getting at what they most wanted to get at on a woman. The way Jonas was trying to get at her now. Hysterical laughter burst out of her.

"What're you laughing at, bitch? Gawdamn, I'll teach you who you're dealing with." His fist struck and searing pain sliced her cheek beneath her eye.

He had gone back to ripping her trousers off when she remembered the bullet wound in his side that Big Red had put there. It would have begun to heal in the three days since the shooting, but it would still be plenty sore.

She ran her hands over his barrel-like midriff until her fingers found the bandage beneath his shirt. Then she doubled her fist and drove it into his wound with all her might.

Chapter Ten

Jonas reared up and screeched like a gutted hog. "You whore! You gawddamned . . . stingy-cunted . . . whore."

Each word was accented with a blow to her face. He'd hauled back his arm to strike her again when there was a dull thwack. His entire body jerked. A heartbeat of silence followed, then he collapsed on top of her, revealing Viola's worried face peeping over his shoulder.

"Tempest, dear? Are you all right?"

"Get this garbage off me." Tempest pushed at the dead weight securing her to the bed.

"You forgot the cinnamon rolls I wrapped up for your Mr. Maddux."

"Never mind the rolls," Tempest cried, "just pull."

Viola shoved her Conlin target pistol into the holster, took hold of Jonas's feet and tugged. She grunted and heaved. Suddenly the boots came off in her hands and she found herself on the floor. "Drat! We won't get anywhere this way."

Viola's good eye took on a determined glaze as she hooked onto the unconscious man's waistband with both plump hands and gave a mighty yank. He slid partway off Tempest and she scrabbled free.

"Oh, Tempest, dear, look at you. Your clothes are all torn and your face is turning purple. Your Buck will have a fit when he sets eyes on you."

Tempest wasted little time in surveying the wreckage of her clothing. She was too busy swiping at her face, her neck, her breasts. "Find me some water and a cloth I can scrub myself with. I've got to get the feel of him off me before I go crazy."

Viola tried to snare Tempest's frantically scouring hands, but it was like trying to catch hold of a whirlwind.

Revulsion sent Tempest into spasms. Angry tears diluted the blood from the cut near her eye, stinging the abraded skin of her cheek. Hysteria edged her voice.

"He put his mouth on me, Viola. He put his mouth on me. I've got to wash. Please, please, help me wash."

"Stop, dear. Oh, do stop." Viola's own face was wet with tears as she snared her friend in a bear hug.

Tempest's hands flailed as she stood stiffly in Viola's fierce embrace. Sucking in a deep breath, she closed her eyes and concentrated on mastering her rioting emotions. Her fists unfurled and dropped to her sides.

"I'm all right." Tempest briefly hugged Viola back, then stepped away. "I'm sorry, I don't know how I could lose control like that."

"You were nearly raped, that's how," Viola retorted. "We must ship him off to Provo or Fort Duchesne so the law can deal with him properly."

"No, Viola, I don't want anyone to know about this. Please, it will only cause more gossip and trouble."

The older woman pursed her lips and stared at Tempest, her brow furrowed. Then she nodded. "All right, dear."

Her hand went to the pistol on her hip. "I'll just shoot him. We can shovel him, like garbage, into that cart of yours, dump him in a ravine, and pile rocks on top of him."

In spite of all she'd been through, Tempest laughed shakily. The image of Viola as a cold-eyed killer was too ludicrous. "Thank you, dear friend, but I don't think that will be necessary. We'll simply leave Jonas here and let him wake up alone to wonder how I got the best of him."

Viola scowled at an imaginary companion beside her. "Yes, Mr. Sims, it goes against all I hold sacred, too, to even think of letting a man go scot-free after what he tried to do to our dear Tempest. There must be some way to punish the scoundrel."

Tempest smiled wryly. "Any good ideas you or Mr. Sims can come up with, I'll gladly consider. In the meantime, how am I going to face Buck, looking like this?" She plucked at her torn clothes. "He'll come after Jonas. Oh, Viola, what if Buck gets sent back to prison for shooting Jonas? What if Jonas kills him? I can't risk it. I can't let Buck find out what happened here."

When Tempest drove the dogcart into the ranch yard, the first thing she noticed was that the barn door no longer hung from one hinge.

Then she saw the cow on the roof of the dugout, calmly ripping grass out of the sod with her teeth. The last time Flopsey had gotten up there, her foreleg had found a weak spot and gone clean through the roof. Tempest had had a devil of a time getting the animal free, and the house had been a mess.

Leaving the cart where it was, she jumped down and ran to the house. She could hear Ethan inside, giggling exuberantly, and Angel shouting, "Gee up! Gee up! Haw! Haw!"

"Holy Saint Mary," Tempest muttered, almost afraid to find out what sort of critter they had allowed inside. The burro maybe, or Grunt, the goat. "Shoo," she yelled at the cow, "get off there, you worthless hunk of coyote bait. Shoo!"

Something crashed inside the house and Ethan shrieked. Thinking her baby had been hurt, Tempest crossed herself, forgetting she had given up the Catholic faith when her mother died and left her to care for her disabled, alcoholic father and a selfish slob of a brother. Her concern for her babies momentarily blocked from her mind all she had endured that day.

The scene that met her eyes when she burst into the room brought her to a dead halt. An overturned stool lay at her feet. On hands and knees, Buck smiled up at her sheepishly, a giggling Ethan perched precariously on his broad back. Angel smacked Buck's rump with a willow shoot and yelled, "Gee up, horsey, gee up."

Keeping his eyes on Tempest, Buck humped his back, one arm twisted behind to hold Ethan in place. The boy shrieked—not in terror but in delight. Tempest's heart swelled. She wanted to cry. Joy, jealousy, and sorrow converged as she wished with every ounce of her being for what could never be. She wanted to throw herself into the middle of them and roll across the floor with them. She wanted to know the same joy she saw on her children's faces, wanted to forget that morning's encounter with Jonas and grab onto the happiness Buck dangled before her like gold at the end of a rainbow.

That it was all pretense struck her as a cruel joke. With her emotions at fever pitch, confused and frightened, desperately needing the solace she knew lay close in his arms— yet so out of reach—she reacted instinctively. Placing her hands on her hips and glowering at the trio on the floor, she demanded, "What in hell's south forty is going on here?"

"Papa Buck wath giving Ethan a horthy-back ride, Mama." Angel jumped up and down. "He let me ride Thpook, and Ethan wanted to, too, but Papa Buck thaid Ethan's too thmall to ride a real horthe, tho he gave him a ride on his back."

" 'Pook, Baba," Ethan cried. "E'fan 'ide 'pook."

"You will not ride Spook." Tempest snatched the child out of Buck's arms and snuggled him tightly to her breast. "You got hurt merely riding Buck's back, remember?"

"No. Ide pook," he whined.

She flashed Buck a furious glare. He flashed back one of his famous grins. A rustling sound took their gazes upward. Dirt from the roof was raining onto the paper that lined the ceiling. Tempest cursed. "Angel, go run Flopsey off the roof before she goes plumb through again."

After the child had raced outside, Tempest turned a malevolent look on Buck. "As for you, *Papa Buck*, can't you find something better to do with your time than play games with my children and get them knocked on their noggins?"

His grin broadened and devilish glints lit his eyes as he scanned her body in the dim light of the dugout. In spite of what her dusty shawl and loose shirt concealed, he'd had her in his arms enough to have a damn good idea what lay beneath. His body tightened. "Sure as hell can."

Shifting her son onto her hip as Buck advanced on her, she backed toward the door. "Don't swear in front of my children. And get that look off your face; I didn't mean what you've got on your lecherous mind."

He stalked her across the room. "Don't you want to ride me, too?"

"No, I do not." He was getting entirely too close. She

thought about being crushed in his arms, about having his mouth on hers. Suddenly it wasn't him she was seeing anymore; it was Jonas. Her eyes widened in terror and, with a sob, she fled through the open door with her son in her arms.

"Tempest? Dammit, what's gotten into you?"

She had nearly reached the dogcart when he caught up with her.

"Whoa, woman. I'm not going to hurt you." Grabbing her arm, he swung her about. "What is it? Why'd you . . . ?"

His jaw locked and his eyes hardened as he took in what the dim light of the dugout had hidden: the bruise on her jaw, the abraded cheek, the small cut by her eye. "What happened to you?" he gritted out from between clamped teeth.

Tempest backed away. Judas, she was terrified of him, he realized. Summoning all his will, he checked his seething emotions. "It's all right, Tempest," he crooned, trying to calm her as he edged closer, the way he would with a green mustang. "You're home now. I won't let anyone hurt you again."

Sensing his mistress's fear, Rooster bared his fangs and growled. Ethan whimpered.

"Down, Rooster." At the firm authority in the familiar masculine voice, the dog flopped onto the ground, his nose on his paws. The fear in Tempest's eyes faded to wariness, and Buck slowly closed the distance between them. One by one he surveyed the evidences of her mishap. Safety pins had been substituted for missing buttons. A length of twine held her butternut-colored trousers closed, but the poorly mended crotch seam gaped to show a silver of white muslin drawers. His fingers shook as they feathered over her swollen jaw, brushing away the flour Viola had applied to conceal the bruise. Tempest winced.

Dropping his hand he bowed his head. When he looked

up again, Tempest saw the desolate pain in his eyes. He was hurting—for her. No man had ever cared enough to feel her pain before. Tears pricked the backs of her eyes— the same tears she had refused to shed after the horrible experience with Jonas. The urge to throw herself into Buck's arms was overwhelming.

"What happened?" Concern tempered the harshness of his voice.

"A . . . a rabbit." Tempest swallowed to ease the dryness of her throat. She couldn't let Buck go after Jonas and risk being hurt. But the lie tasted like straw in her mouth. "It startled Othello and he bolted. The cart turned over, and I was thrown out."

Buck stared at her. Unease gripped him like an eagle's talons, digging into his heart. Was she so afraid of him that she would lie about what had happened? He walked to the cart and studied the wheels, the shaft, the wickerwork sides. The peeling paint was rough under his hand. "On the way into town or on the way back?"

"On the way in." Instantly, Tempest realized the hole she had dug for herself. Anyone in town could tell Buck there'd been nothing wrong with the cart when she'd arrived there. "I mean on the way home," she amended quickly. "About a mile up the road."

The cool blue gaze that trailed down her body was hard and questioning. With his arms folded across his chest, his feet spread wide, his face harsh as granite, he looked more dangerous than a flash flood. Still, she thought him beautiful.

"You always carry safety pins and twine with you?" he asked.

Wheels whirred as her mind delved for a believable answer. Ethan squirmed, wanting down. She clung to him irrationally, feeling she needed him for protection. The bare bottom beneath his gingham dress was warm against her arm. "Why isn't Ethan wearing a diaper?"

"He took it off. Don't try to change the subject, Tempest. I'm not likely to forget about this no matter what you do. Was anyone around when your . . . accident happened?"

"No." She didn't like the way he was looking at her, as if he could see clear to her lying soul. "Why do you ask?"

"Because there's something odd about all this, that's why."

"What do you mean?"

"I mean that the dogcart is in remarkably good condition for having been rolled and dragged. The paint isn't even scratched."

Tempest's laugh came out strangled. "Yes, lucky, isn't it? Of course, as badly as the paint is peeling, a scratch wouldn't show much."

"Yeah, unbelievably lucky. What happened, Tempest? And I want the truth this time."

There was nothing sensuous about the fire burning in his slitted eyes. They blazed with barely suppressed anger. Realizing more lies would only make the situation worse, Tempest sighed. She put Ethan down and patted the boy's bottom, urging him to go off and play. Stalling a few more seconds while she collected her scattered thoughts, she watched her son's plump legs churn as he ran toward a snoozing tangle of dogs.

"Why didn't you put his diaper back on?" she asked.

"Hell, he takes it off faster than I can get it on. Are you going to answer me? It was Jonas, wasn't it?"

The smile that had shaped her lips as she watched her son launch himself onto Rooster's back, his moonbeam bottom flashing in the sunlight as he tumbled over the dog, wilted and her mouth quivered.

"Tempest?" Buck's grip on her arms was surprisingly

gentle considering the magnitude of his fury. "Confound it, woman. Talk to me."

"Yes . . . Jonas." The name rushed out on a sigh of resignation. "He caught me in town. We . . . fought, and he hit me. I didn't want more trouble, so I concocted the story about the cart rolling over to explain my bruises."

His face could have been carved of granite, it was so unyielding. His lips drew back from his teeth in a snarl. "Did he . . . touch you?"

She knew what he was asking. Memory flooded back— Jonas's mouth on her breast, his smell, the scummy feeling his hands left behind on her skin. She closed her eyes on a shudder. "No, I wasn't raped."

He looked so bleak and tortured, she added, "I swear it. He . . . he tried, but Viola . . ."

Buck was no longer listening. His long stride carried him swiftly, purposefully, into the barn. Tempest ran after him. "What are you doing, Buck? Where—?"

He nearly ran over her as he reemerged with his saddle slung over one broad shoulder, a bridle over the other.

"Please, Buck, I don't want more trouble."

Seeming to sense the lethal intensity of his master's mood, Spook stood stock-still while Buck threw the saddle blanket over him and smoothed it with movements as automatic as the blink of an eye. Tempest had anticipated Buck's anger, but she could never have imagined the savage expression now on his handsome features. "Buck? Buck, what are you going to do?"

He spared her no glance. In a voice like a December gale, he said, "I'm going to kill him."

Jonas Creedy wasn't at his ranch or the saloon. It wasn't until Buck ran into Viola that he learned where to find the rutting bastard. With every step that took Buck closer to the Harper Hotel, where the women had left Jonas unconscious, his rage grew. He told himself he would be killing the man for the sake of every woman alive who could or had fallen prey to scum like Creedy. Women like Tempest. Women like Ellen.

His eyes squeezed shut as the pain and guilt of that night fifteen years ago rekindled in his soul. The need to purge himself of those awful memories was so strong he tasted it in the bile that rose to his throat.

Sounds. Smells. Screams. The bite of jute into his wrists. Laughter. The taste of whiskey on his tongue. Fear. Guilt.

Buck clenched his fists as he walked, his knuckles blanched white as old buffalo bones rotting in the sun. The veins in his temples pounded. He yearned to leap onto Spook's strong back and race the wind, leaving the horror of that night behind forever. But he'd learned long ago that there was no escape.

Now he had let another woman down. Would there be no end to his villainy? All those months in the penitentiary, he had told himself he didn't belong there. That he was above the other men whose ruthlessness and savagery so revolted him. Now he wondered. He had never struck a woman, never raped one. Nor was he a thief. But if he beat Jonas Creedy to a mindless pulp, if he killed the man as he so desperately wanted to do, could he still claim to be different from the men he hated?

He came to a dead halt in the middle of Harper's dusty street. A rushing, swirling vortex of hate and fear and confusion threatened to suck him into its bottomless black chasm as he struggled to face the truth deep in his soul. He was oblivious to his whereabouts. Sounds, scents, colors, shapes, all became as muddled and chaotic as his thoughts.

Sudden, angry oaths filled his ears, rising above all other sounds and jerking him back to the present. Brakes squealed against the unrelenting iron of wheel rims as the freighter tried to halt his galloping wagon. Chains jangled. The terrified mules reared threateningly above Buck.

Instinctively recognizing his danger, he threw up his arms, grabbed a strip of harness leather and hung on, dodging slashing hooves and speaking in his most soothing voice while he fought for his life. The freight wagon's entire team lunged to the side, trying to evade him. The harness jerked out of Buck's hand, taking hide with it. He stumbled out of the way of the enormous wheels and watched the wagon career down the street, leaving him coughing up dust and heaving for breath.

As he waited for the drumroll of his heart to slow, Buck knew without a doubt that violence, like Lucifer, extracted a premium he had no desire to pay.

Jonas Creedy awoke to a strange warmth . . . and pain that throbbed from ear to ear. Slowly he opened his eyes. Above him an orange sun glared through gathering clouds that seemed to intensify the harshness of its burning rays, making his head pound more fiercely. His eyes snapped shut and he groaned.

What in hell had happened to him? The last thing he remembered was riding in from Fort Duchesne. Then the soft struggling body of a woman beneath him and—Tempest Whitney!

Jonas cursed. The bullet wound she had bludgeoned with her fist throbbed, but so did his head. What had the bitch hit him with, an anvil?

After several minutes, he became aware of the hard abrasive surface beneath him. He lifted himself onto his elbows and looked about. Above his bare feet rose the crenelated tips of the canyon wall opposite him. How the goddamn hell had he gotten outside? His gaze traveled from his bare toes up his short bowed legs to his squat, hairless chest. *Sonuvabitch!* He was naked. Outdoors. And pure birthing-day naked.

A folded paper, tied with a bright pink hair ribbon, was wrapped about the appendage that peeked from the black nest at his crotch. Swearing worse than a tossed bronco-buster, Jonas ripped off the ribbon. His vision blurred, and the effort to read the paper in his hand intensified the ache in his head.

> Jonas—
> Touch my wife again and it won't be ribbon binding off your privates but good strong wire, drawn so tight you'll be able to sing with the ladies in church on Sundays for the rest of your sorry, unnatural life.
>
> > Skeet
>
> P.S. I wouldn't move too fast if I were you.

Pondering the meaning of the postscript Jonas looked around. He sat atop an enormous flat-topped boulder poised at the tip of an outcropping a dozen feet above the canyon floor. To the top of the precariously balanced boulder was another fifteen feet or so, for a total of twenty-five to thirty feet. A fall might not kill him, but a few broken limbs would be a certainty. He cursed again. Beside him, sharing the sunbaked heat of the red sandstone, a lizard lifted its head and winked.

How the hell was he going to get down without sending the treacherous hunk of rock tumbling to the earth, crushing him on the way?

Carefully, he maneuvered himself onto his knees to better assess his situation, positive the rock teetered beneath him. The lizard skittered away. Jonas peeked over the edge. His head spun. He rolled onto his back and squeezed his eyes shut to still the whirling motion. His stomach churned. As a child, he had been teased unmercifully because he couldn't climb trees like the other boys, and he hated the affliction. When his eyes cleared, he saw a face looking down on him from above. Perched on a rock ledge, looking fat as a cat with a saucer of cream, was the man who claimed to be Skeet Whitney. Smoke from his cigarette threaded the sky as the man calmly surveyed Creedy.

"You sonuvabitching bastard," Jonas screeched. "I'll get you for this. You get me my clothes and haul me off of here or I'll do more than touch that bitch wife of yours, I'll make you wish you were as dead as you're supposed to be."

The man grinned down at him. "Wouldn't advise it, but if it'll make you feel better, do your best. Had a hell of a good time getting you up here and then watching you wake up. My imagination's plumb going wild already with fascinating ideas for finishing you off. I'm downright looking forward to it."

Tipping his hat in a cocky salute, Tempest's husband leaped lithely from rock to rock, then dropped onto his appaloosa's back. "Tell your thugs to watch their backs, because I'll be looking for them. Oh, by the way . . . interesting watch fob you carry. The woman in the picture is a bit homely, kind of reminds me of a hound I once had, but I could definitely see a family resemblance."

Jonas howled vile epithets and demanded to be brought down from his perch. He got the jaunty wave of a hand and a view of the appaloosa's vanishing rump.

"You idiot!" Tempest slammed the lid onto her canning kettle. "Buffalo droppings have more brains than you do."

Buck's beguiling grin never faltered.

Groaning with frustration, she said, "Don't you realize what you've done?"

"I told you Swede and I were careful. Hell, we tried to shove that rock over and it wouldn't budge."

"I'm not talking about how dangerous messing with Balanced Rock could've been. I'm talking about the position you put Jonas in—and through that, us."

Anger glinted in Buck's eyes. "That bastard tried to rape you, and all you can think of is that he might have fallen a few feet? Judas, woman, I thought you'd be furious that I hadn't off cut his balls—"

"If I hadn't been sure it would only make the situation worse, I would have castrated him myself, but . . . Oh, what's the use?" Tempest threw her hands in the air, then raked them back through her hair, loosening more strands. "You don't understand anything."

Buck crossed his arms over his chest, his voice deceptively quiet. "Then why don't you make it clear for me?"

"Fine, I'll do that." Speaking with the slowness and distinction needed to get through to an idiot, she said, "You, my handsome moron, have done the one thing Jonas cannot let pass without serious retaliation. If you had shot off his leg, you could not have made this situation worse. No, you had to humiliate him. Jonas Creedy is an Apache breed with a brain no bigger than his ba—uh, than a walnut—and a desperate need to prove he's as good as any other man. You . . ."

Buck's mouth spread in a dazzlingly sensuous smile.

Tempest faltered. "Why are you smiling at me like that?"

"You think I'm handsome."

"What does your looks have to do with this, and who says I think you're handsome?"

"You do, you called me handsome."

"I called you a moron."

"*A* handsome moron."

Tempest's chin sagged to her chest in defeat.

With one finger, Buck lifted her chin so that she had

to look at him. "If it makes you feel better, I think you're handsome, too."

"Don't be ridiculous. Handsome only refers to men, Buck."

"Beautiful, is that better? Lovely, stunning, gor—"

"You're trying to change the subject."

"This is a better subject."

"No, it isn't."

"Yes, it is."

The sound Tempest made was a cross between a growl and a groan. "Can't you see that you've humiliated Jonas so badly, he won't settle for turning Papa out of the saloon or harassing me. He'll—"

"That bastard touched you." Rage roughened his voice as he cut her off. "The man's lucky he's still alive. He deserved a lot worse than what I did to him. And by God, if he touches you again, he'll get it."

Tempest shuddered at the feral violence distorting his face. She took a deep breath and tried again. "Buck, everything Jonas has ever done has been to prove he's as good as any white man. If you'd burned his house down, he could rebuild. If you'd stolen his cattle, he could buy more. But you took something from him more valuable than anything else he owns—his pride. Only one thing will satisfy him now—your blood pooled beneath your lifeless body."

The anger vanished. His eyes softened. "You're scared for me."

"I'm . . ." Blast it, she *was* scared for him. It was a terrifying thought. She couldn't afford to care that much about Buck Maddux. Or to let him know it. "I have two small children, Buck. Children who live in the same house as you, for the moment, and they could be in danger now, simply by being near you. *That* scares me."

Buck stared at her a moment, his hands on his hips. "All right. What do you think I should do?"

"I don't know. The damage is done. Now we can only keep an eye out for anything suspicious—and be careful."

They glanced about. Although it was only four in the afternoon, the sun had already begun to sink behind the high sinuous canyon walls. Shadows consumed the land. On the sidehill beyond the house, scrub jays called raucously and fought over ripe chokecherries, eager to get their fill before night set in. At the pasture fence, the two mares dozed, each with a hind hoof poised in the air as though they were dainty dancers.

"I'll bring all the animals in close, put them in the barn or the corral," Buck said. "Maybe string some cans across the bridge to warn us if anyone comes across during the night."

"They could come at us from any direction, Buck. You can't string cans around the entire ranch. And the dogs would warn us anyway, unless they're off running after rabbits again."

Buck rubbed the back of his neck, still studying the land. The dogs were unreliable for more reasons than rabbits; Creedy could throw them poisoned meat or even shoot them. If he grew up with Apaches the man was bound to know how to kill silently with a bow and arrow. An alarm system might not snare anything more dangerous than a drunken Scotsman, but at least Buck would feel he was doing something useful. "You're right, it's impossible to completely safeguard the house or the stock. At least, sleeping outside, I'll have a better chance of detecting anything suspicious."

"Oh, I—I'm not sure that's the best idea," she stammered.

"Why not?"

Tempest glanced away. Blast it! She wanted him with

her, but she didn't dare say it so baldly; it would swell his ego until it was bigger than Patmos Mountain. Better to let him think she was only concerned about their safety. "I wouldn't feel safe with you outside somewhere," she said, "where I can't even see you. What better way could Jonas find to get revenge on you than to sneak up and kill you out there under that tree, then come crawling into my bed to finish what he tried to do to me at the hotel?"

"He'll be expecting me to be inside with you," Buck replied. "He'll never think to look for me out there."

"But . . ."

"Now what?"

She wrung her hands on her apron. "He already knows that you sleep outside. Papa told him. That's why Jonas thought I might be receptive to his advances . . . because you weren't keeping me satisfied."

"Advances?" he blurted out, slapping his hands on his hips in disgust. "Hell of a word for attempted rape." Buck didn't care what her reasons were. Just the fact that she wanted him there, sleeping beside her, sent his pulse racing. But he didn't dare let her see how eager he was. "I don't know," he said doubtfully. "To tell you the truth, ever since prison I find sleeping inside windowless rooms . . . stifling. I'm not sure I can make it through a whole night in there."

"Please, Buck."

"All right. I guess I can give it a try."

Oddly stung by his lack of enthusiasm, she said, "Fine, I'll put a shakedown on the floor for you."

Damn!

Chapter Eleven

A freshness in the air hinted of rain as Buck walked back to the house after taking his bath in the creek, making him doubly glad to be sleeping inside tonight. A few feet from the door, Rooster dashed out of the darkness to nip at Buck's heels. Buck kicked at him and missed. The dratted dog was developing a real talent for taking him by surprise. It was a game they had both come to enjoy.

With the door shut safely in the mutt's face, Buck turned to find Tempest eyeing his clean, damp hair with suspicion. He refused to feel guilty about what he had in mind. If he was going to make it through the night in that dark, windowless back room, he would need a distraction. He figured lying next to Tempest, feeling her warmth, breathing in her scent, ought to do the job up right. It would be a hands-off situation, what with the kids sharing the same bed now that Ronan was living there, but he told himself that simply being beside her would be heaven enough. He hadn't wanted to go to her bed dirty and smelling of horse, so he had bathed. Now, feeling her gaze on him, hard and questioning, he tossed his dirty clothes into the corner with his other gear and let the gay tune he'd been whistling fade away.

Angel stood between her mother's knees getting her hair brushed. "Mama made you a bed next to ours, Papa Buck."

"She did, huh?"

Tempest gave her daughter's pale flyaway hair one last stroke with the brush, then patted the girl's bottom. "All done. Go on to bed now."

"Thoon as I kith Papa Buck good night."

Grinning at Tempest, he hauled Angel onto his lap. She wrapped her small arms around his neck and gave him a wet smack on the mouth. "G'night, Papa Buck."

"Good night, dumpling." He breathed in her sweet little-girl smell and swallowed hard as his throat tightened.

The rest of the evening passed with the quickness of a preacher's sermon on a hot Sunday afternoon. Buck read and reread the same paragraph of Homer's *Odyssey*, which he'd gotten in Salt Lake City after getting out of prison. His gaze flicked up to watch Tempest's needle flash in and out of the lamplight as she darned a sock for her father. If she felt any anxiety over the fact that he would be sleeping in her bedroom that night, it didn't show.

"Buck?"

"Hmm?" He tried to appear to be reading.

"I know you'd rather not talk about this, but I'd like . . . I need to know how you ended up in the penitentiary and what Skeet had to do with it."

She was right; prison was the last thing he wanted to discuss. "The posse decided that because I knew so much about Skeet's life . . . your name, where you lived, the name of your little girl . . . I couldn't have been be a total stranger to him. They figured I had to be Skeet's partner. The jury agreed.''

"I'm sorry, Buck. You have a right to feel angry and resentful. I wish—''

"It's over, Tempest, and it had nothing to do with you.'' To his surprise, his anger toward Skeet was gone. For all intents and purposes, Buck had assumed the life Skeet Whitney had left behind, and it suited him fine.

"It made a difference in how you felt about me when you came here, though, didn't it?'' she said, her hands idle in her lap.

"That's over, too. What I feel for you now has nothing to do with Skeet or anything in the past.''

She stared at him, and for a moment he feared she would ask exactly what he did feel for her. Then she dropped her gaze and took up her sewing again. Buck sat there pondering his emotions, and found they were too entangled with fears from the past, his feelings about himself and where he fit into the world, dreams he had long ago given up on. Only his lust for her was clear enough to label; yet even that was complicated by other feelings he wasn't sure he was ready to see. It was enough just to know he wanted her.

The fitted blue calico wrapper she'd donned after her bath was a vast improvement over her usual trousers and baggy shirt. Her breasts swayed inside the tucked bodice when she moved, making his breath stick in his throat. He became aware of another physical discomfort, but decided that the sight of a woman's natural form instead of the stiff artificial look of armored corsets was worth the extra torture. The small naked feet peeping from beneath her hem, with their rosy toes, affected him in an oddly erotic manner. He began his own odyssey as he imagined running his thumb along a gently curved arch, up over a nubbin of ankle bone, and feeling her shiver at his touch. He thought how her feet would feel nestled in his groin, how they would smell fresh-scrubbed, how they would taste.

He could no more keep his mind on his reading than he could his keep his imagination from wandering up those trim ankles to the rounded calves beneath her wrapper, then to the sensitive recesses behind her knees and up the warm satin slope of her inner thighs to the moist secret nook of his dreams.

The room heated up beyond his comfort zone. He told himself to get outside before he burst the crotch out of his pants, but Angel must have spilled hoof glue on his stool; his bottom was stuck fast.

Tempest rubbed one naked foot against the other, and Buck nearly groaned, imagining those feet rubbing his bare legs while he fitted himself to her body and—

"I'm off to bed." Jabbing her needle into the ball of thin darning yarn, she dropped it into her sewing basket and stood.

Buck leaped to his feet as if she had pushed a concealed lever on his hide. He laid the book on the table, unable to recall the title, let alone the subject matter, and turned away to mask the evidence of his arousal.

"Are you coming?" she asked.

"Damn near," he mumbled beneath his breath.

"What?"

"Never mind." Keeping his back to her, he went to the door. "I want to check around before turning in. Leave the lamp, I'll get it when I come back in."

"See if Papa's coming up the road. I'm worried about him. I wouldn't put it past Jonas to use Papa to get even with us."

Buck had had the same thought. He'd considered going out to search for Ronan, but that would leave Tempest and the children unprotected. The fact that she had a gun and knew how to use it gave him little comfort.

The breeze cooled his fevered skin as he stood outside the dugout, letting his eyes adjust to the darkness. A low growl warned him Rooster was nearby. A cat arched against his leg and mewed, hoping for a handout. Buck squatted and ran a hand over its silky fur, wondering if the secret nook at the top of those satin feminine thighs he had envisioned moments ago would feel as soft and warm.

The tin cans and scrap metal he'd strung across the bridge were still in place. The thought of a drunken Ronan stumbling into the rope and getting thrown in the creek and drowned worried Buck. He hadn't seen the old man since Ronan came begging for whiskey late in the afternoon. The Scotsman had been as strung out as Tempest's clothesline. Even though Buck had given him a bigger than usual dose of liquor, Ronan had still taken his mule and gone to find more. Buck only hoped the old man hadn't found more than he'd bargained for.

Before going back inside, Buck drew in several deep breaths, testing his control. He wasn't at all sure he would make it through the night—and not just because of the absence of windows. He wanted Tempest more than anything he had ever wanted before and was afraid to trust himself with her.

If it would make him the kind of husband she deserved, selling his soul to the devil would be a small price to pay. But he wanted more than that. Dammit, he wanted it all: the children, this dank hole of a house, the bizarre canyon with its fantastical rock formations and enigmatic Indian messages, even the menagerie Tempest called her ranch stock. They had all whispered their way into his heart, indistinguishable from the air he breathed, the blood that filled his veins, the sustenance that kept him alive.

That he could come to love two little imps like Tempest's children so quickly amazed him, but no more than the depth of his feeling for their mother. His need for her had grown until it governed his every waking thought, his dreams, his fears. At times it so overwhelmed him that he doubted he would want to live if he couldn't have her. He needed her lips on his, her arms about his neck. He needed her to love him, and with more than her body. How could he touch her, love her, knowing she deserved so much more than he could give her? The fear of letting her down ate at him like acid, leaving nothing.

Judas, if he were a real man—with a man's strength and a man's courage—he'd get on his horse now and ride out of her life. But he wasn't that strong.

And he hated himself for it.

Besides, there was Jonas to consider. Buck couldn't leave Tempest prey to that bastard.

Lamp in hand, he entered the back room, arresting shadows as he went. Slight mounds in the piled quilts showed where Tempest and the children lay. As promised, a pallet waited on the floor, so close in the crowded room that if Tempest got up in the middle of the night and forgot he was there, she'd step on top of him. Her head turned as he set the lamp on the dresser, and their eyes met. Holding her gaze in the amber glow, he sat in the rocker and wrestled off his boots. Then he stood and reached for the buttons on his shirt.

Tempest tried to wrench her gaze away as he worked each button free, exposing a chest sculpted of hard, corded muscle and smooth, warm skin. The days still being warm, he wore no undershirt, so nothing interfered as her gaze caressed each plane, each gentle curve, each masculine nipple nearly hidden in the dark fleece that drifted down his rib cage to encircle his navel, then vanish into his trousers where her imagination swiftly took over. Sensation prickled low in her body, a sweet sort of ache that tickled and teased and tormented. She'd felt this same ache before, a few times with Skeet when he'd been in one of his little boy moods and wanted to pet and be petted. Her body came alive, waiting for something she knew would never come. She tried to stop her brain from wondering if it might be different with Buck, if perhaps he could ease that nebulous needy hunger Skeet had barely touched.

Buck's hands located the top button of his Levi's and she held her breath. She wondered if he wore drawers, or if he slept naked as some men did. Feathers stroked inside her abdomen at the thought that there might be nothing to impede her view of him. The pleasant burning between her legs seemed to melt and flow through her body, like liquid fingers of fire. She gulped, and waited.

Buck smiled as he watched her eyes widen with each button. He stretched the procedure out until he suspected all he had to do was touch her and she would come apart in his hands. He wanted to hear her whisper his name, to feel her hands on him, as greedy as his would be on her. He wanted to know she desired him with the same insane desperation he was suffering. That would be more happiness than he had ever known, or would need to know again. To heighten her interest, he modestly turned his back and peeled off the Levi's.

Tempest was appallingly disappointed by the fine-knitted woolen drawers covering his buttocks and upper thighs. But she reveled in the well-muscled curves of his buttocks displayed by the clinging fit. When he swung back toward the bed, she barely stifled a gasp at what else the stretchy fabric exposed. Heat rushed to places she didn't even know she had. Her eyes took their fill, the drumbeat of her heart trembling the quilts over her breasts. Something powerful drew her gaze up, up, up that long lean torso until it met his.

Buck let his body and his eyes tell her what he wanted. With one word, she could grant him heaven, or condemn him to hell. His breath lodged in his throat as he waited.

An echo of his own yearning flared in her eyes, and his heart cartwheeled. Then she rolled over and presented him her back.

A rumble of thunder muffled Buck's curse.

The walls were squeezing the last of the air from Buck's lungs. He couldn't stay in that dark hole of a room another second without going insane. His mouth was desert-dry, his pulse stampeding. He could almost smell the stench of prison, hear the curses and moans of inmates, along with other sounds too repugnant to acknowledge. He felt the dampness of the stone prison walls and the weight of hopelessness. Self-disgust threatened to destroy him.

Thrusting aside the bed covers, and a dozing Marmalade along with them, he leaped to his feet. He trembled with the effort it took not to tear through the house like a blind madman. He didn't bother with clothes. His fear of humiliating himself with hysterical screams was too great.

The candle and matches he'd had the foresight to place by his bed came quickly to hand. The acrid scent of sulfur filled the room as he struck a match. He shielded the glow to keep from waking Tempest or the children. The last thing he needed was for her to see him shaking and fumbling, panic shrieking from every pore.

Children were afraid of the dark. Babies. Not fully grown men.

Silent expletives clogged his throat as he escaped into the night. Rooster made a half-lunge at him, then halted and backed away, seeming to sense this wasn't the time to argue male supremacy.

In the center of the yard, without a weed to crowd him, Buck planted his bare feet and lifted his face to the sky. Gulping in air he searched for a star, any star, to convince himself he was free and safe. But the sky was as black as his hopes for a normal life. The air smelled heavy and moist. He was trying to unknot his fists when the cans he'd strung across the bridge clanged and clattered. The silence of the dogs told Buck whatever had run into his string of tin cans wasn't dangerous. Still, he moved cautiously through the night toward the bridge.

Soon Ronan Carmichael's scraggly mule clopped into view. The Scotsman lay along the mule's spine, only the hand knotted in Beauty's tangled mane and the precarious balance of the man's bulky body keeping him from sliding off. At first Buck thought he was dead. He pulled Ronan from the saddle and was feeling for wounds when Ronan yawned, opened one eye, and warbled a few discordant notes of song. The rotten-potato smell of whiskey-breath crinkled Buck's nose.

Ronan had found what he'd gone hunting for; he was drunker than a crew of cattle drovers at trail's end.

Rain was falling by the time Buck got Ronan into bed. Donning his clothes and a slicker, he went back out to see to the mule and repair the warning system Ronan had torn down. He considered sleeping in the barn, not at all certain he could return to that airless, dungeonlike room. But Tempest would want to know why he had fled in the middle of the night like a spooked steer, and he couldn't bear to tell her. So he cursed, then ridiculed and shamed himself back to the house.

Lightning splintered the sky in jagged streaks as he approached. Rooster growled from under the wash bench. Buck growled back. "Save that for any real intruders who might come along, you damned mutt. And don't be running off after any bitches tonight."

Ronan was snoring. Buck carried the candle into the bedroom and eyed his dismal heap of blankets on the floor. He was cold and soaked to the skin. Stripping off his soggy underwear, he found a towel, dried himself and slipped, naked, into bed. He was tempted to leave the candle burning, not sure he could last through the night, but in the morning when the candle was all burned down, his prudent Tempest would want to know why. The rain pounding the roof was the kind that flooded creeks and washed out roads. Hard, furious rain that reminded a man he wasn't lord and master of his kingdom after all.

The big bed next to his rustled as Tempest turned over. "What is it? Why were you up?" She sounded sleepy and seductive.

"Your father came home. He was hellbent on singing."

"Is he drunk?"

"A regular walking whiskey vat, stink and all."

"Where did he get it?"

"Some cowhand probably."

"He'll never quit," she said with a sigh. "He was doing so well, with your help, but I was afraid to believe it would truly work."

The bed creaked as she rolled over again, leaving him alone in the stygian blackness of the chilly room. Already the place was musty and damp. The walls crept inward. He summoned his earlier fantasy of shapely feet and secret nooks, but it merely added to his discomfort as his body reacted with bolder demands for a release he couldn't grant. Fighting the panic that had overwhelmed him earlier, he squeezed his eyes shut and lay there, stiff and miserable and scared.

A splat of wetness bathed his nose. More followed. He looked up and saw only blackness. The steady trickle from the ceiling forced him to take refuge under his blankets. Rain-music tattooed his shrouded body. Dampness danced beneath the covers to find him. Mumbling, he crawled out and blindly sought a dryer spot for his bed. His oaths became more audible as his shin met an invisible piece of furniture, the dresser no doubt. He couldn't tell in which direction he was going.

"What are you doing?" Tempest whispered.

"A rain dance, what the hell do you think?" he snarled. "I'm trying to keep from drowning."

"Drowning?" The rain-music orchestrated by the leaky ceiling reached her ears and she sat up. "Oh, no. The cow must have poked a hole in the roof."

"Lot of good it does to know that. There's got to be some corner in this lousy excuse for a house that's still dry, and I'm damned well going to find it." In spite of the fact that her poor housing was none of his doing, he felt somehow ashamed that she had to live this way. She deserved better—a big, sound house of rock or timber, with wood floors and plenty of glass windows. And a real roof that didn't leak. How he wished he could be the one to build it for her.

Concerned for the comfort and safety of the children, Tempest ran her hands over the coverlet. "It's dry here."

Buck froze. Tension hummed in the silence.

She opened her mouth to tell him to forget what he was thinking, but the words died in her throat. She told herself she didn't want her father to assume she was still denying her "husband" his lawful rights. But the truth was, she wouldn't feel safe without Buck in the house. No, that wasn't it either. She wanted to know how it would feel to have Buck Maddux's hot, oversized body next to hers. Close enough to touch, be touched. Heated curls of sensation spiraled through her body. Banishing her wanton thoughts, she said, "I-I don't think there's room."

"There will be if we put the kids end to end."

"But the one at the bottom would smother."

"Not necessarily." He fumbled for the candle and set it aglow. At once, the walls retreated. Wavering light flooded over him.

"You're naked!" Tempest gasped.

"My drawers were wet."

Her hands refused to obey her order to cover her eyes. He was glorious, every inch. Within an instant he thrust to full life beneath her gaze, causing waves of sensation to eddy through her. She clamped her thighs tightly together, but it made no difference. The air sizzled with tension. Buck looked like a cat ready to spring. She thought about the weapons he would use on her: his hands, his mouth, his tongue, his . . . Frantically she tore her eyes from his body and pinned her gaze on his handsome face.

"You can't get in my bed like that," she managed, hating the breathless quality of her voice that exposed her inner turmoil.

"All right." He was too desperate for a dry bed to argue. Leaving the candle on the dresser, he dug into his saddle-bags for dry drawers. Then, decently covered again, he approached the bed. "Get up."

Certain she would rue this decision in the morning, she did as he said. He pulled the covers free at the foot of the bed, then carefully switched Ethan to that end. Tempest folded and tucked two blankets around the small bodies, leaving the children's heads uncovered. The rest of the quilts were arranged over the empty portion of the bed. Buck motioned for Tempest to get in and scoot over.

To Tempest's mind he wasn't "decently" covered at all. If anything, the snug stretchy garment only made him seem more pagan. With wooden, uncooperative limbs she hitched aside, making space for him as he snuffed the candle. Then he was there, lying beside her in the darkness. His warmth seeped into her until her blood steamed and her thoughts scrambled. That he could so easily arouse her was infuriating. If he touched her, if he pressed his warm, soft lips to hers, she would scream. If he didn't, she would die.

She waited.

Minutes ticked past, lost to the music of the storm. He shifted onto his side. His buttocks brushed her hip and she realized he'd turned his back to her. Then she heard his slow, even breathing and knew he was asleep.

Withheld breath hissed out of her, sounding faintly like a curse.

Chapter Twelve

Saturday arrived more swiftly than a raven at a roadkill. Tempest's last hope of avoiding the Stefans' barn dance vanished when her father announced at breakfast that he would be going.

Her nerves were already frayed from sleeping with Buck's warm body next to hers the past few nights. The children had been moved to a smaller bed Buck built for them, so she was alone with him now in the big bed. She knew she should make him sleep on the floor again, but she couldn't make herself do it. Instead, she lay there each night, wondering, hoping, fearing. Waiting. Each night he turned away and went instantly to sleep. One more night like that and she would go crazy. Yet the alternative was equally unacceptable.

Buck said nothing about the dance until the older man left, trailed by the children who were pestering him to help them pull carrots to feed the horses and mules. Ethan, sniffling with a slight cold, dragged his "bankie" behind him. Tempest shook her head. As she scraped dishes into the slop bucket, she tried to ignore the man at the table boring a hole in her back with his gaze. It was useless.

"Weren't going to tell me, were you?" Buck said finally.

The abrasive sound of the knife on the earthenware added to the tension. "Tell you what?" she hedged.

He chuckled mirthlessly. "You know damn well what."

"It's an engagement party . . . the oldest Stefan girl is marrying Ivan Volynskji. Since I don't know them well, and Ethan isn't over his sniffles, I hadn't planned to go. Besides, I have nothing appropriate to wear to a dance."

His chair grated on the floor as he shoved away from the table. The warmth of his big frame and the tingling of her body told her he stood directly behind her. It took a conscious effort not to lean into him. *Touch me. Oh, Sweet Mary, please touch me.*

But he didn't. "Ethan isn't that sick," he said. "According to the Widow Sims, everyone within ten miles is coming . . . partly to see us. She says we need to be there . . . to curb the gossip."

Tempest stared at him. "You mean you already knew about the dance?"

"I was hoping for some hint that you wanted to go with me."

Spinning back to the sideboard, she scraped another plate. "I have no intention of pandering to their morbid curiosity. If they want to see you so dratted bad, let them come here."

"Morbid?"

"You're supposed to be dead, remember? That, and the romantic notion of a bride being stolen from her wedding by a husband more interested in the . . . woman he was bedding than his own wife, is all that interests them."

He nuzzled her neck under her ear. His beard tickled

her sensitive skin, making her shiver. "Do I feel dead?" he asked huskily, ignoring her barb about Lacey.

She whirled and shoved against his chest. "No. You don't look dead, feel dead, or smell dead. Can we get off the subject now?"

Buck didn't budge. He placed his hands on either side of her, trapping her against the sideboard as snugly as a rabbit in a snare. The look in his eyes set her every nerve trembling. It was the look she'd craved for days, a hungry look that said she and she alone could nourish him.

"*You* sure don't feel dead," he whispered, bending to kiss her cheek. "You feel warm and real and good. Kiss me, pretty lady. I haven't had nearly enough kisses in my life and your mouth was made for the job."

He gave her no chance to object. His mouth silenced hers in the most delicious way possible, his tongue stroking the inner surface of her lips with such delicacy she felt cherished and banished all thoughts of resistance. Her hands found their way up his hard chest to the thick hair at the back of his head. To sink her fingers into those silky strands was like a dream come true. They looked like midnight but felt like liquid sunshine, bathing her soul. With light brushing motions, his lips moved over hers, nipping at their fullness. Then he crushed her to him, his mouth demanding, almost bruising as it plundered hers. Tempest thought he would devour her, and she relished it. She couldn't get close enough. Her hips arched brazenly against him, glorying in the proof of her effect on him. She wanted to touch him, to taste him, to climb inside and become part of him.

Buck knew he was out of control. He ordered himself to move away, and cursed his inability to obey. He pressed even more intimately to her, grinding gently, building the heat until he thought he would erupt like a volcano, burning them both to cinders. He'd wanted her too desperately, for too long. Turning away from her each night to keep from touching her had been torture. Now that she was in his arms, his body refused to give up the sweet feel of her against him.

Over and over, he whispered her name, his voice low and tortured. His mouth explored her face while his hands slipped beneath her loose shirt, inched up her rib cage, and found her breasts. Tempest cried out, as if the pleasure were too much. Her head fell back, giving him access to her neck. Beneath her jaw and down the side of her neck, he trailed kisses until he found the seductive hollow at the base that had tempted him so often as it peeked from the opening of her shirt. He bathed it now with his tongue, his thumbs stroking her nipples to hard peaks.

A drop of milk collected on his thumb. A ravenous need to taste it overwhelmed him. He shoved the shirt to her neck, went down on his knees and put his mouth to her breast. Nothing had ever tasted so good.

Tempest gasped as his mouth closed over her nipple. What he was doing was as arousing as it was shocking, in broad daylight with the door open. She could hear the children calling for Grunt to come and get a carrot. What if they walked in and saw Buck crouched there at her feet, her shirt rucked up about her shoulders and his mouth sucking, sucking?

Instead of pushing him away as she knew she should, she held his head more tightly to her. Knowing they might be caught at any moment filled her with a giddy sort of exhilaration that shocked her. He was drinking the milk Ethan no longer wanted, going from breast to breast, suckling them dry, easing the discomfort of their fullness, his hands cupping, squeezing, worshiping.

Out of the corner of half-closed eyes, she saw a shadow cross a sunlit square of the window. "Buck!" She thrust him away.

He came to his feet in a swift, graceful motion, eyes blazing with a hunger that wrenched her heart and increased the ache in the part of her he had yet to touch. A boot scuffed the dirt outside and her father's voice came to them as he spoke to Rooster. Leaning against the sideboard, Tempest stared at Buck, afraid to move and test her trembling legs. He yanked down her shirt and turned her about. "The dishes," he whispered.

Then he vanished into the back room.

A moment later Ronan appeared in the open doorway. Tempest rattled the dishes as she forced her hands to perform what should be second nature, but which seemed impossible at the moment. She couldn't look at her father. Her face was warm, and she knew it must be as red as the paper roses pasted on the wall.

" 'Tis a bonny day," Ronan said. "The bairns are building a wall with rocks so they can play 'fort.' I've a notion to ride up Dry Fork Canyon and visit with the Ancient Ones."

"That's a good idea, Papa," she croaked, then cleared her voice. She felt his gaze on her but couldn't face him.

"Did yer Skeet go back to bed?" he asked.

"No. The roof leaked last night. He's cleaning up the floor."

"Does he need help, do ye think?"

"No," she said a little too quickly. "No, I don't think so."

"Ah. Well, I'm off then."

The moment he was gone, Tempest covered her face with wet, soapy hands. That was how Buck found her when he came from the bedroom. He stood behind her, feeling helpless. He wanted to ask if she was only embarrassed or if she regretted what happened between them. The words wouldn't come; he was afraid of her answer. What they had shared seemed beautiful to him, as beautiful and precious as a desert rainbow. He couldn't bear the thought that she might not see it the same way.

"Who are the Ancient Ones?" he asked finally to distract her.

Tempest straightened and began scrubbing dishes again. "Indians. The ones who built the ruins and carved the designs in the rocks you see everywhere in the canyon. The Utes call them the Ancient Ones."

Buck stepped to the open door and gazed after her father. "Don't suppose any of them left behind some whiskey, do you? Never saw Ronan show any interest in Indian ruins before."

Tempest tried to laugh, but the sound came out strained. "He visits them often, actually. A Welsh grandmother filled him with tales of Celtic druids and witches and magic when he was young. I think the Indian drawings hold the same fascination for him as the strange stone monuments all over Britain no one's ever figured out. A mystery to solve." She sighed wearily. "But you're right to suspect him. He could easily have a bottle hidden in one of them."

Buck knew nothing of druids and stone monuments. Nor were they a subject he wished to discuss at the moment. What he really wanted was to finish what they had started before her father came in, but he sensed that for her the mood was gone. Tense with frustration, he mumbled something about checking on Spook and went outside.

As he walked toward the pasture, he thought about Ronan. Tempest's father had been sober more than drunk lately, even doing some work about the place. If the Stefans' barn dance went the way of most such events, there would be enough liquor floating around to strike every man there booze-blind, let alone one old Scotsman, and there would be no way to prevent Ronan from imbibing.

A sip or two of whiskey would go down his own gullet real well right now, Buck thought. His mind needed numbing. So did his body, but there wasn't enough liquor in the county to kill its cravings. For the millionth time he told himself to mount his horse and get away from Tempest and her canyon. It was insane to stay, feeling as he did. The situation would only end in disaster. He didn't deserve her. Pretending for a while to have a home, a family, a wife had been heaven, even if he did hate himself for the indulgence. Giving up what he'd found here would take every ounce of will power he possessed.

Tonight, he promised himself. He would give himself one more night. Then he'd pay Jonas Creedy a visit. After painting the man a very clear picture of what the half-breed could expect if he bothered Tempest again, Buck would instruct Swede to send for him if Tempest needed help. Then he'd leave.

But tonight he and Tempest would dance and laugh and hold each other close, like any husband and wife enjoying a party. Ethan would fall asleep beneath the chairs the way Buck had as a child, and Angel would make herself sick eating too much cake. He would carry them out to the cart while Tempest said her goodbyes. Then they would go home together.

Home. Was it wrong to ask for one more night to enjoy feeling like a husband and father? Tomorrow would be soon enough to face the loneliness that was all he would have for the rest of his life. For now, he wanted a small taste of what might have been. He knew Tempest wasn't Ellen. His feelings for Tempest went beyond what he'd felt for the innocent young girl he'd married. The girl he had killed.

And after the dance? After they were home and the children were tucked away and Ronan was snoring on his cot in the front room? There was no pretense about what he hoped would happen then.

Closing his eyes he envisioned Tempest leaning against

the sideboard, her shirt shoved up and held in place by the upthrust of her beautiful breasts. Her lips were parted and she was panting. Her nipples were hard and swollen. Reddened from the pressure of his mouth. Her legs were braced a little apart, as though waiting for him to fit himself between them where he belonged. And her eyes—oh Judas, her eyes—big with wonder, sensuous and drowsy, dark and wild with a hunger that matched his own.

Buck opened his eyes and banished the vision. An entire day had to be gotten through before night came. He'd never make it if he didn't get his mind on something else. Like the problem of finding her a dress.

High above, the sun crested the jagged tips of the towering sandstone walls. It glinted off the fanciful spires and castlelike formations, and sprinkled them with gold dust. Buck breathed in the crisp clean air and gazed about as though seeing the canyon for the first time. With the toe of his boot, he nudged the sandy, seemingly infertile soil, then crouched and scooped the dirt into his hand. Off to his left the green of Tempest's irrigated garden—what was left of it after the harvest anyway—proved the land wasn't infertile at all. Only dry. The challenge of this harsh land called to him. He understood now why Tempest fought so hard to hang onto her small ranch. And he wanted the same thing. California and the Pacific Ocean were a dream, one he had needed to get him through prison. But he far preferred the warm, living reality of Tempest and the children. Everything he had ever truly wanted in life was right here.

The evening turned even colder than the previous night and thunder grumbled in the distance, but the revelers inside the Stefans' brightly lit barn were oblivious. Fiddle music and laughter blocked out most sounds. In the loft

children screamed and raced about in a wild game of "it."
Bits of hay from their stomping feet filtered between the
crevices in the loft floor onto the dancers below.

Tempest stood behind the refreshments table passing
out cups of punch, spiked for the men, plain for children
and ladies. Ethan snoozed on a chair nearby, his thumb
in his mouth and his "bankie" tucked under his chin.
Like the other youngsters her age, Angel chased about,
getting underfoot. Ronan had joined a group of men dis-
cussing politics and cattle disease while passing a flask
among them. She wished she could tell the men not to
give him any liquor, but she couldn't bring herself to
humiliate him that way.

Beside Tempest, Viola tapped her toe and hummed to
the music. "You ought to rescue that man of yours, Tempest. He hasn't been off that dance floor for a good hour.
Must be parched as a sun-dried cow chip by now."

Buck's dark head was easy to locate among the throng.
Tempest frowned. Eloise Jensen was clinging tighter to
him than a vine on a trellis. A moment ago it had been
Lucy Bennet. Tempest knew he was only being polite and
sociable, banishing gossip from the ladies' minds, but
country manners did not require a man to enjoy himself
quite so thoroughly. She had to admit he was the most
handsome of the men. His vivid blue eyes were a striking
contrast to his tanned face and the midnight darkness of
his hair, while his strength and self-assurance made him
as conspicuous as the distinctive white streak over his brow.
A hawk among sparrows. Merely looking at him made her
heart leap. But the way he spread his seductive charm
among so many twittering females infuriated her.

"He's not my man," she muttered to Viola while offering
Anna Hopkins a cup of punch. "Besides, I wouldn't dream
of spoiling his fun."

Viola shook her head. "Now, dear, it isn't good to let a

man think you don't care what he does with other women. It gives him ideas."

"He can have all the ideas he wants, as long as they don't involve me."

In a tone of exasperation, Viola spoke to the empty space beside her. "She already knows she's a fool, Mr. Sims. I told her she'd never find another like him. Not around here."

Tempest ignored her friend. She knew Viola was right, but she wasn't about to admit it. Eloise Jensen was leading Buck toward the barn door, her breasts pressed against his arm. Her head was tipped back as she gazed up at him, her lips pouting invitingly. "Skunk-faced weasel," Tempest grumbled beneath her breath. "I absolutely refuse to care what he does." Eloise, on the other hand, Tempest yearned to snatch bald.

Viola followed Tempest's gaze. "Glory be. Doesn't he know what folks'll think seeing him go off with a young girl like that? It's no way to counter the gossip about him and that girl at the Princess. Best go after him, dear, or you won't have a shred of pride left."

"I haven't any now, blast his devil's heart," Tempest retorted. "I can't believe what a bunch of hypocrites those women are, so shocked at having a 'thieving womanizer' in their midst, yet batting their eyelashes and acting like he was an oversized chocolate cake they couldn't wait to gobble up."

Viola smiled. "We women are a contrary lot, as Mr. Sims likes to say. We love dangerous men, especially ones as handsome as Mr. Maddux."

"I don't think anyone believed for one second that he's really Skeet."

"Perhaps not, but they won't say anything to Jonas. There isn't a one of them can stomach the man. Mr. Johansson certainly is keeping his mouth shut. Everyone

knows he and Mr. Maddux have become friends, but no
one can get Swede to say a word about him."

"I don't care what they think, as long as Jonas leaves
me alone."

At that moment Jonas Creedy appeared in the doorway.
Tempest hated the fear the sight of him instilled in her,
and the awful feeling of vulnerability at knowing how close
he'd come to defiling her. That he had seen her naked
breasts and put his mouth on them mortified her to her
very soul. The hair at her nape rose as his gaze lit upon
her. His eyes swept her body, and his snide smile made it
plain he was remembering what he had done to her. She
closed her eyes and turned away, while heat rose to her
cheeks. Suddenly the smells of straw, coffee, perfume on
unwashed bodies, and the other barn scents no amount
of cleaning could erase overwhelmed her, nearly causing
her to swoon. Horrified, she stiffened her spine.

"Gracious," said Viola. "Jonas is heading right toward
us. After what your Mr. Maddux did to him for attacking
you, I'm astonished that the scoundrel has the nerve to
even look at you."

Before Tempest could decide on a plan of action, Buck
walked into the barn. Pretending she hadn't seen Jonas,
she left the refreshments table and merged with the crowd,
taking a roundabout route she hoped would place her in
Buck's path. He saw her and motioned for her to meet
him on the dance floor.

"How sweet of you to break off your moonlight tryst
with Eloise to rescue me," she gushed as they met, her
eyelashes batting coquettishly.

Buck grinned as he swept her into his arms and twirled
her across the floor. "I'm glad you appreciate my sacrifice."

"Why, how could I do otherwise?" Her voice still sweet

as Viola's cinnamon rolls, she added, "You skunk-breathed, two-headed vulture."

"Now, sweetheart, no need to overdo the gratitude. I know you love me."

Under the guise of a dance step, she stomped his toe.

Buck yelped and bit off a curse. "Is that any way to treat your loving husband? And here I was about to tell you how pretty you look."

Her pique vanished and her heart melted. "Oh, Buck, I still can't believe you rode all the way to Price to buy me this dress."

"You really like it?"

"I love it. Yellow's always been my favorite color."

His gaze dropped admiringly to her décolletage that bared a startling amount of bosom and to the small puffed sleeves that revealed slender arms. "It's amber, to match the flecks in your eyes."

Cocking her head, she asked, "What are you after, Buck Maddux? You're too much of a scoundrel to have done this out of kindness." He looked so full of himself she couldn't help trying to knock him down a peg or two. "How did you pay for it? You gave Jonas all your money."

Instead of the devilish grin and ribald retort she had expected, he shrugged. "I didn't go all the way to Price. I met a Mormon family in Wellington. A relative back East had sent the woman the dress, but the neckline was too daring for her. It didn't take much to talk her into trading it for a couple of books I had in my saddlebags." Then came the smile, more sheepish than seductive, and totally serious. "As for what I want, you've always known that."

"Oh, Buck." He looked like a young boy trying to whee-dle his way out of mucking out the barn so he could go fishing instead. She wanted to brush the silver-streaked wave off his forehead and clutch him to her breast. Their eyes locked and they moved closer together. Their legs brushed, and she tingled with sudden awareness of his hard body against her softer one, his large, rough hand engulfing her smaller one, his thigh momentarily inserted between hers as they danced. Her satin skirts whispered, enveloping them as they swirled around the dance floor, lost in each other's gaze as if they were the only two people in the world.

Buck pressed his face in her hair. "Your hair smells good. You're beautiful with it piled on top of your head like this. I like the wisps curling around your face and down your neck." His voice took on a melancholy tone. "Too beautiful for a drifter like me. You deserve a man who can buy you pretty dresses and take you dancing every week. But I'm damned glad it's me you're with tonight, me who'll be taking you home."

Tempest hid her face in his shoulder, afraid to let him see the emotions exposed in her eyes. He made her feel beautiful, soft and feminine. No longer a frontier mother who grubbed in dirt with chapped hands and bred mules to keep food in her children's mouths, but a girl in yellow satin, young and lovely and desired. He crushed her to him and she clung, her heart soaring despite the small voice warning her that she was about to tumble into a deep, deep chasm that could easily swallow her whole. She wanted to be swallowed. Wanted to know the joy Buck's lips and hands and body promised. Wanted him to make love to her, to solve her problems, to take care of her.

When the music ended, he refused to let her go. The fiddler began another song and Buck swept her away. They danced until they were panting, their cheeks flushed, laughing like youngsters intoxicated by their first taste of sensual awareness, reluctant to let go but afraid to hang on and see where the night might take them.

"Having a good time?" he asked.

"Yes. Not as good as you've been having, though, being

pawed and fawned over by every female in the place." Her teasing tone took on a hint of pique. "I can't believe you went outside with Eloise like that."

A dark brow rose. "Jealous?"

"Of course not. I don't give a cat's whiskers if you take Eloise Jensen out in the middle of the dance floor and kiss her till she faints dead at your feet."

As he tipped back his head and laughed, she caught a whiff of night wind and whiskey and silken promises.

"You've been drinking," she said, surprised.

"That's what I was doing while you were imagining me doing Lord knows what with Eloise. She needed to use the necessary. I just escorted her to the barn door, then warmed my blood with a swig from the bottle the men were passing out there."

Tempest gazed about the room, feigning disinterest. "Your conceit is bigger than Patmos Mountain. What makes you think I was imagining anything about you and Eloise?"

"If you weren't worrying about what I was doing with her, why were you so upset that I'd gone outside with her?"

"I wasn't."

"Yes, you were," he challenged with a grin.

"I was not."

"You certainly hustled yourself over to me quickly enough when I came back inside."

Her mouth gaped as she stared at him. "That had nothing to do with Eloise Jensen. I was simply avoiding Jonas. Didn't you see him?"

"No, I didn't know he was here." He stiffened and his eyes narrowed. "The bastard wouldn't dare even speak to you. He knows I'd kill him."

"I'm not so sure of that. He headed right for me."

"Then maybe we should remind him that you belong to me," he growled.

Before she could object, his mouth claimed hers in a kiss so electrifying she could do nothing except kiss him back with every ounce of feeling her body contained.

Jonas Creedy took the cup of punch the Widow Sims reluctantly handed him and watched Tempest go into her husband's arms at the edge of the dance area. His nostrils flared as rage surged through him. She should have belonged to him. Would have, if that bastard pretending to be her husband hadn't come along.

Jonas was becoming more and more sure he was actually Buck Maddux, the man sent to prison as Skeet's accomplice in the payroll robbery. Jonas had sent a wire to the U.S. marshal in Provo asking for information on Maddux, where he was from, and where he was now. Why the hell hadn't there been any answer? He cursed, thinking he would have to take another ride to send a wire to the penitentiary. If Maddux had been incarcerated there, maybe the warden could provide a description to prove once and for all who the bastard was.

So far, Jonas's inquiries had produced no one who could identify Whitney. Jess Barlow, who'd been there longer than anyone else in the territory, would have known the man. Jonas was sorry now that he'd killed the stubborn old codger for refusing to sell him the Carcass Creek Cattle Company. Everyone thought Barlow sold out and moved to California, but he had gone no farther than a grave in his own yard.

Whitney or Maddux, it would be simple enough to kill the bastard. But if Tempest had told the truth about her husband being in prison, he couldn't have spent the stolen payroll, which meant it had to be stashed somewhere nearby. Tempest had paid back the Army, which meant Whitney had a legal right to the hoard. Jonas could only surmise that the thief was being cautious about anyone learning he had so much cash on hand in case they decided to take it for themselves. He smiled. Who deserved it more than him? He would watch and wait. Once the cash was recovered, he would step in and help himself to it all— the money, the land, and Tempest.

Taking a sip of punch, he coughed and spewed the liquid onto the floor. "What the hell did you give me, woman?" he asked the plump widow behind the refreshment table. "This sugar water ain't fit for anyone but brats."

"Or rats," she muttered.

Leaning across the table he snarled, "Watch it, you old bitch. You may find that pig-slop restaurant of yours going up in flames some night."

The hand she rested on the pistol at her hip was completely at odds with her look of wide-eyed innocence. "Why, Mr. Creedy, it isn't wise to threaten me with my husband close by. You never know what might be waiting in the dark for you some night, unheard and unseen . . . like the dead." Cocking her head as though listening, she whispered, "Oh, my, did you hear that? I think I heard an owl call."

Jonas blanched. Beads of sweat formed at his temples, and at the back of his neck. It was all he could do to keep from fleeing the suddenly overheated barn. Damn the woman for using his Apache beliefs against him. How had she known his people were terrified of the dead and that ghosts often spoke with the voice of an owl? He told himself he wasn't Apache anymore, that their foolish superstitions meant nothing to him, but his fingers tightened on the delicate handle of the punch cup until it shattered and the cup dropped into the punch bowl with a splash.

The widow smiled, as though pleased her punch had

been ruined with broken glass. Jonas flexed his hands, yearning to wrap them about her plump neck.

Women turned away as he passed, their hands shielding whispers. He knew they were talking about the way Tempest had humiliated him, walking out on their wedding. They probably all knew about Red's shooting him as well. And the humiliation he'd suffered at Skeet's hands that day at Balanced Rock. A savage sneer distorted Jonas's mouth as he remembered the way his own men had snickered when he'd walked up to the ranch house stark naked. Jonas wanted to show them. He wanted to show everybody. Jonas Creedy wasn't only a half-breed. He was a man to be reckoned with, one smarter and more ruthless than any of them. When he found the lost Spanish gold and became the richest man in the territory, they'd come sniveling to his door, begging for his goodwill.

Tempest Whitney wouldn't consider herself too good for him then. She'd be proud to be the wife of the most successful rancher in central Utah. And the bastard claiming to be her husband would no longer be a problem, because he'd be dead. No one could humiliate Jonas Creedy and go unpunished.

Chapter Thirteen

Buck hugged Tempest so fiercely the buttons on his double-breasted shirt were impressed in her flesh above the neckline of her dress. Her pulse leaped as his mouth took hers, and her knees went soft as biscuit dough.

"Maybe that will get the message through to these women that I'm more than happy with the wife I already have," he whispered when he finally ended the kiss.

"But I'm not your wife."

"Pretend."

Tempest glanced about at the people for whom they were performing this charade. Faces stared back, most of them openmouthed with shock. A few, like Viola, beamed approval, others appeared green with envy. It occurred to her that she was proud to be thought Buck's wife, would be proud to truly be—She didn't let herself finish the thought. It wouldn't be wise.

"Know what I'd like to do now?" Buck asked quietly. "I'd like to whisk you home, tuck the kids in bed, and spend three or four hours showing you all the ways I'd cherish you . . . if you *were* my wife."

The loud thrum of her heart all but drowned out the fiddles and Nathan Olney's harmonica as the musicians began another waltz. Her entire being, body and soul, zeroed in on the feel of his hard masculine body brushing against her and the illicit seduction of his words.

". . . the pulse inside your elbow, I'd kiss that too, before I moved back up to your neck. I'd lick the hollow at the base of your throat, slick my tongue downward until I found your breast and . . ."

His words inflamed her as nothing else ever had. That he was saying them, albeit in a whisper, amidst a crowd of people, heightened their seductive effect. An ache centered at her core, making her want to squirm against the hardness probing her through the layers of her skirts. She hadn't known a woman could feel such lust.

". . . round and round till the tips grow hard as my . . ."

Could they become a real family? She wasn't too old to have more children. Would Buck want children of his own?

". . . and the insides of your thighs. Judas, Tempest, you've no idea how I've wondered what they would feel like. Soft as a puppy's ear? Smooth as satin? Warm, cool? Wide with welcome, or shut tight as a clam? Dammit, woman, let's go home."

Tempest suddenly realized they had stopped dancing. Even through that long heavenly kiss, their bodies had swayed in time to the music. Now they stood alone in the middle of the floor while other couples swirled around them in a cotillion. Her arms were around his neck, her fingers buried in the thick midnight hair. And he was looking down at her, questioningly, and so intensely she felt it in her toes. "W-what?" She had been so lost in her thoughts and the sensations he was creating in her that she wasn't sure what he had been saying, except that it had been sinful and delicious.

"I said, let's go home."

Like his body, his hungry voice caressed every inch of her, inside out, until it was no wonder she couldn't think straight. All she could do was feel, and what she felt was him, chest to chest, belly to belly, thigh to thigh, yearning, craving . . . If someone had asked her name right then she couldn't have answered. She had no identity separate from Buck Maddux, knew only the driving need to become one with him. "Yes, let's go home."

"I'll fetch the cart," he said, as he escorted her to the sidelines.

"Yes, do." She would have agreed to almost anything at that instant. The desire in his eyes and the knowledge that she was the one who had put it there had her soaring higher than eagles' wings. But the moment he stepped away, taking his warmth with him, reality flooded back. "Holy Saint Mary," she murmured, watching him weave through the crowd toward the door. "What am I going to do?"

"I certainly know what I'd do if I were you," Viola said, stepping up next to her.

"What?"

"Why, child, I'd give in."

"Oh, but, Viola, I don't want to be tied to a man again. Getting bedded isn't enough of a pleasure to warrant that big a sacrifice." *At least it never had been before.*

"You don't have to marry him to enjoy his lovemaking, dear."

Viola laughed at the shock on her young friend's face. "No need to look at me like that, young lady. I wasn't always old. Was I, Mr. Sims? And, for that matter, even old folks enjoy a bit of loving now and then."

"Ready, Tempest?" Buck walked up, his arms loaded

with their wraps. "The cart's out front. It's a good thing we decided to leave now, it's going to start raining any second. If we're lucky, maybe we can beat it home."

She let him drape her heavy wool shawl around her shoulders, then went to fetch Angel while he swaddled a still-sleeping Ethan in a blanket.

"Buck, I don't see Papa anywhere," she said when she came back.

"He's passed out in a corner. I don't reckon he'll wake up before dawn. No need to disturb him. Let's just get ourselves home."

Lightning lit the sky as Buck tucked the children into the cart and helped Tempest inside. Spook stomped restively nearby.

"I've got a bad feeling we're going to get soaked," Buck told her as he vaulted into the saddle. "Drive that thing as fast as you can—*without* tipping it over."

His premonition about the storm proved true.

Huge raindrops mercilessly drummed the heads and shoulders of the trio hunched in the cart. The raging storm obscured all sound except the thunder cracking and rumbling overhead, echoing off the cliffs in seemingly endless peals that gradually faded, only to burst once more overhead, deafeningly loud.

Ethan awoke terrified as a particularly noisy clap of thunder exploded nearby. The boy fought his way out from under the quilts and slicker Buck had tucked over the children. Sobbing, Ethan nearly fell from the cart as he scrambled onto his mother's lap. She nestled him close, wrapping her shawl around them both, but in no time they were soaked and shivering. No amount of threatening or cajoling would get the boy back under the shelter he had shared with his sister.

As they neared the house Buck galloped ahead and dashed inside to light a lantern. A bright wedge of yellow welcomed Tempest as she pulled up to the open door. Lifting Ethan from her arms, Buck shouted for her to get Angel inside. Ethan sneezed as Buck set the boy on his bed and stripped off his wet clothes, giving the act no more thought now than he would undressing himself. Frowning, Buck noticed the unusual heat of Ethan's downy skin. Quickly, he dried the boy, dressed him in his nightdress, and tucked him in bed, while Tempest did the same for Angel. Then he went out to take care of the animals.

"I put the coffee on," she told him as he peeled off his wet coat after coming back inside. She herself had changed into a wrapper and soft slippers.

"Good," he said, smiling. "I'll fetch some brandy from my saddlebags to doctor it up with."

"Don't put any in mine. One drunk in this family is enough."

"A thimbleful isn't enough to turn you into a drunk, and it'll go a long way in warding off any chill you may have caught."

Tempest found the doctored coffee surprisingly tasty. After her second cup she decided Buck was right; the alcohol sped through her body like fire on a trail of gunpowder, warming her from the inside out until she felt languid and content, without any overwhelming urge to drain the bottle dry.

"Feel better?" he asked.

He lounged on the floor near the stove, arms folded behind his head, legs extended in a long, narrow vee, bare feet pointed toward the heat. She smiled, thinking how much he looked like Rooster when the hound snuck in the house on a cold night. Except the dog usually thrust all four legs in the air, his hairy belly begging to be scratched. A vision of Buck's naked chest with its thicket of hair, flashed in front of her, bringing a nearly irresistible urge to apply her nails to his abdomen and see if he would groan and writhe with pleasure the way Rooster would. "Yes," she said, smiling, "like a cat who's just had a saucer of cream."

Buck glanced over at her. She did look decidedly feline curled in the rocker, her head relaxed against the pressed wood design, eyes half-closed. Her lips glistened from her last sip of the fragrant brew, making him long to taste her with his tongue. As though she had read his mind, she lazily licked her lower lip clean, and a coil of desire unfurled in his stomach.

"No lingering chill?"

"No, I'm toasty warm from fingertips to toes."

She rolled her head back and forth against the chair. "Is your neck stiff?" he asked, yearning for an excuse—any excuse—to touch her.

"A little. My back, too, probably from bending over that table all evening serving punch."

He sat up. "Come here, I'll rub your neck for you." He patted the floor between his thighs.

Tempest knew she should stay where she was. She would be a fool to become intimate with a man who had made it abundantly clear he would never settle down. But one glimpse of the feverish look in his eye had her blood racing. He wanted her, and she no longer had the energy or the inclination to resist. Giving herself to him would hurt no one but herself. She knew how to avoid pregnancy, and she suspected making love with Buck would provide her with sweet memories for the cold, lonely nights to come, when her thoughts would return to these magical moments of feeling desired, even loved.

Buck closed his eyes, savoring her warmth and the scent of her skin as his fingers explored the seductive curves and hollows of her collarbones and his thumbs gently kneaded the taut cords of her neck. "Relax," he whispered close to her ear. "Lean against me, I won't break." He drew her back until her spine met his chest, then returned his hands to her neck.

After a moment she began to squirm. "Your shirt's wet and the buttons are digging into me."

"That's easy enough to fix." He sat her upright while he swiftly drew the garment off over his head. His denims were wet, too. He considered offering to take them off and decided she wasn't ready for that yet.

The moment he brought her back against his bare chest, his heat warmed her through her wrapper. Then something soft and warm and slightly damp brushed over her nape, and she realized it was his lips on her neck. Swirls of desire eddied through her, making her shiver. She knew she should stop him, but the words wouldn't come. Visions writhed in her head. Dark sensuous visions without substance, dreams veiled in rainbow mists.

Teeth nipped the slackened cords of her neck. Tempest shuddered as need splintered through her. Her head lolled back against his shoulder, giving his lips better access to her neck. He ran his tongue up to her ear, then closed his mouth over the lobe, sucking gently. His breath on her cheek was almost as warm as the tongue laving the inner crevice of her ear. All the while, his hands kneaded her shoulders, liquefying her bones. The heavenly feel of his touch awoke every nerve in her body. She marveled that she could feel so vibrantly alive and totally relaxed at the same time.

"Better?" he whispered in her ear.

"Hmm." She didn't want to answer, afraid he would stop. His mouth moved across her cheek toward her lips. Without thinking, she turned and met the kiss.

Buck moaned. "You taste like sin," he murmured against her lips. Tempest gave a throaty giggle. How could anything taste like sin? Sin had no taste.

He coiled his left arm about her waist and pulled her

more fully against him. The kiss intensified. He pressed
her to open to him and she did. The feel of his tongue
inside her mouth was the most provocative thing she'd
ever known, and she realized it was what she had craved
ever since they'd left the dance. She realized something
else, too—sin did have a flavor.

Buck bit off a groan as desire slammed through him at
her generous reaction, leaving him hard and aching. He
hadn't known women could taste so good, or feel so good,
and he wondered if this was the difference between whores
and good women. Ellen had never allowed his lips to touch
anything except her mouth and cheek. Lovemaking
between them had been an awkward affair conducted in
darkness beneath the bed covers.

The horrible memories of the night Ellen had died filled
him with a sort of desperation, a need to wipe them away
forever, to replace them with new ones he could treasure
instead of abhor. He needed to be loved. To clutch greedily
at all the things he had missed out on with Ellen, the joys
he had never known—like the chance to pleasure a woman
as he never had before. Frantically he buried the memories
in a crypt deep within his brain. Then he sucked in a few
deep breaths and forced his mind back to the woman in
his arms.

But holding her, kissing her, wasn't enough. The need
inside him had exploded into one of such magnitude he
wasn't sure it could ever be sated. Slowly he slid his left
hand up Tempest's rib cage until his thumb brushed the
underside of her breast. Her plump flesh filled his hand
as if created specially for him. He felt it swell, felt her shift
restlessly in a subtly sensuous movement that pressed her
rounded flesh fully into his palm, as though begging for
more. He grew jealous of the fabric that lay closer to her
sweet body than he could. He wanted to feel the silky

smoothness of her naked skin, see the dusky rose of her nipples, taste . . .

Most of all, he wanted her to feel as much pleasure as he did. She'd suffered so much in her life, had been cheated so unfairly. He was sure her husband hadn't made her happy, hadn't given her the ecstasy Buck was determined to give her.

Blistering heat surged to his groin as her nipple blossomed beneath her wrapper. He quelled a bolt of impatience that caused his hand to shake. He felt as awkward and uncertain and out of control as he had the first time he had taken Ellen, when both of them had been unschooled virgins. But he wasn't a boy anymore. He was a man who had been with more women than he could count. What was it that made this one feel differently in his arms? That made *this* breast fuller, tauter, more enticing? *These* lips softer, tastier, more irresistible?

It didn't matter. Nothing mattered except that their lovemaking continue to its natural conclusion.

Tempest never felt the trembling fingers that worked free the buttons of her simple wrapper. She was too lost in the wonder of Buck's kiss. In the sleekness of his inner lip, the soft rasp of his tongue against hers, the evenness of his teeth. She squirmed, seeking some vague something she couldn't name. The brush of scarred fingers on her tender, sensitized flesh warned her of what he was about. Her wrapper was open to her waist and his hand was tugging on the ribbon at the neckline of her chemise. For a second she froze as common sense struggled to claim her. But the delicious memory of his mouth on her breasts kept her still. Then her chemise parted, his callused palm glided over her flesh, and intense pleasure fractured what self-control she had left.

She drew back from his kiss, eyes clenched as she absorbed every nuance of his devil's touch. His lips moved down her throat to the hollow at the base, then lower. Breathlessly she waited, like an eaglet poised for its first taste of flight. Closer and closer he drew to the taut peak that yearned for his kiss and beaded with a fresh supply of milk, while she waited . . . and waited . . .

A sound pierced her concentration. A hacking cough from the back room. The mother in her surged to life, bringing guilt and an unpleasant return to reality. She was trying to disentangle herself from Buck when Angel called, "Mama, Ethan's coughing. He'th all hot and I don't feel tho good neither."

Tempest was gone so suddenly Buck found himself clutching air that felt icy cold compared to the warmth he had been caressing. He stared dumbly at his empty hands for a long moment, listening to his own ragged breathing. His nostrils flared to catch the fading scent of her, musky with arousal.

Damn! The dream had nearly come true.

With a groan he collapsed on the floor, too tightly sprung with need to curse.

Outside, Jonas collapsed against the wall of the dugout. His breath was ragged, his heart racing from what he had seen through the slit provided by the ill-fitting window covering. Rain ran down his dark face and dripped off his chin, but he was oblivious to everything except the scene being replayed on the backdrop of his mind: Tempest's strawberry red nipples swelling, hardening, jutting toward her husband's waiting mouth, begging to be sucked and nibbled and bitten.

His tongue slid along his lips, but it wasn't the rain he tasted. His mouth formed a moue as it enclosed an imaginary nipple. It should be him inside the house. It should be his hands stroking her naked flesh. His tongue tasting her secrets. And he was ready for her. Ah, Gawd, but he was ready.

His hand drifted to the bulge pulsing beneath the soaked fabric of his pants. He squeezed, shuddered, squeezed again. In his mind it was Tempest's hand caressing him, her fingers ripping open the placket and freeing his straining flesh. He didn't feel the cold rain, the cutting wind, only the pleasure of his hand—Tempest's hand—stroking faster and faster.

No, her mouth, it was her mouth on him, that vicious unrestrained mouth of hers, hot and wet and greedy. For him. Only him.

The air in the dugout was thick and steamy from the kettles and pans of water boiling on the cookstove. The odor of mustard and onions permeated the house. From the stove, where Buck was adding wood to keep the room warm and the water steaming, he watched Tempest fuss and worry. In spite of sniffles and a slight fever, Angel was sleeping peacefully, but Ethan's cold had developed into a hard cough that seemed to be growing worse. Buck adjusted the damper and went to stand by the bed, frustrated by his inability to do more. "Is the onion plaster doing any good?"

Glancing up, Tempest shook her head. "No more than the mustard did. I wish I knew what to do. The only time Angel was ever sick was when she caught the measles in St. Louis. The children have both been so healthy."

"I never should have dragged all of you to the dance." His voice was harsh with self-condemnation.

Putting her hand on his, Tempest assured him, "It's not your fault."

"Yes, it is." He jerked away to pace the limited confines of the room. "I knew it was going to storm. When I went outside with Eloise, I saw the clouds boiling in, faster than I had expected. If I'd brought you straight home then, the children would be all right now." Instead he had dragged her onto the dance floor and done his best to seduce her. Lust had driven him home, not concern for her or the children, and he hated himself for it.

A violent paroxysm of coughing convulsed Ethan's small body. When it eased, Tempest spooned a cool syrup made from boiled wild onions down her son's throat, holding his mouth closed and stroking his neck to make him swallow. Feebly, Ethan pushed at her hands. The moment she released him he began to wail.

"He's getting hoarse." Tempest drew the quilts more snugly around the boy. "I think it might be croup."

Something in her voice alerted Buck to her concern, and he tried to ease her fear. "I remember a couple of my brothers and sisters having croup. It didn't seem serious."

The eyes she turned on him were bleak. "It isn't, if it's false croup. Children are always getting false croup. But *true* croup . . . Parents can't always tell the difference until it's too late. A membrane forms in the throat. All of a sudden the child can't breathe, and if no one realizes what's happening, if someone doesn't act fast enough, the child chokes to death. That's how Viola lost her little boy, their only son. I don't think Viola ever really got over the tragedy of it."

Buck studied Ethan for any sign of choking. The boy's breathing was ragged, but he seemed to be getting enough air. "Isn't there anything we can do?"

"I don't know." Tempest tried to remember all she had heard of the illness, but recalled nothing helpful. Aware that fear was taking control of her, she struggled to fight it off. "I don't know, Buck. I don't know."

Kneeling beside her, he wrapped her in his arms. She buried her face in his shoulder, and he felt her tremble as she fought her tears. She'd always been so strong, his feisty little mustang. It tore him to shreds to see her so vulnerable. "There must be some way to clear his throat. Whatever happens, we'll handle it. We won't let him die, Tempest. I promise."

She drew away, knowing this time he was promising the impossible, and loving him for it anyway. "Oh, sweet Mary, I pray you're right."

"I could ride into Price and fetch the doctor."

"That would take far too long. Please, Buck, don't leave me."

Indecision gnawed at him. She needed another woman with her, someone who would be more useful, more of a comfort should anything go wrong. But her eyes pleaded with him, and he couldn't refuse her. He pulled her into his arms again, held her tight. "He'll be all right, sweetheart. He'll be fine." *Please, God.*

Time dragged, making seconds seem like hours as they worked to keep Ethan warm and comfortable. Tempest ground herbs and brewed teas which she forced down the boy's throat. None seemed to do any good. She bustled about, a frantic sort of abruptness to her movements that worried Buck. Her lips moved constantly in silent prayer. He tended the fire and brought in fresh water as it boiled away, cursing the sense of helplessness driving him crazy because he couldn't do more.

Sometime after midnight, Ethan's cough took on a brassy tone, accompanied by a whistling sound. His breathing became labored. He was too hoarse to cry.

"It's croup, Buck," Tempest said as she stroked the boy's brow. "There's no doubt of it now."

"False? Or true croup?"

"I-I don't know. Oh, Buck . . ." She shook her head and put her fingers to her mouth. Dark shadows colored the skin beneath her eyes. She looked bedraggled and exhausted. And scared. So scared he could smell it. Or was it his own fear filling his nostrils?

His throat constricted as he watched the boy move fretfully in the bed. Buck wanted to do something, but didn't know what. He wanted to banish the anguish and fright from Tempest's eyes. He wanted to make her son well. But all he could do was stand there and watch and wait.

Angel woke, complaining of a sore throat. While her mother warmed a cup of ginger tea to soothe the irritation, Buck moved Angel to the other bed where they wouldn't disturb Ethan. Leaning his back against the wall, he gathered Angel on his lap and began a story.

Suddenly Ethan began to gasp for air, his body convulsing with the effort to breathe. Setting Angel aside and telling her to stay put, Buck leaped from the bed and rushed to the boy. His tiny mouth worked like a dying fish's, while his little hands beat at the air.

"Mama, Mama," Angel cried. "Whath wrong with Ethan?"

"Sweet Mary, he's choking." Flipping back the covers Tempest lifted the boy in her arms. She sat in the rocker with him facedown on her lap and thumped his back, hoping to dislodge whatever blocked his throat.

"Mama, Ethan'th turning blue!"

Tempest turned Ethan over and cuddled him to her breast. Panic and grief contorted her face as she watched her small son writhe and gasp in her arms. He choked and wheezed, his face like fine porcelain of the palest blue, his eyes huge and wide open, staring up at her helplessly.

Tempest's tortured gaze cut to Buck, panic screaming from her every pore. "Holy Mother of God, he's dying. *My baby is dying!*"

Chapter Fourteen

Whirling from the sight of Tempest's agonized face and the small boy silently choking to death before his eyes, Buck snatched up a candle and ran into the front room. They had to find a way to clear Ethan's throat. Had to. He'd promised her he wouldn't let her son die. *Please, God, he's so little.* When he returned to Tempest, he was carrying the coal oil can and a spoon.

"Here, hold this." He handed the spoon to Tempest.

"What are you going to do?"

"Saw this used on a prisoner once," he muttered. There wasn't time to talk. He yanked off the potato that acted as a cap for the can's spout in lieu of the one that had been lost and, steadying Tempest's hand, poured oil into the spoon. "I'll hold his mouth open, you give him a couple of drops. No more. If that doesn't do it, we'll try another drop."

"Oh, Buck, are you sure this is safe? What will it do to him?"

"The prisoner stole a vial of morphine from the surgery and tried to kill himself by swallowing the whole thing. He vomited his guts out on this stuff, but he lived. I'm praying it will make Ethan throw up that membrane blocking his throat so he'll be able to breathe again."

Kneeling on the floor at Ethan's head as the boy lay on his mother's lap, Buck held Ethan's jaw with one hand and pried open his mouth with the other. "All right, go ahead."

She closed her eyes, her lips clamped tightly together. *Our Father who art in heaven . . .*

"Tempest, there's no time to waste."

Tempest kissed her son on his forehead. Her heart lurched and her throat constricted as she wondered if it would be the last time she would ever kiss him. *Thy will be done on earth as it is in heaven . . .* Swallowing hard against tears and panic, she dripped the oil down her baby's throat.

Ethan gagged.

Buck snatched the chamber pot out from under the bed and, taking Ethan from his mother, held him over the receptacle. Crouched beside them, Tempest stroked the boy's brow and crooned the usual motherly reassurances while Ethan gasped and heaved. *And lead us not into temptation, but deliver us from evil . . . Please, God, I'll say a dozen Hail Marys every day. I'll find the nearest priest and give my confession, if only . . . Oh, please don't let my baby die.*

"There!" Buck cried. "See it? That mucous-looking stuff? That's what was choking him, I'd bet on it."

Turning the boy over, Buck placed him gently in Tempest's arms. Ethan was exhausted and limp, his color pale but no longer blue. And—*oh, thank you, Lord*—he was breathing! Tenderly, Tempest stroked her son's small face while tears streamed down her face.

Hail Mary, full of grace . . .

* * *

Buck awoke from a half-doze on Tempest's bed, groggy and disoriented, fear gripping his insides. *Ethan! The boy was dying.* He had to do something, had to save him. Swiftly he lurched to his feet and looked about.

Ethan lay in bed next to his sister. His small chest rose and fell with the even breathing of a natural sleep. Full memory rushed into Buck's head. He rubbed his hands over his face, as if to wash away the last dregs of fear left by the awful, frantic moments when he'd thought sure the boy would die.

On the table the candle flickered. Judging from how low the wax had melted, he figured he'd been asleep for hours. Soon it would be dawn.

Tempest sat slumped forward in the rocker, asleep, her head cradled on her arm which rested on the bed by her son. Her other arm was curved protectively about her son's head. For a minute, Buck stood looking at the touching tableau of mother and son, while his heart puddled around his feet like the wax at the base of the candle. Then, yanking himself back together, he lifted Tempest in his arms.

Her skin was pale and drawn, her eyes red-rimmed. Purple half-moons sagged beneath her lower lids. It shredded his heart to see her so worn out. As he set her on her bed, she stirred and opened her eyes.

"What are you doing?" she asked, her voice thick and drowsy.

"Putting you to bed."

"No, I have to tend Ethan." She tried to get up. Buck pushed her back down.

"He's fine. He's sleeping, and that's what you should be doing."

"What about his fever?"

"I'll watch him."

Gently he unfastened the long row of buttons that ran down the front of her wrapper. He was finally doing what he had yearned to do from the first moment he'd set eyes on her—stripping her naked—yet not a single lecherous thought entered his head. His only concern was making her comfortable. He was trying to draw the garment up over her head when Tempest stiffened and slapped at his hands.

"What do you think you're doing?"

"Undressing you. You haven't the strength for it."

"I do, too." She tried to stand and her legs buckled.

This time when Buck started working her wrapper over her head, she let him. "Even I'm not low down enough to seduce you with your son lying sick in the next bed, Tempest."

Hanging between his hands like a rag doll, she said, "I-I'm sorry, I . . ."

Buck dropped the cotton garment to the floor. She looked so forlorn, he couldn't help pulling her to him and hugging her in a fierce embrace. "You're all done in, little mustang," he whispered into the silky hair atop her head. "Stop fighting it, you've already proven you're the strongest woman alive. Let yourself be human for a change, or you'll be too weak to mother Ethan when he wakes up. I'm here, and I'm not going to let anything bad happen to either of you."

With a sigh, she nestled against him, her arms around his waist. For a long time he held her like that, gently rocking her from side to side. It felt good, so good. At last, reluctantly, he set her away from him. Keeping his eyes off the bosom barely concealed by the thin muslin of her hand-stitched, flour-sack camisole, he slipped her moccasins off her feet. Her black cotton stockings were held up by ordinary twine, tied about her thighs just above her knees. Anger and sadness filled him. A yard of garter elastic couldn't cost more than three cents. But he understood; three cents would buy a ribbon for Angel's hair or a whistle for Ethan.

The sight and feel of Tempest's naked feet in his hands broke through the concentration he had used to keep his mind off the bare, feminine flesh he was exposing. Her skin was softer than kitten fur, smoother than polished stone. He stroked a thumb over the delicate nub of her ankle bone, swept his fingers along the concave curve of her arch, over the rounded pad of her foot to her toes, and thought he had never felt anything so sensuous. He was lifting her foot, intending to kiss each toe, when her voice startled him out of the sensual mist that had enveloped him.

"Buck?"

He jerked and dropped her foot.

"All done." He tucked her into the bed in her chemise and drawers, and drew the covers up to her chin.

She gazed up at him, her eyes big as chestnuts in her wan face. "Thank you. I don't know how I would have gotten through this without you."

Guilt slammed into him like a landslide. Tempest was dead on her feet after an endless night of terror, not knowing if her son would live or die, and all he could do was lust after her feet.

Not that her feet were all he wanted. They would only be a beginning. But that didn't matter now. Once more he had proven himself the worthless scoundrel he'd always been. Leopards were incapable of changing their spots, everyone knew that. "You'd have done fine, the same way you've been doing the last two years."

"But I wasn't fine." She squeezed her eyes shut. Her voice was full of emotion and barely more than a whisper. "I was always scared. And lonely, so lonely."

Buck's throat constricted. His voice was hoarse as he stroked her cheek. "You're not alone now, sweetheart."

"I know." She covered her face with her hands to hide the tears welling in her eyes. "Oh, God, Buck, I nearly lost him. In another minute my little Ethan would have been gone."

As if the night's storm had moved inside, the tears came then. The tears Tempest never cried.

"Ah, honey. Sweetheart, don't," Buck begged as her sobs gained tempo. Sitting on the bed next to her, he drew her into his arms. Like a hurt child, she snuggled closer, her arms around his neck, her wet face buried against his shoulder. Murmuring words of comfort and assurance in her ear, he tenderly stroked her back and let her cry out all her fear, all her grief, all her relief. When at last, the sobs dwindled to watery hiccups, he brushed the hair back from her face and kissed her temple. "You need rest, sweetheart, so you'll be able to take care of the kids when they wake up. They still need you, you know."

Red-rimmed eyes peered up at him. "And you, Buck? Do you need me?"

He had been in the process of kissing away the dampness on her warm, satin-soft cheeks. Now he drew back to look at her. Her nose was red and swollen from crying, her skin blotched with deep rose. She had never looked lovelier. "Yeah, I need you," he growled softly, "more than you'll ever know." *More than he could bear.*

"Then hold me," she said quietly. "Let me feel safe and free and . . . and wanted, for just a little while."

If Tempest once considered being wanted by a man the opposite of safety and freedom, she ignored that fact now. Even the first day when he'd grabbed her and slammed her against the door frame in anger she had felt strangely safe in his arms. And she desperately needed that sense of safety now.

"I'll hold you, for as long as you need me," Buck promised, overriding the warning voice in his head.

Because she was struggling to get closer to him, and the quilts between them were in the way, Buck crawled beneath the covers with her. He was fully dressed except for his shirt and wet boots, and he intended to do no more than what she'd asked. A sigh of contentment escaped her as she wrapped herself around him, one leg drawn up over his. They couldn't have gotten any closer, he thought, if she were the skin covering his flesh.

"Buck?" She gazed up at him. "Thank you for saving my baby."

She hadn't thanked him for a single thing he'd done for her, from fixing the privy door latch to rescuing her from Jonas. Her expression of gratitude now testified to the depth of her love for her children. Her request for solace showed how much she had come to trust him. He felt blessed. Buck Maddux was a bastard, a selfish user, a coward. If she saw the truth of him, she would spook like a deer at the click of a rifle being cocked, and he'd never again have the joy of losing himself, even for an instant, in the heaven of her arms.

Buck's gaze slid to her mouth, inches away, soft, swollen from crying. He hadn't meant to kiss her. Yet she seemed to be offering her lips to him, like a sweet benediction on his soul, and he suddenly found himself kissing salty tears from them. The hunger clamoring inside him was only one of the ways he needed her, wanted her, but in that instant, lust overrode all others. With a moan, he deepened the kiss, his mouth moving urgently over hers, pausing to gently nip her firm, pliant upper lip, then the lower. When her lips parted, his tongue glided inside. Her soft moan and the feel of her hands tangling in his hair nearly shattered his control.

The realization that the flimsy cotton of her chemise

and split-crotch drawers were all that kept his hands from caressing bare flesh sent him reeling in a whirlpool of carnal need that further frayed the threads of his control. The plumpness of her breasts pressing into his side, his chest—sweet, sweet pressure—and the knowledge that a few inches higher her knee would encounter his rapidly growing erection didn't help.

Oh, Judas, sweet Judas. Tempest had petitioned him for comfort, not sex. He wanted to do right. For the first time in his life, he wanted to do what was right. But he was only human. There was no hell—he'd just figured it out. Hell was heaven just out of reach. A heaven named Tempest Whitney.

Tearing his mouth from hers, Buck sucked in a long draft of air. What he needed was a good dousing in icy cold rain.

With an indecipherable murmur of protest, Tempest pulled his head back down to hers. Her mouth was hot and demanding. At first Buck tried to keep part of himself separate, aware, in control. The air was thick with the smell of wet earth, lamp oil, candle wax, onion plasters, and warm bodies. Above the rasp of their breathing and an occasional moan or sigh, thunder grumbled in the distance. But beneath his hands was a hungry woman, battering at his emotions, destroying his control, making him tremble with need, and he was terribly afraid he was not going to measure up to the trust she had invested in him.

"Tempest, I don't—"

"Shh." She covered his mouth with her hand. "I don't want to hear of right or wrong, yesterday or tomorrow. I just want to . . . feel."

Judas. Her hands were as busy as her mouth, exploring his naked chest, playing with small masculine nipples, her fingers tangling in his hair. Then her palm slid lower, robbing him of the ability to speak, to think, to breathe.

When she found the hard ridge beneath the fly of his trousers and curled her fingers over it, Buck knew he was finished. A savage sort of frenzy took command. His hand skimmed down her rib cage to the waistband of her drawers, then farther, to the opening that gave access to the satin softness of her upper thighs. His fingers brushed the silky nest of curls hidden within, and she arched into his hand. Buck moaned.

Then she slipped a hand through the placket of his drawers, releasing him to her touch. Like a leaf in a swollen river he was swept away, swirled and wave-tossed and dragged deep deep under, then rushed upward again, tense with need. Afraid she would end things before they began, he removed her hand. Nudging her thighs apart, he levered himself between them. His heart pounded in his ears as he paused, his hard flesh barely nuzzling the soft, humid heat of her feminine opening. Even that much felt like heaven. He braced on his arms above her and gazed down at her flushed face, wanting to drag the moment out. Her eyes were open, watching him. Her hands slid down his back to his buttocks and urged him closer.

Unfortunately, he had hesitated too long. A strange sound intruded into his consciousness, a sort of scratching that seemed to come from overhead, and set the hair at his nape on end. "What in tarnation . . . ?

Tempest went stiff and still. "Centipedes," she whispered.

Every hair on his body prickled. "What?"

"Centipedes. The storm's disturbed them. They've come down out of the sod and are running around inside the paper tacked to the ceiling."

He sat back on his heels, staring up at the dim, candle-lit ceiling. "Judas, there must be hundreds of them."

Buck had seen them, five-inches long and thick as his

forefinger, racing across the ranch yard on thousands of tiny feet. Their bite was said to be deadly. Even the pigs were wary of them. The thought of them falling on him and scrambling over his flesh was enough to kill his ardor. He understood now Ronan's hallucination of centipedes when he had the shakes.

A trickle of water joined the scratching noise. Wood snapped. Mud and water streamed down. Buck leaped from the bed, dragging Tempest with him and shielding her with his body while stones and mud clods battered his head and shoulders. The candle guttered, and went out. Above the roar in his ears, he heard Angel cry out for her mother.

Buck's voice, coming from the darkness, was stark with shock and terror. "Judas Priest! The roof's caving in!"

Chapter Fifteen

"The children, Buck. Get the children."

They slammed into each other in the dark as they dove for Angel and Ethan. Muck and debris pelted them as they untangled tiny arms and legs from bedclothes. Buck tried not to wonder how much of the sludge running down his naked back was mud and how much was centipedes.

"I've got Ethan," Tempest shouted.

He barely heard her above the raw, rippling crack of another pole snapping in two. The jagged ends arrowed downward toward the bed on which Tempest and Buck had been lying seconds before. Mud poured through the newly created gap. After the last rain Buck had thrown shovelful upon shovelful of claylike soil onto the roof above the bedroom to keep it from leaking again. The additional weight, soaked with water from tonight's storm, had proved too much for the roof to bear.

Angel screamed. Ethan awoke in his mother's tight embrace and began crying.

"Easy, honey," Buck crooned to the little girl as he scooped her up in his arms. "Papa Buck's got you, you're safe." Louder, he called to Tempest, "I have Angel, let's get out of here."

He clutched the girl to him, heartened by the small arms that twined trustingly about his neck. Then he wrapped his free arm around Tempest and Ethan, and felt his way through the darkness to the front room. As they escaped the dugout, a deafening roar announced the collapse of the roof, shaking the very ground beneath their feet.

It took three days to clear out the debris left by the cave-in and to fix the roof. Buck borrowed a wagon from John Bennet at the livery and, with Ronan's help, cut enough aspen poles to replace the missing section of roof. Swede and John Bennet helped set them in place. Sod was then cut into blocks, hauled to the dugout and laid on top.

Tempest had washed the soiled bedding and clothing and had cleared out the last of the mud. Other than a smashed ceramic pitcher and basin, the furnishings had escaped serious damage. A bed slat had to be replaced and several precious bottles of fruits and vegetables thrown out. Every corner was searched for centipedes. Each time one was routed, dead or alive, Buck shuddered with distaste. His horror of the creatures invoked smiles from Tempest and gales of laughter from Angel, until he chased them through the house threatening to bury them in a mountain of live centipedes.

"You're no better than me," Buck accused Tempest. "You can't stand harmless house flies. You're as bad as my mother."

"They're ugly and filthy. Have you noticed the kinds of muck flies like to crawl in?" She grimaced. "Heaven only knows what sicknesses they carry. But I'm glad to know you're so fond of them. I won't bother picking them out of your food from now on."

Buck laughed. "If folks got sick simply from having flies around, they'd be sick all the time."

She opened her mouth to argue and he silenced her with a kiss, delighting Angel. The girl danced around them, giggling and clapping her hands until Tempest put an end to the entire scene by kicking Buck in the shins. Ethan, on the cot in the front room, laughed at their antics until his laughter turned into a coughing fit. Tempest shooed the others outside while she fussed over her son, easing his cough with her herbal remedies and making sure his fever hadn't returned. But she couldn't regret the gaiety they had shared. It was the perfect foil for the terror they'd suffered, first with Ethan's croup, then the roof's collapsing. She suspected Buck had instigated the game for that very reason, and she loved him for it.

That night, after the children and Ronan were asleep, Buck sat in the rocker and watched Tempest spread fresh linens on the bed they had been sharing and would share again that night. She felt his gaze on her like a heavy-handed caress and tried to tell herself he was only exhausted, like her, after their long day of strenuous, unending labor. But she knew there was more bothering him. He was too intent. She could almost hear his brain spinning.

"We've got to find a better way to come up with the money we need, Tempest," he said at last. "Earning it is too slow. There has to be another way."

Even though she knew he was worrying about the deadline for making the mortgage payment, Buck's seeming eagerness to solve their dilemma and get out of her life hurt. She had always known he would leave when their pretend marriage ended and there was no more need for him to stay, but after the beautiful things he had done to her in the hours before the cave-in, she had hoped he wanted her badly enough to be reluctant, rather than eager, to go. "I have no argument for that," she retorted, her emotions raw. "But I don't hear you coming up with a solution."

Buck detected the anger and hurt in her eyes. He could have told her that deep down inside he didn't want the solution to come too quickly either. He could have told her how much he cared for her, for the children, even for her drunken father. He could have told her Deception Canyon had come to feel like home. A home he desperately wanted for his own.

But these feelings was too new yet to expose, and he was a coward.

An echo of the fierce anger he'd once felt toward Skeet Whitney for landing him in prison sliced Buck in two, and he clenched his fists. Skeet had been worse than a fool, throwing all this away on asinine whims and irrational fantasies. Only an idiot would treat treasures like Tempest and Angel and Ethan with such a callous lack of concern. Buck wished Skeet were still alive so he could shatter every bone in the man's body, one by one, then squeeze the life out of him a breath at a time. If the devil had appeared at that moment and offered him the power to make Tempest his for the rest of his days on earth, Buck would gladly have signed away his right to eternity. He yearned to claim Angel and Ethan as his own, and to see Tempest's belly swell with his child. There could be no greater joy, he thought. Except, perhaps, for her to love him. He could make her desire him, make her yearn for what his hands and lips could do to her, make her want him inside her. But that wasn't the same as love, and suddenly he wanted it all.

Yet Tempest deserved a man she could trust and rely on, and that certainly wasn't Buck Maddux. He had already proven it by not preventing her near-rape by Jonas Creedy. Though it pained him greatly, he knew if he truly cared about her, he would quit dragging his feet and do whatever he had to do to free her from Creedy's threat. But hours and hours of discussion had produced no better plan than for him to find work, a task he could only accomplish by going to Price or somewhere else too far away to protect her and the children. He'd wasted hours and days searching for wild horses and come up empty. He was beginning to think he should simply shoot Creedy down like the dog the man was, and then get the hell out of Deception Canyon.

The thought of leaving, never seeing Tempest again, made his future look emptier than a beggar's pocket. A loneliness worse than any he'd known before possessed him. Giving up Tempest would be a torture he feared he couldn't survive.

Tempest finished tucking in the top sheet and glanced over at him. "What will you do, Buck, when this is ended? Will you go to California?"

Judas, it was as though she read his thoughts. To think of exposing his true desires to her and being rejected shredded his insides. So, once more, he masked his emotions with a devil's grin. Rising from the chair, he moved behind her, put his hands on her waist and whispered seductively, "Why? Want to come along?"

She elbowed him away and reached for a quilt. "Don't be ridiculous."

His laugh was like the sound of a dull saw as he turned away. Shaking out the folded quilt with a snap of her wrists, she tried again to get him to open up. "You're no Southerner, in spite of all that charm you ooze all over everyone. Where were you born?"

"Does a man have to be from the South to be charming?"

"No, but Southern men like to think they're the only ones who are."

Buck picked up a palm-sized papier-mâché box from her dresser and sniffed the powdery scent that would always be a part of his memories of her. A cracked drinking glass held a well-used toothbrush and a cheap India rubber comb. A plain brush lay beside a small metal box of Sanitary Tooth Soap. No jewelry. No pretty perfume bottles. Not even rose water. Buck swore silently. "You're right, I'm neither a Southerner nor a gentleman. My mother tried to teach me right, I simply didn't learn my lessons well."

"Where is your mother now?"

"Dead. My father died when I was Ethan's age. Mother remarried when I was five, but he died in a year, leaving her a three-year-old stepson to care for, as well as me. A few months later my sister was born. She married again within the year. Roger Kincade. That's how I got my twin brothers, Whip and Cale. Mother died bringing them into the world."

"I'm sorry, Buck."

He shrugged as he watched her smooth the wrinkles from the quilt with her hands and wished it was him she was stroking so lovingly. "I was lucky, actually. My stepfather could've sent us to live with grandparents or put us in an orphanage. Instead, he insisted on keeping the family together. Not many men would take on three children who weren't even related to him. Especially a ten-year-old as wild and rebellious as I was in those days. He straightened me out, though. With a razor strap."

Horrified, she watched Buck stare into the scratched mirror over the dresser as though seeing images from his past play upon his mind like shadow puppets on a wall. Sympathy filled her, but she felt excitement, too. She had yearned to know what put the shadows and pain in his eyes, the reasons he hid behind his devil-may-care attitude and Satan's smile. He had been cruelly abused by his step-father. Now, at last, she could find some way to banish his pain. But he destroyed her newfound sense of accomplishment in one wistful sentence.

"I would have done anything for Roger."

Tempest blinked. "I don't understand. He whipped you with a razor strap."

Buck's mouth curled in a sentimental smile. "Believe me, I deserved it. Mother was like a willow branch, bending every which way, letting me run wild. Roger was an oak tree. He told me to muck out the stable, a chore I still detest more than any other. Being eleven, I decided I was too big to take orders, so I rode into town instead, stole a pint of whiskey and got good and soused. Before Pa caught up with me I'd knocked over three outhouses, caused a couple of girls I'd never liked anyway to wet their drawers, and let old man Simpson's cows out of his pasture. Pa and his razor strap made it plain as sunshine where I stood and what was expected of me."

"Then it must have been losing your wife that turned you so hard."

The smile slid from his face. His eyes were brittle as glass, haunted as a graveyard. Spinning about he stormed into the front room.

"Buck? Where are you going?" She hurried after him.

"Something's walked into the cans I strung up," he said in a voice so bleak it sliced open her heart and left her bleeding for him.

Then he was gone. Tempest shut her eyes and cursed herself, knowing he would find his warning system exactly as he'd left it, undisturbed.

Hours later, Buck returned after several rounds of poker at Swede's saloon and a good deal more whiskey than he'd drunk since his twenty-fifth birthday when he'd shot his horse to death trying to put his rifle in the scabbard. Actually, the horse belonged to his boss who, of course, fired him. Not only had Buck killed his horse and broken the rules by getting drunk on the job, the accidental shot had caused a stampede, killing several beeves. Another shining example of his worth.

By the time Swede shoved Buck and the other drunken patrons from his saloon, Buck had already made up his mind to leave Deception Canyon. But he'd been determined to take care of Jonas Creedy first, even if it meant shooting him in cold blood. So he plotted a one-man assault on the Carcass Creek Cattle Company. Clouds obscured the moon, producing an inky night. Drowsy with whiskey, Buck dozed off and nearly fell from Spook's back. When he came to a familiar bridge across the creek and realized he'd ridden past Creedy's spread, he cursed himself blue. But he was just too tired to go back.

Now he lifted the latch and admitted himself into the house he'd come to think of as home. Half-asleep, he undressed, climbed into bed, and gave himself up to slumber.

It was sometime during the night he awoke to find himself spooned against her back, one arm draped over her waist, a hand curved possessively around her breast. Night after night he had slept beside her, keeping his hunger for her under tight control. But the alcohol in his system weakened his will and his ability to think. It effected his blood like a match tossed into a bucket of kerosene, inflaming the desire that cannonballed through his body. His hand reflexively squeezed the firm, warm flesh it held, and he groaned.

Judas, he was bare-ass naked, and so hard and swollen he could use his member as a fence post. He felt it nudge her soft, cotton-clad bottom and gritted his teeth as he fought the urge to draw up her nightdress and rub his bare flesh against hers. The headache throbbing behind Buck's eyes did not lessen the exquisite pleasure of simply nestling against her. He held stone-still, afraid of waking her. There would never be another moment like this one when he could lie there and revel to his heart's content in the feel of her body tucked so comfortably next to his. The bliss was too precious to squander. He wanted to remember her scent, the texture of her hair, the firm roundness of her bottom pressing his loins. He wanted memories to take with him when he left, memories to treasure on lonely nights when all he could think of was a woman sweeter than anything had a right to be and how it had felt to pretend for one night that he was a husband like any other, snuggling up to his wife in the middle of the night as she slept.

When he finally managed the strength to draw away, he suddenly found his hand imprisoned at her breast by hers. "Don't go," she whispered, turning to him.

Before he could move she had her arms about his neck and her honeyed mouth on his. The pulse pounding in his ears blocked the voice of reason. Need coiled snakelike inside him. His lips couldn't move fast enough or reach enough of her to suit him. The cloth that kept his hands from her naked flesh was an unendurable frustration.

Tempest hadn't known passion could be so viciously wonderful, so electrifyingly intense. She had awakened to the feel of his hand squeezing her breast and had held her breath, hoping there would be more. Praying he would finish what he had started the night the roof fell in. The greed that purled inside her now, demanding more and more of his touch, shocked and thrilled her. She wrapped a leg around him and squirmed closer, trying to affix herself to him so thoroughly they would be inseparable. His scent—night wind, moonlight, and man—fired her senses.

Buck felt her tremble, felt her mouth seek his, her body fit itself to him like a second skin, and knew it was more pleasure than a man could endure. He didn't care how the long placket of her nightdress came open. He lipped a firm rosy nipple, took it between his teeth and let it slowly scrape free. Her hands tangled in his hair, urging him closer until he gave her what she wanted and began to suckle. Mother's milk filled his mouth. He savored the rich flavor, regretting that she was producing less now that Ethan had virtually quit nursing.

Tempest kneaded his shoulders and purred with pleasure. Buck told himself to slow down, make it last, make it good for her, but her lips were as greedy as his, her hands hot and wild and wonderfully uninhibited.

He drew the hem of her gown up her smooth thigh. Her skin was satiny and warm and supple, as he'd known it would be. A desperate need to explore every inch, to conquer and claim and possess, overtook him. A need to make her his in the most elemental way. He stroked her flat stomach and edged downward to the soft nest that protected her most enticing secrets. She shuddered and cried out his name as his fingers slid into slick, sensitive folds. He covered her mouth with his, swallowing the sound.

Colored lights danced behind Tempest's eyes, a rainbow of color, soft and vibrant, harsh and commanding. She held still, afraid he would stop creating such wonderful sensations in her. Then, suddenly, it wasn't enough. She skimmed her hand down his body to close over hard velvet male flesh that jumped at her touch.

He smothered a curse in her hair as he nearly lost control. He snatched her hand away, ignoring her whispered protest. Pushing her onto her back, he shoved her gown to her waist and centered himself between her legs. Braced on his hands above her, he wished he could see her, watch her expression as he entered her. But the room was pitch black. Her hands tugged at his buttocks. He inched forward until he found her sultry heat. His eyes squeezed shut.

Judas, he hadn't thought to ever see this dream come true. Now that it had, he didn't want it to end.

Moaning, Tempest lifted her hips against him. The feel of her inviting him inside, the knowledge that she wanted him, splintered his control. Gritting his teeth, he plunged into the heaven he knew could never belong to him. His last lucid thought as she drew him deep within her was that he belonged there, that her caressing, sheltering, welcoming him, was far better than his dreams. Her passion enthralled him. Tangled thoughts swirled through his head: *Mine . . . I'm home. Ah, Judas, woman, love me. Whisper the words, make the joy last forever. Make it real.*

Somewhere in a corner of Tempest's brain, not yet totally lost to the heat and fantasy of the moment, registered the reality that here at last was the real Buck Maddux. Not the driven, tormented soul with haunted eyes and a bitter heart who hid his need and pain behind a devil's mask. At this moment, he was only a man, as vulnerable to his needs as she was to hers, his soul as naked as his body—and as beautiful, despite the darkness it held.

Pleasure built and intensified. It carried them higher and higher until Buck thought surely they could never return to earth again. The sweetness of it was almost more than he could bear. As he drove himself harder, deeper, into Tempest's hot, slick channel, something swelled inside his chest, opening him up and laying him bare. It seemed to wrench the very life from him, making him over, making him new. He wondered which would explode first, his heart or his loins.

Drawing her legs up around his hips, he fought to hold back. Only when she had reached her pinnacle would he allow himself a release of his own. But the fire blazing so hotly between them was burning him to cinders and he was terrified he would fail her.

Tempest hadn't known such sensations existed. The kind of pleasure Buck was giving her had been beyond her imagination. A metal spring deep inside her was drawing tighter and tighter. She seemed stretched by more than the heated flesh sliding within her and creating a friction she knew would soon hurl her over whatever precipice her body was straining to crest. The intensity of it all frightened her, luring her at the same time, like a dark, forbidden room. Like the love she felt for him. When she thought she could bear no more, her body convulsed and she gave herself up to the incredible rapture pulsing through her.

The strength of her hot flesh gripping his as she spasmed around him again and again stunned him. It triggered his own release, one he knew already would be more fantastic than anything he had ever experienced before. His brain screamed for him to pull out before it was too late. But she tightened around him, causing waves of ecstasy to crash over him, so intense that he gasped. He was incapable of thought, incapable of anything except going with the current that swept him round and round in a whirlpool of euphoria so complete he was taken totally out of himself into a world of sheer physical bliss.

Later, when Buck drifted back to awareness and he was able to think again, he decided he felt much too good to still be alive. Someone had discovered his audacity in trying to claim Tempest as his own, had punished him as he deserved. Then he moved and discovered they were still joined. He squirreled the ecstasy away and yearned for more, even while he cursed himself for failing to withdraw from her in time. He wondered what a child of theirs would look like. Angelic little girl or dark, devilish boy? Would Tempest hate him for planting his seed in her, or would she like the idea of bearing his child?

Shoving aside such nonsense, he vowed to make sure there were no more mishaps like this one. She had given him a gift, a treasure he would cherish the rest of his life, and he wouldn't ask for more.

The covers had been kicked to the foot of the bed, letting the night air chill them. He slid his hands down her spine to her delectable bottom and found it icy. He drew the quilts over them and then lay there, careful not to wake her so he could enjoy every second possible of this incredible joy. The sigh that escaped his lips was one of total contentment. He couldn't remember ever feeling so blissful. If he could lie with her like this night after night for the rest of his life—even if she never learned to love him—he knew he would die a happy man.

Chapter Sixteen

The next morning brought three visitors. The first was a homesteader who wanted to buy a mule and did his best to talk Buck out of Spook. The second was Beaver Hanks, the redheaded, freckle-faced trapper who had helped Tempest finish the dugout and who returned now and then to check on her.

Ignoring the entire season's worth of grease and dried gore the man wore on his fringed buckskins—and the glower on Buck's face—Tempest greeted Hanks with an enthusiastic hug. When they parted, Angel climbed into Hanks's wiry arms and smacked a kiss on his whiskered cheek, while Ethan stood at the man's moccasined feet tugging on his buckskin pants and shouting, "Beeber, Beeber."

Buck hated the man on sight.

"Brung ya some venison," Hanks said, digging into his packsaddle.

Taking the meat from him, Tempest kissed his cheek. "You've a heart of gold, Beaver. Thank you."

Buck uttered a silent snort. The man's heart might be gold, but his lanky body had the substance of a rainbow. He wasn't the type to arouse a woman's passion, Buck assured himself. Besides, he smelled like rotten hides and the musky stink of beaver castoreum.

"Brung you young'ns sumpthin', too." The children jumped up and down in excitement while Hanks pulled child-sized hats of raccoon fur from his pack. The animal's face peered out from the front, and its striped tail dangled down the back. Dew claws from the hooves of a buck deer clattered lightly in the breeze where they hung on short thongs at the back.

"Oh, yippie, Uncle Beaver, you brought me a hat jutht like yourth."

Reverently, Angel placed the hat on her head and beamed up at the adults for approval. Ethan hugged his to his chest as if it were a stuffed toy animal, then rubbed his cheek with its fur.

Buck wanted to puke. He hovered in the background, arms crossed over his chest, feet firm on the ground, waiting for Tempest to remember he existed. There were new moccasins for her and the children as well. With the gay laughter of a child Tempest kicked off her old worn ones and donned the new pair .

Finally Angel turned to Buck. "Look, Papa Buck. Look what Uncle Beaver brought me."

Hanks' flame-colored eyebrows rose at the title the girl had given Buck, but all he said as he extended his hand was, "Folks call me Beaver Hanks, and since it's a helluva lot better than the handle my pappy hung on me, I let 'em."

The man's green eyes held no sign of rancor, only geniality tinged with humor and perhaps a hint of wariness.

Feeling a totally masculine need to establish his territory, Buck drew Tempest to his side. "I'm Skeet, Tempest's husband."

"Well, now, I'm right glad to know she ain't alone no more." Hanks smiled, but the look in the trapper's eye said he hadn't forgotten Skeet's past behavior and was withholding his approval.

"Let's go in," Tempest suggested, her gaze going from one man to the other. "I'll cook up some deer steaks."

As Buck turned to follow her into the house, a hand, the knuckles gnarled with rheumatism, settled on his shoulder, detaining him. Hanks let go and walked a few feet away. Buck scowled, in no mood for the interrogation he knew was coming. Crossing his arms over his chest, which was twice the width of Hanks's, he said, "You have a problem?"

The trapper pursed his lips as if carefully considering the question. "Ain't me I'm a-worryin' 'bout. It's Tempest and them little 'uns."

"Well, put your mind at ease," Buck growled. "They belong to *me,* and I intend to take good care of them."

"Why ain't you been doing it this past two years then?"

"I was in prison, but that's a story I've no intention of explaining to you. All you need to know is I'm back."

Hanks nodded. "Glad to see you feel that way. They suffered a buffler-sized pile o' trouble whilst you was gone. It's time someone looked after them."

Before Buck could reply, Tempest appeared in the doorway, a knife in her hand. "Beaver, you sweet man, this venison is going to be as tender as bread pudding. The knife simply glides through it."

Her face was alight with pleasure, making Buck realize how rare a sight that was. She looked so beautiful it caused a hitch in his heart rate. When he glanced back at Beaver Hanks, he found the man grinning. "What are you smiling at?" he demanded, feeling exposed.

Clapping a hand on Buck's shoulder, Hanks said, "Any doubts I had 'bout you before jest went up in smoke is all, and I'm as pleased as a fly on fresh shit."

Buck shook the hand off. "What are you talking about?"

"Why, hellfire, here I was a-worryin' 'bout you treatin' Tempest right when it's writ all over yer face that ya love her. Fair makes me wanta give a loud ya-hoo. Come on, Skeet, let's go have us some deer meat."

The lanky trapper walked away, leaving Buck to wonder how he'd gotten poleaxed without even seeing the man slip around behind him. Buck Maddux in love? That was more nonsense than he'd heard his whole life.

But deep down, Buck knew it wasn't nonsense at all. He thought of the way the mere sight of her turned his bones to mush, of his near constant state of arousal. He remembered how exceptional their lovemaking had been, how good she'd felt snuggled against him as she slept. Never had he felt such peace and contentment. He remembered thinking if he could lie with her like that for the rest of his life, feeling her warmth against his body, smelling her sweet, earthy scent, listening to her breathe as she slept, holding her—just holding her—he'd die a happy man.

The truth of Hanks's words slammed into him like a runaway locomotive. He couldn't have moved if he'd had to. Inside he was going every which way, half trying to aim his feet toward the house where she waited for him, half doing his best to flee, as though he could escape his fate.

Judas, Buck, where in hell is life taking you now?

Almost as soon as Hanks left, the children, worn out from the excitement, curled into a ball like a litter of kittens and fell asleep. Buck fled the house for the relative safety of the barn, where he seriously contemplated packing his saddlebags and following Hanks's example by tak-

ing off for the mountains. His head throbbed with the
arguing going on inside it. He'd decided to seek the answer
in a whiskey bottle—one a good long way from Deception
Canyon—when the rattle of wagon wheels caught his ear.
Emerging from the barn he found Tempest already outside, shading her eyes with her hand as she stared down
the road and ordered the dogs to be quiet.

"It's Viola," she murmured, recognizing the Jenny Lind
buggy approaching the bridge over Carcass Creek. "And
a man."

Buck squinted at the man riding a magnificent roan
stallion beside the small bouncing carriage. "You know
him?"

"I don't think so."

As Viola brought the rig to a halt in front of them, the
rider veered off toward the well, where he dismounted to
water his horse. Buck felt the man's eyes on him, as hard
and penetrating as a woodpecker boring a hole in a tree.
Unease settled over him as he helped Viola alight.

Tempest hugged her friend. "Viola, what are you doing
here?"

"Found someone who was looking for Mr. Maddux and
decided to bring him out myself." The widow's good eye
sparkled with mischief. "Mr. Sims and I knew the minute
we laid eyes on the good-looking young devil that he would
cause some excitement around here. Let's go inside, Tempest, I reckon these boys might like some privacy whilst
they get reacquainted."

She hustled Tempest into the house, leaving Buck alone
beside the dusty buggy. Viola's sorrel gelding stamped his
hoof, impatient for a drink and a handful of oats. Buck
didn't move.

Get reacquainted? He pondered the widow's odd state-
ment. The stranger tipped back his head as he drained
the contents of the water ladle. Liquid dripped down his

clean-shaven chin onto his shirt. Buck knew no one in Utah, except a few ex-cons like himself, and he couldn't imagine any of them looking him up. Yet the man seemed familiar. He was tall and rangy, with broad shoulders and hips so narrow he could almost be called skinny. His movements were slow and methodical, as if calculated for effect, but there was a tenseness in him that gave Buck the notion the man was full of anger—and therefore dangerous. Buck's unease quadrupled. A professional gun maybe? Pretending to be an old friend to get close enough to earn a hefty fee from Jonas Creedy? Common sense said no; Viola wouldn't bring a gunman to Heartsease. At least, not knowingly.

Slowly he gave the man his back as he led the sorrel toward the corral, every muscle tense and ready as he waited to hear the click of a hammer being cocked. His spine fairly crawled from the impact of the intent gaze on his back. Sweat broke out on his forehead. When Buck turned around, the man was leaning against the low rock wall of the well, arms folded across his chest, head tipped so that the shadow of his hat brim hid his expression. That he looked a great deal more relaxed than Buck felt, irked him no end.

Dammit, who was he?

As Buck approached, the stranger came slowly to his feet. His head lifted. Buck halted, struck again by that vague sense of familiarity. The visitor walked toward him until they stood five yards apart. They stared at each other, waiting for the other to speak first. Blue eyes with a hint of green in their depths seemed to take Buck's measure . . . and find it wanting.

"Don't recognize me, do you, Richard?" the man said finally.

Richard! Years had passed since Buck last heard his given name used. His grandfather's name. Richard Henry

Maddux. How proud he had been to carry that name. How badly he had let the old man down. "Should I?" he said.

The man snorted. He was younger than Buck by about ten years.

"Ma would have kittens, hearing you say that," he said, turning his profile to Buck as he watched a red-tailed hawk soar overhead.

Something clicked inside Buck's brain. His heart began to thud. He stepped closer, examining the man's lean, hawk-nosed face, while memories—old memories put away long ago in self-defense—battered the wall that shielded Buck from the darkness of his past. "Whip?" he asked incredulously.

The man laughed. The mocking tone, as familiar as his profile, levered another brick from Buck's protective wall.

"No, I'm Cale. Whip ... well, he's another story, best saved for later."

"Cale." Buck's voice was soft, a whisper of wind in the leaves. In his mind he saw twin bundles wrapped in flannel, motherless babes who wailed, waved angry fists, and demanded attention, always at the same time. An imaginary missile the size of a buffalo rammed Buck in the chest, near his heart. "Judas. Cale, I can't believe this." He moved quickly toward the half-brother he hadn't seen in fifteen years, his mind so full of questions and emotions he didn't know what to do or say first. "What are you doing here? How did you find me?"

Equally quickly, Cale backed away. Anger emanated from him like a bad odor. "Don't bother to act glad to see me, Richard. I only came to . . ."

Buck watched his brother struggle for control. Joy turned to acid at the back of his throat. The hand he had offered in welcome fell to his side, untouched. Bitterness etched his voice. "You came to what? Tell me what a worthless bastard I am? There's no need, believe me. I tell myself the same thing every day."

Turning, he headed for the barn. He didn't want to hear what Cale had to say. More recriminations, more hate from someone he loved would be unbearable. It would kill him.

"Damn you, Richard, don't you walk away." Cale grabbed Buck's arm. "Not again. Or so help me, I'll—"

Buck whirled, flinging off his brother's hand. "You'll what? Do you think there's anything you could do to me that Pa didn't already do fifteen years ago? That I haven't done to myself nearly every day of my life since then?"

They stood nose to nose, fury glinting in their eyes, fists ready to strike, and Buck thought irrelevantly that the runty little ten-year-old he had left behind had truly grown up. "Judas, Cale, I don't want to fight you." Instinctively, he retreated behind the protective wall he'd created for himself years ago. He grinned. "Tell me what's happened in your life. What are you now? Hell, you can't be twenty-five already. Where did all the years go? Are you married?"

Cale blinked at the sudden change in his brother. Then he scowled. "Wherever the years went, you weren't there to share them. Why didn't you write, Richard? Why didn't you at least goddamn write? All these years, not one lousy word."

Buck shrugged. Suddenly he felt tired, and old. "Didn't figure anyone wanted to hear from me."

"Like hell! How could you think anything so stupid? Shit, Richard, you know goddamned well, no matter how anybody else felt, Lize would want to hear from you. She cried her eyes out for days after you left. Every time she's hurting over something she goes out and sits on that rock by the creek where you taught her to fish."

The words were like knife thrusts in Buck's gut. He hated knowing he had caused even more pain than he'd been aware of. He closed his eyes, battling to shut off the memories he knew would only make him want to cry. He swallowed hard. "How is she?"

If Cale Kincade saw the agony in his older brother's eyes, he ignored it. "I can't think of one damn reason I should answer that. If you were so goddamned interested, you should have written to her."

Buck sighed. "Well, I didn't."

"No, you sure as hell didn't. You didn't write to anybody." Cale's face was harsh with pain and anger. "What happened fifteen years ago, Richard? I want to know what it was that brought this goddamned misery down on all of us. Every one of us suffered because of what you did back then, but Pa's refused to speak a word about it. Ma, too."

The surprise of that was enough to made Buck reel. "He never told you about Ellen? What . . . what happened to her? He never told any of you?"

"Oh, we know she went into labor too early and bled to death. And that everyone blamed you for it. We know you were robbed. But we also know there's more to it than that. Whenever the subject is brought up, Pa clams up tighter than the thighs of an unpaid whore. Says there's no use dredging up the past, that it's best forgotten."

Buck snarled a laugh. "Best forgotten. But not forgiven, right?"

Cale made no reply, and Buck headed again for the barn. He had a sudden need to do something physical. Bashing his head in with an ax came to mind, but he was too weak for anything that noble. Judas, hadn't he wallowed in enough self-pity over the years? He thought he'd finished with that long ago.

The scent of straw, well-oiled leather, and horse manure greeted him as he entered the dim barn. He would give Spook a good brushing, then muck out the stalls. Maybe chop kindling. There was a boxful in the house already, but he needed the exercise. Spook nickered affectionately and tried to nudge Buck's hat off with his nose. Buck jerked out of the way. "None of that now."

Cale came to the door of the stall, his gaze on Buck like a ton of sandstone, weighing him down. What could he say to the kid? That he was sorry? Lord knew that was true enough. But it wouldn't bring Ellen back. Or Buck's tiny son. And he didn't believe it would make any real difference to Cale after all these years either. Buck couldn't bear to talk about that night, couldn't bear to relive it. He'd done it too many times already. Not in the last few years, thank God, but the memories still tore at him now and again, in his nightmares.

"What happened, Richard?" Cale's voice was softer now, less hostile, though no less demanding. But when Buck didn't answer, the anger resurfaced. "Dammit, man, I came hundreds of miles to find you. The least you can do is talk to me."

Buck turned and looked hard at the brother he hadn't seen in fifteen years. "I'll talk to you, Cale. You want to hear about all the horses I've wrangled in the past fifteen years? The steers I've roped? How about all the manure I've scraped off my boots? I'll even tell you about the whores I've bedded. But I *won't* talk about the night Ellen died."

Cale smashed his fist against the wooden stall as his brother turned away and began grooming the appaloosa. "Damn it, Richard. You're as stubborn as Pa."

"If I am, I didn't get it from him. Much as I might have wished I was his blood son, you know I'm not." Buck's hand on the brush stilled. "Maybe that's why it was so easy for him to turn his back on me."

"He didn't turn his back on you." Cale threw an accusing finger in his brother's face. "You're the one who ran out. On all of us. Don't you know you were as important in our lives as Pa or Ma? We looked up to you." Cale crossed his arms atop the stall and buried his face in his sleeves. "Hell, some of us idolized you. Not that you give a damn."

Buck heaved another weary sigh. He rested his back against the wall, one thumb feathering over the brush, feeling the prick of the stiff bristles and wishing they were cactus spines. "I give a damn, Cale. I gave a damn back then, and I still do. But Pa's right, it won't do any good raking up old sins."

After a long time, Cale straightened. He wandered the length of the small barn and back. Sunlight edged through the cracks in the walls, pinstriping the dusty dirt floor at his feet. A chicken darted crookedly after a spider. Somewhere outside, Angel was chasing Ethan, her high little-girl voice imitating her mother as she ordered him to come back and get his diaper on. The ache in Buck's heart eased.

"You marrying that widow?" Cale asked.

Throwing himself back into his work, Buck said, "No. Helping her out for a while is all. I'll be drifting on soon. To California, I'm thinking. Always wanted to see the ocean. Want to go with me?"

"Pa figured you probably headed for the coast when you left home. It was the first place we had the Pinkertons look for you."

Buck stared at his brother. "He hired detectives to find me? Is that how you knew I was here?"

"It was Ma and us boys who hired them. Pa knows nothing about it yet."

"He doesn't know you found me?"

"No." Cale suddenly found something fascinating about the glove on his left hand. "We were told you were in the Utah State Penitentiary, Richard. I went there, then tracked you here."

Ah, Buck thought, pierced with new pain, that's why

he's edgy as a preacher in a whorehouse; he's embarrassed about having an ex-con for a brother.

"We all talked it over," Cale went on, "Birch, Whip, Ma, and me, and we decided one of us should personally check the story out before we told Pa."

Bitterness hardened Buck's tone. "And you drew the short straw. What were you afraid of? That I was a professional killer now? I admit I'm well suited to the job."

"Don't, Richard—"

"Don't what? Speak the truth?"

"No, don't crucify yourself like that. Ellen died in childbirth. Hundreds of women die that way. Our real mother for one, giving birth to me and Whip. Does that mean Whip and I murdered her? Is that how you see it?"

The very mention of the soft, pretty woman who'd sung lullabies with the voice of an angel and was always there to soothe a boy's hurts, was balm to Buck's ragged emotions. "No, that's not how I see it. There were complications, that's why Mother died. It's not the same thing at all."

"Why not, Richard? You tell me how it's not the same goddamned thing. Tell me!"

They were yelling now, toe to toe, and ready to strike blows. They didn't notice they weren't alone anymore—until Tempest politely cleared her throat.

Buck stared at her where she stood in the doorway, outlined by the last rays of the lowering sun. Once again her smallness surprised him. Her courage, her strength, her stubbornness made her seem larger. Her face was pale, her brown eyes enlarged with shock. Her hands were twisted in her apron. He knew they would be trembling.

"I came to tell you supper is ready." Tacking her gaze on Cale, she said, "You'll stay, won't you? You'll have to sleep here in the barn, I'm afraid, there's not much room in the house but—"

"Thank you." At first sight of her, Cale had whipped off his hat. Ever the gentleman. Buck almost smiled.

"Thank you, ma'am," the young man repeated. "But I'm not sure . . ." He glanced at his older brother's hard face and let the words dwindle away.

"We'll be right in," Buck told her.

Nodding, she left, taking the sunlight with her.

A long silence followed. Cale began raking hay with the side of his boot, moving it this way and that like a dissatisfied artist. Buck's knuckles on the grooming brush were blanched. Slowly, methodically, he loosened his fingers, then set the brush on top of the half-wall of the enclosure. When Spook swung his head around and nickered softly, as though offering solace, Buck let out a derisive snort of amusement. What did it say about a man that his horse was the only one to give a damn about him? Buck wanted to believe that wasn't true. Not anymore, anyway. His brother had come a long way to find him. Would he have done that if he truly didn't care? Or had he done it only for their stepmother? "Why *did* you come, Cale?"

The younger man settled his dusty tan hat back on his head and tugged the leather gloves higher up his wrists. "In all honesty?"

"In all honesty."

"I wanted to pound the shit out of you, Richard. I wanted to wring the goddamn life out of you."

Buck threw back his head and roared with laughter. Cale stiffened.

"You think it's funny, Richard? I'm not a scrawny ten-year-old anymore. I can beat the stuffing out of you now."

"Whoa, little brother." Buck threw up his hands. "I'm sure you can. It was me I was laughing at. For having the arrogance to think you might have wanted me to go home with you." Pain shaved the amusement from his voice. "That maybe you all wanted me home."

"Some of us do. Lize's so naive she still believes in you. And Ma wants you back, too. Only she's thinking of Pa. He's been ill a lot since you left, and she has it in her head that seeing you, getting the past resolved, might help."

"I notice you didn't include yourself in that little speech. You still want to wring my neck?"

Cale avoided looking at him. "In all honesty? I don't know, Richard."

"Call me Buck. No one's called me Richard in years."

"Why? Is that your alias?"

With supreme effort, Buck let the taunt slide. "Come on in and have supper. You can bed down out here tonight, and maybe tomorrow you'll have a better idea of whether you want to kill me or simply knock the shit out of me." He started for the door, then stopped, a frown creasing his brow. "Incidentally, folks around here think I'm Tempest's husband, Skeet Whitney." He sighed at the suspicion on his brother's face. "Look, it's a long story, but if you'll listen, I'll tell it to you."

"I'll listen."

By the time Buck finished, the suspicion had fled Cale's face, but not the antagonism. "I'll keep your secret," he said, brushing past Buck as he walked outside to his horse. "But I don't reckon I'll stay. I've got some thinking to do, and that's something I have to do alone." Cale swung up into his saddle and adjusted his hat on his head. A tic twitched in his cheek as he peered down at his brother. "I'll see you in a day or so." Reining his horse around, he galloped toward the bridge, leaving Buck alone in the billowing dust.

Tempest came to the door of the dugout as Buck went to the wash bench. "Is your brother coming back?"

"I don't know." He unbuttoned his pants, pulled his shirttails free, and yanked off his shirt. He felt dirty, inside and out.

With unabashed appreciation Tempest watched him scrub his chest and arms, thinking how wonderful that naked chest had felt pressed to hers last night as they'd made love. The shadows were thick and dark in his eyes again. She wanted to banish them, but didn't know how. He straightened and reached for the towel. She took it from him and dried off his back. It gave her the excuse she needed to touch him, to feel his warmth and vibrancy beneath her hands, and to momentarily ease the ache deep within her.

Buck gazed down at her bare head as she moved in front of him to dry his chest. Her hair was in its usual thick braid, loose ends flying every which way. He lifted a hand to brush them from her face. Then he remembered Beaver Hanks's shocking revelation and let his hand drop. She looked up, her lovely face reflecting his own desperate yearning. The sudden urge to purge himself in her sweetness was so intense it was all he could do not to lower her to the ground then and there. He wanted to strip her naked and bury himself so deeply inside her she would never get him out. The softening of her eyes told him she recognized his need. She leaned close and lifted her face to his. Knowing he shouldn't, but too weak to resist, Buck crushed her to him and took what she offered. Her mouth opened to him and her tongue danced with his. A few years of that sweet tongue bathing him like that and he thought he might feel clean again; her goodness might wash the sour taste of self-disgust from his throat.

"Mama?"

They broke apart to find Angel standing in the doorway staring up at them. Buck experienced a flash of *déjà vu*. But everything was different now from the day he'd first met Tempest. She was willing this time, for one thing. More than willing. He warmed his heart with that knowledge and let it bleed away the tension and ugliness of the confrontation with his brother.

"Who's minding the store while you're gone?" Buck asked Viola as he tossed Marmalade a bite of venison.

"Oh, I have a helper now." She smiled cryptically. "A sweet girl. You must come and meet her."

"Who?" Tempest stopped swirling mashed potatoes with her fork and looked at her friend curiously.

"It's a surprise. You'll find out when you come to town." Putting aside her napkin, Viola scooted back her chair. "I'd best be going. I'm not worried about the girl handling things, but it'll be dark soon, and Mr. Sims doesn't like me on the road alone at night."

"Can't say as I blame him." Buck rose and went to the door. "I'll bring the buggy around."

Shadows were fingering their way across the valley as Buck walked toward the corral. With a half-bark/half-yawn, Rooster hauled himself up to trail after him. Buck smiled. Then he thought of Cale, and the smile fled. What did the boy want from him? Not that Cale was truly a boy anymore. Not at twenty-five. But Buck still found it difficult to envision his brothers and sisters grown up. He wished he knew what they were all doing now. For half a cent he'd saddle up Spook and track Cale down so he could ask.

The ache was back in his heart. Sleep would be scant tonight; there was too much to think about, and he dreaded the nightmares he knew would come.

Tempest stood in the doorway and watched Buck reach down to pull one of Rooster's ears as the dog nipped playfully at his leg. By all appearances, he hadn't a care in the world. Yet she knew better. The voices of the two brothers had been loud as they'd argued, and she'd caught the gist of their disagreement. Panic lanced her at the thought of his going away with Cale Kincade. She knew if he went, she would never see him again.

"He's hurting," she said to Viola over her shoulder. "Something is terribly wrong between him and his family, and he's taken all the guilt of it onto himself."

Viola adjusted her shawl about her plump shoulders. "And because he's hurting, you're hurting. Stop fretting, dear, everything will come out all right. I promise."

"How can you be so sure?" With a wan smile, Tempest waved a hand at her. "Never mind. Mr. Sims again, right?"

Viola winked her good eye. "He's never wrong, you know."

How I pray that's true.

"Mama!" Angel tugged at her mother's shirttail. "Can Ethan and me wear our new hats and play fur trapper?"

Tempest brushed her hand lovingly over her daughter's bright moonbeam hair. "It's too late to play outside, but you can wear them indoors until bedtime, just this once."

"I don't know how can you let the child wear that smelly—" The rest of Viola's comment went unsaid as gunfire shattered the air.

"Merciful heaven!" Viola clapped a hand to her breast.

Tempest paled. "Sweet Mary and Joseph." She rushed to the open door and called out, "Buck, are you all right?"

His voice came from the deep shadows beneath the buggy. "Get back inside, woman. You want to get shot?"

"Just answer me, Buck Maddux. Are you hurt?"

Viola pulled on Tempest's arm, urging her back into the house. "He's fine, dear, but you're a perfect target there in the doorway."

"Get inside and shut the door," Buck shouted again.

The strength of the hands dragging her back from the doorway surprised Tempest. Once they were inside again, she looked down to see the older woman calmly draw her pistol.

"What happened, Mama?" Angel asked.

Picking up the women's fear, Ethan began to cry. Tempest gathered her children into her arms.

"Get your rifle, dear." At the window, Viola nudged aside the thin vellum that substituted for glass, and peeked outside. After soothing her babies, Tempest lifted down the Henry repeater and checked it over as she took up her position by the second window. Silently, they waited. When a quarter-hour had passed with no more shots fired, Viola whispered, "Think the bushwhacker's gone?"

"I don't know. What if Buck was hit? He could be out there bleeding to death."

Viola eased the door open and peered outside. "Mr. Maddux? Is it over?"

"Yeah, he's gone."

Instructing the children to stay put no matter what, Tempest rushed out into the gathering twilight, followed more slowly by Viola. Buck crawled out from under the buggy, his Colt still in his hand. Blood drenched his shoulder.

"You've been shot." Tempest dropped the rifle and tore at his sleeve to examine his wound.

Buck winced. "Easy, woman. You trying to finish the job that bushwhacker started?"

"Of course not," she snapped, her fear turning to anger now that she knew he would live. "Stop squirming and let me see how bad it is."

"It's nothing. Bullet plowed a groove in my shoulder is all. Pack it with something to stop the bleeding and let me go saddle my horse."

"You're not going anywhere. Help me get him into the house, Viola. There's not enough light out here and he may need stitching."

Buck brushed them aside and hauled himself to his feet. "Blasted meddling women. I'm all right, I tell you." He yanked his handkerchief from his rear pocket and folded it into a four-inch square.

"Here, let me." Tempest tried to take the bandage from him. When he slapped her hands away, she merely reached for him again. "Stop being such an obstinate, buffalo-brained bag of—"

"I may be buffalo-brained, but this is my body and I say it's okay. Now leave me be." Thrusting her away again, he stalked toward the barn, pressing the folded kerchief to the wound in his shoulder.

"What are you going to do?" Tempest demanded.

"What the hell do you think I'm going to do? I'm going after that back-shooting son-of-a—"

"And leave Tempest and the children alone, Mr. Maddux?" Viola asked.

"She's not alone, you're here, and they're not after her, anyway. They're after me. But when it comes to that, they didn't mean to kill me or they would have aimed better. It was a warning, nothing more."

Still fussing, the two women followed him to the barn where he fetched his saddle. "I want you to stay inside with the children until I get back," he told them. "Pull the latch in and keep your weapons handy, just in case. I'll be back quick as I can."

Together, the women stood in the darkening yard, watching Buck ride off down the road. Viola took the younger woman's hand and gave it a reassuring pat. "He'll be fine, dear."

"Of course he will." Taking a deep breath, Tempest turned and forced her feet toward the house. "Maybe you should spend the night here, Viola. Whoever that was— and you and I both know it was Jonas—he could come back. No matter what Buck says about them wanting only him."

"Nonsense, child. I can't simply disappear on my new employee that way. She would worry herself silly. When your Buck gets back, I'll have him escort me to town. I think he's right about who the shooter was after. Besides, if we are attacked, I can help." She patted the pistol on her hip.

Tempest wanted to scream. The only two people she cared about in the entire world, except her father and the children, and they were determined to get themselves killed. "You and Buck, you're both obstinate, mule-headed—"

"You're quite right, dear."

Buck returned twenty minutes later, having seen nothing of the ambusher except his tracks heading back toward town. Impatiently, he allowed Tempest to wash and bandage his wound, then he escorted Viola to the buggy. As he rode beside Viola Sims's clattering rig, thoughts and suspicions he didn't want to face crowded his mind. At first, he had assumed the shooter to be Jonas or one of the half-breed's henchmen. Now, another, more insidious notion clawed at his insides.

His brother had come there angry and full of resentment. He had admitted he wanted to wring the life out of Buck. Had Cale decided to simply shoot him instead? Buck didn't want to believe it. Yet the hate he'd seen in Cale's hard blue eyes haunted him.

Chapter Seventeen

The din from the fight going on inside Johansson's saloon ran over into the street, as did stumbling drunks. Fists cracked against flesh and bone. Men cursed. Hard muscled bodies slammed into tables and onto the floor. Wood splintered and gave. Amidst the noise and confusion was laughter and the shouts of wagers being placed on combatants.

Buck entered cautiously, peering through the thick smoke. The sight of Cale leaning against the bar and watching the ruckus rather than participating came as a relief. Buck maneuvered around the thrashing bodies on the straw-covered floor. Cale ignored him, though Buck knew his entrance had been noted.

"Hullo, friend," Swede shouted above the noise. Leaning toward Buck across the bar, the giant confided quietly, "A strange thing this night." He tipped his head toward Cale. "The man was asking to find Buck Maddux. I tell him there is no man here with that name, but I think maybe he find you anyway. Ya?"

"Yeah. Give us both a whiskey."

Buck slid a drink in front of his brother, then lifted his own to his lips. The burning in his throat sharpened his mind and senses. Enough to recognize the sound of running water at the other end of the bar.

Swede was already heading in that direction. "How many times I tell you, Skinner, not to make water in my saloon. There are privies out back for that."

"Ah, Swede," the culprit whined, not bothering to refasten his trousers. "You wouldn't want me to miss out on the fight, would you?"

"Ya, this I want very much, and I think you have done this for last time." He came from behind the bar then, stepping up out of his trench to tower menacingly over his errant patron by at least two feet. Awed by the man's enormity, the brawlers dropped their fists and sheepishly took their seats.

"Care to wager?" Buck murmured to Cale. "I'll take Swede and give you triple the odds."

Cale didn't even look at him. "What do you want, Buck?"

"Same as most men in a saloon." Buck kept his anger under tight rein and attempted to sound casual as they watched Swede toss Skinner into the street. "Did you come straight here when you left?"

"Where the hell else would I go?"

"Up into the rocks near Heartsease, maybe. With a rifle."

Cale whirled to face him, fury and confusion mixed on a face as square-jawed and implacable as his brother's. "What are you trying to say?"

Buck shrugged and calmly sipped his whiskey. "You said you wanted to kill me."

"Someone shot at you from the rocks?"

Turning slightly, Buck showed his torn and bloodied shirt.

Cale's eyes widened. Concern flickered through the blue orbs before the anger returned full force. "And you think I did it? You think *I* shot you?"

Buck didn't, not after seeing Cale's reaction. There was no mistaking the younger man's shock or the distress in his eyes before it was edged out by rage. But Cale gave him no chance to speak. His hand balled and once more the saloon resounded with the crack of flesh and bone striking flesh and bone.

Tempest finished tying a fresh bandage over the shoulder wound Buck had reopened in his fight with Cale.

"I might understand a man your brother's age using his fists to solve his differences, but I thought—hoped—you were more grown up than that."

Buck scowled at her unfair assessment. "He threw the first punch."

"And naturally male pride required you to follow up with the second."

"You'd rather I'd simply stood there and let him pound on me?"

Her smile was cruel. "Actually, there have been a number of times I would have enjoyed such a sight."

Soaking a clean cloth with whiskey, she dabbed at a cut over his right eye. He flinched. "Ow! You trying to kill me, woman?"

"No, I'll leave that to Jonas. Sit still."

She slapped away the hand that tried to keep her from applying more of the stinging alcohol. "How long do you think it will be before your brother tells someone who he is?" she asked. "And, more to the point, who you are?"

Buck grimaced as she treated a scrape on his cheek. "I

explained the situation to him, and he promised not to give us away. Swede bedded him down in his back room."

The boyishness of Buck's grin charmed her. "Cale's not going to be pleased that he still can't beat me . . . especially with me shot up and all."

"I wonder why that fails to worry me?"

Buck ignored her sarcasm. She had been brushing her hair when he'd arrived home with his bleeding shoulder. The golden brown tresses hung to her waist, thick and wavy and irresistible. He yearned to sift its silk through his fingers, bury his face in its fresh-washed scent, sweep it over his naked skin. Reaching up, he pushed the hair behind one of her shoulders, leaving it to hang free over the other. He loved the dance and shimmer of the lamplight in the long waterfall of hair as she moved, almost as much as he loved the gentle sway of her breasts beneath the thin muslin of her nightdress.

"Do you think he'll cooperate?" she asked.

He shifted his gaze to her face as she worked over him, watched her lips part on a gasp as he cupped her breasts in his hands. It was insane, touching her, but he couldn't help himself.

She jerked back, the anger over his foolish brawling still with her. "What are you doing?"

"Ought to be obvious enough."

His voice had grown husky and heated. Almost as blistering as his hands, she thought. She clamped her thighs against an unwanted rush of sultry warmth and sensation, and decided he'd had enough nursing. Slamming the lid shut on her medicine box, she began cleaning up.

Buck watched with hot, slitted eyes. "We've been dragging our feet long enough, Tempest. It's time we set our minds on finding the money to pay off Jonas, before someone gets killed."

Amber flecked eyes yawned with indignation. "Dragging

our feet? Speak for yourself, Buck Maddux. A day hasn't gone by when I haven't given a lot of thought to that particular problem."

Viciously she wrung out the cloth she'd used to bathe his bruised flesh, as though she wished it were his neck. Buck smiled. "Judas, but you're beautiful when you're angry."

"If that's true," she retorted, "then I must be more beautiful around you than at any other time, because I've never been so angry as you make me."

The grin he gave her was satanic. "Proves how perfect we are for each other."

"Raspberry stickers!" The anger was fading. It was impossible to resist him for long. "Your brains could fit inside the head of an ant, with space left over, do you know that?"

"Ever spend much time watching an ant?"

Tempest rolled her eyes. "All the time. What else do I have to do around here?"

"Ants may be little, Tempest, but they're wily as coyotes, maybe even more wily. So I'll consider what you said a compliment."

"You would," she muttered. "Overblown jackass."

He laughed. To keep from reaching for her, he pulled out his cigarette makings. "Seriously, sweetheart, we've got to get our hands on some money."

"Maybe you could ask your brother for a loan, if you're in such a hurry to get out of here."

Blue eyes clouded. Before he asked his family for one cent, he'd simply walk up to Creedy and shoot him.

Rising, he went to the stove. He peeled a long splinter off a log, removed a stove lid with a lifter and stuck the tip of the splinter in the flames. A curl of tobacco smoke drifted upward on the breeze from the ill-fitting window coverings as he drew on his cigarette. He was right. She had to admit it to herself, even if she wasn't willing to say it out loud—she had been dragging her feet. She knew her reasons and prayed his were the same. Once Jonas was paid, and the security of her ranch assured for another six months, there would be no reason for Buck to stay. It was a day she dreaded with every fiber of her being.

Buck opened the door to gaze out at the night. The old suffocation of closed rooms had waned, returning only when he felt trapped by his own increasingly complex emotions. "I keep thinking about the missing Army payroll. It belongs to you now, since you mortgaged the ranch and paid it back. If you only knew where that Pitt place was, we'd be sitting pretty."

"Pitt place?" Open-mouthed, she stared at him. "What Pitt place?"

Buck shrugged, and winced. His shoulder was hellishly sore. "The homestead where Skeet hid the money. The Army couldn't find anyone who'd ever heard of a Pitt family. The troopers scoured every abandoned homestead and cabin for miles around, but they didn't even find a nickel."

Tempest's heart stopped, skittered, started again. "Buck, tell me *exactly* what Skeet said."

The sparkle of excitement in her brown eyes caught his attention. He straightened. "Do you know the Pitt place?"

"Maybe. Just tell me what Skeet said. Word for word."

She looked so damn beautiful lit up like that, he could hardly concentrate on what she was saying. He wanted to kiss her. Frowning, he dug into his memory. "His exact words were 'Tell Tempest . . . look in old Pitt house.' That was all he got out. He tried to shoot himself in the temple then, because of the pain, but he didn't have the strength." Buck turned away, his eyes darkly shadowed again.

Sobered by the image of her husband's last moments, Tempest's tone was quiet and solemn, in spite of the hope growing inside her. "Why didn't you tell me this before? The message was for me. Don't you know what this means?"

One dark brow rose as he studied her. "Seeing that glow in your eyes, I'm hoping it means you know where this Pitt family lived."

"I do, Buck." She danced away from him, swinging her arms in the air. "I do, I do, I do." Her nightdress ballooned about her body. The light showing through the thin fabric gave him a clear view of her curves. Heat swirled through him.

Coming to a halt, she grinned up at him. "He wasn't talking about a homestead, Buck, or a family named Pitt. That's why the soldiers couldn't find it. The money is right here in Deception Canyon. Only not in any kind of building you're familiar with."

His heart began to thrum. "What do you mean?"

"The Indian ruins. The houses were partially dug out of the ground, like a roofed-over pit, so Skeet called them pit-houses. He knew I'd understand. All we have to do is figure out which one the money's in."

"Damn!" He sank down onto a stool. "I figured he'd probably stashed it in the canyon. There's a million places here a man could stash something as small as a payroll pouch, and he didn't have time to do anything else. Just chuck it in a natural hole in the canyon wall behind a bush and hope he could find it again. Judas, Tempest, hiding that money likely cost him his life because it let that Army patrol from Fort Duchesne catch up with him. They lost him when it got dark, but not before he took a bullet. Poor bastard." He shook his head. "Hard to believe he had enough time to get to one of those ruins, though."

"No one else might have been able to do it, but Skeet could have," she said. "You see, Skeet came here to find a treasure an old trader in St. Louis told him about. Lost

Spanish gold. He searched this country until he knew every inch of it, including the ruins. If anyone could have managed to reach one, cache the money, and still get away, he could. The money is here, Buck. All we have to do is find it.''

He stared at her a long time, while his blood slowly began to stir with a different sort of arousal from what he'd felt minutes ago. If Tempest was right, their problems were indeed all but solved.

Chapter Eighteen

Jonas Creedy's lip curled in a silent snarl as he stared out the corner window of Big's Red's bedroom in the Sagebrush Princess. Tempest Whitney had just driven past in her dogcart, Maddux riding alongside—the man Jonas had become more sure was Maddux, which meant he had been tricked into giving up Tempest. No one made a fool of Jonas Creedy and lived to boast of it.

"Jonas?" The rustle of cotton sheets accompanied Red's soft, Southern voice as she lifted herself higher against the bed pillows. Nearly two weeks had passed since Jonas had pummeled her to near-death for shooting him, and she still bore the bruises. Probably would have them for some time to come. Along with the broken ribs. "Please, Jonas, tell me what you're plannin' to do about Lacey."

Tempest pulled up next to the hotel. Maddux dismounted and secured the reins to the hitch rail. He circled her waist with his hands and started to lift her out of the cart, then flinched and quickly released her. Even from where he stood, Jonas saw the grimace of pain on the man's face. He smiled. It seemed Tempest's so-called husband had hurt his shoulder. Thanks to Morgan Paine. *But it's nothing compared to what you're going to suffer before this is over, you filthy interloper.*

Jonas had heightened the ante on Maddux, hoping the added pressure would force the man to show his hand and lead them to the stolen payroll. Maddux must know where it was or he wouldn't be hanging around. Especially since he hadn't started sleeping with Tempest until lately. Maybe the man thought Tempest knew where the money was and he was trying to romance her into telling him. But Jonas was growing tired of waiting, wasting time on Maddux when what he should be doing was searching for the lost gold which was bound to be worth a great deal more than the payroll.

Tempest's brats were jumping up and down in the cart like excited monkeys. The sun glinted off their bouncing curls, making their hair look more white than blond. A hideous, floppy hat hid Tempest's hair, but Jonas didn't need to see it to know it was darker than her children's. The last time he had seen that hat was the day he'd dragged her into the back of the hotel and thrown her onto a bed in one of the rooms. His body quickened at the memory. He would never forget the smell and taste of her. Like fine French brandy compared to a crude home brew.

He wouldn't forget the raging headache he'd awakened with later, either, or the snickers of his men when he'd walked into the ranch yard naked.

"Jonas? Did ya hear me?"

"Enjoy your breakfast in bed while you can, Red, your days of being waited on and pampered by those morons downstairs are over."

Next to Tempest's fair-haired brats, the ebony-haired man with them looked like a raven in a flock of swans.

Or, in this case, a skunk. Folks might wonder how those towheaded brats escaped having black, white-streaked hair themselves, but it was no mystery to Jonas.

His smile was feral as he reached into his pocket and drew out the telegram his foreman had fetched from Price yesterday. The man arrested two years ago as Skeet Whitney's partner and sentenced to prison on a charge of robbery had been released in July—six weeks before "Skeet Whitney's" miraculous appearance in Deception Canyon. It also confirmed that he had blue eyes and black hair with a white streak over his forehead. And he went by the name of Buck Maddux.

"Jonas!"

There was a possibility, Jonas supposed, that the dead man the posse helped bury truly was Buck Maddux and Skeet had assumed the man's identity to evade prison. The driver and passengers of the robbed stage had seen only one bandit, whose face was hidden by a kerchief. Still, that didn't prove anything, which is why Maddux went to jail. Whatever happened two years ago, it no longer mattered if the man with Tempest was Maddux or Whitney. Either way, he was a dead man.

"Ah won't 'low ya to hurt Lacey, Jonas."

He turned and gazed at the woman propped up by a mound of pillows in the center of the bed, a breakfast tray on her lap. Her bruises had turned a putrid purple and yellow, making her appear sickly and unappealing. His gaze followed the trail of her long hair to the voluptuous bosom it barely concealed. Tempest's breasts were smaller, but nursing babies had left the nipples large enough to please even a man's mouth. His groin stirred as he remembered the taste of those nipples.

Moving to the bed he cupped Red's discolored cheek in his hand, squeezed the tender flesh with his thumb, and smiled when she winced. "Don't push me, Red. You know I don't like having to punish you."

His own injury was healing up well, in spite of the setback Tempest had given it with the cruel blow she'd delivered.

Red set the tray aside.

"You hardly touched your food," Jonas said.

"Ah'm not hungry. 'Sides, it still hurts to chew."

The unspoken accusation rankled. His pleasant mood slipped a notch.

"Well, you damned well better eat anyhow. I've lost enough money with you laying up here doing nothing."

Red smiled. "Not to mention what Lacey used to bring in, eh, Jonas?"

That was too much. He backhanded her across the face. Red flinched but didn't cry out.

He walked back to the window. Damn whore. If it hadn't been for threats from Stud and Reuben, he would have had her spreading her legs for customers two days after the beating when it was apparent that she was going to live. How much could it hurt to simply lay beneath a man, broken ribs or no broken ribs?

Down on the street Maddux was kissing Tempest. The memory of watching Maddux fondle her naked breasts brought an element of anger with it. Jonas was the one who should be sharing her bed, not Maddux. Even the physical release he had given himself that night outside her dugout had failed to completely ease his hunger for her. He smiled. His fantasies of Tempest hadn't always included pain, but lately . . . ah, yes, lately he'd thought a lot of how her cries of pain would add to his pleasure as he thrust himself inside her.

He rubbed his hand over the aching bulge in his trousers, but he had no intention of settling again for the kind of relief he'd had to settle for after the dance.

"Come here, Red."

"Why, Jonas?" Her tone was wary.

"I said come here."

The steel-edged voice allowed no room for argument. Red got out of bed and went to him.

"Kneel down," he ordered.

She'd spent enough time at his feet to know what he wanted. Without comment, she knelt and began unbuttoning his trousers.

On the street below, Tempest was watching her pretend husband walk toward the Swede's place, a perfect picture of wifely concern. The boy in her arms put a small hand on her breast. Jonas imagined it was his hand. He felt the delicious suck and pull of Red's talented mouth on his sensitive flesh, his breathing hard and fast now, and thought what it would be like to have Tempest there on her knees before him instead of the whore. His excitement grew. He knotted his hands in Red's hair and pumped hard, ignoring her choked complaint. Then, as if sensing his gaze on her, Tempest looked up at the window. The intoxicating idea of her seeing what he was doing to Red nearly shattered him. When her gaze actually met his through the glass pane, and widened in fear, Jonas's body began to convulse.

When he opened his eyes, the pulsating ripples of a spectacular climax beginning to ebb, all he saw of Tempest was her back as she hurried into the store. Red hitched herself to her feet and went to the washstand. Jonas refastened his pants and sauntered to the door. He was feeling exceedingly good again, making him more generous than usual.

"I'll give you the rest of the day off, Red. Tonight you go back to work. You just proved you was capable of servicing a man. In one way at least."

On his way through the saloon Jonas told Morgan Paine

to come to his office. A simple way of piecing together the last of the Whitney puzzle had occurred to him.

Paine outweighed his boss by fifty pounds. He had a laugh like the bark of a walrus and a triangular face with a low forehead that gave him the look of a moron. But the man was canny as a wolverine, and twice as mean. Traits Jonas admired.

"Come in, Morg." Jonas motioned to a chair and offered one of his poorer quality Cuban cigars. "Got something I want you to do."

Morgan ran the cigar under his nose, sniffing its aroma with audible relish. "Anything you say, Mr. Creedy. Just say the word and it's done."

Jonas smiled. He loved having his boots licked.

There was no sign of Cale when Buck entered Swede's saloon and bellied up to the bar.

"You look for someone, maybe?" Swede asked with a knowing grin.

"Did you talk to him?"

"Ya, I talk. And I think he listen, but he is saying nothing. How is your wound, my friend?"

Buck flexed the injured shoulder and grimaced. "Probably no worse than Cale's head this morning."

Swede pushed a tumbler of whiskey toward him. The glasses weren't getting any cleaner, Buck noticed. He scrubbed at the rim with his thumb before bringing it to his lips. "Where is he?"

"At livery, seeing to horse."

Buck frowned. "Is he leaving?"

Swede shrugged.

Downing the drink in a single gulp, Buck tossed a coin on the counter and gave his friend a nod.

John Bennet's livery was as cavernous and fragrant as

most such places, though less drafty. Buck heard Cale before he saw him. The young man had a deep clear baritone voice that could make him a fortune on the stage back East, if he wasn't so determined to go into their stepfather's import-export business. The song was one Buck remembered their stepmother singing when they were boys, a sweet ballad about a maid with golden hair and swallows in the air.

Cale was in the far stall, brushing down his roan stallion. He barely glanced up at Buck's greeting. John's boy, Beaner, all pimples and Adam's apple, came out of the office. "Morning, Mr. Whitney. Can I do something for you?"

Buck gestured to the man in the stall. "Just came to talk to my brother."

The boy screwed up his face. "But his name's Kincade."

"Same mother, different fathers," Buck explained.

"Oh." Beaner scratched his armpit and nodded. Cale kept on brushing, ignoring them both.

"We could use some privacy," Buck said when the boy continued to stand there.

"Oh. Sure. I was watching the place for my pa, but with you here, maybe I could run over to the eatery and see if I can talk Mrs. Sims out of a cinnamon roll."

"We'll keep an eye out," Buck assured him. "When we're done I'll come and get you."

A long silence followed the shuffle of the boy's oversized feet out the big sliding doors. Finally Cale turned. He leaned an arm on the roan's rump and looked his brother in the eye. "What have you gotten yourself into here, Richard?"

"Buck."

"Richard, Buck, whatever. Are you after the woman, is that it? You just trying to get under her skirts?"

Hearing his brother talk that way about Tempest rankled. Maybe because it made him sound exactly like the scoundrel he was. He nipped the flesh inside his lower lip and waited until the anger passed, knowing it wouldn't be wise to give it rein. "No. I came here only to keep a promise."

During the next several minutes Buck explained how he'd met Skeet Whitney and landed in prison, how he'd come to Deception Canyon to see if Whitney's widow was getting along all right and found her in trouble. Buck skipped over the emotions behind his decisions: the desperate need to avoid responsibility that conflicted with his need to keep promises; the self-hate driving him from job to job, state to state, never letting anyone close to him, never letting himself care, because caring hurt too much when the time came to move on again, and he didn't deserve to be cared about in return anyway. He left out the complex emotions living with Tempest had wrought in him the past few days too: his increasing respect for her courage and tenacity; his growing affection for her children; the frightening need to make her his; and, most of all, the resurfacing of dreams he'd told himself long ago he didn't deserve to see come true—family, home, love, happiness.

When Buck finished, he fell silent and waited for his brother's reaction. Cale's face was hard and calculating, as if he were dissecting every word and seeking untruths. The apparent lack of trust smarted.

"I already told you I wouldn't do anything to hurt your little widow," Cale said finally. "She obviously needs someone's protection."

"But not mine, is that it?" Buck ground out. "Not the protection of a woman killer."

Cale blanched. "I never called you that, Richard. In fact, I've never heard anyone refer to you that way except you. Is it guilt that makes you so defensive?"

"Yes, damn you. The guilt of Ellen's death has eaten at me every minute of every day for fifteen years. It'll keep on eating at me till the day I die. That's something you won't ever have to worry about, though, is it, Mr. Perfect Gentleman?" he sneered. "You don't make mistakes, so you'll never know how it feels to be rejected by everyone you know and love. You'll never know how it feels to hate yourself so bad you want to take a .44 and . . ."

Suddenly the fury waned, leaving Buck weary to his soul, empty. Whirling away from his shocked brother he stood, panting, fighting for control, fighting the sickness in his stomach that made him want to spew up his breakfast.

Behind him, Cale said, "You're right, Buck. I can't know how it felt to be rejected like that, but you're wrong about one thing . . . you weren't rejected by everyone. The folks, maybe, but not us kids. We didn't know enough to turn against you then. It was the way you left, without a word, that hurt us and made us hate you for a while."

Buck's head came up. "For a while?" He turned and looked at his brother. "You don't hate me anymore?"

Cale looked away. "I don't know."

Buck nodded, feeling as bleak as a winter sky.

"Give me time. I told you I don't know what the goddamn hell I feel now." Pinning his big brother with a piercing glare, Cale added, "But if that woman suffers for all these good intentions of yours, I promise, Richard, I'll kill you."

Buck's gut tightened. "A moment ago it was Buck," he said quietly. Buck didn't believe Tempest would be better off in his hands than Jonas Creedy's. That pained him. Almost as much as when his family first turned on him fifteen years ago. He stared at the unforgiving brother he loved, and his voice turned to stone. "If I fail Tempest, you won't have to kill me, little brother. I'll do it myself."

Then, spinning on his heels, he stalked out of the livery.

* * *

Tempest didn't know the two rough-looking men who stopped her outside the hotel and pretended to admire her children, but she suspected they worked for Jonas. That alone made her jittery. Her gaze cut to the window of the Sagebrush Princess where she had seen Jonas earlier, watching her with such savage carnality on his face she had felt as if his hands were on her naked flesh. The window was empty now.

One of the men wore a meticulous brown suit with checkered trousers and a bowler hat. He might have been taken for a clerk or secretary, if not for the cruelty in his pale yellow eyes. The other, larger man looked like a cowhand except for the gun belt strapped low on his hip the way she'd heard gunmen wore them.

"You shore named this 'un right, ma'am," the cowhand said around a chunk of tobacco as he squatted in front of Angel. "If she ain't the living image of an angel, I don't know what is. Ain't that right, Howard?"

"How did you know her name?" Tempest asked, more frightened than ever.

"Uh, musta heard you call her that. Right, Howard?"

The tidy little man called Howard was looking at Angel as though she were frosting on a cake. Remembering Jonas's words about knowing a man who would love to get his hands on her little girl, she drew her children closer. It was all she could do not to grab up her daughter and run screaming for Buck.

The cowhand patted Angel on the head like a puppy, rose to his feet, and turned to Ethan. Tempest forced herself to stand still and not flinch as he stroked Ethan's arm, all but brushing his finger over her breast in the process. The fear lodged in her throat threatened to collapse her lungs. Trying not to be obvious, she glanced up the street, hoping to see Buck. Hoping for anyone who might offer protection.

She tried to assure herself the men wouldn't dare to hurt them there on the street. Their hard, sadistic eyes told her otherwise. She could scream. Someone was bound to come running, but no one could reach her as fast as a bullet fired from a few feet away.

"Had a cousin once with hair that color," the big man said, spitting a stream of tobacco juice into the street, "like bleached-out wheat, you know? Ran in the family."

Eyeing the thick, light brown braid hanging over her shoulder, he added, "Reckon your kids musta got their coloring from their pa, is that right, ma'am?"

Too rattled to think, she mumbled, "Yes, he-he was very blond."

"Ain't that interesting," a familiar voice commented behind Tempest.

She whirled to find Jonas two feet away. His smile was like spider tracks down her back. With a jerk of his head, he dismissed the two men. They didn't bother to tip their hats as they strolled away.

Grinning, Jonas said, "You just gave me the last bit of proof I needed, puss."

"Proof of what?" She managed not to stutter, but barely. He had heard her admit the children's father had been blond—not raven-haired with a white streak over his forehead. Fear crawled over her body like wind-chilled sweat.

"The truth about that husband of yours, of course."

Even though she had expected the words, the air in her lungs froze. He laughed.

"Didn't think I'd figure it out?" His expression hardened, the thin lips curled downward, and the nostrils of his bent, flattened nose flared. "Were you counting on a half-breed being too stupid to see you were lying?"

Fighting to control the rapid flutter of her heart, she

lifted her chin and stared him in the eye. "I don't know what you're talking about."

Jonas grabbed her arm and yanked her close. Ethan began to fuss. "You know, all right."

"Skeet will kill you if he sees you bothering me."

"Skeet is dead."

"No, he—"

Dirty fingernails bit cruelly into her arm. *"Don't.* . . . don't lie to me again."

Tempest clenched her teeth against the pain of his fierce grip, and tilted her chin higher. She would *not* let him see her pain—or her fear. He was like a wild animal, sensing his prey's weakness, using it against her. Drumming up her courage, she spat out, "Get your hands off me, you goat-faced bastard, or I'll—"

"Or you'll what?" he sneered. "Send Maddux after me again? Tell me, has he been keeping my spot between your legs warm and well greased for me? No matter. I'll be seein' to it myself soon—once we're rid of him."

Ethan buried his face in her neck and began to wail. Angel clutched her mother's skirt so tightly Tempest feared the girl would yank the garment off her. Knowing she needed to be strong for them was all that kept her on her feet.

"I'm looking forward to it, you know—" Jonas's low whisper was like the hiss of a snake—"killing that bastard you been spreading your legs for. I ain't looked forward to anything so much since the day I tracked down my mother who thought she was too good to raise me. She died real slow, same as Maddux will, and I'm gonna enjoy every minute of it. Almost as much as what I have in mind for you. Tell him that. Tell him I'll be waiting."

Shoving her aside, he strode down the alley between the store and the hotel.

Tempest closed her eyes and fought for sanity. Ethan and Angel were both crying now. She wished she could join them and let her tears wash away all her fear, but it wasn't that easy. Tears were nothing but emotional rain—useless and unproductive.

Buck. Sweet Lord, if Buck found out about this, he'd kill Jonas. She might be tempted to let him do exactly that, if she wasn't afraid Buck would end up in prison again. What had happened to him two years ago proved the law was not infallible. And she would die if she lost him. It was inevitable, she knew that, yet she was fool enough to keep hoping she could make Buck want to stay, could make him love her. But losing him to his wandering feet was better than seeing him in prison. Or dead.

Taking a deep breath, Tempest stroked her son's back. "It's all right, sweetheart. There's nothing to cry about. It's all right."

Cradling him against her breasts, she squatted in front of her daughter and smoothed the pale hair out of the girl's face. "Stop crying now, Angel. He's gone. Papa Buck would never let anyone hurt us. You know that, don't you?"

Angel managed a nod, and bravely knuckled the tears from her eyes. "I don't like that man, Mama. He'th not nithe."

"I don't like him either, honey. Now listen to me, when we see Papa Buck at Viola's, you mustn't say anything about what just happened, okay? Because if he finds out that Mr. Creedy was mean to us, he'll try to make the man sorry for it, and I think that's what Mr. Creedy wants. He wants to hurt Papa Buck. Understand, Angel? We don't want Papa Buck to get hurt, do we?"

A fresh spurt of tears pearled on the girl's lashes. "I wouldn't never do anything to make Papa Buck get hurt, Mama."

"I know you wouldn't." Forcing a smile, Tempest kissed her daughter's forehead. Then she kissed Ethan and wiped away his tears. "Now, shall we go have some of Aunt Viola's good cinnamon rolls and be happy again?"

The children's brave, watery smiles nearly broke her heart.

Buck didn't go straight to Viola's when he left the livery. Instead, he took a long, dusty hike up the rocky slope behind town, using physical exercise to dissipate the savage fury tumbling his innards.

How could his own brother think so lowly of him? Oh, Buck knew he deserved it. But it still hurt. Damn. If a person truly loved someone, that love should never die, no matter how frequent or serious the mistakes the loved one made. When the disappointment and hurt faded, the love should still be there underneath. But that wasn't the way it worked. Not with his family, anyway. He hadn't realized how much he had secretly counted on being able to go home someday, once he'd regained some self-respect, and find the old love waiting for him. Now he knew he would never go home. Or find forgiveness.

The man who returned to town several minutes later was not the same one who had climbed a hill to work off his anger. This man was colder, harder, more hollow.

He and Tempest had taken three days to finish up autumn chores so they wouldn't be caught unaware by an early winter. A few more days, maybe only one, and they would find Skeet's ill-gotten stash. Then Buck could leave with a clear conscience. He would go without his heart. But then, he'd probably never had one anyway. How else could he have murdered his own wife and child?

Chapter Nineteen

Tempest prayed she would beat Buck to Viola's and have time to recover from her encounter with Jonas before she had to face him. But she scarcely reached the corner of the building before he strode across the street toward her. His face was granite, his eyes so bleak she nearly sobbed at the pain in them. Wisely, she kept quiet, letting the children's babble cover the silence between them while he opened the restaurant door and stood aside for them to enter.

It wasn't Viola who greeted them, but a young woman in her mid teens, with honey gold hair and eyes the color of summer leaves. The moment the girl saw Buck she rushed over, her smile too wide, too joyful to pass as mere politeness to a patron. She didn't seem to see Tempest.

"Buck! Oh, Buck," the girl cried, holding out her hands to him.

A glance told Tempest that Buck had been caught off

guard. "How are you, Lacey?" He didn't take her hands, and kept his tone distant and formal.

Lacey's gaze sidled to Tempest, and her face fell. "I'm fine . . . Mr. Whitney." Her voice was carefully modulated now. "Can I show you and your wife to a table?"

Tempest felt the atmosphere in the room grow dark and tense, like a thunderstorm about to let loose. She wanted to dig a hole and climb inside, but pride wouldn't let her. Briskly she walked to her usual table near the kitchen, then made a production out of removing the children's wraps and seating them, to avoid looking at Buck and the other woman. Woman, hell! Lacey wasn't much more than a child. How could Buck . . . ? Tempest didn't want to think about what he'd done with her. About his hands touching that smooth young flesh, the way they had touched hers.

"What are you doing here, Lacey?" Buck asked quietly.

"Oh, I'm cooking and serving customers for Mrs. Sims. She's so wonderful, Buck. I mean . . . Mr. Whitney." Excitement and easy familiarity warmed her voice again. "I don't work for Jonas anymore. I took your advice."

"Did he give you any trouble?"

"He hit me, but he didn't really hurt me, and it gave me the courage to walk out on him the way you told me I should. When Scotty Carmichael found out I didn't have enough money for a stage ticket, he talked to Mrs. Sims about letting me work here until I earned enough to get to Salt Lake City. I'm so happy now, and I owe it all to you and Scotty."

"I'm glad you're happy. I'd better join my wife now."

"Yes, of course." The formality returned.

Buck saw Tempest's embarrassment and outrage in the tight line of her lips and the high tilt of her chin. Any higher and all she'd be able to see would be the ceiling. The situation was saved by the whirlwind entrance of Ronan Carmichael, with Viola on his arm.

"Tempest! How delightful." Viola's cheery voice diffused the tension thickening in the room.

But not for Tempest. She felt only the additional shock of seeing her father with her best friend clinging to his arm. It was bad enough to endure the presence of Buck's ex-lover without the intimation of an involvement between her father and her friend. The entire world has gone crazy, she thought.

At least Ronan had the good grace to blush when his gaze met Tempest's from across the room. Viola dragged him over to the table. "Mr. Carmichael and I had the nicest walk. The air is so crisp and fresh. I think our lovely fall is about to end. We'll have snow soon. Did Lacey offer you breakfast? She's a wonderful cook."

"No, we don't want breakfast. We came to ask a favor," Tempest said, feeling flustered, foolish, and terribly gauche as her voice cracked and she heard her icy tone.

"Of course, dear. All you have to do is name it, you know that," Viola said.

"Thiminnon rollth," Angel piped up. "We want thiminnon rollth."

" 'Olls," Ethan mimicked. " 'Olls."

Viola put a finger to the tip of each child's nose and leaned close. "And cinnamon rolls you shall have. All you can eat."

Once they had all been served, the older woman said, "Now, what else can I do for you?"

"Don't be grabby, Angel." Tempest tucked a napkin into the neck of her daughter's dress, then scooped a roll onto the girl's plate. It was a movement designed to gain time to compose herself. She had an awful urge to throw every dish on the table against the wall and rail at them all for harboring secrets behind her back. Instead, she forced herself to say calmly, "We were hoping that since you have an assistant now, we might talk you into taking the children for a day or two."

"Second honeymoon?" Viola winked her good eye at Buck.

"Not exactly." He glanced pointedly at the kitchen where Lacey was stacking dirty dishes on the counter next to the sink. "Tempest is concerned about you having enough room for them upstairs though. Maybe you could show her where they would sleep."

Taking the hint of a need for privacy, Viola led Tempest through the kitchen and up the stairs to the living quarters she now shared with Lacey.

Ronan set his tam-o'-shanter on the table and rifled his hair with both hands.

"She'll come around," Buck told him, understanding the older man's sudden case of nerves.

"Aye, I suppose ye're right, but I hadna' expected her to be so shocked."

"I think there was more behind her coldness than your friendship with Mrs. Sims," Buck replied wryly. Ethan shredded his roll, then crawled onto Buck's lap and went to sleep. Angel lapped up every crumb.

Lacey refilled their cups. "Scotty? Thank you again for talking Mrs. Sims into giving me this chance. You have no idea what it means to me, getting away from Jonas and . . . well, everything."

"Ach. 'Twas not my doing, lass. The woman has a heart big as the sky, and she took to ye right off."

"You have a big heart too, Scotty. You simply can't see it for all the pain you carry around inside yourself." She kissed him on the forehead, smiled shyly at Buck, and returned to the kitchen.

Buck cast Ronan a look of speculation. He'd seen the dollop of whiskey Viola slipped into Ronan's coffee before bringing it from the kitchen. "Mrs. Sims has been helping you cut down on your drinking, hasn't she?"

"Aye. She's a good woman," Ronan said. "You've been kind to me as well. I thank ye for that. I know ye didna' think much of me when we first met."

Buck shrugged. "Staying sober was your decision, Ronan. If my encouragement helped, I'm glad." He smiled. "And if I remember correctly, you didn't think much of me either."

The bell on the front door jangled. Buck glanced up to see Swede standing in the opening, looking like a forlorn refugee. The sleeves of his sack coat were several inches too short. Someone had lengthened the trousers for him by cutting the legs off another pair and sewing them to the bottoms. Hat in hand, he did a slow anxious shuffle. Buck waved him over. Swede spit on his hand, smoothed back his blond hair with it and crossed the room in three long strides.

"Are you a giant?" Angel asked.

A smile inched across his face, exposing the large gap in his front teeth, and he relaxed. "I am big enough to be giant, you think?"

She nodded. "You're the biggeth man I ever theen before."

Lacey hurried from the kitchen, wiping her hands on her apron. "Sorry, I was putting a pan of cornbread in the oven. Oh, hello, Swede." She broke into a broad smile. "Would you like some coffee or something to eat?"

Color rose up the long column of Swede's neck. "Ya, please. Coffee."

Buck decided Cupid must have gotten his seasons mixed up. He winked at Swede behind Lacey's departing back. "Come to do some courting?"

Twin spots of rose dotted the blond giant's cheeks. "No. A man needs something to offer a woman before he goes courting. Lacey deserves a better home than my back room." Looking down at the table, he shrugged. "She would not want a man with no teeth anyway."

"You could go to Provo and get new teeth. You could get a piece of land, too, and homestead."

"I have thought of these things, but I make little money in my saloon. Most men go to the Princess because it is so fine. I cannot blame them."

"Lacey could keep her job here. That would help."

Rancor added to Swede's high color. "No! Is bad enough what she has endured. If I make her my wife, she will work only for me . . . for us, making a home for our children. She will work no more for others."

"To a sweet lass like Lacey," Ronan said, "a cave would be paradise, if it held a bit of love."

"Did I hear my name?" Lacey bustled back in to place a cup of coffee in front of Swede, along with the biggest cinnamon roll Buck had ever seen.

He tried unsuccessfully to hide his grin. "Swede was just saying that the Boston Eatery seems to have a lot more to offer lately."

Swede glowered at Buck across the table. A blush colored Lacey's cheeks, but her lush mouth curved in a shy smile. "I'd better go stir the stew."

"Now see what you do?" Swede growled when she vanished into the kitchen again. "You scare her away."

Buck chuckled. The ugliness of the scene with Cale was fading, and he gladly hurried it along. "I don't think a girl like Lacey scares that easily. How do you expect to win her if you don't let her know she's being wooed?"

The bell jangled again. Two cowhands came in and took a table up front. Lacey hurried from the kitchen and stopped short. Revulsion and apprehension flitted through her green eyes.

"Hey, Lacey, gal!" the shorter of the two cowhands

shouted. A puckered scar pulled his mouth down on one side, making his smile grotesque. His hair was lank and greasy. "You change your place of business or something?"

With a pained glance at the other occupants of the room, she edged closer to the table and said softly, "I don't work for Jonas anymore, Hitch. I cook and serve tables for Mrs. Sims now. And that's *all* I do."

Before she could move he snatched her about the waist and hauled her onto his lap. "Aw, now, you don't mean that," Hitch whined. "Not with me. Why, you and me been tighter'n fingers in a glove. Hey, that was one of them double intenders, huh, Billy? Tighter than fingers in a glove. Get it?" He made an obscene gesture with his hands.

Lacey struggled to get up. "Let me go, Hitch."

The cowhand nuzzled his face in her neck and groped for her breast. His friend, a broad, barrel-shaped man with a black tooth center front, laughed. "Whoo-ee! Go to it, Hitch."

"I aim to, Billy, I aim to."

Lacey cried out as he cruelly squeezed her breast, then reached for the hem of her skirt. "Hush up, girl, I ain't gonna do nothing to you I ain't done before. It's been a long time, and I'm hornier than a two-peckered billy goat."

At the back of the room Swede soared to his feet. Buck stood and put a restraining hand on the man's chest. "Better let me handle this, friend. You're likely to kill the bastard."

"These animals *need* killing," Swede snarled.

The cowhands were still laughing and grabbing, while Lacey slapped at their hands and fought to get away.

"Where's your room now, honey? Me'n Billy here'll pay ya double, and you can take care of us both at the same time. That'd be real fun, wouldn't it?"

"Excuse me, gentlemen." Buck's sarcastic tone went over the cowhands heads.

"Wait your turn, mister. The whore's with us. You can have her when we're done."

Moving almost too fast to be seen, Buck plucked Lacey off the man's lap, set her aside, and snatched Hitch from his seat, too angry to notice the pain it caused his injured shoulder. The second cowhand leaped up, knocking his chair backward. His eyes widened as a blond giant appeared behind Buck, ham-sized hands fisted.

Clutching Hitch's shirt front, Buck held the smaller man just high enough so that he couldn't find purchase with his feet. "You're done now." His voice was soft, but with an edge that could skin a rattler. "This isn't a fancy house, and Lacey isn't in the business anymore. Like she told you, she cooks and serves food, nothing more. Now I suggest you find somewhere else to have your coffee."

Hitch went for his six-shooter. Buck slammed him against the wall. "Touch that .44 and you're a dead man."

"Come on, Hitch," Billy said apprehensively. "I think we best get on outta here."

Buck released Hitch, letting him slide down the wall. Anger contorted the cowhand's scarred face into an even uglier visage, but Hitch said nothing as he picked up his hat and headed for the door, Billy at his heels.

"Hey, Hitch."

The cowhand turned back and Buck said, "If I hear of you bothering Lacey again, I'll dig you out from beneath whatever rock you live under and knock every tooth out of that vile mouth of yours."

"No, my friend," Swede said, stepping between them. "This pleasure I want for myself. I tear him piece from piece and let coyotes play with him. Then a *real* punishment I would think up."

Looking a little less cocky, Hitch and his friend escaped out the door. Lacey threw herself into Buck's arms, tears of shame and humiliation raining down her face. He was about to hand her over to Swede's more willing arms when he felt his neck prickle. In the kitchen doorway, staring at him with anger and hurt, stood Tempest.

"How long are you going to keep up the silent act, Tempest?"

Buck braced a hand on the sideboard. A knife flashed as Tempest viciously chopped turnips for supper. He had a hunch she was imagining it was him she was cutting up with such vengeance. She thrust her chin higher and refused to answer.

At first he'd been pleased by her jealousy. It meant she cared, and his heart gloried in that. He closed his eyes and fought the need to touch her, to wrap his arms around her and never let go. It wouldn't be fair. She deserved better. Judas, he thought, how can life go up and down at the same time? To be so close to having everything he wanted yet unable to claim it was the cruelest joke fate had played on him yet. Death would be easier than this torture. He slammed his fist on the counter. "Dammit, woman, talk to me. We have things to discuss, plans to make."

"What's there to plan?" she said, not looking at him. She knew she was acting like a jealous harpy, but she couldn't help it. Seeing Buck embracing Lacey had been a knife thrust to her heart. She wanted him to feel some pain too. "Early tomorrow morning we'll take the children to Viola, then start searching the ruins. Once we have the money, you can return to the dissolute life you're so fond of, and I can resume my own pursuits."

Buck gritted his teeth and let the last part of her diatribe pass. "How do we decide where to start?"

"Considering how little time Skeet had, he probably

didn't get far from the road. So we'll start with the ruins that are the closest and the easiest to reach."

Her calm formality would have amused him once. Now, he wanted to shake her until her head rattled. She wasn't making this any easier. "All right, maybe there isn't that much to plan. Maybe what we really need to talk about is why you've been giving me the cold shoulder ever since we left Viola's this morning."

"There isn't anything to discuss about that either." Chop, chop. More vegetables severed into tiny pieces.

"You're jealous." Suddenly, he needed to hear her say it. To hell with being fair.

"I am not."

"You damn well are, why don't you admit it?"

Her eyes flashed amber fire. Her chin jerked higher. "You aren't my husband, Buck Maddux, which means you're free to sleep with any woman you like. Or, in this case, any child you like, since that's practically what Lacey is . . . a child."

Buck's lips drew back from his teeth in a savage snarl. "Lacey hasn't been a child since her father raped her when she was five years old."

She stared up at him, horrified. "Her own father?"

"Yes, her own father. She ran away with a cowhand when she was twelve and was working a bawdy house three months later. It was that or starve."

Tempest dropped the knife onto the counter and covered her face with her hands. "Holy Mary, Mother of God. That poor girl."

Buck put the table between them to keep from reaching for her. Once he had her in his arms again, he wouldn't let go until he was buried too deep inside her to back off.

After a long minute, she straightened and dropped her hands. "She's in love with you."

"She might *think* she is, but it's only gratitude. I gave her money—"

"It is customary in such circumstances, I understand," she said stiffly, not wanting to hear more.

Buck cursed. "Not for what you're thinking. I told her to hide it, save up a stash until she had enough to get her to Provo or Salt Lake City where she could find decent work, maybe even get married. She's grateful to me, Tempest, that's all."

Without meaning to, he moved closer. He couldn't stand to see her hurting, especially when he was the cause of it. "Hey . . ."

Tempest didn't have to look to know he had donned his devil's mask. She heard it in his voice, like velvet sandpaper. He was hoping to joke her out of her temper. She knew she should let him and put an end to the whole ridiculous subject.

"There's nothing to be jealous of, sweetheart," he murmured. "I'm all yours, heart, soul and"—he winked and held out his arms—"magnificent body."

How she wished it were true. "But you were *hers* first."

The grin never faltered. It was sin itself. "Man's got to learn how to pleasure a woman somehow. You wouldn't want me to be clumsy and inefficient, would you?"

His eyes danced blue fire over her skin . . . and seemed to penetrate deep inside to the very hub of her femininity. Tempest's stomach somersaulted. In self-defense she clung to her anger. "You were married, Buck. If that didn't teach you enough about pleasuring a woman, all the soiled doves in the world aren't going to help now."

But he hadn't pleasured Ellen. In his innocence and selfishness all he'd done was get her pregnant. Then he'd killed her. The fire in his eyes died, leaving only ashes to shadow their depths. His voice was toneless, as dead as he had yearned to be fifteen years ago. As dead as Ellen and their baby. "Can't argue that."

Horrified at the pain in his eyes, Tempest watched him head for the door. A voice told her it was what she had wanted—to hurt him. But it hurt her too. "Buck, I'm sorry. I didn't mean to bring up your wife. I was jealous. There, are you happy? I said it, I'm jealous."

Only the high trill of Angel's laughter down by the creek and the ringing of a hammer marred the silence as Ronan built the children a play fort from broken roof timbers. Slowly Buck turned and gazed at her. Something about the proud, stubborn jut of Tempest's chin contrasted by the vulnerability in her eyes turned his heart to gravy. Tears glistened on her cheeks. For Lacey? For him? She certainly wouldn't allow herself to cry for her own sake. Without meaning to, he found himself beside her. He wiped the moisture from her cheeks and kissed her. His voice roughened with emotion. "You have nothing to be jealous of, Tempest. No other woman has made me burn and ache the way you do. No other woman has put dreams into my head that I haven't dared to allow myself in years. Judas, I want you so desperately it keeps me strung tighter than a whore's corset. Simply being close to you makes me shake all over."

Tempest took his trembling hands in her own and kissed the palms. Her tenderness nearly brought him to his knees.

"Hell, woman." He crushed her to him more tightly. "Don't you know what you are to me? You're fire and rain, summer and sunshine." Bracketing her face with his big hands, he tilted her head up to his. "You're the very air I breathe."

His lips came down on hers, but it was not a tender kiss. Tempest tasted the desperation, the need, the barely controlled power that made his hard muscular body shake. She exulted in the bruising pressure of his mouth, in the passion she aroused in him, in the beauty of his words. Her mouth opened beneath his and her teeth nipped his lower lip.

Groaning with pleasure, Buck tightened his grip. His hands foraged up and down her slender back, exploring her curves, memorizing them. He ached to be inside her. Ached so fiercely he thought he might die of it. A sound, half-moan, half-purr, vibrated deep in his throat as he struggled with his conscience. He had vowed not to let this happen again. "Judas, woman, you don't know what you do to me."

"Perhaps, but I know what I'd like to do." She gloried in the flinching of his powerful muscles and his growl of pleasure as she stroked his chest. Suddenly, his hands were under her shirt, gliding up her rib cage to close over her breasts. She arched against him until she could feel the rigid maleness of him pressing into her stomach.

Buck thought he would shatter. Drawing back, he stared down into her flushed face. Her lips, swollen and rosy from his kiss, were parted, her breath as fast and ragged as his own. Slitted brown eyes, slumbrous with amber-flecked passion, gazed back at him from a thick fringe of lashes. She had never looked more appealing. "Sweetheart," he whispered, "you better get away from me right now, or I'm going to haul this sideboard in front of the door and ravish you in every way there is to ravish a woman." Bending, he kissed her again, hard and quick. "Only I'm afraid, with you, I'll always want more."

Forcing himself to turn away, he went to the door and braced trembling hands on either side of the opening, trying to slow his breathing and bring his body under control before he stepped outside.

He jerked when she touched his back. "Why are you going, Buck? I want you, is there something wrong with that?" She pressed herself against his back and traced the hard planes of his chest through his shirt; the steel waffle of ribs, the flat, iron stomach. When her hands moved lower, he sucked in air and grimaced at the fierce pleasure of her uninhibited touch.

"I've never wanted a man the way I want you," she whispered. "Lovemaking was only a pleasant chore before, not really worth the trouble. But you make me want things I never thought of until you came along."

The ragged purr of her voice sent blood surging to his groin. Her hands seemed to note the change, and she moaned as she tested his masculinity through his denim trousers. Buck groaned. He reached to pull her hands away, and found he couldn't. Feeling the small fragile fingers explore him the way he wanted to explore her most intimate places, he knew he was lost. Yet he had to make her see reason. "I'll be leaving soon. Doesn't that make any difference to you?"

Bone buttons slid from their moorings, and her hand slipped inside. "Yes. It makes me want to enjoy all I can of you while you're here."

"Damn," he muttered harshly, "why isn't there a lock on this door?"

"All you have to do is draw in the latch."

He shivered as her warm breath penetrated his cotton shirt. "Judas."

With one of his lightning moves that never failed to astonish Tempest, he had the door closed, the latch drawn, and her spine pressed to the rough wood. His mouth ravaged hers, while he kneaded her breasts and his hips moved seductively against hers. With more speed than delicacy he tore open her shirt and camisole and buried his face between her breasts. She held him there, a willing prisoner. "Suckle me, Buck. I've needed your mouth on me again. I've dreamed of it until I thought I would go mad."

Teasing her, he kissed and laved her breasts, avoiding the one spot where she most wanted his mouth, until she was panting and whimpering his name. Her breasts were swollen with need, the nipples as hard and aching as the part of his body he yearned to feel inside her. When at last his mouth closed over a proud nipple and he began to suck, she cried out.

"Keep that up and we'll have company we aren't prepared for, sweetheart," he warned, while one hand glided down to the juncture of her thighs. She squirmed and moaned, fueling the fire inside him. He muttered a stream of curses as he fumbled with the knotted twine that held up her trousers, winning a husky laugh from her. And all the time, her busy hands tortured him, promising an ecstasy he wasn't sure he could survive.

"This is one time I wish you wore skirts like other women," he muttered as he knelt to peel the trousers down her legs. For a few moments, he stayed there on his knees admiring her bare legs, running his hands over them and up under her drawers to the softness of her small bottom. "Ah, God, Tempest. You're so beautiful, it makes me weak just to look at you. Tell me you aren't wearing that damned combination thing with the back flap instead of a split-crotch. I'd like to strip you totally naked and spend an hour simply looking at you, but someone's bound to come in eventually, and I can't wait that long anyhow."

Before she found breath to answer, his fingers located the split in her drawers and dipped into hot, humid heaven. Tempest's knees buckled.

"Hang on, little mustang," he whispered. "Brace yourself on my shoulders. I'm going to take you for a ride."

Slipping off her drawers, he kissed her belly and down to the secret nook of his fantasies. Her fingers dug into his shoulders, but he ignored the pain in his wound, knowing she hadn't meant to hurt him. When her legs began to quiver and he knew she was ready to come apart, he rose to his feet and kissed his way from her breasts to her neck and the sensitive spot beneath her ear.

When her trembling fingers found and freed him from his clothes, and her hot hand closed over him, he stiffened with a ragged groan. "Judas, don't move, sweetheart."

"Did I hurt you?"

He leaned his forehead against hers and chuckled. "Yeah, you hurt me all right. You've got me aching so bad, I'm afraid we'll be done before we ever get started."

But keeping still was impossible. She reveled in her power to bring him to his knees with desire for her. She cherished the proof of his passion. Then his hand slipped between her legs again and the world shifted.

Her throaty moan drove him wild. He buried his face in her hair and drank in her scent. Raw turnips, apples, cinnamon, and aroused female made an odd mix, yet it drugged him senseless. Talons of lust shredded what was left of his control.

"The bed, Buck. Now. I want you inside me."

Her words pounded in Buck's brain, echoing the throb of the blood pulsing through his veins. Valiantly he fought for control. He didn't want to take her against the wall like an animal. There was nothing in life but this, he thought dazedly as he struggled to bring himself back from the brink she had driven him to. Too soon. Too soon. He hadn't even thrust inside her yet, and still, the joy, the pleasure, the unending rapture of it all seared him so thoroughly he knew he would never be the same.

He was wrong. Tempest wrapped her arms about his neck and her legs around his waist. Her frenzied writhing found its mark. Buck felt her sultry heat lure him home. The battle was lost. He no longer recalled what the fight had been about, but it was lost just the same. With an agonized groan of mingled pleasure and resignation, he thrust into her moist welcoming heat.

When Buck came back to earth, Tempest's head was nestled in his neck. Her soft, ragged breaths warmed his skin. Her arms clung tightly. Her legs gripped his hips, her ankles locked behind him. And he was still inside her.

Ah, Jesus, what had he done?

She was fire and earth, sweetness and desire, ecstasy and hope. He'd wanted to make love to her, slow and easy, tender and gentle. A physical expression of all he felt for her. Instead, he'd shoved her against a wall and taken her like a whore. Damn his selfish hide. He ought to be horsewhipped. Tempest drew back and gazed at him as if his groan of disgust and agony had been audible. One glance at the brown depths of her passion-glazed eyes and her well-kissed mouth and he felt himself harden again, stretching her slick, hot core and heightening the exquisite sensation of being one with her.

This time his groan *was* audible.

Not only had he been rough and crude, Buck had broken a promise. "I'm sorry," he said into her hair, unable to look at her. "I'm so sorry."

Tempest stiffened in his arms. Judas, he couldn't even apologize to her without inflicting pain. "Not for making love to you," he said on a weary sigh. "I'm sorry I wasn't more gentle. And that I didn't pull out in time to protect you. I don't know what happened. I've never lost control like that before."

Confusion erased the pain in her eyes. "To protect me? You mean . . . withdraw before you . . . ?

Buck nodded. "You ought to pound my head in with that fry pan of yours."

Tempest laid her palm on his cheek and shook her head

in denial. "White Cloud Woman taught me how to protect myself, Buck. Besides, I . . ." She thought better of her confession of love and let the sentence hang. Something puzzled her. He'd said he'd never lost control with a woman before her. Yet, he had been with other women since his wife—Lacey proved that. "Have you always withdrawn . . . ?

"Except with Ellen . . . my wife."

"Even . . . Lacey?"

"Yes."

For fifteen years, he had kept himself from spilling his seed inside a woman. And Lacey had been only one of many, Tempest didn't fool herself about that. Why had he lost control with her? What made her different? Was it possible that he loved her? Tenderness squeezed her heart.

Before she realized what he was doing, he pulled out of her body, removed her legs from around his waist and let her slide to the floor. "It won't happen again. None of this will happen again. It was a mistake."

"Don't say that, Buck. I told you, I can protect myself."

Ignoring her, he stepped away and buttoned his trousers. She stood there staring at the cold, implacable face that had been so tender, so loving a few minutes ago, and struggled to understand.

He found a clean cloth, wet it, and handed it to her without meeting her gaze. She blushed, realizing what it was for. Putting her hand on his arm as he turned toward the door, she begged, "Please, Buck, don't turn this into something ugly. It wasn't, it was beautiful. And it was right."

His eyes blazed, banishing the bleakness and pain. "It *wasn't* right. How could it be? In a few days I'll be gone. I'm a drifter, an irresponsible, no-good bastard who'd ruin your life the same way I've ruined the lives of everyone else I've loved. You and I had sex, Tempest. It was good." He closed his eyes and took a deep breath, unable to keep his hard face from softening. "More than good." His eyes opened and he glared at her. "But it was just sex. The only difference is that I didn't have to pay for it."

With that rapier blow, he yanked her from in front of the door, jerked it open, and slammed it shut behind him.

Left alone in the dim house, Tempest pinched off the flood of emotional rain that threatened to drown her. He didn't mean what he said. He was only running scared. He had given her the treasure of his seed. That had to mean something, didn't it?

Chapter Twenty

On a rocky, precipitous side of Deception Canyon, Jonas Creedy lay belly-down on a flat boulder warmed by the sun, and peered through binoculars at the slope on the other side of Carcass Creek. The man and woman were searching the Indian ruins for Skeet Whitney's stolen money; there was no question in Jonas's mind about that. He would let them find it, then kill Maddux and take the money—and the woman.

A large red ant crawled onto Jonas's dark hand. He flicked it off with a curse. Feeling the gaze of the three men beside him, he brought himself back under tight control. A warrior never allowed minor distractions like insects to break his concentration. The ant people were revered for their strength, their patience, their tenacity. A warrior learned from the creatures who shared the earth with him, he patterned himself after them, made their virtues his virtues, their strengths his strengths, their wisdom his wisdom. Jonas had learned all that as a child in the Apache camp and had proven he was as good a warrior as any of them.

But he was a white man now, with the whites' superior possessions, wealth, and power. Once he had Tempest as his wife, he would also have the respect a white man could expect.

A faint shout and a nudge from Morgan Paine's elbow recalled his attention to the Indian ruins across the canyon. Tempest waved for Maddux to come. She had found something. Jonas couldn't see what she was showing him, but it didn't take much to figure out what it must be. The time had come. At last Jonas could rid himself of Maddux and take what should, by rights, belong to him.

"They found it, boss," Morgan said, sighting down his rifle. "You want me to kill Maddux now?"

"No, he's mine. You and Howard spread out. If I miss, work your way around behind him. But don't kill him. I want that pleasure myself." Lifting his rifle to his shoulder, Jonas sighted on Maddux's broad back. Slowly, his veins surging with the thrill of the moment, he squeezed the trigger.

The bullet whistled past Buck's ear an instant before the report of the gun resounded in the air. Tempest screamed. The Indian water jug she was showing him fell to the earth and shattered. Instinctively, he threw himself on top of her. The sharp edges of the broken pottery slashed his hands and forearms, but he barely felt the cuts because of his fear for her.

"Buck?" Frantically she shoved at him. "Oh, sweet Mary, please don't be dead."

"I'm fine, the bullet missed me." Barely. If he hadn't bent down to get a better look at the pottery, he would be dead now. But Tempest could just as easily have moved into the bullet's path. The thought filled him with terror and rage. "Are you all right?"

"Yes."

"Thank God," he said, then, "Stay down."

He peeked over the rock wall, his Colt cocked and ready. He cursed himself for leaving his Winchester in his saddle scabbard. They'd left Spook and Othello in a nearby side canyon where there was plenty of grass—too far away to reach now. The rifle shot had come from across Deception Canyon and, narrow as the distance was, his six-shooter could do little damage from this distance, while the bush-whacker's rifle would be deadly. He wished he knew how many there were.

"Buck?" Tempest whispered, her voice shaky with fear. "Buck, we have to get out of here. We have to get back to the children. What if Jonas . . . ?" She couldn't finish the thought, it was too horrible.

But she didn't need to finish. Buck's thoughts paralleled hers. He understood her fear, because he felt it too. Last night both children had climbed onto his lap and begged for a story. Then Angel said, holding up three fingers, "I'm gonna be five in thith many more months. Did you know that?" He said no and told her what a big girl she was getting to be. After that she hit him with both barrels. *You'll be here, won't you, Papa Buck? You don't have to give me a prethent. If you'd be here, that would be all the prethent I'd want.* Damn, he thought, why did life have to be so difficult? Leaving Tempest was going to be agony enough. To leave those two small bundles of love, who had accepted him with such open and uncondemning hearts, would shatter him.

Keeping an eye on the rocks on the far side of the canyon, he drew Tempest close. "Stay calm, sweetheart. As long as Jonas and his men are after us, the children are safe. And as long as we stay behind this wall, we will be, too."

He didn't mention how easy it would be for their attackers to sneak down and across the creek, hidden by a bend in the canyon, then climb a draw to get behind them. The rear wall of the pit-house they had taken shelter in had crumbled, leaving them exposed from that direction. Fear hummed through his veins, sharpening his mind and reflexes. Battle instincts honed during his time in the Army fighting Indians, then later as a Montana ranch hand during the range wars, resurfaced. But Tempest's presence left him feeling vulnerable. Keeping her safe had to be his first priority, no matter what that involved.

He studied the scrubby hillside behind them. Higher up, the hill merged with a sandstone wall of rust and ocher sandstone, sculpted by centuries of sun, wind, and rain. On the rim grew junipers and pinyons, but here vegetation was sparse and few rocks were large enough to shelter them. Other than the crumbling pit-houses there was virtually no cover. Within the circle of his arm, he could feel Tempest tremble. Jonas wouldn't purposely kill her, but bullets had a way of finding innocent victims. As long as Buck was anywhere near her, she was in danger.

A hundred yards to their right a ravine cut into the hill, providing the only good cover within reach. Squeezing Tempest's shoulder, he said, "When I give the word, I want you to run like the wind until you reach those rocks at the edge of that side canyon where we left our mounts."

"What are you going to do?"

"Don't worry about me. Just get in that gully and stay there. I'll join you when I can."

Tempest watched him check the load in his .44 and felt a fear she had never known before. Not for herself. Jonas wanted her too badly to let her be hurt. But he wanted Buck dead. She guessed Buck's intentions and went cold inside. He would sacrifice himself to protect her. Her first instinct was to refuse to go, but she knew he would have a better chance if he didn't have to worry about her. Taking his head in her hands, she drew him to her for a kiss. For a long moment they stared at each other, emotion softening the fear in their eyes. There might never be another chance to tell him she loved him. She opened her mouth, but the words were drowned in an explosion of rifle fire and the splintering of rock as a bullet struck the wall. Buck shoved her down and returned fire.

"Now, Tempest. Run!"

For an instant she didn't move, her gaze drinking him in as if to memorize him as he gave his attention to the shooters across the way. Then she gathered her courage and ran.

Feeling her leave his side, Buck's heart stopped. His breath lodged in his throat. Bracing his arm on top of the rock wall, he fired rapidly to force Jonas and his men to keep their heads down until Tempest reached safety. Only when his weapon was empty did he stop. While he reloaded, he looked frantically toward the side canyon, breathing a sigh of relief when he saw no sign of her.

Another shot came from across the chasm. Buck waited, hoping the shooter would fire again so he could get a bead on where the bastard was hiding. The most likely spot was a dense cluster of rocks two hundred feet above the valley floor, almost directly across from him. He aimed and squeezed off a shot. An answering volley came from a few feet to the left. This time he aimed for the flash and was rewarded with the sound of a cry.

Buck reloaded and started for the side canyon, crouching, crawling, taking cover where he could. Dirt flew into his face as a bullet plowed the earth directly in front of him. Momentarily blinded, he swiped at his eyes with his sleeve. Blood smeared the fabric from a nick in his brow.

He lay still, watching, hoping Jonas would assume his quarry had been hit and would expose himself. Nothing happened.

After several minutes Buck took off again, running in a zigzag pattern to dodge the bullets flying at him. When he reached the side canyon, he threw himself over the edge and slid to the bottom where he stumbled and went to his knees. Tempest was beside him in seconds, her arms encircling him. The old wound in his shoulder from the day Cale arrived throbbed from being slammed into the ground, but there was no blood, giving him hope that it hadn't reopened.

"Are you all right?" she asked, helping him up.

She'd nearly gone crazy listening to the shooting and wondering if he'd been hit. A million fears had weighted her mind as she'd waited for what seemed like hours. The only thing that kept her from going back to be with him was the knowledge that she would only endanger him more. When she first heard the scrabbling noises of boots at the edge of the gully above her, her heart leaped with joy. Then she reminded herself the boots could as easily belong to Jonas as to Buck. So she remained in hiding until he came into view. Now he was safe beside her once more, and she felt an overwhelming need to protect him. "We've got to get out of here. Jonas won't give up until he sees you dead."

Buck was too busy studying the boulder-strewn defile to answer. It was rough and narrow, and he couldn't see past all the bends to determine how far it went. But Tempest was right, they couldn't stay where they were. Jonas would come after them. From the right vantage point on the rim above, Jonas and his men could shoot them like ducks in a barrel.

"Tempest, you're going to have to ride to town, get

some help. Damn, why did Cale have to go off now when I need him?"

"I can't leave you here to fight them by yourself," Tempest protested.

"What the hell do you think you can do to help? Dammit, just do as I say. Get Swede and your father, anyone you can. And hurry."

"No. How far do you think they'd let me get before they caught up with me? I'd never make it to town, and you know it. You only want me away from you so I'll be safe. But I wouldn't be, don't you see that? If nothing else, I can reload for you."

Buck ground his teeth in frustration. Unless he could get to Spook and his rifle, he had only his Colt which he could reload by himself. She was right, though. Jonas would never let her ride off for help. He'd take her captive and use her to get him to throw down his weapon.

The air had grown markedly cooler. What he could see of the sky was still blue, but the wind blowing out of the small canyon carried the scent of rain, maybe even snow. Following the side canyon to the plateau was risky, yet he saw no other choice. He had one hope. Praying Spook could hear him, he gave a shrill whistle.

"What are you doing?" Tempest asked.

"Whistling for the horses."

"What if Jonas shoots them?"

"Pray he doesn't. They may be our only chance."

Buck hauled himself to his feet. "Stay here. I'm going to check things out and watch for them."

He hadn't gone ten feet before he heard her behind him. "Dammit, Tempest, I said stay put. I want you out of danger."

"I want you out of danger, too," she retorted, her chin rising.

"I'm the one with the weapon, remember? There's nothing you can do, and no sense placing yourself at risk need-lessly. Understand?"

"Yes, I understand."

He started walking again. The skitter of boots over the rocky ground behind him came as no surprise. If he hadn't been so frightened for her, he might have smiled. She had mettle, his mustang filly. He only hoped it didn't get her killed.

As they drew closer to the main canyon, Buck paused to listen. The sound was faint, but he thought he heard the thud of hooves. He whistled again.

"Are they coming?" Tempest asked, moving up along-side him.

"You don't follow orders very well, do you?"

"If you get hurt you might be glad to have me here." *And if you die, I intend to be beside you.*

He didn't look at her, he was too busy scanning the canyon rim and its mouth for movement—equine or human. But his voice softened: "I'm glad to have you here now, little mustang. I'd rather have you safe is all."

She put a finger to his cheek where it had been nicked by a flying rock chip. Taking her hand in his, he kissed her grubby fingers. He wanted to tell her that her life had come to mean more than his own, that he would rather die than let anything happen to her. The words wouldn't come. He curled his hand around her neck and drew her to him for a quick kiss, trying to show her what he couldn't say.

The unmistakable thud of hooves and the crack of gun-fire wrenched his gaze back to the canyon entrance. Moments later, Spook galloped around the corner and up the dry creek bed, followed more slowly by Othello.

"Good boy." Buck stroked the horse's jaw affectionately. "You've earned yourself a beer, Spook. Providing we get out of here alive."

Othello shoved his black nose under the taller Spook's neck with his own demand for attention. Buck gladly complied.

"What now?" Tempest asked.

He studied the slender side canyon. "Think this draw leads anywhere?"

"I don't know. Skeet used some of these dry creek beds to get up to the plateau, but I'm not sure which ones." Panic jolted her as she realized his intent. She didn't want to climb the plateau. It would take so long, and she was desperate to get home to her children.

Buck glanced up to where low clouds were turning blue skies to pewter gray. He didn't like the idea of Jonas being able to reach town before them, said a silent prayer that Ronan and Rooster were doing their best to guard the children as well as Viola and Lacey. He wanted no one hurt. "We could hole up here until dark, then head home," he said, voicing his thoughts, "but it might start raining. If the temperature drops, we could get snow. It's damn cold now." *And Jonas will be waiting.*

"We have coats and blankets and slickers," Tempest said, determined to put a good face on her fear and not succumb to panic. "We even have food. If we need to, we can start a fire."

"And let Jonas know where to find us?"

"He already knows. If we haven't come out by dark, he'll probably come looking for us." *Or go after my babies.*

Buck flipped the stirrup over the saddle and checked Spook's cinch. "Wouldn't that be nice? We could simply wait and shoot him when he showed up. I'm afraid he'll be a little too cautious for that, though."

Again his gaze traveled up the twisted, narrow defile. Before he could make a decision, rifle fire erupted and a rock splintered behind them.

"Judas!" Grabbing Tempest, Buck shielded her between

his body and the mule's. When the firing stopped, he threw her into the saddle. "Ride, woman. Head up the canyon as far as you can go. I'll catch up with you."

Buck whipped his rifle out of the scabbard and sighted down its metallic length. Othello moved nervously beneath Tempest, but she held him in place. The idea of leaving Buck terrified her.

"Go, dammit, get out of here." Buck slapped Othello's rump.

Tempest fought the confused mule until another bullet whizzed past, barely missing Buck's head and forcing her to realize the danger she was putting them in with her stubbornness. Jabbing her heels into the mule's soot-colored sides, she galloped up the draw, her heart pounding to the sound of gun shots reverberating behind her. The dry creek bed had more twists than a pig's tail. It was too rough to allow her to keep up much of a pace. Boulders all but blocked the passage in spots, and sometimes Othello had to scramble up inclines that, when the creek ran full, would be small waterfalls.

The sound of Buck's Winchester returning fire dwindled as she climbed higher and higher up the snaking rock corridor. It seemed as though she and the mule had been struggling for hours when she realized the shooting had stopped. Terror speared through her. Had Buck been hit? Her heart clenched at the thought. She strained to hear the ring of hooves climbing behind her. Beneath her thick wool coat, her body trembled. Finally she heard what she'd been listening for and her pulse leaped.

But what if it wasn't Buck? What if he was dead, and the man following her was Jonas Creedy?

She wished she had her rifle—or the derringer. She wished she had stayed with Buck. The thought of his life's blood draining into the dry red soil to nurture prickly pear cactus and yucca and spiny greasewood shrubs tore at her heart. She couldn't bear to lose him.

The approaching horse drew nearer. Because of the sharp twists and turns she wouldn't be able to see the rider until he was too close to escape. She thought of calling out, demanding that he identify himself, but her breathing was fast and hard, her pulse hammering in her ears, and she feared she wouldn't be able to utter a sound. Othello moved restively beneath her, sensing her panic. *Don't just sit here, you yellow-livered ninny,* she scolded herself. Dismounting, she searched for the heaviest rock she could lift above her head. Then she climbed onto a boulder at the edge of the turn, and waited. If Jonas showed up, she would know Buck was dead. Nothing short of death would keep Buck from being there to protect her. Stemming the premature grief that closed her throat and twisted her insides, she silently prayed: Please, I'm begging . . . in the name of the Father and the Son and the Holy Ghost, please don't let Buck be dead.

She couldn't go on without him, didn't want to go on. But she would. For her children. She would live for them, though her heart would be buried with the man she loved.

A dark muzzle appeared first, lengthening slowly into a horse's rosy brown head. Tempest's hopes soared.

Spook shied. Out of the side of his eye Buck glimpsed a figure above him on a boulder, ready to crash a rock down on his head. Instantly, his Colt was in his hand, his finger on the trigger. When he saw it was Tempest and how close he had come to shooting her, his heart nearly stopped. Then he wanted to wring her neck. "What in almighty thunder do you think you're doing up there, woman?"

Tempest's arms trembled with the weight of her weapon. Carefully, she lowered the rock to the ground. Now that she knew he was safe, her terror switched to anger. "Defending myself, of course, in case I didn't like who showed up. What did you think I was doing, crocheting doilies?''

"You stubborn fool. I'm beginning to doubt any man could tame you."

"Any man stupid enough to try deserves to have his head bashed in," she retorted. "I'm not an animal to be tamed, Buck Maddux. Or trained or controlled."

A devilish grin broke across his tired, dusty face. A midnight brow lifted. "Or ridden?" he asked.

Tempest scowled. Damn him. She wanted desperately to throw herself into his arms and let him soothe away her fears, but she knew it wasn't the time. "Never mind your nonsense. What happened? Where's Jonas?"

"I didn't stick around to see. Why did you stop here? Is this as far as you could go?" He peered up the defile and saw only boulders and stunted willows.

"No." She climbed from her perch with shaky legs. "I thought it would be better to wait and make sure it wasn't Jonas sneaking up on me."

"It's all right if I sneak up on you?"

"Can't you ever be serious?"

Yeah, I can be damned serious, he thought sourly.

Especially when it came to her being hurt. But it had been too long since he'd let himself feel anything except desire for a woman. He no longer knew how to deal with his finer emotions—if he ever had. Usually he did his best to feel nothing. When that didn't work, he retreated behind his mask of deviltry. Or got angry. Unfortunately, now wasn't the time for either, or for the strong urge in him to take her in his arms.

"Well, what do we do now?" Tempest asked impatiently.

He looked up the steep, crooked corridor toward the top of the plateau. "We keep going, unless you have a better idea."

"We have to get to the children."

Buck heard her desperation. He wanted to reassure her, promise her everything would be all right, but that was a guarantee he couldn't give. "We have two choices—stay here and shoot it out with Jonas ... outnumbered and outgunned ... or try to reach the top and find another way down. You choose."

Tempest bit her lip. "I've never been on top, so I'm not sure where else we can get down, except Dry and Cottonwood Canyons ... and they're far away, clear beyond Heartsease. There are others, we'll simply have to keep close to the edge and find one."

"So be it." He motioned for her to take the lead. If anyone caught up to them, he wanted it to be his back exposed to their bullets, not Tempest's. If he were alone, he'd wait and ambush Creedy when the bastard rode up. But Buck knew Tempest would make sure she was right there in the middle of it all. He had to get her somewhere safe. Then he would deal with Creedy and his henchmen.

Shadows in the deep, ragged canyon thickened as storm clouds sped day toward an early night. The only sounds as Buck and Tempest wound their way up the corkscrewlike course were the ring of horseshoes on rock, the rhythmic huff of the animals' breaths, the creak of leather and an occasional chirp from a startled bird, or the warning bark of a squirrel. Cacti and junipers were replaced with willows and serviceberry bushes, water birch and above, near the rim, pines. The higher they climbed, the colder it became, the promise of snow more threatening. There wasn't room to ride side by side, limiting conversation, even if either had known what to say. Their thoughts were too heavy with worry for each other, and for Angel and Ethan.

Before they reached the top it began to rain. Stopping long enough to don yellow slickers, Tempest silently handed Buck a few hard, dry biscuits to eat. By the time they emerged onto the broad, pinyon-dotted plateau, the rain had become sleet. Night would soon be upon them, and Buck had yet to find them adequate shelter.

Tempest closed her mind to the icy rain and wondered if Angel and Ethan had been tucked into bed yet, if Viola had told them a story. She peered back at Buck, yearning for the comfort she could find in his arms. The kind she wanted to rely on for years to come, years shared with her children and the man she loved. But that simply wasn't to be. The thought left her empty and drained. She slowed Othello, dropping back so that she'd at least be close enough to talk to Buck. Before she could utter a word, a bullet sliced between them, so close she felt the breeze of its passing on her cheek.

"Sonuvabitch!" Buck wheeled Spook about. "That way," he shouted, pointing south. "Ride hard for the trees. I'll cover you."

Tempest knew better than to argue. She rode.

Chapter Twenty-One

Buck paused only long enough to fire an answering shot before he galloped after Tempest. They rode hard, keeping to the dense pinyon forest until their mounts began to tire, then they slowed to a walk. The rain had ceased but it was deadly cold. Mist puffed from the animals' nostrils. Buck signaled for a halt. He strained to hear sounds of pursuit behind them, but could make out only the heavy breathing of their mounts and the thundering of his own heart.

"Do you think we lost him?" Tempest panted.

"We'd be fools to count on it. I'm going to double back and check it out. You stay here." He turned Spook toward the side canyon, then halted. Looking at Tempest over his shoulder, he said, "You even think about following me, and I'm gone. You understand that, woman? I'll ride off and leave you to Creedy."

She knew better than to believe him, but she also knew he needed to focus all his concentration on the task at hand; worrying about her would only distract and endanger him. "I won't follow. I promise."

An eternity later, Buck returned, calling out softly before riding into the thick trees where he had left her.

"What happened?" she asked when he walked Spook up to her. He looked exhausted and cold and as miserable as she was.

"Nothing. Didn't see anyone." White puffs of mist dissipated in the wet air as he spoke. "Come on, let's get out of here. Jonas and his men must be somewhere close, and I'm not too eager to bump into them."

Tempest kneed her reluctant mule out of the shelter of the trees to ride alongside Buck. It was sleeting. She looked up through the stinging crystals at the low, gray sky. "I wish it would snow. I'd feel better if our tracks were wiped out."

Buck didn't point out that, being half-Apache, Jonas Creedy could probably track a duck through water. "If my guess is right, you'll get your wish long about dark. Maybe he'll give up then."

"Are we going to keep going until we find another way down? It would be awfully dangerous trying to descend anything like Treachery Canyon in this weather."

"Treachery Canyon?"

"That's what I've been calling that horrid snake's trail we climbed up. It was treacherous enough dry and in daylight. At night, in the rain, it'll be slick as pig snot, and we'd have to worry about flash floods, too. Snow would eliminate the danger of floods, but we wouldn't be able to see where we were going."

"We can always build a temporary shelter and hole up here somewhere. Don't worry, we'll make out fine."

"I know," she said, trying to sound braver than she felt. "I was thinking about the children."

He didn't doubt her worry over Angel and Ethan. He

was worried, too. But he could do nothing about them at the moment. His first priority had to be getting their mother safely off the mountain. A fierce protectiveness kept his guts tumbling like butter in a churn. The idea of anything happening to her terrified him. "Come on, let's get going," he said, kneeing Spook to a faster pace.

Establishing a meandering course designed to confuse and confound their pursuers, Buck used every means at his disposal to cover their trail. The muddy ground didn't help. He kept to a rocky path as much as possible and at times erased their tracks with a piece of brush. Finally, after two hours of zigzagging and backtracking and praying, the sleet turned to large, fat snowflakes and they breathed easier, knowing the snow would quickly fill in the tracks and leave no trace of their passing until the storm ended. They were following a rocky precipitous ridge when Tempest spotted an odd square-shaped structure.

"Sweet Mary. It's a cabin."

The crude hut was only ten feet square, made of sandstone slabs. Poles laid across the top and covered with brush, sod, and thin sheets of rock made up the roof. Leather creaked as Buck swung himself out of the saddle. The entrance was only four feet high. He crouched and peered inside. "Not much in here," he called as he entered.

The ethereal glow of the snow-white world outside provided a dim light that filtered in through a generous sprinkling of chinks in the rock walls. A crude fireplace took up one end. What remained of an ancient saddle that had housed more than one rodent family, and provided a few winter meals for them as well, cluttered one corner. A few bones lay scattered about, left behind by a much larger predator than a mouse or squirrel. Buck figured it had been decades since any human had taken shelter there. He sensed Tempest standing behind him. Unlike him, she was able to stand upright without brushing her head on the cobwebbed ceiling.

"It's not much, but it will do us fine for one night." Buck knelt at the fireplace and poked at the rubble on the hearth with a stick he found on the floor. A layer of dirt thick enough to smother a man covered what ashes remained.

Together they lugged saddles and gear inside. Leaving Tempest to arrange their belongings, Buck went back out to hobble the horses in a dense stand of pines where they would be shielded from the storm. Much as he regretted exposing Tempest to a night like this in a drafty hovel, he was grateful for the shelter. The tiny snowflakes of a full-blown storm had replaced the first fat tentative flakes as the weather settled in for the night. At least it would hide their tracks and wash away the scent of smoke, allowing them to risk a fire. After three more trips outside, he decided they had enough wood to last the night. With her usual pragmatic efficiency, Tempest had wedged a saddle blanket into the crack above the door, creating a curtain to diminish the cold. Another blanket hung against the windward wall like a tapestry. A small fire blazed merrily on a freshly cleaned hearth, the single note of cheer on a miserable night. Tempest opened two cans of beans and handed one to Buck with a spoon.

"We could set the cans in the coals after a bit and warm the beans, if you want to wait that long," she said as she joined him on the bedrolls spread on the floor.

"Too hungry." Buck spooned the beans into his mouth while he kept one eye out for visitors through the cracks which made fine peepholes.

"I'll cook some bacon and biscuits as soon as there are some good coals," Tempest offered between bites.

"Good, I'm still starved." He dropped his spoon into

the empty can and set it aside. Glancing up at the ceiling, he said, "Suppose there are any centipedes up there?"

She grinned. "You can sleep outside if you'd rather."

"I'll pass." As long as she was with him, he could handle the cramped space and the centipedes. Bean sauce glistened on her lower lip. Without thinking, he wiped it off with a finger. Watching him lick it off, Tempest slicked her tongue over her lips, and instantly a conflagration blazed between them. Judas, he couldn't even look at her without wanting her so badly he shook.

Buck ordered himself to rein in his lust. If he made love to Tempest again, he wanted it to be with gentleness and love, not savagely like the last time. With his blood still racing from the day's danger and fear, he knew if he touched her now it would be with a wild explosive passion having little to do with love and everything to do with a desperately needed physical release.

Nor was he convinced that the herbs she used to prevent conception were reliable. He didn't want to leave her in the same condition Skeet had when he'd got himself killed.

Ah hell, that was only partly true. Buck's dreams lately had taken a new twist. Now he saw them sharing a home as well as a bed, raising Angel and Ethan together, Tempest rounded with his babe. He imagined putting his hand on her swollen belly and feeling the baby kick inside her. He imagined holding it after it was born, a tiny little filly like her mother with amber sparkles in brown eyes, or a boy, dark and raven-haired, except for a touch of white over his forehead, and with eyes like a summer day.

God, how he wished he could make that dream come true. But he loved her too much to burden her with a husband who would only let her down someday—even if she wanted him to stay, which she wouldn't.

"Buck?" Her voice was low, breathy, seductive. The need in her eyes so closely matched his own it ripped at his self-control. She leaned toward him, her lips glistening, begging to be kissed.

Cursing violently, Buck dragged her to him and ground his mouth against hers, tasting beans and woman and desire, an alluring blend he found irresistible. Her tongue danced with his. Her hands raked his hair, her thumbs lightly stroking his temples, then moving down to discover the sensitive spot below his ears. She traced his brows, his cheekbones, his jaw, as though memorizing them. A ridiculous notion, he knew. But his hands were doing the same with her, and he very definitely was trying to memorize her every feminine texture and shape.

And, oh God, she smelled as good as she tasted. He drank in the earthy, homey, bread flour–type fragrance that was her own, tinged now with wood smoke and canned beans.

"Aw, Judas, Tempest," he whispered raggedly. "God help me, I can't turn away from you."

"Why should you try?" she whispered as she reached for his waistband.

He wasn't sure anymore. The reasons were fading, driven out by his all-consuming need to be one with her.

Now and forever.

Their lovemaking was wild and ecstatic, an expression of all they'd endured, all they yearned for in the future, and the fear of never having another chance. Buck told himself this moment alone would be heaven enough for a lifetime. But a small voice within cried, Liar. Each new touch, each sight, scent, and sound was fresh fuel to his need for her. If he lived to be a hundred and enjoyed this pleasure every day, he would never get enough of her.

Shit! Jonas hated snow. The icy moisture found every opening in his clothing, no matter how small. It slithered down his neck and froze him like a brown-skinned icicle. Jonas refused to think of himself as a "redskin." The term redskin outraged him. Anything that reminded him of what he was—and wasn't—filled him with a killing rage.

Watching the snow obliterate the tracks he had been following added to his fury. He tilted his head to study the sky. There was none. The entire world was gray and white, with a touch here and there of pine green, made extra dark by the startling contrast of the pristine snow falling thick as a woman's tears everywhere he looked. Snowflakes landed on his cheeks and melted there. Minuscule icicles clung to his brows and lashes. He lowered his head, shielding his face from the onslaught with his hat brim. Waste of time anyway, looking at the sky.

Jonas steered his horse around and started back the way he had come. He had become familiar with the plateaus in his search for the Spanish gold, but so much of the land looked alike that it was easy to get lost, and he had no hankering to spend the night in a snowstorm. He disliked wet weather. He didn't care how "un-Indian" it was to let something as minor as a little moisture and cold get to him; getting drenched to the skin and slowly freezing, outside in, was pure misery. He had taken pains to hide his weakness from his father's people. The Apache would have blamed such a flaw on his white blood. Jonas preferred to blame it on his Indian blood. As much as he hated the whites, he hated Indians more. Indians always ended up the losers. Jonas intended to win.

Three hours later, after a grueling trip back down the steep, slippery, godforsaken crack Maddux had led him up, Jonas gratefully let himself into the Sagebrush Princess through the back door. The saloon was closer than the ranch house. Not that there was anyone at the ranch to go home to anyway. Thanks to Buck Maddux.

Jonas would get him. Tomorrow or the next day, when

the storm abated. Wherever Maddux and Tempest had holed up, they would have to come out eventually, and he would be waiting for them. Matters would change drastically then. Maddux would be dead. And Tempest Whitney would be his.

Buck awoke in the middle of the night to discomfort in his lower regions. Beneath the pile of blankets and coats covering them, Tempest was wrapped around him like a snake in an apple tree. Her knee, just above his groin, weighed a ton on his full bladder. He eased the knee down, only to encounter a different sort of discomfort. One a great deal easier to live with, however. He lay there, savoring the feel of her in his arms, her naked breasts pressed to his side, her arm draped across his chest in what he liked to think of as a possessive gesture. Her breath on his shoulder was soft and warm, creating faint puffs of mist in the cold air. Outside, coyotes were yipping to announce a successful kill. Life went on. The reassurance added to Buck's contentment as he allowed himself to dream of having other nights like this one. Unfortunately, nature has a way of becoming terribly insistent.

Tempest murmured a protest as he eased from her embrace. He tucked the blankets snugly around her and shivered his way into his clothes. A bit of stirring produced a few good coals hidden beneath the fire's ashes. Carefully he applied kindling and blew on the embers until the sticks caught. Once he had the fire going he picked up his rifle and ducked outside.

Three inches of snow covered the ground, just enough to obliterate the footprints they had left earlier, but the night sky was clearing. The moon peeked from behind a cloud and a few stars sparkled in the ebony sky. Tomorrow would be fair.

Snow hissed and steamed under a shower of warm urine. After refastening his denims, Buck moved to a patch of clean snow and scooped up a handful of the white crystals to scrub his face. Feeling more awake, he headed for their mounts. His boots sank into the white crystalline powder, creating tracks only an idiot could miss. The air had a bite that would do Rooster credit. It seared Buck's lungs as he sucked it in, and it made him cough.

Spook nickered a quiet greeting, as if loath to break the pristine silence of the snowy night. Othello felt no such constraint. The mule's full-throated bray shattered the peace. An owl took flight from the upper reaches of the tree, complaining with an odd, barklike call Buck had heard only in Utah. He chuckled as a branch dumped snow on Othello's indignant head. Nature's payback.

Before returning to Tempest, Buck hiked a wide circle around the cabin, checking for human tracks. He found only blood and bits of fur where a fox had snagged a snowshoe rabbit. The cabin sat in a hollow near the rim of the plateau, hidden by pinyon pines and spicy-scented junipers. A man could pass the spot a hundred times and never know the cabin was there. When Buck lifted the blanket and let himself back inside, he found Tempest in her underclothes, dancing on the icy floor as she struggled to get her feet into her pant legs.

"I'm handier at getting those things off a woman than getting them back on, but I reckon I might help, if you asked me nice."

Her answering glare lacked conviction. "If you were a gentleman, you'd turn your back."

"What are you trying to hide? Already seen everything you've got," he pointed out. "What are you doing up, anyway?"

"I'm hungry. All we had before we got sidetracked was a can of beans, if you'll remember." The memory of all they'd done together earlier in the night fired her cheeks. She hadn't known women could feel such pleasure. Or be so wanton.

"How could I forget?" he asked hoarsely. Before she could pull her shirt on over her head, he had her hands pinned above her head and was nuzzling her breasts through her camisole. "Judas, woman, I can't look at you, touch you . . . I can't even smell you, without stiffening up like a three-day corpse."

"If that's supposed to charm me into taking my trousers back off, you've failed miserably," she said derisively. "You're about as romantic as a maggot in a plate of beans."

"Um, I love maggots in my beans," he whispered in a cougar's purr as he dipped his tongue into her mouth. "The more meat the merrier."

Making a sound of disgust, she tried to shove him away. They laughed as they wrestled on the bed until Buck spied the goose bumps prickling her arms, despite the fire that made soft light dance across her lovely features. "You're cold, sweetheart. Finish dressing." Winking, he added, "Or else take off those pants and we'll find another way to get warm."

"I'm too hungry." Tempest pulled on her shirt. "Besides, I need to brew some tea."

"I'd rather have coffee."

"The tea isn't for you. It's an herb that prevents conception."

Buck sobered suddenly. Taking up a stick, he poked viciously at the fire. "I'll get some bacon going."

Sparks flew and Tempest wondered what had gotten his dander up. She finished dressing, took a packet of herbs out of her saddlebags, and went outside to fill her tin cup with snow. When the tea was ready, she lifted it to her lips, then paused. Would it be so bad to have his baby? She liked the idea, crazy as it might be. Why should she care what other people thought? If they never found out who Buck really was, they would simply believe her no-good husband had gotten her pregnant and gone off again. No one except Buck would know the difference, and he wouldn't be here to find out.

Of course, Viola would know better. And Swede. But they would never tell.

There was her father to think about. Buck suspected Ronan knew the man sharing his daughter's bed was not her husband. Often she caught his tired old eyes on her. They held speculation, perhaps curiosity, but no condemnation. Tempest hated lying to him. He hadn't been the best father, but she had been raised to honor her parents, no matter what. Letting go of precepts drilled into her by the nuns at the School of Saint Francis Xavier was not as easy as it once seem.

Buck was watching her, a hard look in his eye. She lowered the cup. "Would you rather I didn't drink it?"

He reached for the fry pan, averting his gaze. "Has nothing to do with me."

Tempest's mouth dropped open. "How can you say that? It would be your child, too."

"You're the one who would be raising it, Tempest. I'll be gone, remember?"

The back of her throat tickled. She filled her mouth with tea and swallowed, tears and all. "How could I forget? You remind me often enough."

Neither spoke again except in terse, monosyllabic sentences. After they'd eaten, Tempest sat on the rumpled bedroll, her legs drawn up to her chest, her arms wrapped about them as she stared into the fire.

"Moon's out," Buck said after a while. "Warm wind coming from the north. Unless another storm rolls in, the snow will be melted by afternoon."

"Will we be able to get home?"

"I don't know. Snow'll take longer to melt in the draws." He knelt in front of the fire and tossed on a few sticks. "Tempest, I—"

She didn't want to hear what was coming. "I'm not sleepy, are you? Tell me about your family. Was your father in the war like mine?"

A mouse peeked out of a crack in the wall, whiskers twitching. Buck studied Tempest as if considering arguing. Then with a sigh he poked at the flames. "No, he died in 'fifty-four. My stepfather didn't go either. Wouldn't leave his family."

The mouse took a few halting steps inside, its tiny nose testing the air. Tempest tossed it a piece of biscuit from their midnight snack and caught the surprise on Buck's face. "You can't live in a dugout without learning to accept mice and spiders. If you didn't, you'd go crazy," she explained.

He smiled. "What about centipedes? And rattlers?"

"Centipedes are no worse than mice. It's Papa who can't abide them. And you," she added, teasingly.

The mouse finished its snack and skittered over to the decaying saddle in the corner. "Bet it has a nest in there," Buck said, fishing in his pocket for cigarette makings.

Tempest folded her legs under her and glanced about. "You know, this reminds me of the stone cabin Skeet described when he talked about the gold he was looking for up here."

A match flared, adding the smell of sulphur to that of tobacco. Buck blew a perfect smoke ring and watched it drift upward on a draft. "Gold?"

"Yes. Remember I told you about the old trader Skeet made friends with in St. Louis? His name was Bidwell. He had a freighting business there for years. Skeet brought him home for supper a few times. The man wore buckskin with fringe almost a foot long and used his shirt as a napkin." She shuddered with revulsion.

"What about the gold?"

"I'm getting to that, if you'll give me a chance." She scowled at him. "According to Mr. Bidwell his father had been one of the last mountain men from the beaver-trapping days. Once, while his father and some others—"

"Bidwell's father? Or his father's father?"

"Bidwell's father. Stop interrupting. Anyway, Bidwell—*senior*—was scouting Utah Territory for beaver one winter with some other trappers when they happened on a Spanish mine and stole a packload of solid gold bars."

"How much did it amount to?"

Tempest shrugged. "I don't know. I never believed the story so I didn't pay much attention when Skeet talked about it. I do seem to remember him saying something about each trapper having to carry an extra hundred pounds on his horse. He must have been referring to the gold."

"How many trappers were there?"

She frowned, trying to remember. "All I know is, when the whole thing was over, they were all dead except Bidwell. Senior, not junior. At one point they built a rock hut to shelter in. Then Indians stole their horses, and the other trappers were killed. Bidwell took two of the bars, buried the rest near the cabin, and walked out of there. By the time he got to his son in St. Louis the old trapper was too ill to come back for the gold, so he told his son how to find it. And the son told Skeet."

From Buck's expression, she knew he did not believe the story. "Mighty obliging of the man to pass on valuable information like that to a man he hardly knew."

"Oh, Skeet wasn't the only one Bidwell told. Over the years, he'd made deals with other men who were supposed to go find the gold and bring him back a share. None of them ever did, and Bidwell couldn't leave his business long enough to look for it himself."

"Did Skeet promise to share the gold with him?"

"Yes, seventy-thirty, with Skeet getting the larger amount since he'd have to do all the work."

Frown lines still creased Buck's forehead. Tempest could see he was calculating, considering. "What about a map?" he asked finally. "Did Bidwell give Skeet a map?"

Tempest shook her head. "Not on paper. Skeet had a map of sorts inside his head, though, that led him to Deception Canyon. After finding the stone cabin, he was supposed to find a sandstone slab laying over a grave. A map to the gold was supposed to be scratched on the underneath side. But Skeet never even found the cabin."

When she finished her story, Buck gave her a half-cocked smile and shook his head. "That's a hell of a yarn. Your Skeet was a real dreamer, wasn't he?"

Tempest shrugged. It bothered her to hear her children's father ridiculed or maligned. But she couldn't deny the truth. "I suppose he was. He was always coming up with schemes to make us rich. Silver mines that didn't exist. Water divining machines. Once he financed a man who made corsets that were supposed to cure everything from hives to pregnancy."

"A corset?" Buck chortled. "You must be joking. How could anyone think a corset could cure anything?"

Tempest hadn't found it humorous at the time. The money Skeet used included cash she had saved for a bassinet and other essentials for the child she was carrying. Instead, Angel spent her first few months of life sleeping in a dresser drawer and wearing diapers made from an old cotton dress. The same way Ethan had, except there had been no dresser to go with Ethan's drawer. Looking back on those difficult days now, she could see the humor in Skeet's financial lunacy.

"That was nothing," she said, allowing herself a smile, "compared to the Vacuum Developing and Strengthening Appliance he invested in."

Buck flicked his cigarette butt into the fire. "What the devil was that?"

"A little brass air pump attached to a glass tube that supposedly . . ." Her face flushed with heat. In spite of the intimacies she and Buck had shared, she found discussions this personal embarrassing. She wished she hadn't brought it up.

He was watching her with a strange intensity. She thought she could see a hint of humor curling a corner of his mouth. "Supposedly what?" he prompted.

An involuntary smile curved her own lips. She couldn't help it. No more than she could help looking away or keep back the flush that stained her cheeks. "They sold them to men who wanted to . . . enlarge themselves."

"You mean it was supposed to make them grow taller?"

She hazarded a glance at him. Suspicion grew as she spied the glint in his blue eyes. He was teasing her, but she knew how to tease too. "No, it was for enlarging a certain male appendage any woman could easily enlarge without any help at all."

A grin to make a devil proud spread across his face. "Care to show me which appendage you're talking about?" He winked.

"Certainly."

Buck grabbed her hand as it closed over the part in question, but he didn't pull it away. They were both laughing.

"You knew," she accused when she was able to catch her breath. "You made me explain, and all the time you knew what I was talking about."

"I saw an advertisement in a newspaper once. Don't

think I need one though." He pressed her hand to the bulge in his trousers. "Do you?"

Tempest squeezed gently and felt an instant response. Her power over him delighted her. "Umm, I don't know." Wrinkling her brow in somber contemplation, she reached for his buttons. "A bigger size might be nice. I'd have to try both sizes to be sure."

"Witch," he muttered as his lips closed over hers and her hand slipped inside his trousers.

Later as they lay snuggled beneath the blankets, Buck said, "Tell me more about the treasure. I read an article in the *Deseret News* when I was in prison about an old Spanish gold mine in the Tintic Mountains. Said there were other old mines like it in Utah. If Bidwell's story is true, and we could find the gold, our problems might be over."

Tempest gave an indelicate snort. "Might be over? Skeet figured the gold would be worth thousands of dollars. Maybe hundreds of thousands. Enough to pay off my debts, build us a new house, and buy more stock."

Suddenly she sat up, letting the blankets slide from her shoulders. "Do you actually think we could find it?"

Ogling the alluring sight of her bared breasts, Buck smiled. "Won't know unless we try. Right now I have another treasure in mind. One I don't have to go searching for."

"Buck, stop that!" she protested as he pulled her on top of his long naked body beneath the covers. "We have more important matters to discuss."

With a sigh he let her go. "All right. Tell me every detail you can remember about this treasure of Skeet's. If nothing else, it'll give us another way to occupy ourselves until the ground thaws enough for us to get home."

* * *

"Why, good morning, Mr. Carmichael." Viola blushed, knowing her pleasure at seeing the man lit up her face like a lantern in a closet. Standing by the door, plaid cap in hand, and wearing what she imagined to be his best suit, he looked a wee bit, as he would put it, like an elder in the Mormon church demanding donations. His hair had that just-combed look, and his bushy mustache had been trimmed closer than usual.

"Please," he said, "call me Ronan. I feel we be friends now."

"Oh, so do I . . . Ronan. Will you have some coffee?" She indicated his favorite table, the one closest to the kitchen which she used to think of as Tempest's.

"Aye, I'd like that. And one of your delicious rolls, if ye have any left."

Viola beamed as she left the room. Holding his cap in his hand, Ronan took a seat.

"Is that Scotty out there?" Lacey asked from the stove where she was popping a tray of ginger cookies into the oven. She too was beaming. "He missed his usual visit last night, I noticed. I also noticed you've been spending more time than usual peeking out the front window."

"How much time I spend *gazing* out my front window is none of your business, young lady. Now dish me up some rolls for the man while I pour his coffee." Carefully, she lifted the enormous enamelware coffee pot off the back of the stove.

"Would you like me to take them out to him?" Lacey teased.

"Cheeky child," Viola muttered as she marched from the kitchen with two china cups and saucers, and a plate of rolls prettily laid out on a wooden tray. Lacey teased her mercilessly about what she called "Scotty's courtship." The very idea, Viola thought. Getting courted at her age. Why, she would be fifty-seven in March. The notion of being courted at that ripe age was pure nonsense. But secretly she was enchanted. With the idea *and* with the man.

"Here you are." She put the tray on the end of the table and set out the china and flatware and daintily embroidered linen napkins she normally kept upstairs. "I was having my tea when you came in so I brought it along. If you don't mind my joining you, that is." She peered at the slightly rotund man through the stubby lashes of her one good eye, anticipating his response.

"I'd be pleased for your company," Ronan said, standing politely and pulling out her chair. After she was seated he tested his coffee. "Ah, good as always."

Viola smiled. She had added a dollop of whiskey to his cup. It bothered her to think it might only be the whiskey that brought him so regularly to her door. *Now, now, I'm only trying to help the man give up his drinking habit, Mr. Sims. Nothing more.*

"Are me grandchildren upstairs?" Ronan asked.

"Ethan is. He's napping. Angel is over at the hotel playing with the youngest Todd girl."

Ronan picked at a hangnail on his thumb. His nails were clean and stubby, she noticed. Like the man himself. One thick hand lifted to his hair, then dropped, and she hid a smile, knowing he wanted to scratch his scalp the way he did when he was nervous, but he didn't want to mess up his pomaded hair. That he cared about impressing her pleased her.

"Me daughter didna' come home last night," he said finally. "Reckon ye know that, since she hasna' fetched the bairns yet."

He was concerned, as he should be. That pleased her,

too. Reaching across the table, she placed a hand over his. "Now don't you fret, Ronan. No doubt it's the storm that held them up. They probably took shelter somewhere and are waiting for the snow to melt before they head back."

"Aye." He heaved a sigh. "But an old man worries. At least, he does when he's sober," he added with chagrin.

"Of course he does."

Carefully, he fit the same big thumb that he'd picked at earlier through the delicate cup handle and took a long sip. Viola smiled as he scooped a second roll onto his plate. She admired a man with a good appetite. Mr. Sims had always been appreciative of her cooking and had eaten a healthy portion before pushing away from the table to relax with his pipe and a glass of port while he read the *Deseret News*. Funny, she hadn't thought of him much lately. Nor had he visited her. Perhaps it was his way of letting her know he didn't mind her relationship with Mr. Carmichael. She did hate to see his leather platform rocker empty, no papers scattered over the floor. No wine glass on the mahogany side table. She'd taken to smoking his pipe herself just to keep the smell around, though lately she hadn't felt the need so much. She pictured Ronan there in the rocker—minus the wine glass—and blushed at an old woman's silliness.

At the Sagebrush Princess, Jonas Creedy stopped pacing his office floor and looked out the window. Being at the back of the building, the window gave a view of the hill behind town where patches of bare ground showed that the snow was melting. Where was Maddux this morning? Jonas wished he knew what the man might be thinking, which route he would use to get Tempest and himself back home. Were they already on their way?

Damn! He'd been sure all this would be settled and over with by today. Maddux had tricked and cheated him again.

Spinning away from the window, he threw himself into his chair. He rested his elbows on the arms of it and steepled his fingers. At least there was one thing Maddux wouldn't cheat him out of—the lost Spanish treasure. The gold was Jonas's own little secret. No one else knew it existed. He'd made sure of that. Those who knew enough to endanger his goal had found early graves.

A prospector had first told Jonas about the gold three years ago. They had been playing poker in a mining town up north called Alta, and the prospector had lost big. Jonas had generously let the sniveling old drift-dweller off the hook in exchange for a map. But the map had turned out to be nothing more than a bunch of squiggles and circles and lines that led nowhere, making Jonas doubly glad he'd killed the man. After that the gold haunted his dreams, dangling images of wealth and power in front of his nose until he could hardly think of anything else. So he began asking around and learned that Utah abounded with old Spanish mines, and tales of lost Spanish gold. Deeper research, a generous exchange of money, and a few threats whispered in trembling ears, eventually ferreted out the information he wanted. That information had led him to Deception Canyon, where he took over the Carcass Creek Cattle Company and built the Princess to cover his more secret activities—his search for the gold.

Unfortunately the area was a vast maze of canyons and gullies and plateaus. Hundreds of miles of rough country where a man got lost as easy as blinking an eye. Jonas had yet to find the stone hut the gold was supposed to be buried near. It didn't worry him though. He was getting to know the terrain better and better all the time. He would find his treasure soon. Meanwhile, he had created a nice little niche for himself, one that hooking up with Tempest could only improve.

But first Jonas had to get rid of Buck Maddux, once and for all.

Stepping over to his office door, he stuck out his head and bellowed, "Hey, Stud, Howard show up yet?"

"He's here, Mr. Creedy."

"Tell him to get his ass in my office."

When the stocky little man in his dark, tidy suit entered the room, bowler hat in hand, Jonas was standing behind his desk, a position of power he liked to assume in front of subordinates.

"Morning, Mr. Creedy."

Jonas ignored the gunman's greeting. He didn't exchange pleasantries with employees. "The Whitney woman left her children with the Widow Sims at the Boston Eatery. Go see how close an eye they're keeping on the brats. If you can get one of them away without raising a ruckus, bring it back here."

"Sure thing, boss. We taking the kid up onto the plateau with us when we go after Maddux?"

Creedy's eyes narrowed. He didn't like being questioned and had no intention of explaining his change in plans. "No. We'll wait for them to come to us—at the Whitney ranch. The child will ensure Maddux's cooperation."

"What about old man Carmichael? He's spending a lot of time at the eatery. Might give us trouble."

"Get a pint of whiskey from Stud, and doctor it with laudanum. Should be easy enough to get the old rot guzzler out of the way with that. If not, kill him. He'll only be in the way when I take over the place and marry Tempest anyhow."

"I'll take care of it," Howard promised. As he turned toward the door, his mouth curved in a small licentious smile.

Chapter Twenty-Two

He towered a foot above Lacey. A big, beautiful, blond giant. She loved the way his neck went all pink when her fingers brushed his as she put his plate in front of him. And his hands. Lacey loved his hands. She remembered them from the one time he had come to her at the Princess. The first time she had ever seen him. She hadn't expected such gentleness from hands the size of gold pans. She hadn't expected it from any man. Other than Buck, Swede Johansson was the only man who had treated her as if she were a real person, with feelings and needs of her own. If he had a full set of teeth she suspected he'd be almost as handsome as Buck.

Swede stared at the plate in front of him and tried to think of something to say. His throat was dry as a chaste cork. In her pink dress with its bit of lace at the high neck and on the cuffs of her long sleeves, she looked like a confection. Something to display in a baker's window on fancy, hand-cut, paper doilies. What was he doing, a big stupid lump like him trying to woo a woman as fine as her? No matter how she'd been forced to live her life, there was a goodness in her he suspected would grow with kindness and love, like the wild daisies that colored the hills in springtime.

The fork in his hand looked like a child's toy. Lacey tried to think of something to say, a reason to linger and talk with him. His coffee cup was full, his beefsteak and eggs untouched. There were no other customers. She straightened chairs and waited for him to taste his breakfast so she could ask how he liked it.

"You are happy here, Miss Lacey?" he asked, surprising her.

His eyes were blue, like Buck's, only softer and sort of innocent rather than haunted. Blue puppy-dog eyes. "Yes, I'm very happy," she told him. "I love to cook."

"Ya, you are good cook, like my mother." He relaxed. Here was a subject he was at ease with. The pleasure that lit up her face made him grin. "I am good with cutting open cans, but the beans I burn."

Smiling, Lacey said, "I hate opening cans. I always manage to cut myself."

Concern shadowed his eyes. "Next time, you bring cans to Swede. I cut them open for you."

For a moment, as he stared at her, she had the notion he would do anything for her. But that was nonsense. She was a saloon girl. A whore. There was only one thing men wanted to do for her, and that was lift her skirts.

Except Buck, he wasn't that way. He was kind. She would always remember his generosity and the encouragement he had given her to change her life.

You're a sweet, beautiful girl . . . Go to Provo or Salt Lake City . . . find decent work . . . You could start over, maybe even get married.

Could he be right? Could a nice man like Swede ever

want to marry a woman like her? When she'd walked out on Jonas, she'd thought no further than escaping his cruelty. Now new hope blossomed.

"You'd do that for me?" she asked, needing to hear Swede's offer again.

"Ya, that . . . and much more." He turned red and gazed down at his plate. When he looked up again, she saw uncertainty and hope in his eyes.

Lacey's heart fluttered.

"I-I like you, Miss Lacey," he said quietly. "You are good girl."

That made her laugh. "No one else would agree with that."

"Is not your soul they see," he said fiercely. He tapped a finger the size of a sausage roll over his heart. "Is not who you are here."

The tears came unbidden, accompanying a rush of emotion. Swede soared to his feet, and Lacey found herself swallowed up in an embrace as soft as a feather comforter, safe as a mother's womb. She felt . . . cherished. The tears came faster.

"No, no, *älskling,*" he whispered, awkwardly patting her back. He liked the feel of her in his arms, although she was so small and delicate he was afraid he'd break her. He lifted her off her feet so he could rest his head atop hers. "Do not cry. I am big stupid fool. I did not mean to hurt you."

"You . . . you didn't hurt me." She sniffed. "And you're not a big stupid fool. You're sweet and kind and . . . ."

Slowly he let her slide down until her feet touched the floor. One big thumb wiped the tears from her cheeks. "I like you, Lacey," he repeated.

She saw his Adam's apple bob in his long neck, and something melted inside her. "I like you too, Swede. Very much."

He grinned. "You maybe like me enough to walk with me later?"

"Yes, I'll walk with you." *The way Scotty and Viola did when the old man came courting.* The idea thrilled her.

Swede's grin broadened. "You would maybe let me hold your hand?"

Lacey frowned. "I-I don't know. I didn't mean ... I don't do ..."

The big man's face colored like a beet stain. He said something curt she didn't understand, something in his own tongue, then: "No, I only meant to walk, and to talk with you. You do not need to touch me if you do not want."

Sorry she'd hurt his feelings with her distrust, she said, "I like your hands." Taking one of them in hers, she marveled at how small it made hers look. "I remember how gentle they were."

The way he blushed enchanted her. Most men she knew were crude and insensitive. His expression earnest now, he said, "Swede never will touch you again, unless you choose. My attentions are ... honorable, I think is word."

More tears threatened. She was afraid to interpret his words the way they sounded. "I could walk after the lunch rush is over," she said shyly. "At two o'clock, if that's all right with you."

"Ya, is fine." He grinned. "Is wonderful fine. I see you then."

His big feet tangled with a pair of chair legs as he backed toward the door, grinning at her like a child. He caught the chair and straightened it, flushing crimson. It wasn't until she went to clear the table that she saw he had forgotten to eat.

* * *

Cords stood out in Buck's neck as he strained to lift a two-by-three-foot sandstone slab. The warm sun overhead and the strenuous exercise had allowed him to discard his heavy coat. The muscles of his arms and shoulders bulged beneath his shirt until Tempest thought the seams would burst. She was awed by his strength, by the sheer masculine brawn of his powerful body. By his endurance. They had spent hours overturning rocks in search of the map to the Spanish gold. With each stone Tempest held her breath in dizzy anticipation. She held it now.

Buck's lips drew back in a grimace, baring his teeth. He grunted. Then, with a heave, he flipped the huge stone slab onto its back.

"Hell," he muttered, staring at the empty face of the sandstone. "Nothing."

"What about that one over there?" Tempest pointed to a similar rock lying several feet away.

The look Buck slanted her could have boiled eggs. "Tell you what, how 'bout I let *you* try that one?"

She had the temerity to laugh. "And deny you the chance to enthrall me with your magnificent strength?" she said, batting her eyes.

"Judas, woman." He glanced around at the evidence scattered over the ground. "If you aren't enthralled by now, I'd be a damned fool to keep trying."

"I turned over all the ones I could lift." Plopping down on a stone, she added, "Does this mean you want to give up?"

Buck plucked off his hat, wiped his brow on his sleeve and resettled the hat over his dark hair, adjusting it to fit the way he liked. "No, of course not."

As he shrugged into his coat to keep from getting chilled while he rested, he turned a slow circle, surveying the rugged terrain. Most of the snow had melted, the moisture quickly absorbed by the dry, thirsty land. The gentle slopes and flats, dotted with pinyons and sparsely covered with tenacious grasses, tended to end abruptly at the rims of rifts and ravines or to drop hundreds of feet down the face of a cliff. With the toe of his boot, he scraped at the grainy soil.

"Rocky as this dirt is, a man would play hell digging a hole large enough to bury a man," he mused aloud. "Especially without shovels, and I don't imagine fur trappers carried shovels."

"You think the story is all a lie then?" Tempest asked.

"I don't know." Once more he scanned the area. Suddenly his eyes brightened. Shouldering the shovel, he strode off. Excitement rippled off him like lovers shedding clothing, inciting Tempest's pulse to skip. She stumbled, trying to keep up with his long legs as she followed him from gully to gully. Finally they came to a shallow, rock-filled wrinkle in the land. The pinyons and junipers became thicker as the wash deepened, grew rockier, then dipped suddenly in a cascade of tumbled boulders and plunged over the cliff. Snow clung stubbornly to the cool shadows, lowering the temperature. An eerie quiet pervaded the area. Not a bird chirped. No leaves rustled. Tempest shivered.

Buck's expression was intent as he paced up one side of the wash and down the other, seeming unaware of the unnatural feel of the place. With thumb and forefinger he stroked the dark hair on his chin and upper lip. He was on to something, but she didn't have the slightest idea what. He halted by a pile of snow-capped rocks the size of melons, filling six feet of the wash. On top, two large rectangular slabs lay end to end, the square edge of one overlapping the other. He hunkered down and stared at them.

"What is it, Buck?" She knelt next to him, trying to see what had captured his attention.

"Notice anything unusual?" he asked.

"You mean . . . something physical?" she said, thinking of the eerie atmosphere.

"These rocks don't look natural," he pointed out. "Not haphazard enough, a little too concentrated. Those two big chunks on top . . . how do you suppose they got there?" He gave her no time to speak, continuing to say, "I asked myself how I would dispose of a body in ground too rocky to dig in, and decided I'd look for a ready-made hole, like a gully or a cave. Then all I'd have to do is put the body in and cover it with rocks."

"Sweet Mary," she whispered, glancing at the rock-strewn gully with new eyes. "Do you think this could be it?"

"There's only one way to find out." He rose and positioned himself next to the uppermost slab. Tempest stood aside, her hands clutched together over her breasts. She could barely keep her feet from dancing in anticipation.

"Hurry, I can't wait," she commanded.

Giving her a wry look over his shoulder as he spit on his hands, he said, "Want to try it yourself?"

"No, no, you go ahead."

"Thought you'd say that." Amusement sparkled in his eyes before he turned around, gave his body a shake as if to awaken his muscles, then slid his hands under the uppermost slab. Sucking in a deep breath, he braced himself and then heaved.

Too anxious to stand still, Tempest found herself adding her own slight weight to his. Stone grated against stone, but moved only fractionally. She wanted to cry. Instead, she reminded herself the slabs were larger than the others they had overturned. Too large, she thought, for one old man to have put here without some sort of aid. Like a lever or . . .

Buck was already ahead of her. He searched the ground

under the trees and returned with a stout limb. After wedging it between the slab and another stone, he paused to glance at Tempest. With the fur lining of her hood framing her face, and her hands clutched at her breast, she looked like a Madonna praying. He hoped someone was listening. Giving her a wink, he grinned. The pole felt rough beneath his callused palms, rough and cool and strong. He wondered if he were about to hand Tempest the very instrument she needed to pry him out of her life. For a second, he considered faking it, telling her he wasn't strong enough to lift the stone even with a lever. He could come back later, find the gold and wait until the last minute to present it to Creedy so the man couldn't take Tempest's land. She would be desperate by then. Desperate enough to see him as her hero? Desperate enough to love him? Buck snorted. Yeah, she'd love him, all right, the same day Saint Peter welcomed Beelzebub at the pearly gates.

Taking a firm grip, he leaned on the pole, using both his weight and strength to wrest the sandstone from its resting place. At first, he thought he might not have to lie to Tempest. The stone resisted his efforts. Gritting his teeth, he leaned more heavily into his work, giving it everything he had. The instant the slab toppled over, he threw the pole aside and dropped to his knees. Tempest was there beside him, her shoulder brushing his, the white mist of her breath mingling with his. Their gazes met and held. In her eyes he read the same trepidation he felt himself. So much depended on what happened next. And yet, their future didn't solely rest on the gold. Wanting to assure her of that, he said, "There's still the Army payroll." She nodded but her expression remained anxious.

Because the moment seemed to call for it, and because he wanted to, needed to, he put his lips to hers. The kiss was brief, tender, bittersweet. When he drew away, she gave him a smile and caressed his face with her hand.

Then, together, as if at a preset signal, they looked down at the rough surface of the buff-colored stone.

It was blank.

The expletive that rushed out with Buck's exhaled breath was crude and harsh. Without comment he rose and went back to work, repeating the procedure with the second slab. This one was so much easier to move that Buck told himself, cynically, they would find nothing there either. Worthwhile things never came that easy. Not to him. The stone teetered on its side, then tumbled to the ground with a thud.

Tempest's heart pounded and she could barely stand still, yet she was afraid to look. Her breath caught in her lungs. The entire world hung suspended. Within minutes she might be holding in her hands the golden answer to her every problem. The treasure would do more than save her from Jonas Creedy, it would give her the home she had always wanted, as well as a good life for her children. But it would cost her the man she loved. Her joy ebbed. His hand glided over the flat surface of the stone, the gesture slow, almost reverent. A thrill shivered through her from head to toe.

"Is-is the map there?" she asked, allowing herself to breathe again.

Turning to her, he grinned, and she rushed to kneel beside him. "Oh, sweet Mother Mary, it *is* the map," she whispered reverently. "I can't believe it. The treasure exists, it really exists." Clutching his arm, she cried, "We found it, Buck! We found it!"

Rising, he swooped her into his arms and whirled her round and round. She clung to his neck, laughing. Finally, he slowed to a halt and let her feet touch ground. Concern tempered his smile.

"We shouldn't be counting chickens yet," he warned. "This is only the map. We still have to find the gold."

On tiptoe, she kissed him. "I know. And it won't be easy. There aren't any words on the drawing to help us decipher it. That old trapper probably didn't know how to write."

Again Buck knelt. "Not much to the map. This crooked line is probably the edge of the plateau, and the short line here is the wash. The broken one leading south must be a trail."

"The circle at the end looks like a lake," Tempest said.

"Could be." He rose and flexed his tired shoulders. "I half expected the gold to be buried right here with the body . . . if there is a body. Anyway, looks like we have more work to do."

Tempest retrieved the canteen and offered him a drink.

"Know of any lakes up here?" he asked, wiping his mouth on his sleeve.

"I have no idea what's up here, Buck, except deer and a lot of rough country."

"Skeet never talked about things he found when he was hunting for the gold?"

She searched her mind, then shook her head. "He knew I didn't believe the gold existed, so he kept it mostly to himself. It could be a hill, couldn't it?"

"I reckon. Can't imagine there being much water up here, but it could be a dry lake. Damn the old bastard for being so vague." Again he rolled his shoulders.

Going to him, Tempest pushed him onto a rock and began kneading his sore muscles. "Maybe he didn't want to make it too easy. This way, someone accidentally finding the map wouldn't know what it was for. Feel better?"

"Umm, heaven." Buck let his head drop forward and closed his eyes. "How long can you keep that up?"

Tempest smiled. "How long do you need?"

"A lifetime."

Tempest pursed her lips wistfully. A massage each day

would be a small price to pay for a lifetime with Buck Maddux, especially when she enjoyed touching him so much. Lowering her head, she kissed his neck. He smelled of wet earth, leather, and horse. Capturing her hand he pressed his lips to her palm, setting her stomach awhirl. When his eyes met hers, they were soft with emotions she was afraid to believe were real. Then the shutters fell into place, the shadows returned, and he looked away.

"Buck—"

"Thanks, sweetheart." He stood quickly. "Let's go see where the trail takes us. If we even find one," he added cynically.

Tempest followed silently. She wanted to tell him she would follow any road, as long as he and Angel and Ethan were with her. But she was afraid to expose what was in her heart.

They packed their gear in case they didn't return to the cabin. Spook was feisty in the brisk air, prancing and sidestepping, until Buck brought him under control. Othello plodded along in his usual pragmatic manner, only now and then showing a bit of spark as he nipped Spook's tail or sidled up close to Buck for a nose scratch. A squirrel darted across their path, winning a disgruntled snort from the appaloosa. Buck and Tempest nibbled pine nuts as they rode, tossing some of the nutritious seeds to a whiskey-jack that kept abreast of them, flying from tree to tree in a flash of gray feathers and harsh, grating cries. Pines scented the air.

When they had ridden a good deal farther than Buck figured they needed to go to reach their destination, without finding anything, they backtracked to the wash and tried again. This time they rode forty yards apart to cover more territory. Mountain bluebirds, smaller and less showy than the scrub jays that abounded in the area, took wing as Tempest broke from the trees into a small clearing of brown, withered grass. Sliding from the mule's back, she went behind a tree and relieved herself.

Suddenly it struck her that the clearing was round, like the circle on the map. She yelled for Buck. He gazed about the grassy meadow in somber concentration. "Could be it, I suppose," he said. "But what now? Must be something, another map, or some sort of clue to tell us where to dig."

They wandered for some time, searching until, exhausted, they sat down to share the canteen. Buck rolled a cigarette.

"How do we know there aren't two graves, or even two maps?" Tempest suggested. "Maybe the one we found is a fake, to throw us off."

Glancing around, Buck said, "One thing's sure, there are no rocks here big enough to draw a map on." In disgust, he picked up a stick and tossed it at a tree.

"That's an odd scar on that tree," Tempest commented. "It doesn't look like a deer scrape. Do you think it could be a blaze, to mark a trail?"

"Sweetheart, you're a genius." Swiftly, Buck came to his feet, grinding out his cigarette. "It's old," he said, excitement and hope rising in his voice as he ran his hand over the scar. "Very old."

"It almost looks like an arrow, doesn't it?"

Without answering, Buck set off. He found another blaze, and whooped with joy. They followed the marked trees for two miles before reaching a dead end. Hungry, tired and discouraged, they took time to eat cold beans out of a can and discuss what to do next.

"At least it doesn't look like we're in for any more snow," Buck said, glancing at the sky.

"And the cold weather did away with the insects."

Buck grinned. "You mean the flies?"

She shuddered, not trying to hide her dislike of the pests

for once. "The ones around here are big enough to saddle and ride to town."

"Careful, sweetheart. You start confessing things, you might find yourself saying something you'd rather keep secret."

Her chin lifted. "I don't have anything to confess."

He took her chin in his hand and forced her to look at him. Devilish glints sparkled in his blue eyes. "Sure you do, pretty filly. Come on, tell Papa Buck."

"Tell you what, you skunk-faced goat?" The amusement in her voice took the sting from her words. Her hand forked through the silver-streaked hair above his forehead, then glided down his face to tug—not too gently—at his beard. "What should I confess?"

"How much you want me, of course."

"I don't want you."

"Yes, you do."

Tempest tried to frown. The game had become familiar, almost endearing. "You swell-headed prickly pear, what makes you think I would want you?"

He answered with a kiss. His mouth was warm and moist, tasting of beans, and man. Pure, passionate, hungry man. Firm, gentle lips brushed lightly over hers, then pressed more commandingly, and she met them with a firmness of her own.

Buck pulled her into his arms, groaning at the way her coat hid her warmth from him. He parted her lips and dipped inside to savor her taste and tease the tongue flirting shamefully with his.

Tempest melted against him, knowing she'd lost the game. With one kiss he had proven how desperately she wanted him. Would always want him. But she wasn't about to admit it.

"You're lucky it's too cold to run around naked," he whispered as his hand delved beneath her coat. "You'd find yourself on your back." Setting her aside, he stood and in one smooth, lithe movement, leaped onto Spook. "Come on, little filly. A treasure awaits."

Tempest wanted to slug him. How could he arouse her like that and then walk away? Was she the only one affected by their kisses? "Blasted two-headed wolverine," she muttered as she stuffed the remains of their meal into her saddlebags. "If he refers to me as a horse one more time, I'm going to—"

"Called you a filly, not a horse," Buck said with a grin. "Can't you tell the difference between a noun and an endearment? Women are usually experts on endearments. 'Course, your specialty in name-calling leans a bit more toward insults. Maybe I'm going to have to educate you some." Setting his spurs to Spook's sides, he headed south.

Sweet Mary, what am I to do with him? Still grumbling, Tempest mounted and did the only thing she could do— she followed. *Like a dang dog. Not much different from a horse.*

Othello brayed a loud complaint as she dug her heels into him. "Shut up, you long-eared traitor. You're worse than me about tagging after that blasted man." The mule brayed again, set his hooves, and refused to move. Rolling her eyes, Tempest sighed. "All right, I apologize. Now, will you please go?"

When she caught up with Buck, he was sitting sideways in the saddle, one knee hooked around the saddle horn as he stared down at a pile of rocks. "What are you doing?" she asked.

He gave her a quick glance, then straightened. "Those rocks didn't get like that by accident."

Studying them, she said, "You're right. It's a cairn . . . a marker, like a slash on a tree." Excitement banished her weariness as she dismounted. Buck dismounted and reached for the shovel tied behind his saddle.

"What are you doing?" she asked.

"Getting ready to dig up some gold."

"Not here."

He glared at her with sudden impatience. "Why the hell not? You see any other trees around here with slashes on them? Or rock piles? No, there's only this one, and that means the gold is buried right here."

"Okay," she said calmly. "But you're wasting your time."

"And what the hell makes you so smart all of a sudden?"

"I've always been smart. Smarter than you."

Whirling, he came nose to nose with her. He was tired and discouraged and not in a mood to be baited. "Is that so?"

"Yes, that's so." Her stubborn chin rose.

"And just what is it makes you so damned smart?" Buck knew his anger was uncalled for and tried to rein it in. The hours they had traveled that day seemed more like days, and he was sure they had become intimately acquainted with every tree on the plateau. Tempest's eyes were shadowed with fatigue. Hell, they were both tense and worn out.

"At least I'm smart enough to see that the cairn points west," Tempest retorted, "not down!" Smugly, she pointed to a row of rocks nearly hidden in the grass—a perfect arrow, aiming west.

"Judas." Replacing the shovel on his saddle, he mounted without another word.

Twenty arrows and twenty trees later—plus three rock cairns—they emerged from a dense pinyon forest onto a grassy plain. Beyond a range of badlands visible some distance away, the sun was lowering. Buck halted and waited for Tempest to ride up alongside. The afternoon was waning. Buck felt the increased chill, and sensed the hushed, almost reverent quality of the atmosphere . . . as though the setting of the sun were a holy time, a time to pause and pay homage to the power that had created such beauty. He tried to chuckle at his fanciful imaginings, and failed.

"What is it?" she asked as she came alongside. "Why did you stop?"

His only answer was a smile. Spook swung his head around and nickered impatiently. "In a minute," Buck told the horse, patting its long neck. He was studying the lay of the land.

"Do you have any idea where we are?" Tempest said, trying to see what he was looking at so intently. "We could've been traveling in circles for all I know. I'm completely lost."

Buck's chuckle was all chagrin, and no mirth. "Yeah, I have a damned good idea where we are. See that wash over there?"

Tempest followed his outstretched hand. "Yes."

"Look familiar?"

"I-I'm not sure. There are so many up here."

"Well, it damned well ought to. Come on."

The wash led to a pile of rocks Tempest recognized instantly. They had indeed traveled full circle, returning to the grave where their fruitless search had begun.

Chapter
Twenty-Three

"Frog turds!" Tempest blurted. "Bidwell sent us on a wild-goose chase!"

Buck stared down at the rock-covered grave. The slab bearing the map—the first portion, anyway—still lay beside the gully where he'd left it.

Spook whiffled in Buck's ear, then flipped his master's hat off with his nose. Catching the hat midair, Buck cursed. "I'll get you some water in a dadblamed minute, you worthless fleabag."

As if the horse knew he had been insulted, he whinnied loudly. Buck filled his hat with water and held it out. Spook guzzled the water with almost as much relish as he guzzled beer.

Wanting his own share, Othello nipped at Buck's gun belt.

"Close, but no prize." Buck scratched between the mule's ears.

Tempest fetched her own canteen. "What was he trying to do?"

"Show her, you old Arizona nightingale."

Othello bared his teeth and brayed. Then he bent his head, took the handle of Buck's Colt six-shooter in his teeth and drew the weapon from the holster.

"Holy Mary!" Tempest exclaimed.

Laughing, Buck retrieved his Colt. He rewarded the mule with a thorough scratching in his favorite spot. Othello squeezed his eyes shut in ecstasy. "He's a natural, aren't you, boy?" Buck said. "We're working on another trick, but he hasn't quite gotten it yet."

Tempest shook her head with amazement. "I didn't think that mule was smart enough to get in out of the rain, let alone do tricks. Too bad you didn't train him to sniff out gold."

"Yeah." Returning his attention to the grave, he said, "Didn't teach him how to pick up rocks in his teeth either, so let's get busy. I want to get home to the kids before dark."

The children had never been far from Tempest's thoughts during the long day, though she tried to keep her worrying from driving her insane. They were with Viola and Lacey. Her father would be checking on them, and Rooster was there. They were safe. She and Buck had discussed going home before searching for the gold, but had decided there was too much risk of not being able to find the cabin again, let alone the stone bearing the map. Men had searched for the stone cabin for years, but the few who claimed to have found it were never able to find it again. She knew Buck was as concerned about the children as she was, and loved him all the more for it.

There was also Jonas to worry about. Buck was constantly scanning the horizon or gazing over his shoulder to make sure they weren't being followed or about to be ambushed.

She owed him so much. Other than sharing the gold with him, she didn't know how to repay him, but she had a sinking feeling Buck Maddux would never take money from a woman. Even one who loved him.

Squirrels scampered up trees and tossed down pinyon cones, barking now and then in their high-pitched voices, as if to warn away the invaders working below. The thud of rocks hitting the earth punctuated the air. The temperature dropped and thick heavy clouds rolled in from the north.

"We aren't going to have time to find another way down off the mountain," Buck said, studying the sky. "Storm's coming in too fast. We'll have to go back down Treachery Canyon."

Tempest caught his edginess. "You expect Jonas to be waiting for us, don't you?"

He knew better than to try to shield her from the truth. "What do you think?"

She gave him a brave smile. "Then we'll have to be careful, won't we?"

He wanted to hug her. The darkening sky told him he'd better not.

Ten minutes later he uncovered the first metal box.

"The gold! It has to be the gold!" Tempest cried. She covered her mouth with her hands. "Sweet Mary, even after we found the map I was afraid to believe the gold truly existed. Oh, Buck." She didn't care that she was crying. This kind of emotional rain was good; it was happy rain. She threw herself into his arms.

In spite of his own mixed emotions, Buck grinned and hugged her close.

The box was small, yet it took all his strength to haul it onto level ground. Spanish lettering covered the lid. There was no lock. Tempest knelt beside him, her tense fingers digging into her thighs as she waited for him to open it.

A long, meaningful look passed between them. They were both well aware of all that depended on the contents of that box. Buck suspected her heart was pounding as hard as his. Finding her trembling hand, he gave it a squeeze.

Taking a deep breath she said, "Go on, open it."

For a long moment he continued to hold her gaze with his, thinking how their lives might be changed in the next few moments. Part of him prayed the box would be empty or be filled with something worthless. He liked having her need him. But that only proved he hadn't changed over the years, he was still as selfish as ever. Cursing himself, he yanked hard on the rusted lid of the box.

Gold. It shone with an incandescence all its own.

"Judas. Look at it."

"It's beautiful." Tempest's tone was soft and reverent.

Buck lifted one of the gleaming ingots from the box and weighed it in his hands. "It's gold, all right, heavy as sin. Twenty, maybe even twenty-five pounds in each bar."

"But they're so small, not even as big as a regular brick." Tempest held out her hands. When he hesitated, she said, "I'm not going to break beneath the weight, Buck. Who do you think hauled the rocks for the front wall of the house? My wet laundry weighs as much as this gold does. Not to mention Ethan."

"I thought Beaver Hanks helped you build the house."

Her eyes spit amber-colored sparks at him. "So I didn't carry *all* the rocks, I carried enough to nearly break my back. And he was never here long. Before you came I hauled all the water, chopped down sagebrush and greasewood, split it into kindling—"

"All right. Forgive me, I must have lost my head. Here," he said, dropping the golden ingot onto her hands. She grunted with the effort to hang onto it, and he chuckled.

If looks could flay hide, he figured he wouldn't have an inch of skin left.

Tempest held the precious metal bar like an offering to the gods. Along with the jubilation in her eyes, there were also tears. "Oh, Buck," she whispered, "it's almost over, isn't it? The trouble with Jonas—it's finally going to be over."

"Yeah, sweetheart. Almost over." He didn't bother pointing out that they still had to get the gold, and themselves, home safely. Or that the gold meant an end to their pretend marriage.

Placing the gold on her lap, she wrapped her arms around his neck, too overcome with her own emotions to hear the sadness in his voice. Her tears wet his cheek.

"Hey, no need to cry." Judas, she'd have him bawling too in another minute, he thought. "You'll be safe now. You're rich. You'll never have to worry about how you're going to feed your kids again. You can even build a new house. A real one . . . made of wood."

"A real house," she repeated wonderingly. But he wouldn't be sharing it with her. She would be alone again. Her joy faded. "How are we going to get it home? The box must weigh two hundred pounds."

"Damn close. I suspect there's at least a second box."

"You're right," she said with a new burst of excitement. "There are no bars missing from this one, so there has to be the one he took the bars from to get back to St. Louis."

Again he looked up at the sky. It would soon be dusk. "Unless we want to spend another night up here, we're done searching for today. It'll be raining in another hour. Need to travel fast if we want to get home tonight. An extra hundred pounds each is going to be hard on the animals and will slow us down."

"We'll take what we can easily handle and come back for the rest," she said.

"Yeah, if we can find it again."

"If we can't . . . well, even a few ingots will pay Jonas off and leave the children and me fairly well set. We don't need much, really." *Except you to share it all with.*

He was studying the terrain. "Country up here all looks alike. There aren't enough landmarks to go by."

"We could leave signs . . . slashes like Bidwell cut into the trees," she suggested. "And cairns where there are no trees."

Exactly what he had in mind, but he wasn't going to tell her that. She looked too pleased with herself. Grinning, he kissed her. "Judas, but you're smart. 'Course you already proved that by falling for me, but—"

Tempest slugged him. "I did not fall for you."

"Sure did. You look at me as though I were a bowl of ice cream on a hot day."

"I do not."

"Do too."

"You're insane."

They divided the bars between their saddlebags, Tempest taking the biggest share since mules could carry more weight and she was lighter than Buck. Then the box went back into the grave and the stones were replaced to make the spot appear as untouched as possible.

As they rode past the cabin, Buck's heart filled with regret. They had made love in that hut. Within its drafty rock walls he had allowed himself a few minutes to dream and to hope. Tomorrow, if they escaped Jonas, they would take the gold to Price. The bank there would buy it from them or advance what money they needed until a buyer could be found. Creedy would be paid off, and Buck would have no more reason to stay in Deception Canyon.

He tried, to no avail, to work up his old enthusiasm for the sights he had planned to see when he left prison. Even the idea of seeing the ocean left him cold. Soon he would ride off into the Utah desert, leaving Tempest and the children behind. But he would not leave in one piece. His heart would remain here.

Jonas rubbed his gloved hands up and down his arms and snuggled deeper into the limited shelter of his rock hideout. Frigging wind was colder than his cursed mother's heart. He hoped the sky would clear up before Maddux appeared. Jonas wanted to see his bullet rip through that meddling bastard's body, wanted to watch Maddux realize he was a dead man.

Howard was late showing up with the brats. If that sonuvabitch had stopped to play his games with that little girl, Jonas would carve him into tiny pieces and feed them to the coyotes.

It wasn't handling Maddux alone Jonas was worried about, but having to kill the man too soon. Jonas had games of his own he was eager to play, games that would reduce Maddux to a shivering heap. Apaches were experts on tortures that guaranteed plenty of pain and a nice long death. Tempest would be the salt he would rub in Maddux's wounds. Jonas chuckled, thinking of the pleasure it was going to give him to rape her before that skunk-marked bastard's eyes. Not that rape would be necessary. With her girl in Howard's clutches, Tempest would do anything Jonas asked. He couldn't wait to see her on her knees before him.

An owl hooted overhead. Jonas shuddered. He wondered if his white mother still scorned Apache beliefs now that her spirit had joined those wandering restlessly, earthbound because they had been mutilated when they died. If any specter haunted him, it would be hers.

His hand went to the locket he wore as a watch fob. Blackbird would have railed at him for taking his mother's

locket from her body and wearing it on his own. Apaches
burned the possessions of the dead to avoid ghost sickness.
Superstition, he told himself, as he glanced nervously at
the trees. The fob was only a reminder to him of all that
he hated in this world and of all he intended to do to get
even with those who had wronged him.

Including Buck Maddux.

With a soft nicker, Spook pranced nervously at the opening to Treachery Canyon. Buck leaned forward to pat the
appaloosa's neck. Night had fallen and the air was redolent
with the scent of the coming rain.

"Buck?" Tempest's voice came low and quiet through
the darkness. He turned to look at her.

"Nearly there, sweetheart," he assured her. "You all
right?"

"I'm fine. I just want to get home. Why did you stop?"

"Studying the terrain to make sure of where we are."
Reaching over, he gently squeezed her knee. "We've
reached the canyon, so it won't be long now." *Unless we
run into trouble—spelled with a capital* J. Wordlessly he prayed
that wouldn't happen, or if it did, he would be able to
keep her safe. A nudge of his knee started the appaloosa
forward.

"Wait, Buck."

He looked at her over his shoulder.

"I . . . can we talk?" she asked. "There's something I
need to say."

Turning Spook, he came up alongside her. "Now? It's
freezing cold, about to rain, and you want to talk?"

"Yes. Please, it's important."

Even in the darkness he could see the earnestness in
her eyes. He knew he should insist that they go on. Talking
could wait until they were safe at home—or at least down

that narrow chasm and onto the main road. But after tomorrow he would have no place in her life. Her home would no longer be his. Until then he could refuse her nothing. "All right, let's move deeper into the trees where we'll be out of the wind a little."

Othello needed no urging. Like a puppy, he followed the gelding. When they were inside the pinyons and junipers, Buck dismounted. He lifted Tempest from her saddle and sheltered her with the warmth of his body. "Okay, woman, what is it you need to say?"

Twisting her hands in the lapels of his sheepskin coat, Tempest gazed up into the face of the man she had come to love. She searched for a sign that he was truly willing to listen, but saw only patient indulgence and the same wariness he'd shown whenever she tried to get him to be serious about something. "I know you don't want to answer this, but I have to know what's going to happen once Jonas is paid off. I need to know what you plan to do."

Buck's heart pounded. He had hoped she would ask him to stay, but he hadn't actually expected it. Not that it mattered. He couldn't stay. And if she knew him, knew his past, she wouldn't ask. The cocky devil's grin didn't come so easily now, but he curved his lips and lowered his head close to hers. "What do you have on your mind, little mustang? Got used to having me in your bed, and now you're reluctant to let me go?"

She flinched as though struck, and Buck hated himself for putting the pain in her eyes. His throat ached with the need to tell her he didn't mean the ugly words he'd said. But he held to his purpose and kept silent.

Tempest had expected flippancy, but not crudity. Gritting her teeth, she refused to let her tears surface. "Don't, please. Don't make light of the beautiful thing that's happened between us."

Stepping back, he glanced away, afraid the yearning in

her eyes would make him weaken. Afraid she might see the yearning in his. "Why not, Tempest? We both knew it couldn't go anywhere. I told you, I'm a drifter. Settling down isn't in me."

"You told me. That doesn't mean I have to believe you."

The words were soft and tremulous, underscored with a tender sort of understanding. Guilt knotted his throat. His jaw ached with the effort to keep from blurting out his true feelings. Determined not to reach for her, he shoved his hands into his coat pockets. He didn't dare look at her.

A small hand cupped his face, trying to turn it toward her. Her ungloved fingers were cold. "What we shared was more than sex, Buck. I know the difference. You made love to me. I've never felt so cherished as I've felt in your arms. You could be happy here, if you'd only let yourself. The children adore you and—"

"We've been all over this, Tempest." He didn't dare let her continue. Shoving away from her, he needlessly lifted the stirrup and adjusted the cinch on his horse. "No point trampling it into the ground. I'm no good for you, that's all there is to it. Now, if you're finished, let's get going. It'll start raining any minute now, and I want to get out of that deathtrap of a canyon before we get caught in a flash flood."

Tempest wanted to stamp her feet—on his chest. "Blast it, Buck Maddux. Why do you have to be so stubborn?"

He glared at her. "Because I know what's best. You have no idea who I am. Judas, woman, I'm an ex-convict, doesn't that tell you something?"

"Yes," she shouted. "It tells me our justice system isn't fair. You didn't belong there, Buck. You didn't steal that money. Skeet did."

The stirrup slapped against Spook's belly as Buck

dropped it back into place, making the horse shy. "Forget it, Tempest. You don't know anything about it."

"I do too. How can you argue about this? You were innocent."

Spinning around, he towered over her, his face contorted in a grim mask. In the shadows he looked larger than ever and more dangerous. "I'll tell you how innocent I was: They imprisoned me for theft, but what they should have done is hang me."

The barely leashed violence in him tightened the fist knotting Tempest's stomach. Her heart thudded. She knew he wouldn't hurt her, not physically, yet she was afraid. "You're only trying to frighten me, Buck. You're no murderer."

"You damn well *should* be scared. If you had an ounce of sense, you'd climb on that mule and run like hell."

Her smile was small and sad. "I can't, Buck. I love you."

He squeezed his eyes shut against the joy and the pain her words gave him. Before he could give in to the overwhelming need to reach for her, he swung away. She didn't mean what she said. She couldn't. But, oh, God, how he wished she did. The wanting in him was so large it filled his entire being, making the loneliness in him unbearable. His insides felt scrambled, as though he'd been thrown by a bull and stomped to boot. He swallowed sudden moisture and blinked back tears. Bracing his arms on Spook's back, he begged for strength. "Listen to me," he said in his harshest tone. "I *am* a murderer, Tempest—three times over. Do you hear me? I've killed three people. One a baby not even born yet. Can you still say you love me?"

He laughed at the shock on her face, but the sound was hard and cold and without humor. "Never mind, I know the answer." Jamming his left foot into the stirrup he hoisted himself into his saddle. Small hands clutched at his leg.

Tempest glared up at him. "Don't you dare presume to know what's in my mind, Buck Maddux. If you killed anyone, it was an accident. You could never kill anyone on purpose . . . unless he deserved it."

A raindrop landed on her upturned cheek and slid downward like a tear. He resisted the urge to wipe it away. "Did Skeet deserve to die?"

Confusion creased her brow. "No, but . . . You didn't kill him, the posse—"

"No!" He grabbed her arms and lifted her until they were nearly eye to eye. His fingers dug cruelly into her flesh. Spook pranced sideways, snorting a protest. "The posse put a bullet in his stomach, Tempest. But it was *my* bullet that ended his life. A bullet I purposely fired into his brain."

Tempest stumbled as he dropped her onto her feet. She caught herself and straightened, staring at him in horror and disbelief.

"Now do you understand?" he snarled. "I put my Colt to your husband's head and pulled the trigger. *I* killed Skeet Whitney."

"There . . . there must have been a reason," she stammered, her mind seeking an explanation. "He'd been shot in the stomach. Even I know a stomach wound means a long, painful death." Understanding dawned in her eyes. "You put him out of his misery, didn't you? That's why you shot him. So he wouldn't have to suffer anymore. That's not murder, Buck. That's a very painful sort of kindness."

Looking away, he yanked his hat lower over his eyes. Obviously, she needed more convincing. "What about the other two, Tempest? I said I murdered three people, remember?"

When she didn't answer, he pinned her with eyes that

were darkly shadowed, cruelly savage. "Ask me. Go ahead and ask me who the other two were."

The hat brim failed to hide the anguish in his eyes, an anguish so deep, so brutal, she could hardly bear to look at it. The words he flung at her like a well-aimed dagger tore her heart to shreds. She held her breath, afraid to speak, even more afraid to hear what else he would say. Then it came:

"My wife! Do you hear me, Tempest? I murdered my own wife, and with her, our unborn son."

Chapter
Twenty-Four

Buck kneed the appaloosa forward, but Tempest latched onto a stirrup and held tight. Confused, Spook tried to sidestep the woman.

"No!" She shook her head, stark denial in her anguished eyes. Spook tossed his head and whinnied. Tempest held on. "That can't be . . . you wouldn't do something like that."

"Go ask my family. They'll be more than happy to tell you all about my sterling character." Acid burned Buck's throat. The horror on her face, and the knowledge that he'd put it there, was killing him. He couldn't bear any more or he would take back everything he'd said and beg her not to let him go. He prayed she wouldn't force him to share the dirty details of his sins. Judas, what he had already divulged should be enough to send her running like a rabbit with a coyote on its tail. Reaching down, he tore her hands from the stirrup.

"Buck! Buck, please."

"Forget it, Tempest. There's nothing more to say." He spurred Spook to a trot, not even looking to see if she followed.

Stunned, Tempest stood there, watching his broad shoulders fade into the rain. Then she climbed onto Othello and plodded after the gelding, the mule so slow she feared she would lose Buck in the storm. A hard kick hiked Othello's speed to a jolting sort of canter that jarred her teeth. When a speckled rump and a long tail ghosted into view, she breathed a sigh of relief. She slowed as she drew abreast of Buck. He stared straight ahead, ignoring her.

"I have to know what happened, Buck. I need to understand."

"All you need to understand is that I'm no good. For you, for your children, even for myself. You should be damned eager to see my back."

"I already saw your back, riding off into the storm without me, and I was terrified. Blast it, Buck"—her anger rose as swiftly as the rain fell—"you have no right to decide what's good for me."

"I have no rights over you at all, which is what's best for both of us. Drop it, Tempest. It's over. You have the gold. Heartsease is safe. You don't need me."

"Stop telling me what I need! I make my own decisions."

Treachery Canyon yawned before them, black and sinister in the spectral mist of the storm. Without pausing, Buck spurred Spook into the dark defile, forcing the mule to fall behind. Tempest wished she had something to throw at him. Blast his hide, why did he have to be so stubborn? "Buck!"

There was no answer. "Damn you, Buck Maddux," she hollered into the murky shadows. "You listen to me. No matter what you do, no matter what you say . . . I'll still love you. I'll *always* love you."

His broad back vanished again, this time around a corner. Tempest found herself isolated in an inky hole. Malevolent walls hovered over her as she descended the steep incline. Jagged projections reached out to snag her. She was alone, with nothing to accompany her but a shattered heart and ravaged dreams.

Jonas heard the cry and smiled. The voice had been human, and female. He positioned himself on one knee behind the rocks, steadied his rifle on the wet crag, and sighted down its barrel. The brightness of the slick, gleaming stone wall across the canyon would make a fine backdrop to outline Maddux's silhouette as he rode into view, giving Jonas a perfect target.

The original plan had been to let Maddux and Tempest ride past him, trapping them between him and Howard down below. The children would have ensured a quick surrender. Then they would've taken the captives to the Whitney ranch and Jonas could have some fun before killing Maddux with long, slow torture. Since Howard hadn't shown up with the brats, Jonas would have to take advantage of the one thing he still had going for him—surprise—and get Maddux with his first shot.

Damn Howard. The fool would have been welcome to the brat, as long as his fun hadn't interfered with Jonas's. Jonas didn't care what happened to the girl once she'd served her purpose. Children had as much appeal for him as a bucket of piss. Now Howard would have to be punished.

Howard cursed and slid his gun from its holster as the yellow mongrel came closer, its nose sniffing the air. If the dog gave him any trouble he'd shoot it. Two hours he'd hidden in the bushes behind the Boston Eatery, waiting for a chance to grab the little girl. Now it was raining. He wasn't going to squat there getting soaked forever. If he couldn't get the kid soon, he'd give it up. It was past time for him to meet Jonas, and Howard didn't want to make the man any angrier than he would be already. He had some pay coming. Angry men had a tendency not to pay up.

The dog took another step toward him, growling deep in its throat. Howard cocked his six-shooter, then eased the hammer back into place. A gun shot would rouse the entire town and ruin everything. He'd pistol-whip the mutt instead, then slit its throat.

Howard had the gun raised and was ready to bring it down on the snoopy dog's head when the back door of the restaurant squeaked open.

"Rooster. Here, Rooster," a small, high-pitched voice called.

Howard froze. Angel. Standing in a wedge of candlelight from the door, her pale hair and pristine nightie limned with gold, the child truly looked like her namesake. He had to have her. Forgetting the dog in his lust for the girl, Howard rose onto the balls of his feet, ready to lunge for her. Growling, the dog blocked the way. With a curse Howard whipped the gun down toward the animal's head.

Buck leaned back in his saddle for balance as Spook maneuvered a steep, tricky stretch of the rocky stream bed. He didn't need to look behind to know Othello was there, Tempest clinging to the thick barrel of his sturdy body. The mule's steps rang eerily in the darkness as his metal shoes struck stone, echoing the gelding's hoofbeats. The appaloosa stumbled on loose gravel, caught himself and went on, his ears swiveling to Buck's murmured praise and encouragement. The clatter of the rocks skittering out from under the horse's hooves created another echo in the deepening sandstone walls of the narrow passage. A few soft plunks told Buck the gravel had found water. It had rained hard for several minutes, magnifying Buck's fear of flash floods. When the rain slowed and turned to sleet, he uttered a silent prayer of thanks, but he wasn't fooled into thinking the danger was over. A light rain here didn't preclude a heavy rain up top somewhere, which could still flood creeks like this one.

Soon Spook rounded another bend and entered the icy water. The sides of the finger canyon were too steep to avoid the stream. Water rushed and gurgled around the gelding's fetlocks, then rose to his knees.

At the next curve, the horse snorted and balked. "Come on, you beer-guzzling bag of horse meat," Buck crooned, raking the gelding lightly with his spurs. "There's nothing down there that's any worse than what we've already been through." Ears laid back in protest, Spook placed one hoof in front of the other and braved the dark unknown.

The rifle shot in the close confines of the rocky cleft nearly deafened Buck. He felt the bullet strike his hard skull, nearly knocking him from the saddle. He tightened his legs about the appaloosa's girth and clamped his jaw against the pain and descending darkness, but even as he tried to turn Spook back up the canyon he knew it was no use. He was dead. The blinding agony in his head made it impossible to see, muddled his thoughts. His brain registered Tempest's frightened call to him, but he hurt too much to reply.

Another bullet exploded. Spook screamed. Pain ripped through Buck's lower leg. Rock splintered behind them. Frantically, the horse sought safety. Buck hung onto him, fearing his faithful steed had been hit and waiting for Spook to go down, taking Buck with him.

Tempest's panicked voice seemed more distant now. He tried to answer and couldn't find the breath. His jaw clenched so tightly against the pain that he couldn't get any words past his teeth. He suspected the thick, warm dampness in his left eye wasn't rain. Beneath him Spook plunged and scrambled and clambered like a green bronc with its first rider. Hump, boil, crow hop. Jackknife. Hump again. Buck's bronc tried them all. Clamping his legs tighter around the horse's thick barrel-like body, Buck clung like a leech. His hands were growing numb. Hell, his entire body was growing numb. Except the parts that hurt. It was becoming more difficult to stay mounted. He could barely feel the reins in his gloved hands, but he knew they were escaping his grip. His body listed to the side. He was going to fall. He tried to stop it. His brain insisted that his life depended on keeping his butt glued to the saddle, but he could do nothing to prevent the humiliating tumble. At least, he consoled himself, once he was on the ground he could sleep.

Tempest. Where was Tempest? Can't sleep. Got to get to her. Got to keep her safe.

Buck was sliding, sliding. He couldn't stop. Judas, he was going to die. His brain was turning to water, flowing away from him down the creek that swirled about Spook's fetlocks. The inky black night closed in on him, pulling him down, dragging on his limbs, exhausting him. He made a last effort to get a firmer grip on his seat, and failed. Oblivion followed him down.

The distressed whinny came from directly in front of Tempest. Othello brayed an answer. She screamed Buck's name and received only silence. Suddenly, a huge dark wraith appeared before her, bearing an empty saddle. Spook reared as he nearly collided with the mule, snorting with fear. Swallowing her panic, Tempest dismounted and went to the horse.

"Easy, boy, it's only me." She crooned softly and inched closer until at last she managed to grab hold of his halter. Gentle strokes and calm words soothed the appaloosa. After securing the animals' reins to a crag, she went in search of Buck.

She didn't have to go far. He lay on his stomach, his face pressed to the wet, icy cold ground, the water of the creek swirling about his legs. His hat was missing, washed away by the creek. Stark terror left her throat thick and dry. Dread froze her heart as she knelt beside him. "Buck? Buck, can you hear me?" *Sweet Mother of God, please don't let him be dead.*

He was so still. Praying silently, she dragged him from the water and tenderly rolled him onto his back. The roar of the quickly swelling creek, and the steady drum of rain on the rocks around them were so loud that even with her ear pressed to his chest, she could detect no heartbeat. Tempest didn't try to stop the tears mingling with the moisture on her face, but she refused to believe he was dead. Life couldn't be that cruel.

Damn Jonas Creedy! He had done this.

Fresh fear surged through her as she realized the half-breed would come looking for Buck to make sure his bullet had done its job. She would have to hide Buck, find a way to get him dry, and tend his wound. She would protect him, and she would see that Jonas paid for his villainy.

A brisk search of the immediate area disclosed no cave, no overhang, nothing that offered shelter. She would have to rig a sort of tent using the gutta-percha tarps their bedrolls were wrapped in, hoping the storm and the dark night would help to conceal them. The stubborn fool didn't even have his slicker on. It made little difference now—he was soaked clean through—but she fetched the bright yellow slicker from behind his saddle anyway, and laid it over his still body, tucking it beneath his bearded chin as if he were a child. She stroked his dark hair from his forehead, and her fingers came away coated with warm sticky liquid the rain swiftly washed away. *Blood. Oh, Sweet Mary, so much blood.* He would die if she didn't get the bleeding stopped. If he wasn't already dead.

No! He couldn't be dead. She wouldn't allow him to die. "Blast you, Buck Maddux, don't you dare die on me."

Using rocks she anchored one side of a tarp to a jutting four-foot-high boulder, the opposite side to the ground. She laid his slicker on the wet ground, worked his limp, heavy body onto it, then knotted her hands in the sleeves and dragged him under the crude shelter she had created. Then she began to strip off his clothes so she could get him dry and make sure the wound in his head was the only one he'd suffered. She had removed his spurs and boots and was unbuckling his gun belt when the tarp was suddenly wrenched away.

"You're wasting your time, puss."

Looking up, she saw Jonas leering down at her out of the darkness.

"If your lover ain't dead yet, he soon will be," Jonas taunted, a .38 double-action revolver with a sawed-off barrel pointed at her. "Hand me his gun belt."

"No!" Overwhelmed by fury and frustration, and ignoring the vicious weapon he held, she leaped to her feet and threw herself at him, her fingers trying to gouge the eyes from his head. "You killed him, you filthy bastard."

"Damn you, cut that out." He grabbed her arms and threw her from him. She slammed into the jagged wall and crumpled to the ground, taking the rest of the tarp with her and leaving Buck exposed once more to the storm.

Jonas's eyes on her felt like dirty hands. "Careful, puss, or you may find yourself meeting the same fate he did."

Keeping the .38 leveled at her, he looked down at Buck. "You sonuvabitch," he muttered, as he bent to pull Buck's sidearm from its holster, "you weren't supposed to die. Not until I'd had some fun with you." Standing again, he drew back his boot and repeatedly kicked the limp body lying in the rain.

Screaming, Tempest lunged at him again. "Leave him alone. Haven't you done enough?"

Holding a gun in each hand made him awkward, but he managed to wrap his arms around her and trap her against his chest, her arms caught between their bodies and rendered helpless. "No, I ain't done enough," he snarled. "I had some right fine plans for giving him a nice, slow death. Maybe I'll just use 'em on you . . . after I get what else I want off you." He smeared his wet mouth across hers, then bit her lower lip. She refused to show the pain he enjoyed giving her.

Shoving her away, he said, "Bring me the rifles from your saddles."

"Get them yourself." With the back of her hand she wiped his kiss from her mouth. The blow came so suddenly she didn't see it coming. Her head jerked with the impact of his hand against her cheek and she cried out.

"I said get them rifles," he repeated, aiming the .38 at her.

Glaring at him, she did as he said. He opened the chamber and magazine on each gun and dumped the bullets into the creek. Then he handed the empty weapons back with an order to replace them in the scabbards.

Rain dripped from Jonas's dark hat. "You're being a real good girl, puss. I think I oughta reward you with a kiss."

Quickly she stepped away. "I don't want any rewards from you."

Malice radiated from him like flames from hell. "That ain't being smart, puss."

She saw his intent in his buzzardblack eyes and knew she should have allowed the kiss. Perhaps if she cooperated and kept him well occupied, he'd let down his guard enough for her to disarm him somehow, knock him out. She watched him make a fist and draw back his arm, her heart thundering in her ears so loudly she didn't hear the approaching horse until Jonas whirled toward the noise. From the darkness came a disembodied voice: "Mr. Creedy? It's me, Howard. I'm coming in."

The squatty, bespectacled gunman appeared at the bend, a buckskin gelding behind him.

"Where's the brats?" Jonas asked.

Tempest's heart lurched, but she kept silent.

Howard's gaze flicked to the sidearms his employer held—a sawed-off .38 in one hand and a .44 Colt in the other. He licked suddenly dry lips. "I tried, Mr. Creedy. I barely missed grabbing the girl at the hotel, but the old man beat me to her and took her back to the eatery. After that, they never let either of the children outside for a second."

Jonas marched toward the man, oblivious to Tempest's gasp of horror. Howard shrank before the angry half-breed. "What you mean is you failed, ain't that right, Howard?"

The runty man shuffled his feet and knotted the reins in his hands. "There wasn't any chance—"

"Never mind," Jonas barked. "I don't want to hear your whining. If I didn't need you I'd end your miserable life right now." He stared at the hired gunman a long moment, his crafty eyes narrowed as though debating whether he really needed him or not. Finally he turned away, tucking Buck's .44 in his waistband. "We'll finish this later. For now, get over there and make sure Maddux is dead."

The relief on the gunman's face was evident even in the shadow of his dripping hat. Tempest thought him a fool.

Howard laid an ear to Buck's chest. "He's dead, Mr. Creedy."

Tempest turned to the wall and buried her face in her arms, the words, like bullets, puncturing her heart. Until that moment she had held to the belief that Buck was still alive. Now the strength drained out of her. Without him, she no longer cared what happened to her.

"All right," Creedy said. "Make sure there ain't no other weapons hid in their saddlebags."

Spook shied and rolled his eyes as the man approached. Blood glistened on his rump where a bullet had creased him. Going to the mule instead, Howard untied a flap on the saddlebags. Tempest knew the instant he found the gold. His gaze darted from her to Jonas and back to her. She knew he was wondering if she would give him away if he kept the find to himself. His eyes seemed to be offering her some kind of deal, protection perhaps, maybe even a share of the gold, but Tempest remembered the unspeakable things this little man wanted to do to her tiny daughter. Narrowing her eyes, she turned toward Jonas. Before she could speak, the runt squeaked out, "There's something here you might want to see, Mr. Creedy."

Jonas's mouth dropped open at the sight of the gold ingot Howard held. For a moment he stared at it; then he spun toward Tempest. "Where did you get that?"

"We found it."

Two long strides brought him face to face with her. He grabbed her, his jagged nails digging into her arms. "Don't play games with me, puss. You can't win. Now, where did you get it?"

Tempest glared at him. "Figure it out for yourself."

"Damn you!" He slapped her so hard she reeled from

the blow. "That was *my* treasure. You had no right to even know about it. How did you find out anyway?"

Before Tempest could answer, he snapped, "Never mind. It's mine now, that's all that matters." He rushed back to the mule, shoved the .38 into his holster, and began emptying saddlebags onto the ground. Tempest's extra shirt floated through the air like a banner and was swept away by the creek. The fry pan clanged against the rock wall and fell unheeded to the ground. Keeping her gaze on the two men, she edged toward it.

Howard had moved to the other side of the mule and was emptying the other bag. "Here's another ingot, Mr. Creedy."

Jonas snatched it away. "Mine. Mine at last," he said, kissing the cold, gleaming metal. Smiling at Tempest, he said, "The gold, your spread, and you . . . all mine." His laughter raised gooseflesh on her arms.

While Jonas petted and caressed his new prize, gloating over his luck, Howard tucked a gleaming ingot inside his coat. It no longer mattered to Tempest who got the gold. All that mattered now was getting back to her children alive. To do that she needed to get away from these despicable men, and the little gunman—not so tidy now with his suit and bowler hat soggy and limp—had just handed her the means to send him to his grave. "Do you really think Jonas will let you keep that gold?" she inquired coldly.

Spinning toward his man, Jonas whipped out the .38. "What are you up to, Howard?"

"Nothing, Mr. Creedy." Howard backed toward his horse, his hand hovering over his own weapon. "She's trying to cause trouble between us, is all. I wouldn't be stupid enough to steal from you."

Casually, Jonas strode toward the man. "That's good, Howard. I'd hate to have to kill you. Come over here now and help me make sure there isn't more."

Howard hesitated. It was a mistake. A predator to the core, Jonas saw that and made his play. With his fists full of coat lapels, he slammed Howard against the wall, holding him in place with a well-positioned knee that wrenched a howl of pain from the man. Extracting the gold from Howard's coat, Jonas shook his head. "What a disappointment," he purred. "I'll have to kill you after all."

His face contorted with pain, Howard pleaded, "Please, Mr. Creedy. I—"

Jonas laughed. Tempest edged closer to the heavy iron fry pan.

Slowly, Jonas raised the snub-nosed revolver and took aim. Howard covered his head with his arms and sobbed. Letting the sound of the shot cover her action, Tempest snatched up the fry pan. Howard jerked as the bullet slammed into him, then slowly slumped forward, one arm dangling in the creek. Blood ran over the wet rock, clouded the water for a instant, and was washed away.

Her heart pounding, Tempest prayed for forgiveness for her part in the man's death. Jonas walked to the body and stared down at it dispassionately, then nudged it with his foot into the creek. It floated a few feet, caught on a snag, and stuck. The rush of water around the new obstacle filled the silence, lending a touch of normalcy to a nightmare Tempest knew would be forever imbedded in her memory.

Turning to her, Jonas said, "How many more ingots are there?"

"Five in my bags, three in Buck's," she stammered.

Jonas frowned, his thin lips pinched. "Had to be more than that. You sure you ain't trying to hold out on me?"

Tempest stared at him thoughtfully. If she convinced him there was no more gold, maybe she could get away later and get it herself. It could be her ticket to freedom. One Buck had given his life to help her obtain. Suddenly

she knew she would do anything to keep Buck's death
from being in vain. "If there's more, we didn't find it."

"Then there's nothing else to be done here, except have
a little fun." His small eyes glinted with evil as he aimed
the short-barreled revolver at Buck's still body.

"What are you doing?" she demanded. "He's already
dead, what good will it do to . . . ?" She ground to a halt,
realizing Jonas was baiting her. He knew she couldn't bear
to see Buck's body riddled with more bullets.

Jonas smiled. There was no humor in the curl of his
thin lips, only demonic pleasure. "It'll do me a lot of good,
seeing my bullets tear into his flesh the way I've been
dreaming it."

She didn't give herself time to think, she simply acted.
Bringing the fry pan from behind her back, she swung it
at Jonas's head with all her might. He saw it coming and
ducked. The force of her swing carried her in a half-circle.
The pan clanged into the rock wall, sending teeth-jarring
vibrations up her arm and all through her body. Gasping,
she dropped it and rubbed her tingling hands.

"That wasn't very smart, puss. Not smart at all." Rage
distorted Jonas's features. "I oughta punish you for that,
but I want you fit when you pleasure me tonight. Might
be other ways to tame you, though, and almost as much
fun." He turned the weapon back on Buck.

"No!" Without thinking further, she threw herself over
Buck's body. "You're right, there is another box. We
couldn't carry it all."

"Where?" Jonas asked.

"Under a pile of rocks in a wash near a stone cabin."

He smiled. "Take me there."

"I-I will." Looking down at Buck's handsome face, she
asked, "Can I just have a minute?"

Giving her a keen considering glance, Jonas said, "How
bad do you want it?"

"What do you mean?"

He stepped close and pulled her to her feet. She smelled whiskey and onions as he squashed her against him. The brims of their hats collided. His voice was quiet, underscored with menace. "I got a fantasy about you, 'bout what I'd like to see you do with that sassy mouth o' yours." She flinched when he took her hand and placed it over the placket of his trousers. Movement beneath the dark wool fabric told her he was becoming aroused. "I want you eager, sweet puss. *Real* eager to please me."

Something inside her shriveled and died. Never had it been more clear to her why some women chose death over rape. Willing or not, each time he touched her, she would feel violated, and she would want to die. But she didn't dare let herself dwell on that now. If Jonas caught any hint of the revulsion she felt, he might start looking for additional ways to punish her and keep her in line. Like threatening her children. No matter what, she had to keep her babies safe. She lifted her chin and prayed for strength. Then she closed her hand over the growing bulge in his trousers and gently squeezed. "I'll be eager, Jonas. I'll make you happy."

He closed his eyes and arched into her hand. Rapture erased the ugly malevolence from his face, startling her with a glimpse of the man he might have been, had his life gone differently. She would have jerked her hand away if he hadn't chosen that moment to place his over hers and rub it up and down his erection. She swallowed convulsively and closed her eyes, willing herself to see this through, to not let Angel and Ethan down. Finally he released her and she opened her eyes.

"Get your goodbye over with quick," he rasped, his eyes white-hot still with desire. "Let's get to that stone cabin where we can be more cozy. I been waiting for this night for a long time, and I don't wanta waste a single minute of it.''

Kneeling beside Buck, she rubbed her hand on her denims in a vain effort to wash away the feel of Jonas Creedy's body. Lying where she'd left them, Buck's spurs glinted in the rain. Leaning over him, letting her slicker hide her movements, she slipped one of the spurs into her coat pocket. Then she kissed Buck's wet mouth, surprised to find his skin soft and warm yet. Her throat ached and grew tight as she fought back tears. They could have been happy together, she was sure of it. But she would never get the chance to convince Buck of that now. She stroked the hair from his eyes, glad it had stopped raining, even if it made no difference to Buck now, and whispered, ''I love you, Buck. I'll never forget you.''

''That's enough, for Christ's sake. The sonuvabitch is dead,'' Jonas growled. Grabbing her arm he yanked her up.

''I'll get you for this someday, Jonas,'' she vowed in a voice devoid of emotion.

He laughed. ''You'll get me, all right. Every inch, deep and hard and swift, whenever and however I please. And you'll learn to like it. Now get to emptying them saddlebags. Howard's, too. Take the food and what other goods we'll need and throw out the rest. These horses are gonna be our pack animals. I ain't leaving one bar o' that gold behind. Which bag has the Army payroll in it?''

The unexpected question threw her. ''Army payroll?''

''Don't play dumb with me. I know you found it in them ruins. You was all excited and yelling for him to come see it.''

Tempest frowned. When realization came, she burst out laughing.

''Stop that, you stupid bitch.'' He slapped her so hard her neck snapped. ''Nobody laughs at Jonas Creedy.''

Needles of pain iced her cheek where he'd struck her. Donning a look of contrition she forced out an apology. "I'm sorry, Jonas. It's just that I'm so tired, and it suddenly seemed horribly funny that the payroll was what Buck and I started out to find, but with everything else that's happened, I'd completely forgotten about it."

Jonas's tense body relaxed fractionally. "Well, I ain't. Now where is it?"

"I don't know. You were wrong. It wasn't the payroll I found, but a beautiful piece of Indian pottery, completely intact. They are so rare, and I was excited."

His calculating gaze was like fingers stripping her naked, probing her secrets.

"I'll empty the saddlebags and show you." She edged toward the appaloosa. Jonas waited silently as she went back to work. Soon three piles littered the ground, necessities in one, gold in the second. The third was not so tidy. When Jonas had finally accepted that she was telling the truth about the payroll, he cursed vilely and kicked the pile of dispensable goods, sending everything flying. Disgusted at his childish show of temper, Tempest jammed the items they would take with them into her saddlebags, including the iron fry pan. The gold went into Jonas's bags.

When all was ready, she climbed onto Othello and gazed down at Buck, feeling as if she were leaving behind a part of her soul. It killed her to simply ride off and leave him like that. What if coyotes got to him, or a flash flood washed him away, battering his body against the rocks as it roared down the twisting, narrow canyon?

Jonas mounted, holding the reins of the two extra horses. "You first, puss. I don't trust you at my back."

As she dug her boot heels into Othello's sides to get him moving and turned her gaze away from the still body of the man she loved, her throat burned with the effort to fight back her tears. But she refused to give Jonas the satisfaction of seeing her cry.

Everything within Buck protested as he watched Tempest disappear into the dark with Jonas Creedy. He had regained consciousness in time to see Creedy cold-bloodedly shoot down his own hired gunman. Knowing his and Tempest's best chance depended on Jonas believing he was dead, Buck gritted his teeth and held silent. Now, shivering violently, he struggled to get his feet under him and stand up. His ribs ached as if he'd been kicked by a bull. His left leg was stiff and hurt like the devil. When he tried to put weight on it, it buckled beneath him. His throbbing head reeled.

Sucking in deep breaths, he eased himself back down and gingerly felt his head while he waited for the dizziness and nausea to pass. His fingers came away sticky with blood. The bullet had gouged a groove in the side of his head above his right ear. Another had gone through his calf barely missing his boot. But he was grateful the bullet had passed all the way through.

Eyes slitted against the pain, he searched for a crutch to help him stand. His vision blurred and he had to blink several times before he could focus. The rain-spawned stream had washed away much of the accumulated debris in the dry creek bed, leaving nothing of value within reach. There was no sign of his hat. The one thing he could be thankful for was that he lay only a few feet from the water. A drink would give him strength. He sat up cautiously. When the world stopped whirling, he tried to get onto his knees. Moving his left leg was like driving a spike from his calf to his groin. His teeth clamped so tightly against the pain that his jaw throbbed. Merely dragging himself close enough to the water to drink left him panting. Judas, he was weak as one-bean coffee.

The collar and front of his sheepskin coat was stiff with dried blood. In spite of the coat's warmth, he felt frozen from head to toes. His lower body was rain soaked. Liquid squished within his boots, both water and blood. At least it had quit raining.

Damn that half-breed bastard for taking Spook. Buck wasn't sure he would have had the strength to haul himself into the saddle, but he would have had a better chance of catching up to them on horseback. On foot, he doubted he could make it to the top of the plateau. If he had been less woozy, and Creedy less cautious, it might have been possible to jump the bastard. As it was Buck had had no choice but to play dead, watching through slitted eyes as Creedy mishandled Tempest. To not be able to protect her better grated harshly against his pride—and his ego.

The pain eased and he got his wind back. He took off his glove and scooped water into his mouth. At once his stomach revolted. Vomit splattered off the rock and onto his coat. The stench brought up more bile. When his stomach was finally empty and the spasms had ebbed, he bathed his face and dried it with his neckerchief. Then he summoned what strength he had left and began an agonizing crawl to a high, jutting chunk of rock. Hand over hand, using the rockface as a ladder, he dragged himself up.

His mind was so muzzy he could hardly think, and he realized he was seeing double. Unthinkingly, he shook his head to clear his eyes. Pain stabbed through his head, and he reeled backward. He was unconscious before he hit the ground.

Chapter Twenty-Five

Buck managed to walk, crawl, and drag himself a hundred feet before he heard the muted ring of a horse's hooves on rock. The echo made it difficult to tell if the rider was approaching from above or below. He didn't figure it very likely that many people would be riding up this particular side canyon in the middle of a cold, wet night. It had to be one of Creedy's henchman.

Biting his inner lip against the pain, he bent in a half-crouch, keeping his injured leg as straight as possible, and searched the ground for a rock that fit his palm just right. Then he positioned himself behind an outcrop. It took forever for the plodding animal to reach him. His fist clenched and unclenched on the rock he held. He smelled the animal before its black nose emerged from behind the outcrop, followed by its long-eared head. Abruptly the animal halted, tossed its head and brayed. A mule. A man's thick brogue came out of the darkness: "Mr. Maddux, be ye there, son?"

Buck barely stopped the blow he had been ready to inflict. "Ronan?"

"Aye." The burly Scotsman dismounted.

"Judas," Buck muttered, dropping the rock. "I nearly killed you."

"Aye, I ken that, and I'm mighty glad ye didn't."

Buck chuckled, but the sound was ragged. The strength drained from him like milk through cheesecloth, and he leaned heavily against the mule, panting.

"Where's me daughter?" Ronan asked, glancing about anxiously. "I came to warn ye Jonas was up to something."

"Too late. Jonas has her. Took her up top after the gold. My horse too."

"Gold, ye say?"

"I'll explain later. Let me get my breath and we'll go after them."

For a few minutes Buck clung to Ronan's saddle; then he slowly slid to the ground. The mule sidestepped his crumpled form. Ronan knelt beside him. "Be ye hurt, lad?"

Buck groaned, and put a hand to his throbbing head. Seeing the makeshift bandage he'd applied, Ronan clucked his tongue. "Ach, been shot, have ye?"

"Head was grazed." The world was a red whirlpool of pain. "A bullet went through my calf too."

Ronan examined the head wound and replaced the bandage. " 'Tis stopped bleeding. We can count our blessings for that. I'll see to your leg now."

"No time." Buck struggled to stand up. "Have to get Tempest."

"Ye're in no shape to go after anyone, son. We'll ride double back to town and fetch help."

"No . . . Have to save Tempest. Can't let her suffer like . . . Ellen. Rather die."

" 'Tis yer pain talking, lad," Ronan said. "I dinna' know

this Ellen, or what she has to do with me daughter, but I know when a man's pushed himself beyond his limits. 'Tisn't wise, you know. Ye got two serious wounds, and I'm an old man with only one arm. We need help."

Buck had to convince him. Sucking in a deep breath and gritting his teeth, he braced a hand on the man's shoulder and heaved himself to his knees. Then he rose shakily to his feet. "I'm all right. While we're riding back to town, Jonas could be raping her. I won't risk that. Just give me what weapons you have, and I'll go on alone."

"I'll no' be lettin' ye do that. She's me daughter. Somehow, we'll find a way to rescue her together."

An unspoken understanding passed between the two men as Ronan handed over a Remington .44 Army revolver. Buck clasped the older man's shoulder with his free hand and nodded. After satisfying himself that the sidearm was clean and loaded, Buck slipped it into his holster. He took hold of the pommel on Ronan's saddle and placed his left foot in the stirrup. "Help me up, and climb on behind."

Ronan gave him a boost up, moved to the mule's head and took hold of the bridle. "Beauty canna' carry us both up this incline."

"Can't leave you here." Buck started to dismount.

Quickly the Scotsman shoved the younger man back into the saddle. "Dinna' be a fool, lad. Ye're hurt. Ye'd only slow us down on foot. 'Twill be soon enough to ride double when we reach the top."

Buck nodded, knowing Tempest's father was right. "How did you find out about Jonas's plans?"

"Big Red caught me as I was leavin' town and told me Jonas was layin' for ye. I came fast as I could."

A strained chuckle erupted from Buck's chest at the idea of the old man and the mule racing pell-mell up the mountain. "This old plug isn't capable of moving fast."

"Me Beauty is a game lass. She does her best."

"Yeah, well, I'm grateful as hell for her tonight. You, too. Not sure I would've made it if you hadn't found me."

"Ye've been good to me daughter, Mr. Maddux. 'Tis I who should be grateful to you. And I am."

The Scotsman fell back as the mule struggled over a rough spot. When Ronan came alongside again, Buck asked, "How did you know I wasn't Skeet?"

Ronan laughed. "I may be old, lad, and missing an arm. But I'm not a complete fool. When I first came here Tempest mentioned that her Skeet was fair haired, like the bairns. A man on the run might dye his hair, but I doubt he'd go to the trouble o' streakin' it white. Then there's yer eyes. But I woulda' known anyway. Didna' have to meet Skeet to ken that he was weak. Whatever else ye might be, lad, ye're not weak."

Buck didn't bother arguing that last point. He didn't have the energy. But the need to block out his fear of what might be happening to Tempest kept him talking. "Why didn't you say something?"

" 'Twas obvious as the tassel on me tam-o'-shanter that me girl be taken with ye. And ye with her. She's been cheated enough in life, I wasna' about to cheat her of a chance at real love."

Buck snorted derisively. *"Real love?* No woman could love a man like me. Not if she had any brains in her head."

The older man was quiet a long time. The scrape of horseshoes on rock and the hoot of an owl filled the gap in the conversation. "I canna' guess what ghosts be haunting ye from yer past, lad. But I ken the torture inside yer soul. 'Tis much like me own, I fear." Ronan paused as if assembling his thoughts. "Ye told me I could start over, and I thought ye crazy. But I know now what ye said was true. I can start over, and be a better man for it, I'm wagering. No reason you canna' do the same."

"Too many ghosts, old man," Buck replied wearily. "Too much pain. I don't deserve ..." He didn't finish. To say he didn't deserve Tempest's love was too much like admitting how desperately he wanted it. He couldn't say the words. If he did, he might never be able to take them back, and he loved her too much to saddle her with a devil like himself.

"Ach. Forgiving yerself yer own sins is not so easy, is it, lad?" Ronan chided. "Well do I know that. But I'm beginning to see the right of it. 'Tis a far bigger sin to waste yer life wallowing in self-pity. 'Twas you helped me see that. Same way ye helped me kick the whiskey. Do ye expect me to believe ye canna' do it for yerself?"

Buck forced a chuckle. "You telling me I should give up whiskey, old man?"

Tempest's father refused to rise to the bait. His tone remained sober and somehow damning. "A man can run from responsibility. He can run from the loved ones he's let down through cowardice and selfishness. But no matter how far ye run, ye can never escape yerself, lad. Yer sins follow ye wherever ye go, like the skin on yer back. Ye can reach back and scratch it, but ye canna' tear it off ye no matter how ye try. And even if ye could, 'twould only be yerself ye'd be spiting."

An eternity of tense silence fell while they rode along before Buck said quietly, "You've come a long way in the last week or so, haven't you, old man?"

"Aye, lad, that I have, and 'tis damn proud o' meself I be."

As the flames of the bonfire leaped and danced, Tempest imagined them the very fires of hell. Within them Jonas Creedy writhed and screamed, while she watched and laughed and gloated. He had murdered the only man she would ever love. No punishment could be too harsh.

Burying her hands in her coat pockets, she encountered the spur she had taken as a sentimental keepsake. Her heart tumbled at the brutal finality of her farewell to Buck. She couldn't believe he was gone. That the devilish glints in those summer blue eyes would never sparkle again. To know he was lying there in that dark, damp defile, alone and forgotten, hurt more than she could bear. Jonas could have it all, the gold and her land, if she could just have Buck alive. He was where her happiness lay. Her heart ached with love for him. He had loved her too, even if he hadn't admitted it. She'd been foolish to think the land was everything. It was nothing, nothing at all.

In the shifting light of the fire she watched Jonas tear into the old grave like a madman, and she envisioned how she would take her revenge on him. The rowels of the spur in her pocket were blunt enough not to injure a horse, but they could be lethal used on a man's face. He giggled as he heaved rocks every which way, so absorbed in his work he seemed to have forgotten her.

Inch by inch she edged closer to Spook, choosing the appaloosa because he was faster than Othello and she would need speed. The mule would follow on his own as he always did. Spook tossed his head as she approached. She whispered soothingly to keep him from alerting Jonas. Othello nudged her with his nose, unable to understand why she was paying attention to the gelding rather than him. She decided to take all the horses. Jonas couldn't catch her on foot. She had started to swing herself into Buck's saddle when a coarse voice cut through the darkness.

"What d'ya think you're doing, bitch?" Jonas said.

Startled, she fell. Her foot tangled in the stirrup. Spook pranced and she called to him softly, terrified he would bolt and drag her behind him. When she freed herself and climbed to her feet, Jonas yanked her toward him, nearly pulling her arm from the socket. "Going for a ride without me?" he snarled.

He struck her so hard she reeled and found herself on her bottom again on the cold, wet ground.

"Take my horse and leave me stranded, will you? Damn you, I'll teach you to cross me." Again he reached for her.

"Hold it right there, Creedy."

Tempest gasped and whirled toward the unexpected sound. The yearned-for voice she had thought she would never hear again.

Buck Maddux limped into the flickering light of the bonfire, a revolver in his hand and death in his eyes. He was pale, the bandage on his head bright with blood. But he was alive!

"Put your filthy hands on her again and you're a dead man, Creedy," Buck promised, his voice as cold and piercing as icicles.

"Buck! Oh, Buck, thank God you're all right." Tears of joy crowded her eyes as Tempest started toward him. Before she'd taken two steps Jonas snatched her in front of him, at the same time drawing his sawed-off .38.

"I must be getting old, letting a man slip up on me like that," Jonas sneered.

"Shouldn't trust others to make sure a man's dead," Buck said.

Jonas nodded. "You're right in that. Even left you with a sidearm hidden somewhere, eh? No matter. Just means I'll have help hauling them rocks." With one hand he twisted Tempest's arm behind her back until she cried out in pain. "Unless you want to see this slut hurtin' worse'n she is now."

Buck's jaw tightened. "Let her go, Creedy."

Jonas laughed. "Think I'm crazy? Naw, reckon I'm the

one with the upper hand, just the way I like it. Toss the six-shooter over here, real easylike, or your whore's gonna get a bullet in her back."

Buck cursed. Rage had banished common sense when he'd seen Tempest go down beneath Jonas's heavy hand. Now she was suffering for it. Suffering because of another of his mistakes. There would be no more. He would get her out of this mess—or die trying. Setting aside his emotions he studied the situation with a cool, ruthless eye. Ronan was somewhere in the darkness, working his way toward the appaloosa and the Winchester in Buck's scabbard. Buck needed to keep Jonas distracted and buy Ronan some time. "Oh, I know you're crazy, Creedy. Otherwise you wouldn't mess with that treasure. It's cursed, you know."

"What're you talking about?"

"Spaniards always put curses on their gold . . . to discourage theft. Didn't you know that? Dig up the box and see for yourself, it's written right on the top. Or can't you read Spanish?"

Jonas watched Buck with small, wary eyes that showed a hint of fear.

Buck smiled. "Doesn't matter. Tempest can read it for you. She learned a bit of Spanish serving vittles to freighters in St. Louis. Didn't you, sweetheart?"

"Yes. Yes, I did, and I remember reading the curse when we found the box." Catching on to what Buck was attempting, she dug deeply into her imagination. "It was so terrifying, I don't think I'll ever forget it. 'Anyone who touches this gold with evil in his heart will die a slow, agonizing death.'" She faked a shudder. "Each of the trappers who originally stole it did die horribly. Two at the hands of the Spaniards, another tortured by Indians. And the old man who buried it here—the last of the thieves— he starved to death because of some strange malady that made him vomit up everything he ate." She shuddered again, and this time for real. The curse was fictitious, but the trappers had died exactly as she'd described. Remembering what he'd said about having hunted for the treasure for years, she guessed Jonas would know everything about it, including how the thieves had died. Hopefully, that bit of truth would convince him of the rest.

For a long time Jonas stared at Buck. Then he laughed, a shaky, humorless chuckle. "You're lying," he accused. "*You* dug up the gold, and I don't see you dying no horrible death."

"I took the gold to help a defenseless widow and two little kids keep a half-breed bastard from taking their land away from them," Buck replied calmly. "The only evil in my heart is wanting to see you dead for the way you've treated Tempest. Can you say the same, Creedy?"

The flickering firelight distorted Buck's face, making him look anything *but* an angel. "You have any goodness in your heart, Creedy?" he prodded. "Or just greed?"

Creedy's eyes took on a wild glint that put a hitch in Buck's pulse. The man was insane, and that terrified Buck. There was no telling what a madman might do. He could kill Tempest for the sheer pleasure of it, and with such coolness Buck might not see it coming in time to act. *Ronan, old man, where are you?*

"I don't scare so easy, Maddux," Jonas warned. He gave Tempest's arm a fiendish twist. She managed not to cry out, but couldn't keep the pain from showing in her eyes. "Now drop the six-shooter like I said, or I'll bust her arm."

Buck felt sick inside. He was afraid to push the man any farther, he couldn't risk getting Tempest hurt. The side of him that needed desperately to prove he had the courage and gumption to save the woman he loved protested the need to once again knuckle under to an assailant, but another part of him knew pressing Creedy now might easily bring about a fate similar to what Ellen had suffered. He would do anything to avoid that. Courage wasn't enough. He had to use wisdom as well. He threw Ronan's revolver at Jonas's feet.

Still holding Tempest, Jonas crouched and picked it up. "Nice. Remington .44 Army. Prefer the Colt myself, 'specially my Moll here," he said, gesturing with the sawed-off .38. "Short barrel like this is a real advantage in a close fight. Not only deadly, but damned hard to take away from a man." His custom-designed holster was too short for the .44, but he shoved it in anyway, keeping the .38 on Tempest. He sounded almost normal now, though his eyes were still wild.

Buck's wounded leg was trying to buckle on him, and the pain in his head caused colored sparkles to dance before his eyes. If he pretended to collapse, Creedy might relax and give him the advantage he so needed. Struggling not to collapse for real, Buck let himself droop with a weariness that was much too real. "I'm feeling kind of weak. Mind if I sit down and have a smoke?"

"Go ahead. You're gonna need your strength to haul the rest of them rocks out of the grave. Just make it quick, and don't try nothing stupid."

Turning his gaze on the grave as he lowered himself to a rock, Buck fished in his coat pocket and came up with his fixin's. The extra rifle ammunition he'd kept there was missing. He wondered again where Ronan was. The few extra minutes the cigarette would buy them was the best he could do to give the old man the time needed to retrieve the Winchester and load it with the spare ammo. "Doesn't look like I'll have to haul too many rocks. You were so close to that box it's a wonder it didn't jump up and bite you." A satanic smile etched his face. " 'Course, it's usually you snakes who do the biting, isn't it?"

"Bait me all you want, Maddux. I'm too close to getting everything I ever wanted to let you ruin it for me now."

"Yeah?" Buck tapped Bull Durham tobacco onto a cigarette paper. He took his time, making a production of pulling the drawstring on the tobacco pouch closed with his teeth and rolling the smoke neat and tight. "Too bad you won't live long enough to spend that gold you're drooling over."

"No?" Hysteria edged Jonas's laughter. "What d'ya figure is gonna stop me? You? Might be kinda hard, since you're gonna be dead soon."

Remembering something Viola had told him about Creedy, Buck made another attempt to rattle the man. "You believe in ghosts?"

Jonas blanched and Buck knew he had struck a nerve.

"Ain't no such thing," Jonas snarled.

Buck nodded. "Back East when I was a boy, we lived in a house almost two hundred years old." He tapped ash from his cigarette and took a long drag. The flaring tip was brilliant in an otherwise black and white world. "House had been through a long succession of owners. Seems nobody stayed long. See, the original owner died there. Found out his wife had been sleeping with another man while he was off fighting the British—and beat her to death. Then he shot himself. Folks insisted he haunted the place. Watching for the other man, so he could kill him, too."

Tempest heard a twig snap behind her and waited for Jonas to spin around to see what was there. But the man was too taken up with Buck's story to hear. She waited, knowing something was about to happen. She could see it in Buck's eyes. He'd been stalling, but now the stalling was over. A flash of red arced through the air as Buck tossed his cigarette into the darkness. He caught her gaze, then shifted his eyes to something behind her. Hope flared. He hadn't come alone.

"Saw that ghost once," Buck continued. "Scared the piss right out of me. Wore a Revolutionary War uniform, like George Washington wears in the paintings of him. You know who George Washington was, Creedy?"

"O' course I know who he was. Quit your babbling and get to hauling rocks."

Out of the darkness to their right came the hoot of an owl. Jonas whirled toward the sound. He was shaking, and Tempest knew it wasn't because of the cold. The man was terrified. The snub nose of the Colt wavered as he sought a target. Slipping her hand into her pocket, she closed her fingers over the spur. Suddenly Jonas yelped and loosened his hold on her. Tempest broke away in time to see a black wraith shaped like a mule cross through the firelight, a .44 Remington clutched in his big yellow teeth. Taking advantage of Jonas's surprise, she whipped out the spur and slashed it across his face. Howling, he released her.

Everything happened quickly then. Jonas was shooting wildly in every direction. Buck shouted for her to get out of the way, but she leaped up and grabbed the short barrel of Jonas's Colt. A fierce blow landed on her jaw. Still she clung to the gun for all she was worth. They fell to the ground and rolled in the mud, fighting over the six-shooter.

On the sidelines Buck yelled frantically for her to let go, trying at the same time to get a frightened Othello to let him take the Remington from him. Finally Othello surrendered his prize. Aiming at Creedy, Buck shouted for him to give up. Grunting and groaning, Tempest and the half-breed continued to struggle. She was afraid to let go. Jonas had fired several shots, but she couldn't be certain he was out of ammunition.

In a desperate measure, Buck thrust up his arm and fired into the clouds. Jonas jerked as though struck. His grip loosened. Tempest snatched the stubby weapon away and dragged herself free. Then Buck was there, helping her up, the Remington held steadily on Jonas. Wild-eyed, Jonas lay on the ground, panting as he stared at the six-shooter aimed at his heart.

"Easy, Creedy. It's over." Buck's hand itched with the urge to pull the trigger and blast the man straight to hell where he belonged. "You all right, sweetheart?"

"Yes." She snuggled into his embrace, exhausted, bruised, and terribly, terribly grateful they were both alive.

He hugged her tightly and kissed the top of her head. "She's something, isn't she, Creedy? My little mustang." The tension in Buck's body eased, but the way he leaned into her told her he was nearing the last of his strength. Othello decided it was time he received a little applause for his heroics and butted him in the back.

"Whoa, you long-eared Lothario." Nothing would do but that Buck scratch the mule's favorite spot and give him the praise he deserved. "You did good, boy."

Tempest laughed, marveling at the way the mule had lifted her father's Remington out of Jonas's holster with his teeth and run off with it. "I knew someone was behind me. I saw you signal with your hand, but I never expected your accomplice to be Othello."

Buck had taken his eyes off Creedy for only a second. Suddenly, firelight glinted on polished steel in the half-breed's hand. Buck spun, dropping to a crouch and shoving Tempest aside at the same time. Before he could fire, a shot exploded. Jonas grunted and lurched backward. Dropping the knife he'd been about to throw at Buck, he clutched at his chest. A red stain spread over his brocade vest, soaking the watch in his vest pocket.

A man emerged from the shadows.

"Papa!" Tempest shouted.

" 'Bout time you got here," Buck said, barely able to push himself to his feet.

"Sorry, lad, that horse o' yers is as skittish as a bagpiper with a mouse up his kilt. Wouldn't let me near 'im. Loading a rifle with one hand isn't so easy either."

"You did fine, old man. Just fine."

On the ground, Jonas gasped for air. Blood trickled from a corner of his mouth. Pain contorted his face as he stared with dazed eyes into space. Looking down on him, Ronan said, "He'll soon be meetin' up with those ghosts ye had 'im panicking over."

Buck laid a hand on the shorter man's shoulder. "Thanks to you. That owl call you gave was perfect."

"Glad I could help, lad."

Jonas's eyes widened with sudden terror. "Mother?" he whispered. A strangled sound came from his chest, his legs spasmed, then he lay still.

Ronan knelt and felt the man's neck for a pulse. "He's dead."

The raw strength, built of will alone, which Buck had been drawing on ever since he'd regained consciousness abruptly left him. His gun hand fell limply to his side, and the Remington slid to the ground. He staggered as he turned and tried to walk away, cursing his body for betraying him. Everything began to spin.

"Grab him, Papa," Tempest cried as she came to her feet.

Ronan slipped his good arm around the younger man, taking his weight. Tempest rushed to Buck's other side, and he looped an arm around her neck. They sat him down in the warmth of the fire.

"Oh, Buck, look at you. You nearly killed yourself trying to save me." Affectionately, she raked the silver-streaked hair off his forehead with her hand. "Your face is so tight with pain you look like death itself."

He attempted one of his famous grins. "Reassuring to know you still find me handsome, sweetheart."

"Quit your nonsense. You're not out of the woods yet. We have to get you home where I can take care of you."

"Home," he murmured softly as the blackness took him.

Chapter Twenty-Six

Pain. Fog. Echoing voices ordering him to drink. Darkness. Each time Buck awoke it was the same. His mind was so befuddled he couldn't think. He knew he'd been shot, but that was all.

Except for the hands. Gentle, soft, soothing on his skin. Bathing his face with coolness. Vague glimpses of Tempest, brief, shadowy, and accompanied often by a bitter liquid poured down his throat. The hands belonged to her. Sweet, sweet hands. Doing sweet things to his body that made him feel better. Buck was in love with those hands.

Ronan was there, too, but his presence meant being jostled about painfully. Then there was a tiny moonbeam of an angel who called him Papa Buck and kept insisting he get well.

Buck wanted to get well. He hated the weakness that kept him so drained he could barely lift his head. He hated the fog that clouded his mind and made him want to sleep all the time. Seconds. Hours. Days. There was no telling how long he had been bobbing in and out of that haze. Even when he'd thought the pain had lessened, he'd been too groggy to move. All he could do was sleep. Then, finally, he awoke one day to see Tempest's lovely amber-flecked eyes gazing down at him, and he knew he was going to live.

"How long's it been?" he asked, licking dry lips.

"Four days. You had a concussion. Here, drink this."

He frowned. "What is it?"

"An herb tea with a touch of laudanum in it."

"No. No laudanum. Stuff's poison."

Smiling patiently, she said, "I know. It's as addictive as alcohol, but it makes the pain bearable, and I've been careful not to give you too much."

"Don't want it." The moment he shook his head, the world began to spin and he closed his eyes. After a moment he said, "Gotta get up."

"You're in no shape to get up."

"Got to." He struggled to lift himself and nearly passed out from the pain in his head.

Pushing him back down, Tempest scolded him: "You empty-headed mule, you're not going anywhere."

"I'll wet the bed then."

"Oh." She pulled the chamber pot out from under the bed, then sat down beside him. "Here, I'll help you. You won't need to stand."

It was all he could do to remain conscious as the room whirled around him, but he managed to sit up. When Tempest reached for the opening on his underdrawers, he slapped her hands away. "Some things a man has to do for himself."

"If you black out before you're finished, you'll make a mess," she complained.

"Then sit behind me and hold me up, but you're damn well not . . ." He didn't see any need to finish the sentence.

She braced him from behind while he saw to his business, then helped him lie back down. As she picked up the chamber pot to take it outside, he mumbled, "First time I stopped a woman from laying her hands on me. Must be getting old."

Each day after that he was able to stay awake a little longer. Except for the fading effects of the concussion, his head wound was healing fine. The tiny stitches she'd carefully sewn above his ear were removed, and the infection in his calf was gone. Even though the pain had let up, his leg was stiff and still very sore. Slowly, he began to gain strength, but he wasn't an easy patient.

"How long are you going to keep me tied to this bed, woman?" he said a week after the shooting, arms crossed over his naked chest, face scowling at her.

She wanted to say, Until I can convince you to stay. Instead she held out the cup of broth she had brought him. "I don't see any ropes holding you down."

Buck ignored the cup. "Don't need ropes. That lug of a cat of yours lays on top of me all day, and if I try to get out of bed, you sic Rooster on me."

"As if that dog would harm a hair on your head. You're not well enough to get up. Quit pouting and drink your broth."

"Men don't pout. And I'm sick of broth. How do you expect me to get any strength back when you won't give me any solid food?"

With a sigh of exasperation, Tempest sat on the side of the bed and tried to put the cup to his lips. When he shoved it away, beads of brown liquid splattered onto his bare chest.

"Now look what you've done." Tempest set the cup on the bedside table and reached for a napkin. Grabbing her wrists he held her still.

"Lick it up," he growled.

"What?"

"Lick it off. I'll show you how well I am."

Feeling the strong grip of his hands she wondered if she'd misjudged his condition. She watched the glistening droplets meander through the hair on his chest, down his flat belly to the waistband of his underdrawers, and felt slow heat spread through her body. Ignoring it, she said, "Don't be silly, Buck. You're not well enough for that yet."

"Try me," he rasped.

But she was right. He was still weak as one-bean coffee.

Unused to being idle, he fussed and griped every minute of the day, demanding all Tempest's attention and generally driving her crazy. Ronan spent most of his time tending to the animals or courting Viola, and the children, especially sensitive little Ethan, quickly learned to give their Papa Buck a wide berth. Left alone, while Tempest saw to outside chores or went to town, Buck idled away the lonely hours brooding over the future.

No one in Harper knew yet about the Spanish gold. When Ronan had delivered Jonas's body to the Carcass Creek Cattle Company, he'd said only that the man had shot "Skeet Whitney" out of jealousy and revenge, and had wound up mortally wounded himself. The gold was buried in the garden until Buck was well enough to accompany Tempest to Price where they would deposit it in a bank. They would report Jonas's death to the local constable there. Once word got out about the treasure, the news would spread clear across the West. Ronan had suggested that the descendants of the old fur trapper who'd first buried it might try to claim it as theirs, but Buck doubted it. If anyone had a prior claim, it would be the Spanish government. Since there was some question about the law allowing Tempest to keep the gold, she was refusing to even consider it hers. But even she couldn't resist dreaming of how she would spend it.

All Buck would agree to take was twenty-four dollars and six cents. Without Tempest and the children, he didn't care where he went or how he lived. Simply thinking about it left him feeling hollow and miserable. Life had given him a glimpse of heaven. Where else could he expect to go now, except down?

She said she loved him, and Buck believed it, but would she still, if she knew the bitter truth of his past, the truth about Ellen? The more he worried and stewed over it, the grumpier he became. He lay awake nights. He refused to eat, which infuriated Tempest. More arguments ensued each time she caught him out of bed and trying to force strength back into his leg by walking before she considered him ready. The tension between them grew thick as axle grease. Watching them, Ronan would shake his head and take the children away until their anger blew over.

Then one day Angel crawled onto the bed beside Buck, a few straggly lavender daisies in her grubby hand. "What are those for?" he asked, frowning.

"To cheer you up tho you won't be mean to Mama anymore," she said.

His frown deepened. "You think I've been mean to Mama?"

"Un-huh." Angel began plucking petals from one of the daisies. "You yell at her all the time. Don't you love uth anymore?"

His heart broke, and he gathered her close. "Of course I still love you, dumplin'. I love all of you, especially your mama. I'm sorry, I guess I don't handle being laid up very well."

"Ethan was grumpy when he was thick, too." Heaving a heavy sigh of acceptance, she said, "I gueth it's a man thing."

Buck chuckled. "What do you mean, a 'man thing?'"

"Mama asked Aunt Viola how come men are thuch

babies, and Aunt Viola thaid it was jutht one of those 'man things' we women have to deal with.''

Putting back his head, Buck roared with laughter. After that, he was a model patient. Quiet, painfully polite, somber as a mortician.

It wasn't Tempest's fault he was laid up. Or that he was hurting because his time with her was almost over. He'd brought enough trouble into her life; the least he could do was make their last days together as pleasant as possible. He didn't sleep any better at night, and his melancholy deepened, but he was careful to act cheerful enough around the others and to keep his inner pain to himself. When he was finally able to walk all the way out to the privy without the crutch Ronan had made him, he kept the news to himself. In spite of dizziness and occasional flashes of double vision he was well enough to drag himself onto Spook and ride away. He simply couldn't make himself go.

On a cold, blustery Sunday morning in October, Ronan took the children into town to have lunch with Viola. There was no sign of Tempest. Buck assumed she was outside hauling water from the well to do the washing, or feeding the stock, or doing some other chore. Left alone, Buck rose and began exercising his leg. A fire blazed in the stove, keeping the room warm. He was hobbling back and forth in his underdrawers, grumbling over the stiffness and continuing weakness of his leg when the door opened and Tempest stepped inside with a pan of freshly dug potatoes. She stood there a moment, staring at him before putting the pan on the table. She hung up her coat and hat, then turned toward him. Her hair was flying about her face as usual, her trousers were stained with mud from the garden, and her shirt hung to her knees, hiding her shape. She was so beautiful, his heart clenched and his throat grew tight. This could easily be his last view of her, he thought.

All he had to do was open his mouth and tell her about Ellen. They were alone. It was the perfect time.

He remained mute.

Tempest crossed the room and stopped in front of him, close enough to touch. Close enough to smell her earthy, feminine scent. "What is it, Buck? I know something's troubling you, something more than the slowness of your recovery. Please tell me."

His jaw tightened. He ordered himself to speak of what lay so heavily on his heart, but what came out was: "I hate being idle is all. I'm restless and . . . and frustrated." Limping past her, he sat on the bed and rubbed his sore leg.

"Muscles take a long time to heal," she said, kneeling at his feet. "Here, let me."

She sat back on her heels and placed his foot in her lap. Then she gently massaged the tender muscles around his wounds. Seeing his bare foot so close to that feminine heaven he never quite succeeded in getting off his mind, and her breasts moving inside her shirt, a fierce thrust of desire shafted through him. He knotted his fists in the sheet to keep from reaching for her. Then she lifted her face to him and smiled, and he was lost.

With a growl of frustration and need, he pulled her onto her knees between his thighs and took her mouth with his. Pressing closer, she wrapped her arms around his neck and returned the kiss every bit as fiercely. After a moment, as if they realized no one was going to tear them apart, the kiss gentled and became a slow exploration, a reacquainting of themselves with the joy and pleasure they had yearned for and missed so desperately since his injury.

Outside, a light sleet was falling. The branches of the cottonwoods were bare. Fiery spikes of willows colored the creek bottom, and the hills resounded with the bugled challenges of bull elk guarding their harems. Secretly Tempest prayed for an early winter that would make travel impossible and would keep Buck at her side a little longer.

"Judas, but I've missed you," he whispered hoarsely as his mouth raced over her face.

Badly enough to stay? she wanted to ask, but his teeth were gently nipping her neck the way she loved, his tongue soothing each spot. She could hardly think for the sensations he kindled inside her.

"I'm sorry," he whispered into the hollow above her collarbone. "I've been a bastard, but only because I don't want to leave you."

Her heart soared. "Then don't. Stay with me, Buck. I love you. I love you so much."

His throat was too tight to speak, and he was afraid. He stretched out on the bed, drawing her on top of him. She didn't wait for him to remove her trousers. Her lips never left his as she tore at the knotted cord around her waist. When she was naked, he kissed and caressed her until she moaned and writhed, her legs straddling him as she tried to join their bodies and find the rapture she knew awaited.

White-hot fire seared Buck's veins, centering in his loins. He groaned as she positioned herself so that her sultry heat barely cradled the tip of his erection. For a long time they gazed at each other, drawing out the moment. It seemed momentous somehow. Pivotal. As if this joining of their bodies would seal them to each other for all time. As if, from this day forward, they would become indivisible. Not two halves of a whole, but one entity. All Buck's years of lonely wandering, of unspeakable yearning, of blindly seeking something he couldn't name—didn't believe existed—had been for this. For Tempest.

"*This* is my treasure," he whispered huskily. "You. You're all the treasure I'll ever want."

Her heart turned to honey and she bathed him in it, in her love.

Later, Tempest awoke curled about Buck as he lay on his back, one arm slung over his face. The covers had been dragged partially over them, but there was no hiding their nakedness or what they had been doing. Her gaze flew to the clock as she imagined her father and the children walking in on them. She sighed with relief at how little time had passed.

Buck stirred. He snuggled her more closely to him, one hand stroking down her arm, then drifting over the curve of her hip to the satiny thigh she'd draped across his. Still half-asleep, he adjusted their positions so that she was spooned with her back to his chest. He kissed her shoulder and murmured what sounded like "Treasure."

Had he meant what he'd said during their lovemaking? Was she all he would ever want? Or would his restless feet eventually call him away from her? Her heart sank at the thought. She wished she had something to give him, a token of the beauty they had found together, something he could wear close to his heart. Mentally, she rifled through the few treasures she had kept over the years: the tiny beaded purse White Cloud Woman had made her, a silver charm shaped like a buffalo that her brother Rule had given her on her sixth birthday; or better yet, the obsidian spearhead she'd found when Skeet had dragged her to see his favorite Indian ruin. The stone was as black as Buck's hair and would be a wonderful keepsake of Deception Canyon. She could have a hole drilled so he could wear it on a thong about his neck. She recalled her exhilaration the day she'd found it, the new insight she had gained into Skeet's fascination with the canyon. The ruin was so well hidden that—

"Holy Mary!" Suddenly Tempest scrambled from his embrace.

Startled, Buck sat up and stared at her. "Where the hell are you going?"

"The stolen payroll!" Her voice trembled with excitement as she grabbed for her clothes. "I know where it is!"

Buck fell back onto the bed and closed his eyes. "I think I heard this once before." He tried to pull her back down on the bed, but she shoved him away.

"Don't, Buck, I'm going after the money."

"Now?"

"Yes, now."

"What's the rush?" Frustration edged his voice. "You're already rich. Come back to bed."

Yanking on her shirt, she said, "You know we may not be allowed to keep the gold. The payroll will pay off my loan with enough left over for a small log house. With windows . . . and a wood floor." She grinned. "This solves everything, don't you see? You refused to take any of the gold, but it's only right that we share the payroll money. You earned it, Buck. You spent two years in prison because of it."

"I don't care about any damned money. I just want you. Come on, sweetheart," he pleaded, "I need you."

"I'm too excited," she protested.

"So am I." He gestured to his aroused body.

Laughing, she said, "I promise I'll make it up to you when I get back, but I have to know if I'm right, if it's really there."

Buck grudgingly swung his legs off the bed. "All right, all right. Let me get dressed."

"No. You're in no shape to climb rocks. I'm going by myself."

"Like hell! Jonas Creedy might be dead, but there are plenty of other dangers for a woman alone out there."

Tempest led Buck a mile beyond Treachery Canyon to a particularly rugged side canyon that made a single twist, then ended abruptly. The east wall formed a sandstone ridge atop a steep rocky incline. After forming the inner curve of the twist, the wall sprouted straight up in a towering mass of fragmented stone, eroded by time and weather into crumbling battlements. The west side was a more gentle, juniper-covered slope wearing a sandstone crown. Leaving Spook and Othello to nose out edible grasses amongst the debris of the corroded mountain, Buck shouldered a pick and shovel and limped behind Tempest up the east side to the base of the rocky ridge on which Indian rock etchings abounded.

Above them as they followed the ridge, the wall rose in irregular layers of beige, russet, green, and purple. In places the rock looked as though it had been partially melted and a black stain poured over the exterior, creating a gruesome pock-faced facade with pale hollow eyes peering out of the black, like something from a nightmare. Sweat dripped down his temples beneath his hat brim as he hobbled along the steep, rugged incline in Tempest's meager shadow, forcing his still-healing body to perform feats for which it wasn't ready. His breathing was ragged. Tempest's was easy, unlabored. The tools on his shoulder grew heavier, and his leg began to throb. Detesting his weakened state, he growled, "You sure you know where you're going?"

"Yes." She stopped and pointed. "See that flat rock there, the one that creates an overhang at the base of the ridge? Underneath it is a big pit-house that's almost entirely intact. I think that's where Skeet hid the money."

"I don't see anything."

"That's why it was his favorite. He called it his secret ruin because it was impossible to see until you were practically on top of it. He even dragged Angel and I up here. She was Ethan's age then. Can you imagine bringing a child that small on a trek like this?" Tempest shook her head. "Skeet never had much sense, I'm afraid. He wasn't much more than a child himself in some ways."

"It's farther off the main road than I figured he'd go," Buck said, trying to hide the fact that he was panting. "Hell of a climb too. Can't imagine him having time to get up here and hide the gold before the posse caught up to him."

"That's why I didn't think of it at first. Actually, it's been so long since I've been to any of the ruins, I've forgotten where most of them are, except the ones that are visible from the canyon bottoms." Tempest peered at him anxiously. "You look peaked. I told you you weren't up to this yet."

Glowering, he retorted, "I could have been up and regaining my strength a long time ago if you hadn't kept me drugged with your witch's brew." He grimaced. "Tasted like rotten chicken guts boiled in coal oil."

Tempest laughed. "You're not even close."

"Judas, I hope not."

Since the overhang formed the roof, access to the ruin was through a tiny, ground-level opening barely large enough for Buck to crawl through. Inside, the light was dim, but the room was cool and although the ceiling was too low to allow him to stand upright it was surprisingly roomy. There was no sign of the floor having been disturbed. They concentrated their search on the rubble of a partially collapsed wall and soon hit pay dirt. Under a few stones, still in perfect shape except for a few mouse holes, lay a leather pouch marked Property of U.S. Army. Gold and silver coins cascaded out of the chewed openings as Buck lifted it. Tempest laughingly let the coins sift through her fingers onto her lap. "Oh, Buck, have you ever seen anything so beautiful?"

He smiled. He adored the childlike enthusiasm lighting up her face. The gold's gleam echoed the amber glints in her eyes. He decided to have some of the coins fashioned into baubles she could wear about her neck and wrists. "No," he said, staring at her hungrily. "I've never seen anything more beautiful." Then he clenched harder at his control and said, more somberly. "You're even richer now. You mortgaged Heartsease to pay back the stolen money, so this is rightfully yours."

"No. *We're* richer, Buck. And I don't want to hear anything more about it. I wouldn't have found this or the Spanish gold if it weren't for you. It wouldn't be fair for me to keep it all."

He thought of the stubborn pride keeping Swede and Lacey apart. He thought of all he wanted to do for Tempest and the children before he left. He thought of California. "Tell you what, put a thousand aside for me, and we'll see."

"A thousand isn't enough," she said, and stuffed a handful of ten-dollar gold eagles into his coat pocket. While he dug them out, she slipped more into his other pocket.

"Tempest!" He snatched at her hands but she evaded him. The cold coins slid down his chest through the open neck of his shirt. "Hey, that's cold," he complained.

Her joyous laughter was contagious, and his own deep rumble joined hers as he got even by filling her trousers with silver dollars. She gasped and jumped to her feet. A shower of jingling coins poured out of her pant legs onto the ground. When she pulled up her shirt to extract a coin stuck in her waistband, Buck glimpsed the under curve of a breast, and his laughter ebbed. Desire careened through him.

He pulled her onto his lap, a hand closing over her breast as he kissed her. Her arms came around his neck, and she demanded as much as she gave.

They were panting when he finally drew away. Looking down into her flushed face, he brushed a thumb across a taut nipple. Her eyes half closed, and she let out an earthy moan. Enjoying her unbridled reaction, he rubbed the nipple again. "This alone is worth every coin in that pouch," he whispered, nibbling her ear. "And more. So much more."

Her eyes opened. "You couldn't buy me with all the gold in the world, Buck Maddux. But I gladly give myself to you."

Groaning, he kissed her again. There was no sweeter or more giving woman in the world. Love filled him to overflowing. His heart felt ready to burst. But before he could tell her what was in his heart, he had to make her understand exactly what she was getting. She hadn't believed him when he told her he had killed his wife and baby. He couldn't ask her to entrust her life to him until she knew the truth. Yet the words wouldn't come. He began gathering up the money and putting it back into the pouch. "Let's get out of here. The walls are closing in on me."

"Oh, Buck, I'm sorry. I forgot what closed places do to you."

He'd forgotten, too, actually. He couldn't even say when he last felt the oppressive sense of panic at being shut into a windowless room. Tempest had banished that nightmare. She had made him whole again. In so many ways.

When they were back out in the fresh air, transferring the money from the mouse-chewed pouch to the security of a saddlebag, Buck suggested she give her father some of the money. "Living off his daughter is hard on a man's pride. Being able to hold his head up again might help him make a clean, permanent break with the whiskey."

"I already told Papa I wanted him to have some of the gold. He refused . . . out of that same stubborn pride you're talking about. I think he's afraid to trust himself with money yet. Even one double eagle would buy a lot of whiskey." She picked out a large gold coin and ran a thumbnail over the embossed eagle on its face. "I told him I'd hold it for him until he's ready."

"If he could resist the money, he's already kicked the booze. All he needed was self-respect, and he got that saving my life and helping to free you from Jonas Creedy. I never would have made it that night without him and that ugly old mule."

Studying him from beneath her lashes, Tempest said, "Odd. That's what Papa said *you* needed. Self-respect. What did he mean, Buck? It has to do with your wife and baby, doesn't it? What really happened to them?"

It was the opening he needed. Buck sat down with his back against the sun-warmed rock of the Indian ruin and watched a fox amble across the hillside on the other side of the little box canyon. Tempest deserved the truth about Ellen; he needed to tell her. But fear of losing her tied his innards in figure eights. Whatever affection she felt for him would die once she heard the details of that horrid night. He couldn't bear that. Yet he had to tell her. It was time.

Chapter
Twenty-Seven

"I was eighteen when I met Ellen," Buck began, draping his arms across his bent knees. "My stepfather tried to talk me into waiting, but I insisted on marrying her right away. I was so hot to get her into bed. She was the first woman I . . ."

The fox surprised a mouse and gave chase. "We were too young to know what we were doing, but we were happy. At least I was. Ellen wasn't fond of cooking and hated the one-room house that was all I could afford. She complained a lot. I was too insensitive to understand her feelings, I guess. I was working for Pa at his warehouse in Memphis, so I didn't spend as much time in that little house as she did, and when I was home, all I thought about was . . ." He shook his head. "It wasn't making love. I didn't know what love was back then, let alone how to pleasure a woman."

Buck's smile was sad, and a bit self-deprecating. Tempest listened quietly, tamping down the foolish stab of jealousy she felt at the thought of his being happy with another woman. Making love to another woman.

"Ellen cried when she learned she was going to have a baby, but I was overjoyed. I'd always loved children and looked forward to having my own. When Pa asked me to go to New Orleans to pick up a shipment, I was like a kid at Christmastime. I was going to take my wife on a side trip to see the ocean when we got there." He sighed. "She didn't want to go, and I sure as hell wish she hadn't."

His eyes filled with such pain and self-loathing Tempest felt it in her soul. He straightened his long legs and began plucking up weeds and tearing them apart. She knew he didn't want to dredge up the awful memories of that time, afraid he might never be rid of them. She slipped her small hand in his to offer him what comfort she could. He closed his eyes, blindly lifted her hand to his mouth and pressed a kiss to her palm. Then he let her go and looked away as if to put distance between them. Knowing it would make the telling of his story easier for him, she ignored the pain that distancing brought her.

"I was so damn cocky," he said, shaking his head ruefully. "Too damn immature to realize I didn't know everything. On the way to New Orleans I got into a poker game with a few men at the inn where we stayed the first night. Ellen hated it when I drank. She didn't want me to play with them, said they looked sinister, but I told her I could take care of myself." He covered his face with his hands, muffling his words. "Judas, but I was stupid. So damnably stupid. And Ellen paid the price."

He dropped his hands and continued. "I bragged about going to New Orleans to pick up a valuable shipment of goods, as if I were a big successful businessman. French silks and laces, Limoges china, and perfume. They were impressed. Oh, yeah, those men were really impressed."

The fox caught the mouse. It tossed its prize into the

air, like a cat. Buck picked up a stone and threw it at the animal. The missile fell far short, of course. The fox never even heard it hit the earth.

Buck was quiet so long, Tempest thought he wasn't going to continue. When he did, his voice was ragged, almost too low to hear, yet she couldn't miss the pain behind his words, and she ached for his suffering.

"The next night I was looking for a place to pull the wagon off the road and make camp when a rider appeared in front of us, another one behind. Stupid as I was then, I knew we were in trouble. They boxed us in at a spot where trees crowded the road and there was no way to escape them. Ellen was trembling and clinging to me. I could feel her fingers digging into my arm through my coat." Buck's voice was flat, wooden. He no longer watched the fox, looking inward instead, at visions of the past.

"The one they called Captain was older and had the manners of a gentleman. Outwardly, anyway. They'd fought side by side for the Confederacy and had been riding together ever since. The captain was friendly enough, and there were no weapons visible, but I knew my winnings weren't all they meant to take from me. The way the captain kept looking at Ellen scared me so bad I was sick inside."

Buck put his head in his hands, and Tempest saw his throat work as he swallowed and fought for control. "Judas," he said, looking up again but still seeing only the past. "I can't believe . . . How could I have been so stupid and cocky . . . ?" He shook his head and swallowed again. "My revolver was in my valise, in the back of the wagon where I couldn't get to it. I tried to bluff them into believing the only money I had was what I'd won from them, plus traveling expenses. They didn't go for it, they wanted my money belt too. I laughed and told them there wasn't any, that my stepfather had arranged for me to get the money for the shipment directly from his bank in New Orleans. The captain stared at me a while, then nodded to the others. The next thing I knew, Ellen was screaming and I was being dragged off the wagon seat. I curled into a ball to protect myself from their blows, but they kicked me and pummeled me until I was barely conscious. I felt them tearing at my clothes searching for the money belt. When they found it, they gave me a few parting shots, enough to knock me unconscious.''

Again Buck shook his head, and Tempest knew he was unaware of the tears running down his cheeks. She ached inside. She wanted to touch him, comfort him, but she sensed he wasn't through with the awful story he was telling, and now wasn't the time to remind him of her presence. He wasn't truly here beside her; he was on a lonely road north of Louisiana near the Mississippi River. And he was scared and hurting and ashamed. She didn't realize there was moisture on her cheeks, or that her hands were knotted in her coat to keep from reaching for him. She was terribly afraid she already knew where the tale was going.

When he began speaking again, his voice was hoarse, ragged with pain and tight with bottled up tears. She wasn't at all sure he was going to be able to continue, and almost prayed he wouldn't.

. . . *The pain didn't seem much improved when Buck woke up, and something sharp was pricking the skin under his jaw. He saw the one called Arkansas kneeling over him, his knife at Buck's neck. The man laughed and spit out a wad of tobacco, barely missing Buck's head. "Captain says we can have us some fun now. Didn't want you to miss out."*

Ellen screamed then. Buck tried to get to her and found he couldn't move. His hands and feet were tied. Snickering, Arkansas walked away.

Buck blinked away the fog in his head and saw Ellen. She was struggling in Charlie's grip, while the captain looked on. Arkansas joined Charlie, and they threw her roughly to the ground. When she tried to get up Charlie struck her in the face. Ellen screamed. Charlie pounded her in the stomach again and again. Buck yelled for them to leave her alone, but they ignored him. Arkansas braced one knee on her right arm and held the tip of his knife to her throat. The blade glinted silver in the moonlight, and Buck held his breath.

"Lay real still now, ma'am, and don't make a sound, or you'll likely find your throat slit, you hear?"

Ellen sobbed as Charlie tore away her clothes. When she was naked, her dress in tatters about her small body, Charlie stood. No words were spoken between the men. Obviously this was a familiar routine. The captain knelt between Ellen's legs and unbuttoned his pants. Her pale legs thrashed and she started to scream, but Arkansas growled another threat.

Buck struggled to reach her. He shouted every epithet he had ever heard as he tried to drag his bound body closer to his wife. On his elbows he hitched himself over the ground. He had to stop what was happening. He couldn't let them hurt Ellen. But he couldn't get to her in time.

The captain handed his cap to Charlie. Then he fitted himself between Ellen's thighs. Buck screamed.

Too late. Too late.

He cried. Like an infant, he cried. For Ellen? For himself? He didn't honestly know.

The men took turns. After a while Ellen stopped sobbing. She lay still and quiet. As though dead. Buck knew she was probably praying that she would die. But she had to hang on. For the baby's sake, she had to survive.

The baby. Buck's throat was raw from screaming and crying, but he rasped out more curses as he thought of his tiny babe inside that battered body.

When it was over, the men cut him free, got on their horses, and rode off. Buck finally reached Ellen. She was blessedly uncon-

scious. Her face was bruised and streaked with dirt, blood, and tears. Her breasts had been savagely bitten. Between her legs blood glistened.

Buck wished with all his heart that they had killed him. How would he ever look her in the eye again? How would he face his stepfather? His foolishness had lost him the money for the shipment. His selfishness and stupidity had gotten his wife raped . . .

Even now, fifteen years later, he knew he hadn't deserved to live that night. And now, he told himself, Tempest knew it, too.

Tempest remained silent a long time after Buck's voice died away. The horror he had described was unspeakable. It clogged her throat until she could hardly breathe. Sweet Mary, what he had endured. And Ellen. Poor Ellen. It was no wonder he suffered still from the horror of that awful night. Surreptitiously, she wiped the tears from her face as she struggled for composure. She hurt so badly for him she couldn't move. Buck hadn't moved either, and she could feel the tenseness radiating from his body. At first she thought he was just waiting for her reaction. Then she realized the story wasn't finished. "What about . . . Ellen?" she whispered. "How did Ellen die?"

His tone was cold and harsh, as he gave only the bare details, keeping his emotions locked inside. "She went into labor there on the road. The baby . . . my son . . . was born dead. I couldn't stop the bleeding. Ellen bled to death in my arms."

Tempest swallowed the lump blocking her throat and she squeezed her eyes shut. Her heart ached for poor Ellen. For the baby that had had no chance to live. Most of all, she ached for Buck.

* * *

Neither spoke on the ride back to town where Ronan and the children waited. Tempest's mind whirled with all Buck had told her. The knowledge that he had carried this burden of guilt for so long tore her apart. She could understand now why he believed he was worthless. For fifteen years he'd been telling himself he was a murderer who didn't deserve happiness. For him, that was reality. Tempest didn't see it that way.

Buck's foolishness had led to the death of Ellen and their baby. But he had been only twenty years old. Old enough to marry, old enough to sire children, old enough to take on the responsibility his stepfather had entrusted to him. Old enough too, maybe, to know better than to let on to strangers that he was carrying a large sum of money. Yet, even the elderly made mistakes. Age had no corner on that market. And while being young didn't excuse what he'd done; it did make it easier to understand, and easier to forgive.

Tempest didn't need to be told that Buck's family had rejected him because of what had happened. She could only imagine the devastating grief his family and Ellen's must have suffered. It was a tragedy, a terrible, terrible tragedy. The anger they'd felt was understandable. But forgiveness was a part of love. She was certain his family hadn't stopped loving him. How could they? They had simply reacted to their anger, disappointment, and hurt, saying things they didn't truly mean. If Buck hadn't vanished on them, he would have had their forgiveness years ago. Maybe then he could have forgiven himself.

He expected her to reject him as his stepfather had, Tempest knew that. The shadows haunting his eyes were deeper and darker than ever. No devil's smile graced his face. The facade of carefree womanizer no longer offered him any shelter. His sins were out in the open. His restless gaze darted everywhere as if seeking a hole to crawl into. Not once had his eyes lighted on her. Shame made him afraid to face her. How could she convince him that whatever he may have been at twenty, today he was as good a man as God ever made. A man she loved with all her heart.

A mile out of town she came to a halt. He reined in beside her. "Buck, before we get to town, I have something I must say."

"Not now, Tempest," he said raggedly. "Please, not now."

She wanted to argue, but he looked so tired, so beaten. Perhaps he needed time to recover from the ordeal of reliving the awful experience he had related to her. "All right, tonight then."

Angel and the Todd girl were playing jacks on the front porch of the Boston Eatery when Tempest and Buck rode into town. Seeing them, Angel gave a glad shout and jumped up to wave. Tempest waved back. To her surprise, Buck slowed the appaloosa. For a brief moment his gaze met hers; then it flicked away, as if he couldn't bear what he saw. Or what he expected to see.

"I'll stay at the hotel tonight," he said.

The words came as a shock. She hadn't anticipated this. The scoundrel knew it, too. He'd counted on surprise to freeze her tongue to the roof of her mouth, the same way he was counting on her not arguing with him in public. Panic swung her heartbeat into triple time. What on earth was he up to? What was he planning? She couldn't bear the answers that came into her mind, and became determined not to let him get away with his tricks.

"It's best this way," he said in a bleak voice that ripped at her heart. "I'll be leaving in the morning at any rate. Long drawn-out goodbyes only make things worse."

"Damn you, Buck Maddux." Because she knew he was too stubborn to listen to anything else, she used the one weapon she knew would reach him. "You see that little girl over there? What do you think it's going to do to her if you simply walk out of her life without a word?"

Buck glanced at Angel who was still jumping up an down and waving. His heart sank. All the way back to town he'd tried to come up with a way to make this parting easier for the two of them. He hadn't thought about the children.

"It will be hard for Ethan too," Tempest said. "He's too young to understand. They're both too young. Angel had barely stopped asking for her father when you came into our lives. Now she thinks of you as her papa. How are you going to explain to her why you're leaving?"

He glared at her. "You knew I'd be going. All this time, you've known. Why haven't you prepared them?"

"Maybe I was hoping it wouldn't be necessary."

He wanted to ask what she meant, but time was running out. Angel was racing toward them, too impatient to wait any longer on the porch. As Buck watched, Viola emerged from the restaurant with Ronan, who was holding Ethan, all wearing enormous smiles of welcome. Judas. He shook his head. How had things gotten so complicated?

"Okay, I'll stay at the dugout tonight so I can spend some time with the kids and help them understand. But tomorrow I'm leaving." He scarcely had time to get the words out before Angel got to them.

"Papa Buck! Papa Buck!"

She held up her arms, and there was nothing he could do but reach down and lift the child onto his lap.

When they returned home to Heartsease, they found more than they had expected. The door stood open. Inside, the house looked as though a herd of brahma bulls had stampeded through it. Knocked-over stools, kindling, and dried herbs ripped from where they'd hung littered the floor. Dark syrupy sorghum dripped down the front of the sideboard onto a mound of white powder from the overturned flour bin where a pig wallowed. A hen was pecking at a bowlful of sugar cubes on the table. Sticky Cat tracks trailed across the counter, up the walls and across the floor. Sorghum and flour-covered felines and dogs were racing round and round the room as if they'd gone crazy on locoweed. Tempest's first terrifying thought was that someone had been there searching for the gold. The true cause was a bat, flying just below the ceiling while the frenzied animals leaped to catch it. The bat had probably flown in through the window and, hearing the cat chasing it, the ever-curious dogs had jumped at the door until it swung inward, letting them, and the pigs, join the fray.

"Blast," Tempest muttered, staring at the awful mess. "Papa, keep the children outside. There may be broken glass."

The animals paid scant attention to her as she began straightening stools. Buck reached for the broom. He watched the bat circle the ceiling, waited for it to come around again, then smacked it with the flat side of the broom. It fell to the floor where the cat pounced on the carcass, fighting off the dogs with bared fangs and slashing claws. She bounded out the door with the prize clamped in her teeth, only to lose it to one of the pigs.

Tempest grumbled about the waste as she swept up glass from a broken lamp. "You can afford a hundred lamps now," Buck pointed out.

"Just because I have the money, doesn't mean I need to go squandering it."

He knew better than to argue. She was too stubborn to listen. But the stress of his imminent departure caused him to take a fatalistic viewpoint on everything. It soured his disposition as well. "Doesn't mean you need to turn into a miser, either."

Slapping her hands on her hips, she said, "If all you're going to do is harangue me about my spending habits, I'd just as soon you went outside and got out of my way."

"Fine with me." He stomped out the door.

With a sigh, Tempest glanced again around the destroyed room. Her initial surprise at seeing Marmalade and the dogs lunging for the bat had alleviated the strain hanging about them like a cloud of gnats on the ride home. Now all was as it had been before. At least, between her and Buck. Tension. Anger. Hurt. Poor Papa must be wondering what on earth was going on.

Buck probably figured that his story about Ellen had killed her love for him. It wasn't true and she needed to let him know that, but she wasn't sure how. The matter needed to be handled with the delicacy of bufferfly wings, the diplomacy of a queen. Tempest prayed she was up to it.

As Buck headed for the barn with Spook in tow, he told himself the day would be easier to get through if he didn't torture himself watching her, knowing in a few more hours he would leave and never see her again. Yet he was already starved for the sight of her.

A diminutive hand slipped inside his, and somber brown eyes peered up at him. "Are you gonna unthaddle Thpook, Papa Buck?"

"Yes."

"Good. I don't want you to go nowhere."

He frowned as he gazed down at the girl. "What makes you think I'm going anywhere?"

Angel looked him straight in the eye. "Mama has plenty of money now, tho you don't need to pretend to be my daddy anymore.'' Moisture pearled on her long, pale lashes. ''But I don't want you to go away.''

It was as if the imp had reached inside his chest and squeezed his heart. His throat constricted. Hunkering down in front of her, he smoothed the flyaway hair from her sweet face. ''You don't?''

''Nuh-uh.''

It was foolish to ask. The answer was bound to hurt, but he found himself nudging the words out from around the lump in his throat, needing to hear them. ''Why not, buttercup?''

Raking tiny fingers through his beard, Angel thrust her lower lip out in a pout. '' 'Cauthe I want you to th-th . . . I don't want you to go away like my real papa did. He'th not ever coming back, and me and Ethan need a papa.''

''I know you do.'' Buck hugged her close, his eyes shut against the pain. It had hurt even more than he'd expected, hearing her say she wanted him to stay. If only Tempest felt the same way. He sought the words to explain why he had to go, but his mind was too full of hurt.

Angel's slender arms snaked around his neck. Her voice was soft, quavering with the blossoming of tears. ''I love you, Papa Buck. Pleathe don't go.''

His own tears came as a shock. Buck hadn't shed tears since he was a boy. He had denied himself that solace fifteen years ago and on every empty, pain-filled night since. But there was no stopping them now, and, strangely, he didn't want to.

That night, Buck lay awake on the cot in the front room long after everyone else had gone to bed. He folded his arms behind his head and stared up at the ceiling as he savored the sweet memory of Angel's declaration of love.

He wasn't at all sure he could leave her and Ethan. Or their mother. Especially their mother.

Maybe he could find a job around Price and come calling. In time, Tempest might learn to love him again.

Judas. Who was he fooling? Spook might sprout wings too, and fly him to the ocean. But it wasn't likely. Stupid to even hope he still had any chance with her. If she could have put aside the ugliness of his past, she would've done it by now. He had killed her love for him, as surely as he'd killed Ellen.

He should get his rear out of bed that instant and into his saddle. He could be miles away by morning. The children would forget him eventually. So would Tempest, though it was a painful truth to acknowledge. It must be close to midnight now and everyone was asleep. He could hear Ronan snoring softly in the back room where he slept in the children's bed. Now that everything was out in the open and there was no more need to pretend to be Skeet Whitney, it had seemed prudent for Buck to sleep in the front room. It had also been the most convenient bed to get a half-conscious man into when they'd brought him down off the plateau. He could slip out into the night and—

A sound came from the bedroom. Buck looked toward the doorway. The moonlight shining through the two velum-covered windows was too weak to penetrate the shadows, but he knew someone stood just out of sight. Then Tempest stepped into the room, the whiteness of her nightdress like a beacon lighting his soul. His heart thudded like a tom-tom, so loudly he could barely think above the sound. His entire body grew tense, his throat dry.

Her bare feet made no sound on the hide rugs as she moved toward him. Buck scooted into a sitting position, his back to the wall. He needed its support. He rubbed his suddenly sweating palms on the quilt. His eyes never left her face, trying to pierce the shadows to see her expression.

She stopped beside the bed, and Buck swallowed convulsively as he waited for her to say something. Her scent tantalized him—that odd combination of baby powder, wild herbs, bread dough, and woman he found so seductive. His breath came quick and hard. Nerves, stretched to their limit, caused his foot to jerk. He tried to work up enough saliva to speak. He didn't have the courage to ask what she was doing beside his bed in the middle of the night. She had probably decided it would be best for him to leave right then.

Before he could moisten his mouth enough to talk, she lifted the covers and slid in beside him. Anticipation froze him to the wall. Then her hand touched his face. "Did you really doubt that I would come to you tonight?" she asked quietly.

Numbly, he stared at her.

"Did you think I would let you walk away tomorrow without trying to change your mind?" The softness of her voice took the sting from the admonition.

"I-I didn't know what to think."

"Oh, Buck." She snuggled closer to his tense body. "You thought I would turn away from you because of what happened to Ellen, didn't you?"

The painful lump in his throat began to dissolve. He gulped. In one quick easy movement, Tempest threw aside the covers, hiked up her gown, and twisted so that she sat facing him, straddling his thighs. Lacing her fingers into the dark hair on his chest, she bent and kissed him. "What will it take to convince you I truly love you, Buck?" she whispered against his lips. "That I'll always love you, no matter what you did in the past."

He was afraid to believe. This could be a dream. In a

few minutes he would wake up, his body hard and aching with a need only she could fulfill.

She kissed him again, this time running her tongue over his lips until they parted, then, as he had taught her, dipping inside. Her woman's center wriggled against the hard ridge in his underdrawers. The air left him like an escaping balloon, and he moaned softly. Wrapping her in his arms, he buried his face in her hair, and clung to her tightly. "Aw, God, Tempest. I don't deserve—"

"Hush," she said. "I love you, and nothing you could say or do is going to change that. So, just love me back, Buck. It's all I'll ever ask of you."

Words failed him. He let his hands and lips answer for him, the only way he knew how, with slow, almost painful tenderness. Giving and taking pleasure. Giving and taking love.

Tempest snuck back to her own bed in the wee hours of the morn, but she was too happy to sleep. After dressing, she wrote a note to let her family know she was going herb hunting. She had promised the Eisenbeins she would restock their supply before winter put a stop to her collecting. Her gaze strayed often to the man asleep in the bed across the room. His hair was tousled, one arm slung over his eyes, a foot sticking out from under the blanket. Like a little boy, she thought fondly. As she took up her basket and let herself silently out the door, she made a decision— there would be no more herbs for preventing pregnancy. Not for her.

Half an hour later, Buck awoke to the tickle of a feather on his nose. Keeping his eyes closed, he clutched Tempest in a bear hug and started to kiss her. But the wriggling, giggling creature in his arms was too small. Opening his eyes, he found Angel staring down at him, an impish smile on her face.

"You were thleeping, Papa Buck."

"Trying to, anyway. But I know how to get even with you for waking me up."

Angel screeched as he tickled her. Soon she was gasping for air from laughing so hard. At some time during the melee, Ethan joined in, giving and taking his own share of tickles. The three rolled over the bed until it was a tangled mess. The frenzied barking of dogs ended the game. Going to the window as he dragged on his trousers, Buck peered out into the pale morning sunlight. "I'll be damned," he muttered.

"That'th a bad word, Papa Buck," Angel chided him.

Ignoring the girl, he hurried to the door and flung it wide. "Cale! I didn't expect you back," he said hesitantly. The children followed him outside. Ethan clung to Buck's leg and sucked a thumb as he stared up at the stranger, while Angel stood quietly waiting.

Swinging down off his horse, Cale Kincade turned to face his older brother. Ethan edged behind Buck. For several seconds the two men stared at each other, uncertain how to go on. Cale had one arm slung across his saddle, the other on his hip. He wore striped trousers, with a butternut shirt and a brown leather vest. His mouth was soft, rather than rigid with anger as it had been on his previous visit. A masculine version of their mother's mouth. The sight of it eroded the hardness Buck had lived with so long, and it eased his trepidation at seeing this bitter young brother again.

A tiny hand slipped into Buck's. "Who'th he, Papa Buck?" Angel asked, peering up at him with wide brown eyes.

"He's my little brother," Buck answered softly. "One I'm damned glad to see again."

Like river mist in morning sunlight, the tension dissolved. Wearing a small smile, Cale gave the girl a formal bow. "It's always a pleasure to meet a pretty lady," he pronounced over her tiny hand.

Angel giggled. "He'th nithe, Papa Buck. I like him."

Sensing the more pleasant mood that settled over them, Ethan emerged from behind Buck's leg. A grasshopper bounded past them and the boy gave chase, followed by his sister, leaving the two brothers alone.

"I went to Price," Cale said after another moment of awkwardness. "Wired Ma that I'd found you."

Buck went totally still, unaware that a pig was nibbling at the hem of his denims. The tension returned. Like a condemned man awaiting sentencing, he stiffened in preparation for the worst.

Chapter
Twenty-Eight

Cale reached inside his vest pocket and handed him a yellow slip of paper. Buck's throat went dry and his pulse kicked into a lope. Slowly, dreading what he would find there, he unfolded the paper, smoothed the wrinkles, and read the wired message:

Everyone thrilled. Pa cried. Bring Richard home. Only he can help put past behind us and heal family. Tell him Dr. Jakes says problem with baby brought on early birth, not rape. Ellen probably would have died anyway. Tell him we love him and forgave him long ago.

Love, Ma.

Carefully, Buck refolded the paper. His eyes stung. The wind, he told himself. After a moment, he cleared his voice to disguise a sniff, then glanced up, knowing Cale was watching and waiting for a reaction. "I don't know what to say. For fifteen years, I . . ." He couldn't go on. Swallowing hard, he looked away.

"I know, Richard. I've done a lot of thinking since I left here, especially after getting that wire. As little as Ma said there, I've still got a fair picture in my mind now of what happened. All I can say is, I'm sorry. I had no right jumping you. Lord, it must have been awful, your wife raped and . . ."

Buck turned away as the sting in his eyes worsened. His throat was tight and aching. The grasshopper had flown into the empty corral. Ethan was crawling beneath the pole fence to go after it, his bottom as bare and pink as a pig's nose.

Cale's hand came to rest on his brother's shoulder and gently squeezed. "As Ma said, it wasn't your fault. You've been tearing yourself up over this all these years. Now you need to put it to rest. Come home with me, Richard, help us be a real family again, a happy family like we used to be. Everyone's missed you."

Slowly, Buck faced him, a small, sardonic smile curving one side of his mouth. "Including you? Or do you still want to throttle me?"

Cale grinned, then sobered. "Truth is, I missed you as much as anyone. If I hadn't cared so much, I wouldn't have gotten so angry. It's probably why I volunteered to come to Utah to find you." Holding out his hand, he added, "Friends?"

Buck looked from the extended hand to Cale's anxious face. "We're a whole lot more than that, I hope," he said as he enveloped his brother in a bear hug.

When they broke apart, each man glanced away, blinked his eyes and cleared his throat. Finally Cale said, "How about it, Richard, will you come to see the folks?"

"Eventually, but my place is here now. I'm going to

marry Tempest. Stick around and be best man at my wedding. I have a million questions to ask about the family."

Regret shadowed Cale's eyes. "I'm glad for your happiness, Richard. I wish I could be here for the ceremony, but I'm afraid there was another reason I came West." He took a deep breath before continuing. "Whip is missing."

"Missing? Judas, why didn't you tell me sooner?"

Cale gazed about them at the man-sized greasewood shrubs and the towering, battlemented walls of the canyon. "I told myself you wouldn't care. And I figured you didn't deserve to know anything about any of us." Looking back at his big brother, he added, "I'm sorry for that. I'm sorry for everything. But I've got to find Whip. My gut tells me he's in trouble."

Buck thought of the young boy Whip had been the last time he'd seen him, quiet and sensitive, much like Ethan. Aware of other people's pain, he took it on himself, seeming to think it was his responsibility to make it go away. Then Whip and his best friend "Frog" Morton went hunting with the twins' Uncle Timothy. Somehow Frog had been mistaken for a deer and had died in Whip's arms. Whip was never the same after that. He was quieter than ever, all bottled up inside, like a firecracker. Buck kept waiting for Whip to explode, but he never did. "Each of you always did seem to know what the other was feeling. How long has he been gone? What happened?"

"It's a long story, Richard. Why don't you ride to Price with me? I'll tell you on the way."

"How urgent do you think it is to find him? Could it wait until after the wedding?"

Cale's brow furrowed. "When's it going to be?"

A hint of devilishness brightened Buck's eyes. "I don't know, I haven't asked her yet."

Chuckling, Cale said, "Tell you what, give me a month

to find Whip and I'll come back and stand up with you. Who knows, maybe Whip will come, too."

"Make it two weeks and you've got a deal." Buck thumped his brother on the back.

Cale chuckled again. "You drive a hard bargain, big brother. I guess that would give me enough time to get to San Francisco and back."

As they shook hands, Buck said, "Give me five minutes to find Ronan, saddle my horse, and harness up Tempest's dogcart. There's something I need in Price, and we can talk more on the way."

"Hope whatever you're getting is small, if you plan to haul it in a dogcart."

"Actually, it's big as a house, in a manner of speaking," Buck said with an enigmatic smile as they walked to the barn. "I need the dogcart for the kids. Tempest is off hunting herbs, and Ronan is busy working on her root cellar, so I figured to take the kids to Mrs. Sims in town. It'll give my future father-in-law a chance to do a little sparking when he goes to pick them up."

Before leaving, Buck wrote a note for Tempest on a piece of paper Viola had used to wrap up the dog bones she'd saved for them at the eatery. He tacked the message to the door with a nail so she couldn't miss it when she came home.

The dogcart had barely cleared the bridge before a long-legged mutt became intrigued with the smelly paper on the door. Standing on its hind legs, he pawed at the missive until it tore loose from the nail and drifted to the ground. Disappointed to find it was nothing more than paper, the dog trotted off after better game. A pig waddled over, nosed the paper, and gobbled it down.

Two hours later, Ronan put away his shovel, washed up,

changed into suitable "courting clothes," and rode into town.

Tempest returned home, her basket half full of herbs and wild onions, her back sore from all the digging she'd done, to find the yard deserted, the house empty and ominously silent. Going to the barn, she saw that Othello and the dogcart were gone. So were Spook and her father's mule, Beauty. They had all gone into town for some reason. It irked her that they hadn't been thoughtful enough to leave a note. She could saddle one of the mares and join them, but she had work to do, as always. And they would surely be home soon.

She washed and hung bunches of biscuitroot, onions, sego lilies, yampa, salsify, mullein, and yarrow from the ceiling to dry. Later the mullein would be used in a soothing lotion, the salsify juice would be sold as an aid to indigestion, and the yarrow prepared as a poultice for wounds or made into a tonic. The rest would be added to their food stores. Noon came and went. No one returned to share dinner with her. She wandered the house, worry clawing at her. Perhaps Angel or Ethan had been hurt. Buck might have taken them to Viola or to the doctor in Price. Panic nibbled at the edges of her composure. The house showed no sign of a mishap. No blood splatters or stained clothes, no broken glass.

Finally she couldn't stand it any longer. She rushed outside, intending to ride to town and came to a dead halt halfway to the barn. Pressed into the dusty soil was a strange, but not unknown, hoofprint left by a horse missing a nail from one shoe. Sweet Mary. Cale Kincade. Buck's brother had been there this morning. Turning, she ran back to the house. Panic knotted her insides.

Buck's bedroll and gear were gone. The red spice can that had contained his portion of the stolen payroll money was empty.

A voice in her head kept shouting No! No! He wouldn't leave. He couldn't—she loved him too much. He simply couldn't go off and leave her, giving her no chance. Giving *them* no chance.

Saddling Mother Superior, she headed for town. There was no sign of the dogcart. Her fear grew. Bursting into Viola's eatery, she rushed into the kitchen. Lacey looked up from where she was bent over, basting a roast in the oven.

"What is it, Mrs. Whitney? You look scared near to death. Is something wrong?"

Tempest wasn't about to ask Buck's previous lover where he was. "Where's Viola? Is my father here?" Without waiting for an answer, she turned toward the stairs that led to Viola's private quarters.

"They're not up there."

Lacey's words stopped Tempest in midstride. She turned to look at the girl. "Where are they?"

"Scotty took her and the children for a ride in the dogcart. They'll be back for the supper rush. Is there something I can do for you?"

"Is Buck with them?" She was too upset and frightened to realize she'd used his real name. Not that it mattered any longer; everyone in town had known the truth by the time all the hullabaloo over Jonas's death had blown over.

A federal marshal had come from Salt Lake City to talk to everyone who knew Jonas. They had been searching for him for three years in connection with several unsolved murders. But the long list of names he'd used confused and misled authorities. Not until the report came in that a treasure of Spanish gold had been found, and a man killed, were they were able to pick up the trail again. No one ever learned his real name. Jonas had borrowed the name Creedy from the missionary who had taken him in as a youth. Only one thing was certain; he had left a string of dead men behind that, laid end to end, would have gone nearly the full length of Treachery Canyon.

"I don't know where Buck is," Lacey said. "I saw him earlier this morning, riding toward Wellington with a younger fellow I remember coming through town a few days ago."

Tempest stifled a groan. "Was the younger man around twenty-six, tall, rangy, with light hair and blue eyes with just a hint of green in them?"

"I didn't see his eyes, but the rest fits well enough."

"What about his horse?" Tempest asked. "Was it a big roan?"

Lacey smiled. "Now that you mention it, it was. One of the prettiest I've ever seen."

Moaning, Tempest dropped her head into her hands. "Cale. Sweet Mary, he's gone off with Cale."

Concerned, Lacey knelt beside her and patted her knee. "Please don't be upset, Mrs. Whitney. I'm sure they'll be back soon."

"No. I've lost him, he's never coming back." Straightening, Tempest tried to fight off the tears gathering behind her eyes. Why she should suddenly feel so comfortable talking with this girl was beyond her, but she couldn't seem to stop herself. "He's gone home with his brother . . . to Memphis."

"But, surely . . . even if that's true, he's bound to come back. He loves you."

Giving the girl a sad smile, Tempest said, "I thought he did, but now . . ."

"Why, it's plain as frost on a pumpkin, Mrs. Whitney. I saw it the first time you came here together. His eyes take on a warmth when he looks at you, a warmth I've never seen in any man's eyes before." Lacey sighed wistfully. "I don't think I've ever seen a man more in love with a woman."

"What about Swede? Buck says the man is crazy for you."

She blushed delicately. If Tempest hadn't known better, she wouldn't have believed the girl had ever worked as . . . as what she'd been at the Princess. In her simple, high-necked, cream dress and ruffled apron, Lacey looked the picture of innocence. Tempest remembered what Buck had told her about Lacey's father, and her heart went out to the girl.

"Yes," Lacey said hesitantly, "I think Swede does love me, but . . . it's a sweet, gentle kind of love. What Buck feels for you is fire and passion—the kind that lasts forever."

Tempest looked down at her small, work-worn hands. Could Lacey be right? Tempest had been so sure last night when he'd made love to her. He hadn't said the words, but every touch, every kiss had seemed to say so. Yet, what if she was wrong? What if he didn't love her enough? He had been separated from his family for so long. Once he was back with them, he might never want to leave them again. Would he send for her?

"What are you going to do, Mrs. Whitney?" Lacey stood watching her, her basting brush still in her hand.

Tempest snorted indelicately. "What can I do? Go chasing after him?"

"I certainly would . . . if I loved him."

Staring at the girl, Tempest realized Lacey was right. What woman ever got what she wanted by sitting around waiting for a man to come along and give it to her? They might back East where men weren't so hard and life followed more traditional paths, but not here. Here, women learned to take care of themselves. They learned to fight for what was theirs.

"You're right," she murmured as she drew her riding gloves back on. "I'm not going to let him do this to me."

Halfway out the door, Tempest turned. "Thank you, Lacey."

"You're welcome, Mrs. Whitney."

Returning the girl's shy smile, she said, "Please, call me Tempest."

As she rode toward Price, she remembered all the times he'd told her it wouldn't work for him to stay. He was a drifter. No good for anyone. Incapable of settling down. Even last night, through all the passion they'd shared, he had never said he would stay. Sweet Mary, he'd never even spoken the word "love." If only Cale hadn't come back. For fifteen years, Buck had carried the guilt of his wife's death like a hair shirt, exiled from his family, from everyone he loved. She didn't begrudge him his chance to be reunited with his father, but she'd be damned if she'd let him go without attempting to convince him it was here he belonged. And telling him what a rotten coward he was for sneaking off without a word.

"What do you think? Do you like it?" The pretty young woman turned her head from side to side, modeling the bonnet that had, until a few moments ago, been in the milliner's shop window.

Buck stood back and studied the bonnet. "It looks very pretty on you." It would look even prettier on Tempest, he thought. The heart-shaped brim would complement the delicacy of her face, the seal brown color would set off her dark blond hair, and the roses tucked into the spangled gold net at the crown perfectly matched the amber flecks in her eyes.

Carefully lifting the straw hat from her head so it wouldn't disturb her coiffure, the young woman said, "If you don't like the color, we can make it up in any shade you choose. And the spangled net could be replaced with tulle for a little less money."

"No, I like the net. And the color."

"Excellent." Smiling coquettishly, she took a hat box from under the counter and placed the bonnet inside on a nest of tissue. "I'm sure your wife will be very pleased."

"Yes." Buck smiled back, enjoying the idle flirtation. "Soon as I get one."

"Oh." The salesgirl brightened. "You're not married?"

"No. Now, how about a dress to go with the bonnet?"

She secured the lid with a string. "This is a millinery, Mr. . . .?"

"Maddux."

"Mr. Maddux, I'm Alice Dray. We don't make gowns here. But I'd be happy to show you to the dressmaker's and help you choose something. I've my noon break coming up."

"That's kind of you. I'll wager you could direct me to a store where I could find a doll too."

"A doll? Certainly. You're buying gifts for your family then. Are you here on a visit?"

"You might say that." Buck hid his smile at her artless attempt to find out who would be receiving the bonnet.

Alice handed him the box. "I'll fetch my shawl."

Buck bought two ordinary day dresses Alice considered boring, then chose a dress with a jacket of brown striped wool, gored and pleated at the back, then flowing into coattails over a bustle. The bodice was of gold wool, matching the two overskirts which crossed in front to form deep points over a brown striped underskirt. He had paid for his purchases and was about to leave when a picture in an open fashion book lying on a table caught his eye. The picture showed a woman wearing what looked like a skirt, but was actually a cleverly made pair of wide-legged pants for riding astride.

"Do you have any of these made up?" he asked.

"The split-skirt? Only one which I made for an order that hasn't been picked up yet. Would you like to see it, sir?"

He paid extra to convince the woman to part with the

riding outfit, assuring her she would have time to make another one—though he had no idea how long that might take—before her customer came for it. As they left the store, his arms full of packages, he was too preoccupied with thoughts of Tempest in the new outfits he'd bought her to notice the proprietary way Alice Dray looped her hand through his elbow. As they stepped onto the boardwalk, he bent his head to hear something she was saying. He felt good. Life, he decided, couldn't take him much higher than this—buying gifts for the family he intended to make his own. The click of a rifle being cocked snapped his head upright, and he found himself staring down the business end of a Henry repeating rifle thrust at his nose.

"Judas!" Backing up, he nearly knocked Alice through the dressmaker's window.

"Buck Maddux, you're the lowest, lyingest, snake-tongued devil of a jackass it's been my misfortune to run into."

"Whoa there, Tempest." His eyes were on the shaking hands aiming the rifle directly at his heart. At her feet Rooster bared his teeth at him. He saw her gaze flick from him to the girl clutching his arm and back to him again. "Now, sweetheart," he stammered, "things aren't what you're imagining."

"Just what in blazes are they then?"

Her hat and clothes were dusty from her hard ride to Price. Wisps of hair flew about her face and stuck out of her braids like bristles. The hard set of her mouth and the fury in her eyes gave her a wild look that belied the delicacy of her face. She was breathtakingly beautiful. He loved the fire in her eyes, the endearingly stubborn slant of her mouth, her scent that drifted enticingly to his nose. This fiery little mustang was his. She loved him. He wanted to laugh with joy, but thought better of the idea. Now wasn't the time. "That'll take a minute to explain, Tempest. If you'll listen."

She glowered at him. "Start talking."

He glanced at the frightened girl beside him, the dressmaker in the doorway, the people on the street who had stopped to watch. "We could use a bit of privacy," he said loud enough for their audience to hear.

Tempest didn't care about the growing crowd. She glared at the pale-faced girl gripping Buck's arm and debated which of them to shoot first.

"Think you could put the gun down?" Buck asked her.

"No. And don't rile me. You know what happens when I get upset while I'm holding a rifle."

He knew all right. Her finger got jittery, which meant he could end up being shot for no good reason. They were back where they'd started a month ago. Suddenly, her lack of trust infuriated him. That he felt guilty maddened him even more. Judas! He hadn't done anything wrong.

"Dammit, Tempest. Stop this nonsense right now. Put down the Henry and let me explain."

"I'm not the one who's stopping you from explaining, you two-faced billy goat." Tears pricked the backs of her eyes. She blinked them away, refusing to let them dilute her anger. "How could you, Buck? You haven't even been gone a day and you've already taken up with another woman. Are you pretending to be *her* husband, too?"

Alice gasped, jerked her hand from his arm and stomped off down the street. A steel-eyed look from Buck sent the dressmaker scuttling back inside her shop. A few people on the street edged farther away, but curiosity and amusement kept them hovering. Price was small yet and offered little in the way of entertainment.

Buck set his packages at his feet, then, thrusting a finger at Tempest, he growled, "Now you listen to me."

"I'm not hearing anything worth listening to."

Heaving a sigh, he said, "I'm not here for the reason you think."

"Oh? And just what is that? To spend your money on another woman, then go off with your brother, free as you please? Why, Buck? After last night, how could you—"

"I'm not going anywhere with Cale."

She shoved the rifle a few inches closer. "You came here with him. Do you deny that?"

"Judas, but you are the contrariest, most bullheaded . . ." Yanking the Henry from her trembling hands, he emptied the bullets on the ground and propped the gun against the building. Then he grabbed her by the arms and yanked her close. "You're going to listen to me whether you like it or—"

"Sic 'em, Rooster!"

Buck yelped as the dog's teeth clamped onto his leg. He tried to shake it loose. "Dammit, Rooster, I thought we were friends."

"Let go of me, and he'll let go of you," Tempest informed him stonily.

Buck let go. The dog released Buck's pant leg and sat on his haunches, tongue hanging out as he gazed up at him with a big doggy grin. "Traitor," Buck muttered.

"Your little friend forgot her purchases," Tempest said with a pointed glance at the packages scattered around Buck. "But then, I suppose you can take them to her later, after you're finished with me . . . provided you're still in one piece."

"I'm never going to be finished with you. And for your information, these aren't hers. They're mine." Bending, he picked up a long, narrow box. He ripped off the string and flipped open the lid. "I doubt she'd be too interested in this, do you?"

Tempest stared at the beautiful doll with the painted china face and fancy ruffled dress. Her pulse quickened. Hesitantly, she reached out to touch the lace trim on the doll's sleeves. "For Angel?"

"For Angel. And this"—he disclosed a pouch of Lone Jack, her father's favorite pipe tobacco—"can you see Miss Dray using this?"

Tears threatened. Tempest fought them, afraid to believe what her mind was telling her. What *he* was telling her. "Were you going to mail them before you left for Memphis?"

Buck sighed. "No, Tempest."

"Then what, Buck? I know your guilt over Ellen torments you, but if you stayed, I could heal your pain. I know I could—"

"You already have, sweetheart." He took her by the arms and drew her close, his heart seared by the agony on her face. "Don't you know that? Aw, Tempest, I'm living proof of your healing touch, and I have no intention of going anywhere."

"Oh, Buck, I want to believe you, but—"

"You can. I'm a legitimate businessman now, after all. Half owner of the new Johansson and Maddux Saloon."

"Johansson and . . . You bought into Swede's saloon?"

"Actually, we're taking over the Sagebrush Princess. I'm backing it financially, and Swede will run it." He shrugged. "It was the only way I could get him to take the money he needed to set up housekeeping with Lacey. He's buying the Carcass Creek Cattle Company, too. Want to go to the wedding with me?"

She ignored the invitation. "Why did you leave with your brother this morning then, without saying a word? I knew he wanted you to go home with him so I simply assumed—"

He shook his head. "You assumed wrong. Cale has already left on the afternoon stage for San Francisco, to look for our brother Whip. I'm not going anywhere except home—to Deception Canyon. I have a house to build."

"A house?"

Putting his arm around her, he pointed her toward the street. The crowd, eager to see what he was showing her, parted and peered around each other's shoulders to see. "That big freight wagon loaded with lumber is what I came here for," he said. "Getting to spend more time with Cale was just an extra bonus."

She tried to tamp down the hope springing up in her heart. "But what are you going to do with a house?"

"I'm going to live in it . . . with you. And the children, of course. I didn't say anything about it in my note because I wanted to surprise you."

She stared at him. "Your note? There wasn't any note."

Buck frowned. "Something must have happened to it. I left a note telling you I was coming to Price to see Cale off and that I'd be home late tonight. Now, are you ready to help me get that lumber back to Deception Canyon so I can build my family the house they deserve?"

Amber-flecked eyes, brilliant with unshed tears speared him. He saw the fear in their brown depths and understood. Fear and Buck Maddux were old companions.

"Your family?" she said tremulously. "Us?"

"If you'll have me." His mouth spread in a devilish grin. "Unless you prefer living in sin," he added with a wink.

"Go on an' marry him, lady," someone yelled from the street.

"Yeah, say yes!"

Tempest glanced at the cheering crowd, then back at Buck. It was real. He wanted to marry her. Smiling and crying at the same time, she threw her arms around his neck. "Yes. Oh yes, yes, yes. I'll take you, to have and to hold, from this day forward, till death do us part," she whispered so softly only he could hear.

Buck kissed her. "I love you, Tempest. I promised Cale I'd go home soon, but when I do, I want you beside me as my wife."

"Oh, Buck. I love you, too. And I'm going to do everything I can to make you happy."

"That won't take much, sweetheart." His lips nuzzled her ear. "All you have to do is keep saying that one little word that sounds like heaven in my ears."

Her body began to sing with need. "What word is that?"

"Love," he said softly. The devil in him had fled. He was totally serious now, his gaze on her so tender it bushwacked her heart.

"Love is something I haven't had much of for a long time," he said, "and coming from you, it's the prettiest word in the world. So all you have to do to keep me happy is snuggle up close, put your lips to my ear, and whisper 'love.' "

* * *

About the Author

With her novels Charlene Raddon has turned a childhood fascination for people and the "olden days" into stories of hopes, dreams, pain, joy, and the human struggle, not only to survive, but to excel. Her writing has won several awards, including Golden Heart Finalist in 1991. When not writing she and her husband spend as much time as possible camping, fishing, exploring new roads and enjoying wildlife. Her hobbies include needlepoint, gardening, dying Ukrainian type eggs and, of course, lots of reading. Charlene lives in the Salt Lake Valley of Utah with her husband and a very fat and demanding, but affectionate, cat. Her many loyal fans and a head full of story ideas is what keeps her going. She loves nothing better than hearing from readers. Write to her at PO Box 900724, Sandy, Utah 84090-0724. For a signed bookmark or bookplate and, for as long as her supply lasts, a free arrowhead, please send a #10 SASE.